Peril

RUBY BARNES

Print Edition

Published by Marble City Publishing

ISBN 10 1908943033
ISBN 13 978-1-908943-03-3

.

Mercy

To be honest, I've had a skinful. I find myself in an area of derelict buildings around the back of Dublin Heuston Station, close to the river. Cloud obscures the moon and stars; the Liffey's matt waters absorb rather than reflect light. This doesn't look like the same river I cross every working day. The tide is out and the wide flow has reduced to little more than a stream in places, flanked by bulbous mounds of shining mud. Night dwellers, rats and others, scamper along the bottom of the stone walls. I become disorientated and wonder if this might be the River Dodder or some other tributary of the Liffey. Perhaps I've somehow wandered a few miles off course, walking drunk for half an hour instead of a few minutes. It won't have been a first.

What to do? I don't know Dublin well. Retrace my steps.

I turn and walk straight into the end of a stick that knocks the wind out of me. Bent double, I can just make out the end of a crutch and a socked foot. It's the Romanian beggar I had heated words with on the bridge this morning.

'Ticalos! Bastard!' he growls. 'You give me money.'

As I try to catch my breath, there occur to me three reasons why I'm not going to hand over any money. Firstly, lack of politeness. Secondly, I'm drunk and angry at the fucker and, thirdly, there's nothing left in my wallet.

So, I shove him back. I push the cripple hard in his chest with my clenched knuckles. I know that sounds mean, but I have my reasons.

Well, bad move. His shorter, wizened leg and deformed foot don't prevent him from discarding the crutch and standing on two feet, albeit in a strange and lopsided stance. And he has fists of iron. They rain down upon me, despite his lack of height, like punishment from the Gods. I block a few punches, mostly with my ears and chin, and even manage a vague counter attack that threatens his peculiar way of standing, but he shuffles crablike around and, shaking off my drunken slaps, hammers at my ribs and head. A roundhouse punch connects with my jaw and, through the haze of alcohol, I feel a tooth loosen. The next blow numbs my shoulder, reducing my defences to one arm.

Two and two come together in my blurred brain. The addict I read about in the newspaper, he was found beaten to death somewhere around here. Choosing a recent murder scene as your toilet is never a good idea.

A knee in the thigh gives me a dead leg, eliminating my preferred combat tactic of fleeing the scene, and I fall sideways. Death has come creeping behind Heuston Station. My wife is about to be widowed. An elbow, I think it must be an elbow because it feels like a pointed hammer, drives into my spine and knocks me flat to the ground. His snarl is audible, like a dog when you try to take away the bone. I begin to recall childhood events and the first time I met Jo, then our wedding and setting up home in Ireland together. Most clichés have an element of truth. My life flashes before me. It hasn't all been shit.

A fist gropes and tangles itself in my hair, lifting me just long enough for another fist to punch the side of my skull with a crunch. He drops my head to the ground and I manage to instinctively turn, taking it on the cheekbone but preserving nose and teeth. Then I see salvation, underneath an old pallet, just within hand-reach. A rusty two-foot metal bar.

His breathing is laboured now, he's tired. I grab that metal bar from under the pallet and, backhand, swing it hopefully into the black space over my body.

It connects.

There's a sound like a rotten floorboard splintering underfoot in a derelict house. I have no idea where the blow landed but he crumples into a heap on the ground and I drag myself sort of upright. Arm and leg are working again and I have no broken bones. I wield the bar in the Star Wars style of a Jedi Knight battling Darth Vader, make a few swishing practice passes through the air and then deal him a series of blows to the body. The bar is heavier than I had expected. Meaning to leave him with one last memento, I swing the bar over-arm and let it land with its own weight on his good leg.

Now, when I say the man yells I mean all the pain of his life and every demon in hell emerges from his mouth in a scream that splits the air. His shaking hand reaches down towards the socked foot that looks as though it will soon detach itself from the childlike leg. No shoe. How can that be? I look down confused and then realise I've shattered the beggar's crippled leg. But the screaming doesn't stop. It just goes on and on and on.

It's in my power to end it. I swing the metal bar in a high arc over my head and bring it down like a medieval executioner. The base of his skull is my target. Then the screaming stops. Oh, mercy! I drop the bar and lean, panting, against the river wall. After eons have passed I realise that the guy isn't stirring. Looking at his back, there's no heaving, no sign of breath being drawn. I move to feel his pulse. The neck is cool and greasy, no pulse. I pull back the eyelid that isn't pressed to the ground. It reflects back the light of the moon. Pupil fixed and dilated as they say on the television.

Well, what else can I do? Carry him to nearby St James's Hospital? Call an ambulance? I throw his body over the wall, onto the mud of the riverbank thirty feet below. The tide is still out.

A little about me

When I'm finished you will likely have no respect for me. What not to do with your life by Gerard Mayes. There will be a warm feeling that it happened to me, not you, and that I deserved it. Fair judgment, trust me on this if nothing else.

There are many clichés about the Scots. They're short and dour. They have sandy hair, ruddy faces, keep their money next to their groin in a hairy purse called a sporran and wear string vests. I personally don't favour the string vest, otherwise that's me. Oh, and hard working. That's another allegedly Caledonian attribute excluded from my portfolio. I'm Gerard Mayes, out for an easy life. Be a pal and call me Ger. One other thing, I adore women and, strangely enough, they tend to go for me. It must be pheromones or something. But that's not what left me lying amidst a tangle of dead bodies and a pile of cash with the finger of guilt pointing at my head. No, it was penny wise, pound foolish did for me.

I was brought up to believe a penny on the pavement belonged in the pocket of the finder. Not that there were any unclaimed coins on the cracked and weeping footpaths of Port Glasgow, alongside those decrepit shipyards and the abandoned River Clyde. If there were, you wouldn't be able to see for the frenzied bundle of young and old fighting over the Queen's head. Even a stray Green Shield stamp, stuck to the ground, would have had a gaggle of grannies trying to lick it off.

Charity is central to my story but I never encountered it back home. A supplicant on the streets of Port Glasgow would have had his beggar's bowl robbed and received a dead leg from the steel capped boots of the locals. Quite right too. That's the way of thinking I was brought up with.

Then I moved to live and work in Ireland, home of begging extraordinaire. Anyway, let's take a look at those bodies at a time when they still drew breath.

Giving up, giving in

Five people for dinner, an awkward number. All the recipes are for even numbers. That irks Jo, my wife, as she's not the best at maths and can't adjust the ingredients, but I'm happy enough because the extra portion usually lands on my plate. And, anyway, there isn't a dinner guest born who could partner Aunt Mary, our special visitor this weekend. So odd we are and odd we remain.

Tom and Renée are the other 'couple'. Renée is Jo's friend from college and Tom is my mountain walking partner. It's a sort of sport to bring them together. Renée has never had an enduring romantic relationship to my knowledge. Tom had a long-term partner but he died in a car accident about five years back.

There's an edge to this little gathering only three of us are aware of. Aunt Mary is our future benefactor - Jo is her only niece and it's no secret amongst family that she features predominantly in the old bird's will. Aunt Mary is our meal ticket; it's just a matter of time. Then, last week, a story started the rounds that an old friend of Aunt Mary's had left her inheritance to charity. So I had Jo on the phone to her aunt, inviting her down for a few days. Nip things in the bud.

We're enjoying an aperitif in the back lounge whilst Jo puts the finishing touches to dinner. Our place in Bagenalstown is too big for the two of us but the space is handy for entertaining.

'Not too much for me, Gerard dear. I'll only get giddy.'

Aunt Mary feigns moderation but gives me a wink and holds her wine glass out a little longer. I pour and try not to look at her pink scalp through the short, thinning curls of her blue rinse. Aunt Mary is a periodic feature at our house and friends regard her as they would a venerable piece of furniture. Antique leather.

'My giddy aunt,' Jo calls from the kitchen. She's mocking my British turn of phrase.

'Don't mind them, you're a treasure.' Tom lays his hand on Mary's and she giggles like a girl.

'Buried treasure,' I mutter.

I pour Prosecco for Renée, the bubbles fizzing up close to the rim. She concentrates on the wine and I have a brief chance to study her face unobserved. Up close her lips are perfect, slightly parted with just a touch of white teeth showing. Then the glass is overflowing.

'Whoops. Sorry! Here, I'll get something to mop that up.'

I'm back in a flash with kitchen paper and mopping the floor in front of the easy chair where Renée is sitting, poised, her girlish legs crossed. There's a splash on her knee and I wipe it dry with my hand, so quickly that even Renée doesn't realise.

'Hah!' Tom coughs across the room, choking on his Prosecco.

'Are you alright, dear?' Aunt Mary asks.

There's a spluttering sound as he clears his throat.

'Yes, fine thanks. I was just laughing at the waiter.'

'Hmm. Yes, he is a little clumsy.'

I look Tom in the eye and his crows' feet crinkle. He knows what I'm up to. Renée has always been my fantasy fuck.

'So, Josephine dear, your impossible husband thinks I'm buried treasure. Not very Christian. Have you managed to get him to church recently?' Aunt Mary projects her voice loudly towards the kitchen and then rounds on me. 'Gerard, you should go with your wife sometimes and listen to a sermon or two.'

'Why leave the house for a sermon when I can get one here and now from you?'

It's just banter. The old bat and I usually take chunks out of each other in this way.

'The ten commandments are a good place to start. And there are other details, such as respect your elders.'

'I do respect you, Mary. I have to respect anyone who has survived as long as you have. Two world wars and all that.'

Aunt Mary laughs as Tom clears his throat.

'I can only agree, Ger needs to improve his manners. But if you do go to the church, Ger, don't expect to see me there. Not after last time.'

'Oh? Why dear, what happened?' Aunt Mary asks.

Jo pipes up from the kitchen. 'It was that visiting priest from Dublin, he went on a rant against homosexuality. Said it was an abomination.'

'Abomination,' I mouth to Tom with mock disapproval.

'Chance would be a fine thing,' Tom mutters. 'It's water off a duck's back to me, but I don't need their bigotry.'

Aunt Mary stares at the floor. I know she's thinking of her late companion, Philomena. The church would never have blessed that union.

'Well,' I say, 'the last time I went to church was up in Tallaght at Jo's parents. And it'll take wild horses to drag me back. The priest was recounting his early years in England and said the British were fierce unfriendly.'

'But you're Scottish dear. I mean, I know that's part of Britain but it sounds like he was really complaining about the English,' Aunt Mary is back with us.

'It's not who he was insulting that's important, it's the fact that the priest could show such a lack of whatever it is, that his own behaviour wasn't exemplary.' I find myself on a soapbox.

'Such moral rectitude. Truly admirable,' Tom smirks.

Renée has nothing to say on the subject, but stands looking out of the French windows onto the garden. She's distant, demure. Her allure is tangible like perfume.

'Are you okay?' I ask quietly, moving beside her.

'Sure. You have the garden nice. It must have taken ages to plant all those bulbs. You have green fingers, don't you?'

'I'm glad you like it.'

Different coloured blooms are poking up through the grass at the foot of the trellis and archway, others crowding the raised beds. I've no idea what any of the varieties are called but I do recall crawling drunk on hands and knees to plant a miscellaneous selection of bulbs, after weeks of Jo nagging at me to get the job done.

'Well,' Jo says above the sizzle of a pan on the hob, 'dinner is served. Ger, would you do the necessary?'

I herd our guests into the dining room, open some red wine for the table and help Jo to bring in the plates. The starter is my favourite, goat's cheese and caramelised red onions on breakfast mushrooms.

'Is this cheese fresh?' asks Aunt Mary. The pungent taste makes her old face pull comically and everyone laughs.

'It's meant to taste like that. It's goat's cheese,' I explain.

'Good Lord! It tastes, well, I don't know!'

'Ever been downwind of a mountain goat?' Tom asks the table. 'Pretty bad, actually.'

Jo disappears off to the kitchen to serve up the main course and I follow her.

'This is Aunt Mary's and this is for Renée.' I take the two plates from Jo. She kisses me lightly on the lips, like a sibling, and brings two other plates.

I could just poison Aunt Mary's dinner and solve our problems. But there's never a vial of untraceable toxin to hand when you need it.

Back at the table I pour red wine into the larger glasses at each place setting.

'What do we have here, Miss Josephine?' Tom looks at the tower of food on his plate.

'Sea Bream, pan fried, topped with black olives, bulb fennel and tomato, on a base of crushed potatoes.'

Renée laughs but not unkindly. 'You sound exactly like the menu in that pretentious new restaurant in town. Doesn't she?'

'I'll be glad when this fad for putting the mash under the meat, fish, whatever, is over,' I complain, sliding my double helping of fish off the mound of potatoes.

Someone gives me a sharp little kick in the ankle but I can't tell who the culprit is. It has to be Tom or Renée, they're both in range.

'Well, if it tastes as good as it looks, Jo, then I think you have a great future as a chef,' Tom says. I guess he kicked me.

It does taste good and there's little conversation as we tuck in. Aunt Mary manages to find the only bone and starts to choke. I pour some water into a glass and hand it over, but she's too busy coughing to take it. Then things go worryingly quiet with Aunt Mary. Jo looks at me and I give a nod to say she's your aunt, you save her. Jo gives Aunt Mary a flat-handed slap on the back which knocks the offending bone out onto her dinner plate, together with her lower false teeth.

'Thank you dear,' she says, replacing the dentures as though nothing has happened. Cool as a cucumber is Aunt Mary.

I offer the water again and this time she sees it and takes a deep draught.

'For a second there I thought we had lost you, Mary.'

'Wishful thinking, Gerard.'

'Last week's sermon was interesting,' Jo says, too obviously changing tack I think.

'What was that, dear?'

'Well, the priest read out a letter from the Bishop on the subject of charity and giving money to people on the street.'

I throw a warning look at Jo. We do need to know Aunt Mary's position on the subject but this is a danger zone. The discussion mustn't sound too manufactured.

'And pray, what did the Bishop have to say?' Tom prompts.

'He said the congregation should only donate to charities that are run by religious organisations. And we shouldn't give to people begging on the streets.'

'Not give to beggars?' Renée asks. Her profile is so perfect from my angle. 'What reasons did he give?'

'If I remember correctly he said,' and Jo puts on a pious tone, 'it is society's task to care and, furthermore, giving to people on the street undermines the structures designed to support the needy.'

'But surely it's an individual's decision whether or not they give money to someone who holds out their hand? I think I can judge if somebody is in real need of my charity.' Aunt Mary is very discerning when it comes to handouts. That's why she's wealthy. Mean and wealthy. Give it to us, Mary.

'Well, I personally disagree with the Bishop's letter,' Jo says and then turns to face me. 'I don't appreciate being dictated to about my few small acts of charity.'

'Well, the reason I try to stop you from giving to every beggar in Carlow and Kilkenny is most of them are tricksters,' I reply.

Tom picks up the local paper from the seat of the empty chair next to him.

'There was a piece in here last week that said gangs of beggars are coming in by train and car to capitalise on the volume of tourists. And pickpockets working with the flower sellers. It's a business. No-one should give money to these people, that's for sure.'

'What about registered charities?' Aunt Mary asks.

'No, it's an industry. Young do-gooders on their gap year, driving SUVs into the jungle, delivering a wet feed to villages in need of livestock and electricity, not vitamin-enhanced porridge.' Tom can be very forthright.

'But what about Oxfam, Concern, Trocaire, Bothar and the others?' It sounds like Aunt Mary has been looking into the subject, right enough.

'Sir Bob Geldof?' I suggest.

'Mary, if you read any recent book on Africa, you'll get the same story. Michael Palin's Sahara, even Sir Bob's own book. They're unanimous in their view of the ineffectiveness, inappropriateness and futility of the charity industry. Those countries need good government, not food handouts. Food donation is a solution for famine relief, but these countries end up reliant on the large charities as a social welfare system.'

I'm impressed by Tom's memory of my Africa books on the shelf behind Aunt Mary.

'Bring back the Commonwealth, the Empire,' I throw in, to universal condemnation. Always guaranteed to get a rise.

Aunt Mary seems thoughtful.

'But there are people begging who are poor and hungry, aren't there?' Renée says. 'You must have seen them in Dublin, Ger, when you get your daily train. Right?' She gives me an eager look that needs pleasing. Please, please me.

'I've seen some of them, right enough, around the station. Addicts. You could drop a stone in the cup and they wouldn't notice the difference. Spaced out. I think it's totally irresponsible to give them money, just so they can get another fix or a can of cheap lager. More wine anyone?'

'I've seen them too, Gerard,' Aunt Mary adds. 'Some are in a trance, that's for sure. But others hang their heads in shame. It's a terrible predicament they're in. Perhaps we should give them the benefit of the doubt.'

'No, Mary, you're wrong. Addicts don't need money, they need treatment.' Tom speaks like someone who knows.

Rather than let him discuss his recreational cocaine habit with Aunt Mary, I decide to throw in another perspective.

'What about buskers? Anybody have a view?'

'They get what they deserve. If it sounds good I always give. I'm a big fan of live music, aren't you?' Renée's smile beams around the table. 'Go on, Ger, play a tune for us and we'll see if you deserve payment, shall we?'

I look at my guitar, hooked up on the wall, but Jo gets in before I have a chance.

'Don't encourage him, Renée.' We all hear the beeping of the oven timer. 'Anyway, dessert is ready.'

Jo heads off to the kitchen with the dirty plates, accompanied by Renée. I stay put this time.

'Gerard Mayes, I do believe you have a mean streak in you. I'll wager you've never given any money to anybody on the street.'

'You'd win that bet, Mary. Not a penny, except a busker, and then rarely. Most of them can't hold a tune. As for the junkies who sit on Heuston Bridge and the gypsy types, well, I have no problem passing them by.'

'It's not right to walk past these people without it pricking your conscience in some way,' Aunt Mary scolds me. 'It's not Christian. These are people in need, even if you don't agree with what they're doing about it.'

I'm saved from further embarrassment by the return of Jo and Renée with the dessert, a hot blueberry pudding.

'You're right, Mary. Ger doesn't have a charitable bone in his body.' Jo serves from the steaming dish she has placed in the middle of the table. 'I'm used to that but it doesn't stop me wanting to give. When I see those people on the street, so desperate they'll ask complete strangers for money, no, I can't believe it's an industry. Some of them must collect just a few cents an hour.'

'If I'm honest,' and I rarely am completely honest, 'I think it's a sop when you give to someone on the street.'

'What do you mean a sop?' Aunt Mary says.

'I mean throwing a few cents in someone's begging cup is a way of easing your conscience, but it doesn't deal with the real issue. The person is forced to beg because of their circumstances. Society should support people in need, should help address their circumstances.'

'Good Lord!' Aunt Mary exclaims. 'You agree with the Bishop! Well I never.'

'There, you see. I reach the right conclusion on my own without even going near a church.'

Jo shakes her head and I give Renée a smile.

Aunt Mary excuses herself and heads to the bathroom.

Renée pipes up.

'Changing the subject, I've bought a new home theatre system but I haven't a clue how to set it up. Your wife has agreed to lend me your services tomorrow, haven't you Jo?' Renée's hand descends on my thigh under the table, her expression all innocence.

'No problem. It's just a question of the right plug in the right socket.'

'Well, it might be a little more than that. The wires for the speakers need to be run around the skirting boards and everything. No, it's too much to ask, isn't it? I'll get a man in.'

'Listen, it doesn't matter if it takes you the whole day, Ger, because I'm away on my cookery course. He's all yours, Renée. Be gentle with him.'

Renée's face takes on a warm pink colour, like a young girl after exercise. Her hand is still on my leg below the table. Tom's foot cracks my shin again and I yelp.

'Sorry, matey. My foot slipped,' he says.

'Apology accepted.' But it still hurts.

'Well it's time for my beauty sleep,' Aunt Mary announces on her return. 'So I'll bid all you young people good night.'

We endure a round of wet kisses and Jo gets a big hug before Aunt Mary clops up the bare oak stairs to the guest room. Renée decides to take her leave and Tom offers her a lift home. I'm surprised when she accepts, because Tom is definitely over the limit, another bad habit of his. Tom has his own rules.

'Around ten in the morning then?' Renée kisses me on the cheek. Oh boy.

'Have the kettle on. I'll bring my toolbox.'

I shake Tom's hand.

'Okay, captain?' he asks.

'Thanks,' I say.

They head out of the driveway in his big Mercedes.

~

Whilst we're getting ready for bed, Jo quizzes me.

'Were you flirting with Renée earlier?'

She has a twinkle in her eye I don't often see these days.

'Listen, it's you offering your husband out to the highest bidder.'

'Well, whet your appetite where you have to, but eat your dinner at home.'

Jo code for all systems go. I make sure to brush my teeth a bit extra, freshen up the unspeakables and dab on some aftershave, like a trail of crumbs in the forest.

Jo and I have been trying for kids for a while now, without any luck. Apparently my little sperm fellas are mutants, some double headed, some without tails. Not good for the libido on either side. So, when a bit of unexpected passion arises like this, we both leap at it. Not that my appetite for Renée's surround sound system installation is in any way diminished. On the contrary, a man's sexual greed is infinite.

The handshake

My father's appetite for handshakes was infinite. A first memory is of standing in pyjamas, little black dogs on sky-blue winceyette, and shaking his big, cool hand. And my baby brother David, not yet able to sit up unaided, having his hand shaken as Mum held him up for the ritual.

'Goodnight, Gerard.'

'Night, Daddy.'

'Goodnight, David.'

Mum did kiss us, on the forehead.

Our goodnight handshake was physically the closest I ever got to my father, except for a series of punches when we had our first teenager versus adult confrontation over a table-tennis ball.

Hmm, I hear the Freudians amongst you. Problems with intimacy and emotion. Not entirely accurate. As we grew into little men there was intimacy. Hours spent together down in the shed, working all kinds of wood into different shapes. Dad knew young hands would struggle to work hardwood with hand tools, so he started us on balsa softwood and then we moved on to white deal and pine. Whilst other kids were swinging in the playground, David and I were in full attack across our quarter acre garden. My Saracen's scimitar whirled against his sturdy Crusader's sword, blades as sharp as wood can be.

'Re-sharpen, re-sharpen,' David would call when our finely honed edges became dented.

No doubt the neighbourhood of retirees was annoyed to hell by our noisy antics as David and I were the only kids in the street. Mum and Dad had moved the family to an affluent retirement area, a zone of natural wisdom. Next door Denis, a retired bank manager, was building the concrete hull of his dream boat in a garage. He built it too wide to get out of the garage. How wise was that?

We played sports, but never with other kids. Just us and Dad, at weekends. Dad had good eye to hand coordination, as did we, but what he didn't have was two functioning legs. As a child he had contracted polio and his right leg was grotesquely withered. This led to a strange gallop when he had to run, and a tendency to lunge with his weak leg. According to him, this had lent itself to fencing and boxing at university. No team sports.

The surgeon's remodelling had reshaped his foot many years earlier but the result was continuous wear and tear due to an unnaturally high instep. He was always at his foot, scratching and peeling the dry, hard skin from the ball and heel. That gave me a phobia of other people's bare feet. Unless they belong to a beautiful woman.

But Dad's interest in one-on-one sports made sense to me. I could see how he would have had to defend himself from bullies throughout his life.

The first week in high school I found myself under attack. A tall, scruffy boy named Daly spat all over my new school blazer as it hung in the sports changing rooms. The gap between his front teeth was perfect for spraying spittle and he had all the lads laughing at my expense. Daly was bottom of the barrel and looking for someone to exchange places with.

'After school, Daly,' I said.

When sports period was over, the tough guys tried to get us to fight in the classroom but I resisted. Daly looked worried.

'Let's forget it, Mayes,' he said.

I shook my head. The insult had to be paid for.

At the home bell I followed him down the field to the school buses and, just before he tried to board his bus, I kicked him repeatedly in the thigh until he went for me. Then I pulled on my black leather gloves and went to work.

Daly hadn't a clue. I danced around him, in the lopsided style of Dad, and let fly with clinically accurate punches, mostly at eyes and mouth. The exchange was almost soundless and he didn't land a blow. It felt so very good.

Joking Jo

A voice in my head is telling me I'll never manage to change Ger. I still think he's made of good stuff. The first time, in the pub in Killarney, when he appeared out of the myopic mist and kissed Mam's cheek on first introduction, I knew he had the husband makings. But somehow I lost the recipe.

Sure, he's gut-bustingly funny at times, especially in company. I can see from the audience's reaction. And there's nothing sycophantic about their mirth. Ger doesn't attract sycophants, quite the opposite. All my friends know he's a disaster. I think that's why they don't judge me over the Ciaran thing.

Look at Ger's work situation, wallowing in a job more suitable for a school-leaver than a man who should be raising a family. It won't last. None of his jobs ever do. He'll fall out with the new boss, this Deirdre woman. One to three years is all he ever manages and then it's a new start at the bottom of a ladder somewhere else.

This house here in Bagenalstown, bought on the promise of future earnings and built to accommodate a tribe. What a waste. We could have stayed small and lived a good life, a childless couple travelling the world whenever the mood took us. Ger's words and I hate him for the truth of it.

I've spent the years thinking a child would make all the difference to Ger. He would finally grow up and settle down. Now I'm not so sure of it. There's still a chance, despite his mutant sperm as he calls them. But I no longer laugh along with the guests at our dinner parties. Ger doesn't even notice.

It was Ger's idea that I should take up some new, body-enhancing sport activity. I've seen the way he looks at Renée with her bird legs and wasp waist.

'No, there's nothing feminine about her,' he said one night after sneaking glances at her all evening in the pub. The feigned disinterest was just a tactic, he was looking for a shag off me at the time. And in typical Ger fashion he tried to switch the subject from his lust to my insecurities. 'Hey, if you're so hung up about your figure, why not try something new? Yoga or something.'

I know he would just love to get to grips with her bones. There's no chance I would ever have Renée's figure, not even if I starved myself. To be honest, I like my curves compared to that anorexic look, and I know Renée has a reason for her figure that no one would envy.

But a little trim and tone never goes amiss.

Pilates was advertised in the local free paper. Call Ciaran now to enrol. Twenty women working up a sweat, on their backs on padded mats in the school hall, as Ciaran circled on his carved from solid legs, adjusting our postures. He managed to keep an asexual attitude during the classes. I even thought he was gay for the first few weeks until I saw his car had child seats.

Ciaran's face seemed familiar. Then he brought his kids to school one morning and I remembered I had seen him, on occasion, there in the playground at delivery time. Nice looking, unremarkable until

Pilates had revealed how long, toned and flexible he was.

'I hope you're doing your moves at home,' he confided in my ear as he passed me that day in the playground. There was a flutter in my stomach I hadn't felt for a long, long time.

The next week we had a girls' night out at the tapas wine bar in Kilkenny. The second glass of Rioja started to loosen tongues and the husbands came in for a lashing. Domineering, controlling, lazy, sports crazy, brains in their pants.

'Well, I think you're very lucky to have Ger,' Ella said. 'He's just so funny and, well, uncomplicated. I love his accent.'

I saw Renée's eyes drop demurely to the table.

'It gets a bit wearing after ten years,' I said. 'Sometimes I wish he would go away for a while, then I might appreciate him more when he comes back.' And I meant it.

'What about Ciaran?' Jill asked.

'How do you mean?' I felt the heat rising under my polo neck.

'Come on,' she said, 'we all see the way he looks at you when you do the pyramid.'

There were nods in agreement. Me included. I picked up a wine mat and fanned my flushing face with a laugh. Renée's eyes caught mine and narrowed.

Did we make an unspoken bargain at that moment? Ever since the first time Renée met my husband they've been circling each other in a mating dance. Shouldn't I be more possessive, protective, jealous? Does it mean I don't care? It has a necessarily limited lifespan, if they do start a liaison. I don't feel threatened by it.

Ciaran is caring, passionate and divorced. He brings me to a sweat in minutes, in a way Ger never has. We make love to the same tantric music he plays for the ladies at Pilates. Last week I even came in the class as everyone was touching the ground behind their heads with straight legs. No one noticed, except Ciaran. We're great together. It's just sex. But Ger had better shape up or he's toast.

Surround sound

I arrive to install Renée's home-theatre system. Her place is on the outskirts of Bagenalstown, a two-story modern townhouse with no front garden. Feeling conspicuous, I approach the door with my toolbox.

The front door opens before my finger can press the bell button.

'Right on time. You heard the kettle, didn't you?'

Renée beckons me in.

I had intended to kiss her on the cheek and linger, perhaps get a full kiss, drop the toolbox and, well. But she's virtually hiding behind the door as she opens it. So I decide to go for plan B, which is to play the role of rough and ready workman – hopefully seduced by randy householder.

'Morning Madam. Sound system installation at your service. Right then, show the dog the bone.'

She gestures with a delicate hand towards a far corner, as the front door opens right into her living room. I carry my toolbox over and make as though examining the Japanese branded cardboard boxes piled there, although I'm aware of Renée's fluid movements in closing the front door.

'Tea or coffee?' she asks, leaning against the kitchen door jamb in attempted nonchalance.

'Tea please. Any biscuits?' I know she has bought some specially, I saw them on the kitchen counter as I passed.

Renée brings a big steaming mug of tea and some dark chocolate biscuits on a plate. I'm huddled over a pile of wiring at the rear of her television but I sense her within my personal space. As I straighten up to take the tea my back protests and I groan, a hand reaching for the ache. Like an old man.

'Don't overdo it. Jo won't thank me if I send you back damaged, will she?'

Renée hands me the mug and puts the biscuits on the TV unit. Her blue jeans are painted-on tight and the T-shirt above them is too short to reach the waistband. A glimpse of flat stomach like an athlete and a navel that would hold a diamond. She pauses just long enough for me to catch a sense of musky warmth.

'This shouldn't take too long. There might be some shouting and swearing though. Bad habit of mine when I'm doing DIY.'

'Well, shout away, I won't disturb you. I'm going upstairs to get a shower, hope you don't mind?'

Her grins disarms me, I'm all a-fluster.

I unpack the home theatre units from the box. Footsteps patter across the floor above. She's light on her feet, walks on her toes like a ballerina, but these houses are so flimsy I hear every move. I close my eyes and imagine her undressed, clothes on the bed. Then she pads over to the shower and switches it on. This fantastic creature is naked and getting soapy just a few feet above my head.

The tangle of wires and equipment on the floor looks like an insurmountable challenge and I feel a hot sweat building on my chest and back. I have to get this job done or she'll finish up her shower and go out shopping or something. I spread the instructions out flat and look at the various components. Then, whilst scanning the room for likely spots to place the speakers, I see there are already sockets installed in the four corners of the room. Either the builder or a previous occupant has ready-wired the place. Good news, but I don't have all the necessary connectors to use those sockets. So I'll have to make a quick, temporary installation and come back another time with extra bits and pieces. Suits me fine.

I place the DVD unit in the TV cabinet and soon have everything connected, with the four speakers and the bass unit in makeshift positions around the room. Almost no shouting and swearing involved. The sound of the electric shower is still coming from upstairs. Just to test now with a DVD. I pick one at random, which turns out to be Austin Powers – The Spy Who Shagged Me, and place it in the unit. A fiddle with the remote control and the picture comes up on the TV. Then sound explodes from the speakers, causing me to shout in surprise. I had the volume up full.

'Ger? Are you okay?' Renée's voice calls down the stairs.

'Yep. It works. It works.' My heart is thumping.

'Can you do me a favour? Come up and get my towel, I forgot it. In the hot press, the big blue one, can you?'

'Sure, won't be a second.'

I bound up the stairs and look for the hot press, or airing cupboard. There are five identical doors off the upstairs landing. One of them is ajar, presumably Renée's bedroom. I find a box-room office, two guest rooms and a bathroom before finally locating the airing cupboard, grab a big, fluffy, light blue towel and stand uncertain by the open door.

'I have your towel,' I call through the crack.

'Thanks. Just, well, wait a minute will you?'

The door yields slowly with an agonising creak as I push it a bit further open, hoping to catch a glimpse.

'Listen, not being funny but would you cover your eyes when you hand me the towel?'

'Sure, no problem.'

I'm standing in her bedroom now and can smell the shower gel she's been using in the en-suite. Fruity and exotic. I take a look around the room, it's not especially feminine but modern, minimalistic. The bed linen is cream, quite plain, but looks like silk. There, on the duvet cover, is a black blindfold of the type airlines provide for long-haul flights. I pick it up and slip it on, grope for the towel and fumble my way towards the en-suite.

'Ha! Very good.' Renée must have seen me.

I feel a wave of moist, warm air as she opens the shower door.

'Wait a second, I have to get something, okay?'

There's a brief wet touch on my hand.

'There. Would you hold the towel out for me please?'

'Sure.' My voice sounds disembodied. I take the corners of the towel and spread my arms wide. Her damp hands move inside mine as she takes hold of the towel and I release it.

'Can I take this off now?' I move my hand up towards the blindfold but it's intercepted by hers.

'Not yet.'

She takes my hand and leads it up to her face. I feel silken material wrapped around her head. She's blindfolded herself with a scarf or something. I place my hands on her naked shoulders and I can feel the towel is wrapped around her, under her arms. She lifts my hands.

'No, I'm the boss. You're my humble hired help.'

Her hands slip under the hem of my T-shirt and push it up. I raise my arms as she lifts the shirt carefully over my head, without dislodging the blindfold. Even barefoot she's nearly as tall as me. Then I feel her lips on my chest, her neat teeth finding my right nipple and tugging at it, an exquisite pain. I try to run a hand through the back of her wet hair, up from her neck, but find the knot of the scarf is in the way. So I let my fingertips run lightly down her neck and between her shoulder blades. Then she straightens and her lips are on mine, tentative, as though we have all the time in the world.

Her mouth pulls away and I feel her hands fumbling with my belt and trousers, which drop to the floor. My toes instinctively find the tops of my socks and push them off. A hand grasps me firmly through the fabric of my boxer shorts, the first sign of urgency.

'Come on. Let's move to the bed.'

I'm led by the hand, out of the en-suite. There's a soft thump on the floor, which must be her towel, and I stumble onto the bed. With a laugh she guides my right leg over hers and I'm on my hands and knees over her. Still blind.

'My neck. Start with my neck.'

I lower my head and find wet hair, an ear and then the side of her neck. The aroma of whatever she has used in the shower is so delicious I try to lick it from her skin.

'Oh, God. That is so good.'

Her hands rub firmly down the side of my ribs and then reach up to my head, guiding me down along her body. Her breasts are smaller than Jo's but firmer, the nipples much bigger and very pointy in her excitement. With my lips I can feel the edge of her ribs at the concave dip of her stomach and I find a small pool of nectar in her navel. The shower gel residue is making my tongue tingle.

Further down, her hair is shaved except for a narrow strip running down the middle. I reach the end of the hair and then move off to the inside of her thigh, leaving her gasping.

'You tease, Ger Mayes. Just you wait.'

'There's time. All the time in the world.'

I kiss along her thigh, and stroke with my hands. Her muscles are tensed and her leg quivers. All the way to her toes with my tongue.

'I do believe we have a little foot fetish going on,' she says.

'I have a Renée fetish. All parts of Renée are fetish material. Roll over Madam, if you please.'

She does, letting me investigate her back, from the soles of her feet to the nape of her neck. The muscles ripple and twitch under my touch. I brush my lips over the light down between Renée's shoulder blades and take a firm mouthful of her buttocks. Then I lick down and between her cheeks.

'Oh…my…God!'

She rolls over and pulls my face into her groin. Renée tastes as sweet as I've so often imagined.

'I'm so wet. I need you inside me now!'

The blindfold is pulled off my head and her arms under mine urge me up, face to face. It's unbelievable, like awakening from an erotic dream to find myself making love to the object of my fantasy. Her thin, nimble hand slips down between us and guides me inside her. Immediately she's arching and moving in a way I've never known before. It makes me feel masterful.

'There, right there. Oh God!'

Although I'm excited to the point of palpitations, Renée comes twice before me. When I finally manage it, the blood is rushing in my ears and I collapse in a shuddering sweat.

'Gerard Mayes, I do believe that we made love.'

Renée lays on her side, head on one hand, and her long, slim legs stretch out forever. We both know there's novelty to our passion, but that doesn't diminish it. I pull her towards me and we kiss long and deep, the kind that requires good breathing technique. Then she breaks and traces kisses down my chest and stomach, and the whole game starts again. Oh boy.

~

The fine tuning of Renée's home theatre system requires another visit. I complete the cabling of the speakers in semi-professional fashion and our investigation of each other's nooks and crannies also reaches new standards. A lot of potions and lotions are employed. I'm pretty much infatuated with every inch of her milk and honey body, feet included.

We decide the time we spend together should be concealed from Jo. So I start to 'go to the gym' more frequently. It's no surprise if I come home tired from my exertions and fragrantly wet from the shower.

I've found out some things about Renée. She's a lonely soul who craves affection and intimacy. The sort of man she likes is too intimidated by her appearance to approach her when she goes out and, despite my recent evidence to the contrary, she's not a regular man-eater. I guess that's where I fit in. I say the things she needs to hear and, in return, she gives herself to me.

What does Renée see in me? Why has she betrayed her friend, my wife, Jo? I'm not sure myself. It was a bit of a surprise when she made her move at the dinner party, after all the time I've known her. She confessed a secret, long-held desire but something made her step over the line. My body broadcasts scent, so I've been told, and I was wearing Hugo that evening. That could have been it. No point in over-analysing, a door opens and you step in.

'Not a good idea, captain,' says Tom. 'Fantasy and reality need to be kept apart, mate. If you sleep with your fantasy fuck then what is there left to fantasise about?'

A new fantasy fuck, I guess. So that's another job on my list, window shopping.

Unappreciated

Tom was right and now, after a few weeks, it's beginning to feel mundane with Renée. She is gorgeous with her platinum blonde hair, slim figure and fine face, but Renée isn't as witty as Jo. And her interrogative ending of every sentence is like living in an Australian soap opera.

Renée and Jo, I need them both, to satisfy different needs. I know the thing with Renée can't go on forever. We'll get caught or else she'll eventually realise she can do better. And now I need something else. My work, my job, is mind-numbing. There has to be more to life. Is it still called a mid-life crisis if you recognise it happening?

'Come to the casino, captain, the one I go to in Dublin,' Tom suggests. He knows about the meaninglessness of life, Tom does. Gambling and coke keep him going. I'll have to give it a try.

~

Monday I take the second train of the morning to work. It's crammed with summer day-trippers and the air conditioning isn't working, again. I play my regular private game as the passengers get on and off, eyeing women and mentally keeping score.

Would, wouldn't. Wouldn't, would.

As usual, I'm the last passenger to leave the train at Heuston station, final destination. Just because I travel with the herd it doesn't mean I have to mindlessly follow their trail of spore.

The air on the platform tells me how the day is going to be – warm, still and humid. I exit the station at the river doors, where the smokers congregate, and cross between two parked double-decker buses to the river wall. There's a smell of engine oil and axle grease, the perfume of mechanics. Thirty feet below that wall the Liffey's waters run low, swirling downstream amongst rocks and stones, broken tree branches and a museum of shopping trolleys and traffic cones.

Behind me there's a ring of bells as the Luas tram approaches. I move away from the tracks, closer to the balustrade, and almost trample a character sitting under the dedication plaque in the middle of the bridge. He's one of the drug addict types, head down, in a trance. There's not a sound from him until, stepping too close, the heel of my shoe jogs his cardboard cup and rattles the couple of cents in it.

'Thanks, boss. Thanks a million.'

I've been acknowledged as a contributor. So I stop and turn, thinking to correct his error. The chap emerges slightly from his trance and turns his face up to me. At first glance he could be taken for middle-aged but he is more likely mid-twenties. The eyes seem focused on something far behind my head. His body is wiry, clad in grubby denim, and the weather-beaten skin of his hands, neck and face has an unusual tone and colour, as if he were some other kind of animal. He mumbles something unintelligible. I've no wish to engage him in conversation and doubt it would be possible anyway. So I turn on my heel and resume the walk to work.

On the other side of the bridge people seem to have a spring in their step. There's music on the air, accompanied by the heady smell of damp old stone wafting up from the river walls. A small man, leaning seated against a clothes recycling container, is cradling a Spanish guitar in the crook of his right knee. His eyes shut, fingers flying across the strings and frets. Now, in all modesty, I play pretty good guitar myself and can recognise a virtuoso.

'What's your name?' I've waited for a pause in his playing.

He tunes one of the strings and looks up at me. Brown eyes of friendship.

'Ilie. My name is Ilie.'

Like Ilie Nastase, the 1980's tennis player. He must be Romanian.

'You play well, Ilie. Here.'

I bend down to place a ten Euro note in his collecting cup. Ten is a bit excessive but it's all I have. Then I notice his right foot is shoeless, clad in a long, thick, woolly sock. I've a nasty feeling he's about to bare that foot and do something unpleasant.

'Thank you, thank you.' He beams at me and starts to play again. With an effort I ignore the socked foot, stay to listen some more and then glance at my mobile phone. Time for work. He sees this, understands I must go and wraps up with a flourish. We both raise a hand of salutation.

My office is just up from the bridge. Once there I ignore the lift, that's for smokers and wimps, and take the stairs up three flights.

'Nice of you to join us, Ger,' fat Deirdre calls to me from her office as I work my way across to the cubicle where my life wastes away Mondays to Fridays. I deposit my rucksack under the desk and head for the tea room. Whilst the tea is brewing, I head into the gents' and re-hang all the toilet rolls so the dangly bit hangs away from the walls. I have an ongoing toilet paper style feud with a worm named Brian.

Back to the tea room, hot mug of tea in hand, I chuckle for the thousandth time at the Gary Larson cartoon printed on it. Two fat cartoon cowboys in tall hats, one is blowing up an inflatable cow by mouth. She's looking good, Vern.

Then I wander into fat Deirdre's office where the other eight team members are squeezed around an oval table meant for half that number. The Monday morning meeting.

'Right, well. As you all know, Jim has moved on and I've been fortunate enough to be selected as the new manager of this unit.'

Eight faces look back at Deirdre. Two of them struggle to conceal animosity. I'm one. Caroline is the other.

'Caroline, you'll remain as team leader for new applications.' Caroline's animosity eases a little. 'Taking up my previous role as team leader for complaints will be…Brian.'

'Thanks, Deirdre-uh,' the obsequious Brian acknowledges. He has a strange way of ending his sentences-uh.

I'm furious. This is my reward for going up against fat Deirdre and Caroline for the manager's job. Marooned in a cubicle with the bottom feeders.

The meeting goes on but I don't hear it, distracted by seething thoughts of injustice. I know I've only been with the Railway Procurement Agency for a couple of years and at a lowly grade. In my mid-thirties I was a mature entrant and I'm surrounded by young ones leaving me behind. Can nobody see my potential? It must have been close with the interview panel. Caroline was second and I could credit that. She's a candidate for the prized and vacant position of fantasy fuck. But Deirdre? A woman with a waist three times the size of mine? Certainly she provides better value per kilo than I do. Probably the main selection criterion.

'What do you say, Ger?' the object of my scorn is asking a question.

'Sorry, what's that?'

'Brian suggests we move the Monday meetings to nine o'clock. Okay for you?'

There are sniggers around the table. Everyone knows I take the late train in on a Monday. Well, most days. Brian raises his Neanderthal brow and grins. I fantasise about whether it's possible to break a nose that has no bridge to it.

'Sure, I can do nine. As long as the train is on time.' I lie. This is a direct attack on my work-life balance by Brian. He has hated me since I arrived in this God-forsaken hole and started to hang toilet rolls correctly.

Surprisingly, Caroline comes to my rescue. 'It's a problem for me. I have to drop the kids at school before I come in. Most days I could make half nine but when it's raining the traffic can be very heavy.'

She gives me a look that says you and I, we're allies. Maybe we could be more.

'Ah yes, Caroline. Sorry, I forgot,' Deirdre apologises. She forgot about Caroline's obligations because she, Deirdre, has no kids. Because she's too fat to copulate. An image of Deirdre and Brian testing that idea floats into my mind. Caveman and hippopotamus. Cross-species fertilisation, impossible.

The meeting fizzles out with no real changes except Brian's team leader appointment, which is totally within Deirdre's gift. I wander back to the tea room to refill my mug. Talk in the tea room is all about a body the Guards found near the station last night. It's not an uncommon occurrence in the rougher parts of the city.

'Beaten to death, I heard-uh,' Brian says, nodding wisely.

Brian lives nearby in an unsavoury area, which suits his character.

'The fella was known to the Guards, as they say, lived on the streets, one more scumbag off the planet-uh.'

I add fascist to my mental shortlist of Brian's attributes and return to the workplace.

'Mayes, your days of laziness are numbered-uh,' Brian slimes in my ear as I sit down on my cubicle's swivel chair.

'I'll have you for bullying,' I reply with a smile, rising back up onto my feet. I'm not a big fella by any means but Brian is a titch. He looks like a chimp.

'We'll be counting hours, Ger-uh,' he retaliates while scampering away. 'Counting hours, we will, starting today-uh.'

Brian is a worm, a coward. But I know this means trouble. I'm supposed to do seven hours a day, which might make some people laugh. Even if I add the frequent tea breaks and lunch to my hours, I generally only manage about six. Actual work hours? Well, to be honest, maybe four. Is it my fault Irish Rail doesn't have a frequent enough train timetable? Hardly.

The important thing is this: does Ger Mayes get his work done? Well I do. Okay, I don't. There's just too much of it, even if I did ten office work hours a day. And in any case, handling complaints from the public is a drag. Never ending. I don't have the aptitude for it. I should be management.

Before I realise, lunchtime is here. It's across the road to the pub where I order the usual soup and a sandwich.

I find a quiet corner where I can read my book undisturbed. The table girl comes by and I hand her the token for a pot of tea. That's the way things works in the Nancy Hands pub. She's back almost immediately.

'That was quick,' I say and look up to find it's not the table girl but Caroline.

'Mind if I join you?' She flashes a smile I haven't seen before, nice teeth.

'Be my guest.'

She smoothes her knee length skirt over her thighs and slides onto the other side of the L-shaped bench. Caroline is tall, even when seated. Statuesque. It goes with her normally icy office persona.

The table girl arrives with the tea and Caroline orders another for herself.

'Aren't you eating?' I ask.

'No, I had something earlier.'

I can tell from the hungry way she is looking at my sandwich that Caroline belongs to those who maintain their figure at the expense of near starvation. All the same to me. She looks good on it.

'Listen,' she says whilst pouring her tea, which has just arrived. Her left hand is trembling slightly, a wedding band on the third finger. 'I know you went up against Deirdre and me for the job...'

'And the best man won.'

She laughs and preens a little. Ice maiden is melting. The blonde hair isn't natural but who is natural these days?

'You should think about burying the hatchet with Deirdre.'

'I might bury it in Brian's snail head.'

'Yes, that was a bit tough, Deirdre choosing Brian. I'm not too fond of him myself.' Her mouth tightens a little. She looks good when she's serious too. Good looking woman.

'What do you have in mind?'

'What I have in mind is a kind of alliance.'

'A kind of dalliance?'

'You wish.'

I do wish.

'Yeah, Caroline, you wish.'

We hold each other's gaze. I know I'm no oil-painting. But I'm Ger Mayes.

'I don't know what it is about you. But there's something...indefinable.'

'Whereas your charms are more obvious.' Her blouse is open two buttons and I know she has sprayed Light Blue perfume on her throat because I can sense it rising with her temperature. I almost have her in the Renée place.

'Perhaps it's your eyes.' She looks into them and I see hers are grey blue. 'Or perhaps it's that you're a lazy bastard who gets away with it.'

The moment is gone and she's telling me what she came here to tell me.

'Deirdre and Brian are out to get you, if you don't pull up your socks.'

'Tell me something I don't know.'

'Seriously now, I think that's one reason why you didn't do so well on the promotion panel.'

'Deirdre told them about my hours?'

'I guess. So you need to address the issue.'

'You mean an alliance, to get Deirdre?' This sounds like fun.

'No, I mean you have to get your hours up.'

'And why are you telling me this?'

'Because I like you. You're good at your job and you add something extra to the team.' That's crap. She clearly has the unaccountable hots for me.

'Thanks.' I'm genuinely flattered by her attentions.

'Well,' she drains her teacup, 'I must be getting back. Hey, it was nice to chat. We'll have to do lunch again sometime.' Do lunch? She had a cup of tea.

'Sure. Thanks. See you.' I half stand, lady leaving the table.

Odd. The best looking woman in the office came on to me in the pub, under the pretence of my working hours. I linger for another twenty minutes. Then I wander up to the Phoenix Park and sit on the upper step of the Obelisk, contemplating life. Jo is happy, Renée is happy, it looks like I could make Caroline happy. The casino visit with Tom is coming up. I feel on the edge of greatness.

Back at the office, lost in a reverie, a rare event occurs: I miss my usual train home and first realise when the clock reaches half past four. My train left five minutes ago. So I go for the umpteenth mug of tea. As I approach the tea room I hear the door of the ladies toilet open and, on instinct, I quickly back away around the corner.

Caroline's voice. 'I told you, flattery is always effective, even when it's insincere.'

'Well, whatever you said seems to have done the job. He's stayed on for the next train.' Deirdre's voice is as fat as her face.

By five o'clock the scheming cows have left the office and I'm all alone. The next train isn't until half-six and there's no point in hanging around the station. I'll be tempted to spend money on coffee or something. So I do a little internet research on the charming Caroline Lynch and find out a few things. I always like to research my next target.

She's into horse riding, has medals for it. Looks good in the couple of published pictures I find, standing next to her horse. Lives in Kildare. I find her facebook page and wonder if I should invite her as a friend. Then I'll have access to more pictures of her.

So I do so. I can see her friends and there's a Feargal Lynch, her husband I guess. He looks like a farmer. The ice maiden is married to a farmer.

At six, having wrapped up my surfing, I stroll down to the station and take in the river as I cross the bridge. The water is up, not flowing but swirling, the incoming tide clashing with the downstream. There's no sign of the guitar player with the sock or the addict beggar from this morning. I buy a chicken breast burger with curry chips at SuperMacs in the station and eat it on the train.

Once the food is finished I drift into sleep, thoughts of Caroline, Renée and Jo mixing in my mind. Could I sleep with all three in one week? How might I manage that? Surely it can be done. When the train pulls into Bagenalstown I wake with a start, dazed. Hard day at the office.

~

'You gave money? To a beggar?' Jo is incredulous.

'Not a beggar. He's a musician.'

'A busker then. But this is one of the guys on the bridge, right? How much did you give him?'

'Two Euro.' I have to lie. Ten sounds ridiculous. 'You should hear this guy play. Something else.'

'Yeah, well, I'll take your word for it. Listen, Renée was round here earlier.'

'Oh, right.'

I look and listen for any hints of danger. Jo seems tense but I don't think she's onto me. She just wants me to be sympathetic.

'I think there's something seriously wrong with her. She was throwing up and everything, in a lot of pain. If you're heading to the gym will you look in on her, check she's okay?'

Holy moly! Playing straight into my hands.

'Sure, if it'll help, no problem.'

'You're a kind man, Ger.'

She gives me a soft kiss on the lips as I head out the door with my gym bag. At times like this I think maybe Jo and I do have a future after all.

The fall

The next day I take the later train, not wanting to let the coven of office witches think their spell has worked on me.

I exit the station and try to squeeze between two buses parked improbably close together, misjudging the gap. The African driver of the rearmost bus gives me the crazy eye. There's a moment of panic as I imagine myself crushed by a whimsical press of his accelerator.

Onto the bridge and different scents rise with the steam of earlier rain. Sweet spearmint of chewing gum. The farmyard odour of a reconstituted patch of Garda horse droppings. That horse deposit is right on the spot where the dazed addict sat yesterday, but of him no trace.

The chap with the socked foot is there again by the clothes recycling bin, but without his guitar. He isn't wearing a baseball cap today and I can see bruises on his face, the type that come from fist fighting. But he has the other foot on display, the left one, I'm sure it's the alternate one to yesterday. A few mumbled notes of a tune emerge from his mouth, slightly oriental.

Plain old-fashioned begging with a bogus disability. Ludicrous and disappointing. I have to laugh out loud.

'Funny? You think this is funny?' He shouts at me as I walk on briskly, eager to get away from the maniac. 'Scum!' He shouts after me. So much for our musical camaraderie of the previous day. It's like he's a different man.

By the time I get to the office, the storm clouds have gathered again and a deluge begins.

I spend the whole day snowed under with work. Brian piles it on thick and there's no sign of Caroline. I flatter myself to think she's avoiding me.

Work sucks and yesterday's feeling of elation has evaporated. I'm back in my rut. The hours drag until my usual train time, no chance of me missing it today and I'm out the door.

The earlier storm has broken but the street is a scene of devastation. Rivers of water that I had to negotiate at lunchtime to get to the pub have washed up over much of the pavement and left behind a layer of detritus. Mud, sticks, rubbish and God knows what all over the place.

I'm so busy picking my way through the gunge I almost walk into something or someone coming up the street. The low shape hisses at me, like a cat surprised by a dog, and I step away instinctively. It's him, my adversary of this morning, the pathetic beggar. He's around four inches shorter than me, hunched over two metal crutches. One leg, the left one, is held hanging off the ground and bent at the knee, withered. He's truly crippled. The dark blue sock is squeezed into a sports shoe but the laces remain undone and dangle to the ground.

My mind flashes back to childhood images of my father. His withered leg, left thin as a stick from polio. The deformed foot and everything associated with it. Peelings of hard skin gathered on the arm of his favourite chair every evening.

I'm truly repulsed by the Sock Man. He recognises this with all the hypersensitivity of a cripple.

'Ticalos! Son of bitch!' he snarls in his pidgin and struggles on up the street through that slippery mess of pavement. I feel as though I've kicked a dog. Then another figure approaches and a hand grasps my shoulder.

'Ger! Heading over?' It's my brother-in-law Alex, Jo's brother. He helped me get my job a couple of years ago. It sounds like I'm supposed to know what he's talking about.

'Across the road?'

'Yeah, Nancy's and maybe Ryan's after. You got the email right? Today was my last day.'

In truth Alex has never much liked me but here I am in receipt of a spur-of-the-moment invitation to the pub. A rare event.

'Sure I'd love to, Alex, but I have to get the train.'

'It's not the last train to Bagenalstown. Even I know that. Come on, just a pint. My last day in the job. You might save me from drinking alone.' He jests. Alex is popular.

'Well, I could murder a pint to be honest.'

'Good man, Ger, good man.'

We stand shoulder-to-shoulder, waiting for a gap in the traffic and then stroll over and in through the faux-antique double doors of the Nancy Hands. Inside it's heaving with people from the Railway Procurement Agency. Some top knobs included. He's well connected.

'What'll it be, Alex?'

'No, my treat. I've a tab behind the bar.'

'What? I can't buy my favourite brother-in-law a drink?' It's a standing joke. He's my only brother-in-law and I never buy. 'Ah well, I'll take a Smithwicks.'

The chosen pint arrives much more promptly than a Guinness would.

'So where are you off to again, Alex?' I feign lack of knowledge but I'm well aware he's heading off to be Communications Director of another State body. Alex's career progress is meteoric, much to my chagrin, but Jo doesn't point it out. Not too often.

'Food marketing. Bord Bia. Cheers. Glad you came along.'

We clink glasses and I feel the warmth of a room full of people celebrating somebody else's good fortune. Three women want me at once I want to shout, but I wouldn't be heard above the din.

'Gotta mingle. You know how it is. Just order at the bar when you need another.' Alex moves off into his various circles of friends.

Now I'm alone in a crowded room and so I try to adjust my posture to something nonchalant. There's not one face I recognise. A mixed blessing. I've no desire to bump into fat Deirdre or Brian the brain but it would do no harm to stumble across Caroline.

'Hey, you work in our place, don't you?' I turn to see a bright-eyed young thing with her brunette hair in a bob.

'No, never seen you before in my life.'

'Oh, I'm sorry. It's just you looked familiar and I don't see anyone else I know.'

'Just kidding. You're Karen, aren't you? I'm Ger.'
I know very well who she is. A graduate on her work experience year, a junior in Caroline's team. Cute.

'Ger? Right, yes, Ger.'

'Alex is my brother-in-law. Let me get you a drink.'

'Oh, thanks. Vodka and Lucozade.'

'Vodka and what?'

'Lucozade. That's what everyone is drinking these days.'

'Right. Okay. Don't go away.'

Two girlfriends of Karen's have arrived by the time I return with the drinks. We're all soon best friends and laughing about office politics.

Alex spins off from the throng in our direction. He points at my empty glass.

'Don't be a bore. Forget your train and relax. Let me give Jim and Marie a call, they'll be only too happy to put you up for the night. Get another round in.'

Jim and Marie are Jo and Alex's parents. The Outlaws I call them. I occasionally abuse their hospitality when I have a night on the town. After Alex has set me up with them, I call Jo and explain her little brother is keeping me out. She doesn't seem too perturbed, probably she'll enjoy a quiet evening without me.

I'm not quite sure what happens to Karen but, as the last orders bell is rung, I find myself deep in a philosophical discussion about rolling stock with several male colleagues whose names I can't remember. There's a rush to get in a final round of pints and then the cool night air hits as the barmen coerce us out the doors and home.

'You'll be okay? Get a taxi.' Alex is very much the worse for wear, body swaying. Or am I swaying? He's one of those guys, though, whose voice stays sober to the point of unconsciousness.

'No, not a taxi. Too bloody dear. I'll take the Luas, it's still running.'

Behind us on the pavement two of the company directors look ready to start a drunken scuffle. One is a big meaty guy and the other small and wiry. Alex and I look at them and then at each other, concluding without words that it's not our business. A taxi comes down the street with the roof light on and Alex steps out with raised arm.

'Thanks again. Don't be a stranger.' He opens the cab door, turns to give me a man hug and then sits into the back seat.

I look back at the two fellas now locked in a tussle and turn away.

~

City railway stations always attract a certain category of night-time loiterer and Heuston is no different. At the Luas stop I find myself in the midst of a handful of characters, perhaps in their early twenties, who have already burnt the candle of youth at both ends. Fuelled by drugs, alcohol and God knows what else, if there is anything else. Glue perhaps.

A derelict female approaches me.

'Got any spare change for the Luas, Mister? Get a girl home?'

Through the alcohol befuddling my reasoning I see a chance to make recompense for my meanness to the crippled beggar. Before I know it, all the change from the several rounds of drinks comes out and I thrust it into her cupped hands, probably some ten euro or more.

An older man in the motley group exclaims 'You're a gentleman, you are. A real gentleman. To help a lady in need.'

I've probably given that lady in need enough money to kill her few remaining brain cells.

'Would you know where the nearest loo is?' I ask my new acolyte. Having neglected my end of evening pee before leaving the pub, I'm now close to bursting.

'Try the station, boss. No, wait.' He struggles to read the time on the Luas information display. 'The official bog'll be closed now. We'll keep sketch for the Guards if you wanna use that wall.' He points vaguely at the river. 'Else round the back is more private.'

'Thanks, mate.' I'm already walking away.

An impending release of urine after several pints of cold beer is amongst the sweetest of anticipations. I trot around the building and, finding a dark wall, go about my business. It's only after a minute of relief my eyes adjust to the darkness and a makeshift shelter of metal and cardboard sheets becomes visible. The flimsy dwelling's occupant hurls a few choice obscenities as my filtered Smithwicks splashes and trickles. A vague shape, possibly female, emerges from the darkness and slopes towards me. My task substantially completed, I turn and trot off, slowing to a walk when it feels safer.

I find myself in an area of derelict buildings close to the river. Cloud obscures the moon and stars, the matt waters of the Liffey absorbing rather than reflecting light. This doesn't look like the same river I cross every working day. The tide is out and the wide flow has reduced to little more than a stream in places, flanked by bulbous mounds of shining mud. Night dwellers, rats and others, scamper along the bottom of the stone walls. I become a little disorientated and wonder if this might be the River Dodder or some other tributary of the Liffey. Perhaps I've somehow wandered a few miles off course, walking drunk for half an hour instead of a few minutes. It won't have been a first.

What to do? I don't know Dublin well. Retrace my steps. I turn and walk straight into the end of a stick that knocks the wind out of me. Bent double, I can just make out the end of a crutch and a socked foot. It's the Romanian beggar I had heated words with on the bridge this morning.

'Ticalos! Bastard!' he growls. 'You give me money.'

As I try to catch my breath, there occur to me three reasons why I'm not going to hand over any money. Firstly, lack of politeness. Secondly, I'm drunk and angry at the fucker and, thirdly, there's nothing left in my wallet.

So, I shove him back. I push the cripple hard in his chest with my clenched knuckles. I know that sounds mean, but I have my reasons...

~

And the rest you know already. I throw his body over the wall, onto the mud of the riverbank thirty feet below. The tide is still out.

There's a scurrying sound from the darkness behind me and I turn but see nothing. In my dazed confusion I forget that metal bar - the murder weapon, covered in his blood, my blood and my fingerprints.

Two hours later I arrive at my Outlaws house, dishevelled and obviously drunk. It's not much different from the state they're used to seeing me in but they're already in bed. A scrape on my cheek and blood oozing from grazed knuckles are all I notice in the bathroom mirror before I crash to sleep.

~

The next morning I wake with a mighty headache and my limbs are like lead. At around 10 a.m. my father-in-law Jim brings me in a cup of tea.

'You look rough. I don't think you'll be going to work today.'

'Thanks, Jim. Yep, had a rough night. Hope I didn't wake you.'

'Not at all, Marie is still out cold in there. She sleeps like the dead.'

Jim is right, I'm too sick for work. I pick up my mobile and call in, reaching Caroline's voicemail. I should call Brian, as he's supposed to be my line manager, but no chance of that. As I leave a message asking Caroline to tell Deirdre I'm sick, my voice sounds like my throat is full of sludge from the Liffey. Convincing enough.

I lie in late, then struggle out of bed and put on last night's clothes. The trousers are wrecked, muck all down them and holes in the knees. My jacket is in a similar state but my keys and the wallet with my rail season ticket are still in the pocket. No money whatsoever.

Marie is still in bed and Jim has gone off to play golf so I grab some tea and toast then walk the five minutes to the Luas stop, each step discovering a new ache somewhere in my body. Half an hour ride into the city and then the next train home to Bagenalstown. Other passengers ignore me in my dishevelled state. It makes me fell less of a murderer.

The countryside looks different as it rushes past the train window. Perhaps it's the light, I don't normal travel down country midday. The ticket collector comes by after an hour and eyes me suspiciously.

'Tough night?'

'You could say that.'

Athy, Carlow and then the train pulls into Bagenalstown station. I wake from a doze and break into a sweat as I realise my car-park ticket will have expired early this morning. That'll mean a clamp and a big fine to deal with. I see the white van of the security company driving around the car-park as the train brakes to a halt. There's a gaggle of grannies getting off and I'm unable to fight my way through them to get out quickly. In any case they're moving faster than me, my legs have stiffened up after one and a half hours of sitting. But, in a stroke of good luck, the clamping man has chosen a big Mercedes to be his first victim and I'm able to drive off in my Passat, unpunished. Close call.

Jo's blue Golf is on the driveway as I pull up. Home for lunch I guess.

'Hello? Surprise, it's me,' I call as I step into the hallway, but there's no answer, just the drone of the electric shower upstairs. Strange.

I look around and hang up my ruined jacket. Coats on the coat-rack, unpaid bills in the mail holder. I have that feeling of having been away and the disappointment nothing has changed.

Those oak stairs seem steep today and I have to haul myself up with the banister, like old Aunt Mary does. Jo's sports gear is lying on top of the dirty washing basket and the shower is still running. She must have been for a lunchtime run. This fitness thing is becoming a bit of an obsession.

I kick off my shoes, wander into the en-suite and sit on the toilet seat, leaning my head against the wall. From there I watch through the misty glass as she rubs shower gel down her thighs and over her breasts. My own private show, although the lad doesn't seem to be responding properly.

'Holy shit!' Jo sees me when she rinses the shower cubicle door. 'What the hell are you doing here?'

I open the door and step in.

'Jesus! You still have your clothes on, are you mad?'

She steps out and shuts the door. I let the water flatten my hair, soaking through my shirt and down over the ragged trousers. After an undefined number of minutes I open my eyes and stand up, away from the tiled wall against which my head was leaning. It's difficult to take off the wet clothes and in doing so I discover there are deep bruises blossoming on my shoulders, thighs, ribs and back.

When I emerge from the shower I have to call on Jo for my towel.

'What's going on? Look at the state of you and what are you doing here at lunchtime?'

It's time to apply the complex, well-thought-out story that has been bumbling around in my head on the train journey down.

'I was mugged.'

'You look like you've been steamrollered. Are you sure you weren't in a drunken fight?'

'Well, you should see the other guy,' I joke. Not really funny.

~

After two days' recuperation at home, I'm battered but mobile. The news carries the story of a crippled Romanian beggar who has been found in the River Liffey near Heuston, beaten to death with a blunt instrument. The Guards haven't yet found the murder weapon. I feel the fabled long arm of the law reaching out across four counties for my throat and a fever sets in.

The weekend looms and provides me with a further remove from what happened behind the station, such that I begin to wonder if it really did happen. Have you ever had a dream in which you murder someone and struggle to conceal the body? Then you wake and there's no body, no evidence. It didn't happen.

Building canoes

When delirium grips you, dreamland becomes a fantastic place. As a kid I had a particularly bad dose of something and thought I was lying in a vat of peeled, live snakes. No idea how I came through without a snake phobia, but I can't stomach spiders.

This time I don't have any reptile dreams. No, something far worse. A replay of real life events that haven't haunted me for a decade.

Dad always had a passion for boats and water. He was fascinated by our neighbour Denis's concrete-hulled boat but thought it was a monstrosity.

'Boats should be built of wood,' was Dad's mantra.

On the day of that boat's dry launch, Dad and I went around next door to help Denis try and extract his hull from the garage. I can remember clearly how the bulk of it tilted on the trailer as it hit the doorway.

'It's not going to make it through!' Dad shouted, his forearm caught between the smooth concrete hull and the rough red bricks of the garage wall. 'I can feel my bone bending!'

But it didn't break, lucky for him.

Wood, the natural medium to float on water. It was Dad's intention to build a river boat out of wood but it never came to fruition. A start was made with canoes. We drove out of Port Glasgow and way down to the East of England. Ottersports Canoes was on the fringes of a market town called Bury St Edmunds in the flat Suffolk countryside. We guessed it was the site where St Edmund was buried.

Dad, little David, me and Brett, our golden retriever, all squashed into our family's old MGB GT 2+2. The tiny sports car fairly raced along on our way out but was sluggish once Dad had loaded the coffin-sized wooden canoe kit onto the roof-rack. On the way back we twice had to stop at a service station and let the overheated engine cool off. A hell of a long day, off at six in the morning and not home until midnight.

For the next six months the huge garage attached to the side of our house became a place of wonder. Wood shavings, fibreglass matting, fibreglass resin, varnish – these were the origins of the strange odours that permanently took up residence there. At times we were allowed into the garage to watch the process.

'What's this, Dad?' I would hold up a strange shape.

'It's part of the cockpit rail.'

'It doesn't look like wood to me.' David was used to the solid lumps of wood we fashioned into toy swords.

'That's because it's marine ply. Thin layers of wood sandwiched together with a waterproof glue.'

I loved the look of the edges where Dad had hand-smoothed the plywood to a silky finish. It reminded me of liquorice allsorts.

Pieces of the giant jigsaw were offered up, trimmed and positioned. He built jigs to hold the pieces whilst the matting, soaked with resin, was laid in place to make the bonds. Those jigs sometimes consisted of David and myself holding pieces in position. Other times he lashed pieces together with thin rope and became obsessed with mastering every knot known to mankind. When things didn't go so smoothly, we were chased away with a flurry of expletives.

The garage-come-workshop was a place of wonder even before the canoe building. It had a six-foot pit in the floor to facilitate car repairs. A scary thing for kids, dark and damp, full of the biggest, hairiest spiders. Sheets of plywood covered the drop as a rule – Dad wasn't much into car mechanics. When we were younger we had fooled around over the pit.

'I dare you to step on it,' I would say to David.

'There, easy. Now you.'

David was smaller, lighter and fearless. I had the stronger fear of crashing through and my hesitancy would draw Dad's attention.

'Gerard, don't step on there. It might not take your weight. We don't want any accidents, boys. If you want to mess about then do it outside. Or go play with the train set.'

Up above was a large loft with exposed beams under the pitched roof. The timbers were oversized by the builder and several were good to take the weight of an engine on a block and tackle. Dad had floored that loft and built a large table, on which there was a huge electric train set. Pride of the set-up was the Flying Scotsman, an engine that could actually blow steam through some contraption if you filled it with water. The train track, engines, carriages and buildings had been there since I could remember. That must have been Dad's hobby before he became obsessed with boats, wood and knots.

The first output of our canoe workshop was a single kayak, the sort with a hole in the top where the person sat. Every outer surface of the craft was mirror smooth and it glided through the murky waters of the sea lochs like a barracuda. Dad was so impressed with his own handiwork he embarked upon another two canoes in parallel, one single and one double-seater with the idea of family canoeing holidays. I recall those holidays as times of extended numbness of the bum, after hours sat on a hard wooden seat.

Our little fleet was still in near new condition when we lost our captain. Things had not been going well with Dad's employer, a company called Rank Xerox. I never really understood what he did for the company, some kind of upper management job, but the upshot was the company had to shed a third of its employees globally due to business difficulties.

One day he came home from work in jubilant mood.

'They're looking to let go any manager aged over fifty!'

Mum seemed to think this was great news. Dad found himself retired early with a silver parachute.

I was seventeen years old. The facts were there to see, the reasons why Dad was so pleased to retire early, but my vision was blurred by the hormone-induced autism that is adolescence. Granddad had died of a heart attack at age sixty-five, within months of his retirement. My dad was expecting a similar fate and the redundancy program at RX gave him the chance to enjoy the few years he thought he had left.

Well, fate don't like smart people. We took a family holiday, budget style as usual, to Butlins holiday camp in North Wales. It was at Pwllheli in Gwynedd – how on earth is that pronounced? The Welsh aren't into phonetics, but Butlins were adept at removing all ethnic authenticity and the camp could have been anywhere in the UK. The red-coated entertainment staff were from all over. It was a strange choice of holiday venue, and one seemingly at odds with Dad's slightly bohemian take on life, but it was an unbreakable tradition his parents had established. I resolved it would be my last family holiday as I was ready to fly the nest, at least for those two weeks a year.

There were few age-appropriate activities in the camp for two teenagers like myself and David. We had never been to a disco and weren't into team sports. The few youths that hung around the place looked tough and smoked cigarettes. One night, after four days most of which Mum and Dad had spent drinking in the bar, I lay awake in the chalet bedroom I shared with David. His regular breathing across the room told me he was already in the land of Nod and I was contemplating a hand party, motivated by thoughts of a slinky girl I had noticed amongst the smoking youths. The bed conversation of my parents came through the gaps around the ill-fitting adjoining bedroom door.

'Are you okay, love?' Mum said in a low voice.

'No, Mary. My back's sore again. Give it a rub would you, pet? Just there, a bit harder. Oh.'

This was something of a ritual.

According to Mum, Dad just laid his head on her shoulder and fell asleep. That was the position I found them in, sitting up in bed, when I ran in to Mum's screams. Dad's head was turned towards her chest but I could see the side of his face was a pale gray-blue colour.

To their credit, Butlins did have medical staff on call but there was nothing to be done. The coroner subsequently found Edward Mayes had suffered a massive heart attack and died instantly.

I think Dad would have appreciated it, had we hauled him in his coffin the six hours home to Port Glasgow on the roof of the MGB GT, just like the trip with that first Ottersports canoe kit. But it wasn't to be. I drove our car the entire stretch back up to Scotland with my magnetic Learner plates attached. The writing on the packet was accurate – they were good for up to seventy miles an hour. David hugged Brett in the back seat whilst Mum sat silently in the front, a shrunken half of a couple.

I don't remember us making arrangements with a funeral home, or how and when Dad's body made its way back home. I do remember the funeral and crematorium. A gaggle of distant, estranged relatives making an appearance, most of whom I hadn't seen for five years or more. David and Mum wept openly at the service, leaving me feeling a little dysfunctional that the tears weren't flowing for me. Later, we all exchanged pleasantries outside the crematorium, the dust and smoke from Dad's remains swirling from the chimney and blowing back over the mourners.

~

Our big house had never been a place of particular mirth, but it felt very empty and quiet without my father's presence. Mum's grief became the dominant household personality. We lads were perfectly able to prepare our own food when we wanted it, and she calmly cleaned up after us. When Dad died we were promoted to young men, supported by a duteous mother. There was none of the scolding and cajoling that had characterised our life prior to Pwllheli.

When she wasn't washing, ironing or cleaning, Mum continuously played an old favourite song on the record turntable, Alone again - naturally by Gilbert O'Sullivan. She would sit in the back lounge and let O'Sullivan's plaintive tones fill the room whilst she drank her tea. Then there might be an episode of Coronation Street she would watch on the TV, followed by O'Sullivan again.

I look back now and wonder why I couldn't have been more lucid, why David and I left Mum to handle her own grief and depression. She did go to the doctor and prescription bottles of pills began to feature in the bathroom. One time our family physician Dr Crawford came out to the house and sat with us for a little chat.

'Boys, your mother is still in the grieving process. Just give her the time and space she needs, but take care of her. She's a wee bit depressed.'

The time Mum spent in bed increased but she was non-invasive and that suited us teenage boys just right. There were no aunts or uncles on the scene. Mum was an only child and, for some reason, Dad had established a distance between himself and his two siblings long since before we were born.

'Have you seen Mum today?' David asked me one afternoon.

He was nearing his final exams and had spent the day in his room, allegedly studying. A musky odour that shrouded him suggested he was smoking something for the stress.

'No. It was your turn to keep an eye on her, remember?'

I had spent the day working at Faslane Naval Base, my first full-time job. Trainee radio technician was to be just the first of many career routes I managed to eliminate.

'Uh huh? Yeah, well I've been here haven't I? She wasn't in the kitchen or the lounge when I came looking for a sandwich at lunchtime. What's for tea?'

David started to root through the fridge, pulled out a jumbo packet of wafer thin ham with just a few shavings of meat left in it and held it up in the air.

'There's nothing in here. Why isn't Mum doing any shopping these days?'

I hadn't noticed, having my lunch at the new job and going out most evenings via the chip shop. Gilbert O'Sullivan was moaning his song from the sitting room. I headed out to look for Mum.

'Hey, and turn off that record would you? It's been playing all afternoon, driving me nuts,' David said through a mouthful of ham scraps.

The music stopped as I approached the door, then restarted.

'In a little while from now, if I'm not feeling any less sour...'

Miserable bastard, O'Sullivan. I opened the door and expected to find Mum asleep on the sofa, as usual, but no sign of her.

The curtains were drawn and gave the impression of night time, it being a gray and drizzly day as it mostly is in The Port. Dad's chair was still in position to one side of the old fireplace. On impulse I sat in it, my hands rubbing the faded upholstery of the arms upon which he used to pile the pieces of hard skin from his tortured feet. The record played on. I tried to imagine what must be going on in Mum's mind.

'I cried and cried all day. Alone again, naturally.'

Gilbert finished up his dirge and I lifted the repeat lever to switch it off. Perhaps Mum had gone shopping. I decided to search the house for her and went from room to room. The bedroom door was shut so I knocked gently and then eased it open, but there was no huddled form under the duvet. Every room in the house was unoccupied except for my brother's room and even he would have noticed if Mum was in there.

Our front garden was mostly laid to lawn, with a sandy coloured gravel drive in the shape of a Y. Dad's car was lying dormant on one branch of the driveway, its insurance and MOT certificate expired. The other branch was occupied by a glass fibre river boat on a trailer, one of Dad's projects that had survived him. This boat had been my refuge on a first outing to the pub two years previously, Dad highly unimpressed to find me the next morning in the front cabin and a puddle of puke in the cockpit. I doubted Mum could even climb up onto the trailer and into the boat but I checked anyway. No sign of Mary.

Out back there were just the shed and the garage, and a big old walnut tree in the middle of the lawn. I thought she might have just sat down against the tree trunk and her heart given out, like in the Forsyte Saga, but the saggy shape in the long grass at the tree's base was Brett the dog, busy cleaning his privates. The neglected shed, scene of boyhood woodwork, was fastened on the outside with a rusting padlock. I held the lock in my hand and was wondering where the key was when I heard a crash and a shout from within the garage.

The smell of resin and glass fibre dust still hung in the air. As soon as I opened the door I saw what Gilbert O'Sullivan had driven my mother to. At the far end of the garage, above the pit, a rope hung from the rafters and down into the hole. It was taut with weight and creaked like the rigging of an old wooden ship. The plywood boards that had covered the drop were in a broken, splintered jumble around the brick edge of the pit.

A low moan came up from the depths. She might yet be alive. I ran forward and grabbed the rope, not quite sure what to do, and looked down.

'My ankle, Gerard, I think it's broken.'

It seemed like the most words my mother had spoken to me for weeks. She looked up from a kind of kneeling position on the floor of the pit, a hangman's noose around her neck. I walked down the steps at the front of the pit without fear of spiders. First, I loosened the rope from under her throat. It was pulled tight, as though she had continued to try and strangulate herself whilst on her knees.

'Gerard, love. I wasn't really going to do it, you know. The wood snapped under my weight.'

'I can see that, Mum. I can see that. Here, let's take this thing off you.'

She lifted herself slightly with a groan and let me raise her chin so I could take the noose from her head. The pit was damp and stale like a grave.

'Can you stand?'

'Let me try. I'm sorry, love. As if you need this trouble on your plate. No, I can't get up.'

I had to call the ambulance service. In the twenty minutes it took them to arrive from Gourock, I managed to free the rope from the rafters and dispose of it in the dustbin. My name isn't Hercule Poirot, but I noticed the smoothness of the wood, where the top of the rope had been knotted. Mum's hanging rope hadn't been too long after all, it had just slipped.

The medics confirmed Mum's left ankle to be broken and lifted her out of the pit with some difficulty. They had to cut off the straps of her shoes. They were cutting into the already swelling flesh under her light tan tights.

I went with Mum in the back of the ambulance to the accident and emergency department of the Inverclyde Royal Hospital. It was a huge brown building up on the hill, dominating the town. There were signs at every corridor junction and I noticed there were two acute psychiatric wings of the hospital. What would happen if they found out Mum had nearly died at the end of a rope? I thought of myself and David, running amok in the house. Smoking, drinking and girls. Washing, ironing and cooking. We weren't ready for independence.

It was an ambulance return journey too, a few hours later with Mum's leg in a cast. She took to bed with some painkillers and I went to take another look at the garage.

Mum's wrecked shoe was still next to the pit and I picked it up absentmindedly. Then I saw the broken pieces of plywood that had covered the pit were marked with small triangular indentations. They matched the heel of the shoe. Mum had jumped up and down on those boards until they'd given way.

I felt angry with her, that she would try to abandon David and myself. At the same time I was worried Mum would find another method of suicide less reliant upon her skill with knots.

She never made another attempt upon her own life that I knew of. Instead, she just dissolved over the years. We all drifted along like flotsam on life's tide. David left home first, after he finished at Stirling University, and then I moved south of the border for work. Mum eventually suffered a massive stroke and was found dead by a neighbour. Alone again, naturally.

The price

I know I've recovered because the ribs of the plastic shower base no longer cause pain to the soles of my feet. It's great to stand here, naked and comfortable, under streaming hot water. The mess of sweaty linen on the marital bed has taken on a greyish hue and the cheesy odour of confinement has impregnated my sinuses after three bed-bound days.

'Let's call out the doctor,' Jo had said on day two of my thirty-nine and a half degrees temperature.

'Save your money. You'll need it when I'm dead.' I didn't want the quack coming and probing the remnant injuries from my mugging. As if he would somehow divine the truth from my bruises.

'A serious case of man-cold,' Renée had declared on day three and, making sure Jo had gone downstairs, smoothed my mad hair and moistened my dried lips with hers.

I give Renée credit for my recovery because that kiss elicited my first hard-on for days and brought the fever to a crisis.

~

Today I feel almost normal. I've slept through past midday.

'You're feeling better then,' Jo says when she comes home for lunch at the back of one, after a gym session or something. 'Welcome back to the world.'

'Ha, ha. I'll probably go into work tomorrow at this rate.'

'What? Finish taking the week off, surely. Why would you go in?'

'Because I'm feeling better, because I have responsibilities at work.' Jo pulls a face of incredulity. 'Because I'm a bit stir crazy after four days.'

'Well, if you're feeling better you can start this afternoon by changing the bedclothes. They're rank. I have to sleep in that bed too you know.'

'No problem.'

I've had enough of playing the invalid. The truth is that, since my mind returned from the delirium of the last days, I've been keen to get back into Dublin and put things back on the simmer. With Caroline, naturally.

After we've both eaten the lunch Jo has made, and she's returned to work, I head upstairs. It takes a good while to locate what looks like a sheet, pillowcases and a matching duvet cover. The sheet turns out to be the wrong size. It's for the sofa bed in the spare room. Ditto the duvet cover. Then the pillowcases don't match the right sized duvet cover and, anyway, I have the expected difficulty in getting the duvet cover on. When all is finally done, to what I believe will be Jo's satisfaction, I'm exhausted and collapse on the freshly made bed. What was Jo thinking of, giving such a demanding chore to an untrained convalescent?

The next sound that penetrates my consciousness is the front door closing. Jo's home from work. I've slept the whole afternoon.

'Ger?'

She runs on her toes, child-like up the stairs.

'Just testing my handiwork,' I explain as I emerge from under the duvet and try to smooth its symmetry.

'You missed Renée, look.' She hands me a folded piece of paper.

How's the sick one? Renée, kiss kiss.

'Kiss, kiss eh?' Jo comes to me with a twinkling eye and places her lips on mine for a brief moment.

'We could mess the bed,' I smile.

She flinches. 'Did you clean your teeth? It's just, well, your breath is pretty bad.'

'You mean from the fever?'

'I guess so, although it wasn't great before.'

'But...' Renée doesn't seem to mind, I nearly say.

'If your wife can't tell you then who can?'

'You could have told me before.'

'Mouthwash. Try some mouthwash. How about Chinese for dinner? I can't be bothered cooking. And maybe a bottle of wine?'

Well, that'll do a lot for my bad breath.

'Yeah, sounds good. I'll go get it.'

'Are you sure? Do you feel okay to drive?'

'Yep. If I'm going to work tomorrow I'll have to drive to the station, so it'll be a good test.'

Jo calls in the order, as usual, because they always have problems with my Scottish accent and things get mixed up. While she's still on the phone, I launch my car off the driveway and begin to realise things are not quite as they should be. The pedals and the steering wheel feel spongy under my feet and hands. Cars appear as if from nowhere, travelling alarmingly fast. This seems strange indeed as I normally consider myself to be dominant on the road, something of a Driving God. I manage to get to the Golden Sun without crashing but am honked by a granny in a Micra. How the mighty fall.

On the way back I stop at Lidl and pick up a very good bottle of Rioja for a keen price. Just one bottle, as I'm still not well. The other folk in the shop seem to be staring but I don't return their looks.

Jo opens the front door to greet me.

'Look at the state of you!'

I hand her the paper bag of food and the wine bottle, then I look in the hallway mirror. Six days of beard growth, which is a mix of ginger and grey, and my overcoat is inside out.

'Will you dish?' she calls from the kitchen.

'No, sorry, I need to sit down. Will you do everything?'

I install myself on the sofa and we have a lazy evening of takeaway, wine and television. The only conversation is about whether to flick from one inane TV program to another. Then, when we stagger up to bed, Jo decides to favour me with a shag. Once I've cleaned my teeth.

'This is purely for therapeutic purposes,' she says.

'Well, you'll have to do all the work as I'm still convalescing,' I say hopefully. In fairness, I've done my part by using the mouthwash.

And the request is granted. Lying flat on my back, an occasional thrust being all that is required, I'm treated to the vision of Jo getting what she needs on top, whilst her right hand rubs the place I can never seem to reach when I'm in the saddle. It doesn't take long, her hips grind into mine and her breasts bounce together as she builds up speed in a heaving rhythm. When she comes it's such a tightening that I follow her involuntarily. Of course it's not unpleasant, but I feel ridden.

In the morning, still a little spaced out, I make it to the 8:37 train in one piece. For a change I take a seat facing the back of another and, Jo's borrowed MP3 player connected, close my eyes to the sound of Norah Jones. When I next open them, I'm the only one on the train except for a Chinese guy who is collecting rubbish left behind by the now departed passengers.

It feels like I've been away from Dublin for a long time. The Liffey is swollen and charging seaward, like a huge artery full of brown blood. No sign of all the usual debris that clutters the river bed at low flow: shopping trolleys, traffic cones, children's bicycles, dead Romanians.

There's a breeze crossways over Heuston bridge and an earthy smell leaps over the Luas tracks. I don't hear the music until I'm across the other side and then I stop short, both captivated and cautious.

Ilie's face is serene as he coaxes the melodies from his guitar's strings. He sees my shoes and lifts his gaze to mine. I hesitantly smile at him. This is real, he's here playing guitar. It's how things were before. I only have two Euros in cash so I bend and place it in his cup. He says nothing and there's no change to his expression. This can't be the man who attacked me behind the station, if it ever even happened. His crippled leg is intact, the crooked knee cradling the round swell of his guitar.

I straighten and step forward but then two things happen at once. The music stops and I let out a shout. Something hard has struck me painfully in the shin.

Stepping back, I stoop to rub my shin and see a plastic carrier bag. Ilie is holding it to block my path. He drops the bag to the ground with a clank and parts the plastic to show something metal and heavy inside, bent and stained dark brown in several places. It looks very much like a murder weapon.

Self preservation tells me I should grab the bag from Ilic and hurl it into the Liffey, but my body is not responding to the instinct. Instead I start to back away, only to find a hand on each of my arms. Two youths flank me, clad in sports gear. They're both taller than Ilie but the family resemblance is unmistakable.

I look around the street, hoping for some authority figure to rescue me from my predicament. Ilie barks a little laugh and rises surprisingly easily from the ground with the aid of his crutch. He holds up the evidence bag and says 'Follow me.'

We move in the direction of Phoenix Park and I have to hurry to keep up with his surprising pace. Heavy traffic forces us to wait in a gaggle at the Coyningham Road pedestrian crossing. I'm hemmed in by the three of them. On a good day I would fancy my chances in a fair fight with any one of them, maybe even two, but it's not a good day. My brain is floating in a bowl of soup and the old bones feel detached from their muscles.

The man turns green and we shuffle forward across the junction. Now we are immediately outside the new Criminal Courts of Justice and there's no shortage of authority figures to appeal to. Garda Síochána cars are everywhere, as are TV news vans, reporter crews setting up cameras and testing microphones. There must be a high profile criminal case in the offing. That could be me. Two officers on the top step of the entrance gaze over our heads from the saddles of their mountain bikes. Ilie gives me a narrow-eyed look over his shoulder. Make your choice. Us or the law. I don't break my stride.

Once in the Park, I let Ilie walk ahead and develop a distance between us. There's a steady flow of cars down the middle of Chesterfield Avenue, the thoroughfare that transects these 1750 acres of parkland. It's quarter past ten in the morning and I wonder where all the traffic is going at this hour. The kerb is lined with parked cars of every size, shape, age and colour. A car thieves' paradise if it weren't for the ever-present mounted law officers, two of whom are slowing up the traffic as their huge horses clop steadily along the tarmac. Once the horses pass by, a shove on my shoulder brings me back to reality. The two lads are right behind.

Ilie weaves slightly along the footpath, avoiding the drooping branches of trees heavy with fresh growth. Beech trees at a guess, I'm no horticulturist. As I endeavour to follow the scampering Romanian musician, Wellington's Monument rises hugely up on our left. Several degenerates are sunning themselves on the giant, sparkling granite steps whilst drinking cans of beer. More Guards on foot are heading towards the morning drunks. I consider again the choice between incarceration and Romanian revenge, but Ilie has second guessed my hesitation. He stops, turns and holds the bag aloft. I'm firmly in his grip.

We move on apace. A warm breeze helps the sweat to form on my forehead and I get a whiff of something earthy. Can it be me? Or is it my escorts? A burst of resonant snorts and trumpeting explains it: we're about to pass the elephant residents of Dublin Zoo. Like them, I'm enclosed in a yard of my own shite.

The distance we've covered already is much further than I would normally walk in these work shoes and blisters are beginning to form on the backs of my heels. I feel this through a haze as though the feet belong to someone else. The fever of the last few days has addled my brain.

The white steel of the Papal Cross catches the sunlight over west. It's only half the height of the Wellington obelisk but it would seem a more fitting place for the Romanians to string me up. A wave of panic stops my march. What are they really going to do to me? Surely I had better turn myself in. The Garda Síochána headquarters are somewhere in this park, but I'm not sure whereabouts.

There's a gap coming up in the metal railings to the right. I make a break for it and start to run, holding one strap of my backpack to stop it bouncing. There's a small lake and I pelt towards the northern end, already out of breath. Behind me is a steady patter of running shoes. I glance over my shoulder and see one of the Romanian lads on my heels, so I slip my left arm from the strap of the backpack, stop and step to the side, swinging the bag hard with my right hand. But there's nothing of any weight in it and the impact on my pursuer is comical. He stops and rips the backpack from my hand. The other youth appears on the scene from the opposite direction, panting hard. He's run around the other side of the lake.

'We go…Maze,' the first lad says, handing me my backpack.

'Where?' There's no maze in the Phoenix Park I know of but it would just be perfect at this point. A murderer pursued through a maze by vengeful members of the victim's family.

'We go… Gerard Mayes.'

Shit! Somehow they know my name.

Ilie appears on the scene, a smile on his face.

'You come with us, you have no choice. Is better for you, believe me.'

I square my shoulders, chest still heaving from the attempted escape. The youth who ran around the lake produces a flick-knife, holds it discretely against his trouser leg, then as quickly puts it away. I have no choice.

It seems Ilie's plan is to walk me to death. The heat rises from inside my jacket and the sweat is so hot beneath my backpack that I'm tempted to throw it in the undergrowth. At last, just as my heartbeat has made itself audible, my torturer leaves the path near the Castleknock exit and disappears into a copse of thorn trees. The youths are close enough behind me to make it plain I should continue and follow Ilie along a track through the trees. I bend my head to avoid the thorns at eye level.

The path broadens out into a clearing, the ground covered with a patchwork of mats and rugs. This reminds me of the sort of den my brother and I would fashion out of a thicket on the hillside back home. Ilie stands in the middle and waits for me to join him. Then he squats down and gestures for me to do the same. Between us lies the bloodstained bar with which I killed his brother.

I look at the evidence and contemplate my fate. They'll kill me here, during normal daylight, and no one can save me. It's happened before in the Park. No one can hear you scream. There are soft noises behind me and I turn to see we now sit in a circle of ten or so people.

'With this you killed my brother.' Ilie speaks factually, no discernible malice. He brandishes the alleged murder weapon. 'I know what happened. You are a murderer.'

He's surprisingly eloquent. I wonder where Ilie has learned his English and how long he has been in Ireland. But it doesn't seem the right time for small talk. Then he continues.

'Alin was a bad man, my twin. He brought us trouble many times. But you threw my brother's body into the river.'

'No!'

Someone must have seen my fight with the beggar, Alin. Then recovered the metal bar from under a pallet or wherever. I should have searched for it and thrown the thing down over the wall with the body. Let the tide come in and bury it forever in the Liffey sludge.

No one answers my denial. I sit in silence. This doesn't seem to be a kangaroo court. There's no murderous intent in the air, only the story of a murder.

Ilie confers briefly with the circle in a language I cannot understand but some of the words sound vaguely French. The talk dies down and he turns his impassive face to me once more.

'You will pay us compensation for Alin. For my brother.'

I look at Ilie and those gathered around me. As well as the two youths that were my park escort, the circle includes children, a dwarf, two other cripples and a woman with a moustache holding a baby doll. It's a fucking freak show. Then I consider the metal bar lying, bloodstained, in the middle of the circle, within arm's reach. The sun, breaking through the clouds and the trees, glints off the blades of a knife here and there in the audience.

'What makes you think I killed your brother?'

'You were seen there. By Nadia, behind the station, seven nights ago.' Without averting his eyes, Ilie's open, outstretched hand indicates a young girl. She's no freak and, by the look of her, she may well have been selling favours at the rear of Heuston that evening. The girl hangs her head and he continues. 'Nadia could do nothing. Alin meant to kill you. You were lucky. He was unlucky.'

I feel pretty unlucky.

'Why do you think it was me? It must have been dark.'

Ilie waves his hand at the murder weapon. 'This. Your blood, Alin's blood. Police will find your fingerprints.'

'No, maybe Alin died from a beating with this metal bar but my fingerprints, my blood, they're not on it.'

He shakes his head. 'I showed you this. Your face said guilty. I said follow and you did. Nadia saw you kill Alin. Alin said he would hurt you. It was you.'

'Oh no,' I reply quietly.

'Of course we can give this evidence to the authorities and tell them about you. Your life will be ruined. You should jump in the river and join Alin. No, better for you, a private arrangement for compensation. Has to be better for you. Better for your family.'

So this is what it has come to. A moment's weakness, a few euro in a beggar's cup and now my life in their hands. I wait for Ilie, surviving twin of Alin, to speak again.

'You will do two things. First, you will come back here in exactly seven days with one hundred thousand euro in cash. The second thing we keep for later.' The group murmurs assent.

I groan. One hundred thousand euro. Our house has enough equity to borrow against. But in just one week? And if they want more I don't have it.

'How am I supposed to get that sort of money? I'm not a rich man, I'm just an ordinary guy.'

'This is your problem. You killed Alin, you bring the money. One week.'

The circle is silent. I rest my chin on the steeple of my clasped hands.

'I can get fifty.'

'Don't bargain with me, Ticalos!' He spits at me, no longer constraining his temper. 'One hundred thousand. Seven days. Or this goes to the police and your lazy, comfortable life goes to prison.'

So, the situation isn't negotiable.

'What's the second thing? I don't have any more money. I'm not a rich man.'

There is murmured conferring amongst the group again. 'The second thing will be something we ask you to do. We will not ask for more money.'

'Will it be something illegal?'

There's a flutter of laughter around the circle. Involuntarily, I smile at the amused audience.

'Yes, something illegal.' My face must be an open book as he continues, 'No, we will not ask you to kill someone. You have already done that.'

I rise from the grass to leave. Leave the Park, leave Dublin, leave the country? Again Ilie has sized me up.

'Do not run away from us, Gerard Mayes of Bagenalstown. It is only money. You still have your life. One week from now, bring the money here,' he points to the ground beneath him, 'and then I will tell you what else. Now you may leave.'

The circle parts and I wander through the bushes, the thorns tearing at my backpack.

One week.

Renée and the whole weight of everything

They tell me nothing can be done. I had already sensed it. I've long expected the return of my old enemy.

In the dusty corners of my mind there's a vague recollection of Mum and Dad having a particular argument. It would have been before I started school. The exact words elude me, so I'll fill in the blanks.

'Not now, Andy. Renée will hear. For Christ's sake, not now of all times!'

Dad says nothing for a while but his silence is like a great wet towel, laid upon us. I'm in my bedroom, kneeling on the bed and listening hard through the wall. I hear a wardrobe door opening, the clatter of coat-hanger hooks and then two clicks. He's going on another trip and that brings a smile. Presents, he always brings me presents after a trip.

'For pity's sake!'

And then comes Dad's voice, impossibly deep and deliberate compared to Mum's shrieking. Not that her shrieking alarms me, it's commonplace in our house.

'Linda, we both know it would be better if I went. Better for all of us.'

'Run away then. Go on. Leave the whole weight of everything on me.'

The last phrase is verbatim. For a long time I imagined Mum was lying on the bed, underneath something heavy, and she needed Dad's help to get the heavy thing off her. Like the way people were tortured, in olden times, by placing heavy stones on their chest until they betrayed their king or confessed to witchcraft or died. I had to endure my own personal torture before realising the whole weight of everything was actually me.

'Your father's gone on a trip.'

'He'll bring me the swing-ball this time. I know he will. He always knows what I want. I love Daddy. And you, Mummy. But Daddy brings me stuff.'

'Yes, sweetheart. I don't know about the swing-ball. It's not the season.'

'What does season mean?'

It was a season of sickness that fell upon me like Autumn. First a chill and a damp feeling in morning's first breath. Then, like the leaves, my hair began to fall. A common nightmare for children and adults alike is their hair comes out in clumps when they brush it. For me it's a memory. My flaxen strands were all over the house.

'Mummy, what's happening to my hair?'

'Don't worry, sweetheart. Our bodies change. Look at James next door, his teeth are falling out. Doesn't that look funny? But he'll grow new teeth and you'll grow new hair.'

My body changed. The little fat tummy Dad used to pat and say 'chocoholic, just like your mother'. My tummy vanished as if Dad had taken it with him. My appetite for chocolate and just about everything else left me for good. Perhaps the trigger for hunger had been surgically removed, along with the tumour, from my four-year-old stomach.

In teenage and adult years I was often mistaken for anorexic and then later, when the trend in popular disorders changed, bulimic. Even today, eating remains a mechanical task I can easily neglect.

Dad did visit me in the hospital. I think he did. That's the way I remember it anyway. Mum maintained he didn't, he was too busy chasing young skirt, enjoying his new-found freedom. She remained bitter about him up until her death last year. Had I ever managed to persuade her to visit a psychiatrist, I think she would have finally articulated the thoughts that had buried her motherly love. Dad left because of me. She lost her youth and beauty because of me. It was all my fault. Then she'd have seen it wasn't, and we might have had peace with each other.

When I came home from hospital, Dad wasn't there. But he did visit and he did bring the swing-ball and set it up in my bedroom, much to Mum's disapproval. I watched him bat the thing around like a maniac and laughed for the first time since he had left.

The next year I started in school and the whole weight of everything placed itself on my shoulders like a greatcoat.

'My mum says you had cancer.' It was Tim Steele in the playground. An over-energetic lad was Tim, these days probably diagnosable with some anachronisable syndrome.

Most of the other kids looked at me like I was a leper, but I carried on skipping and chasing with the two girls who lived in my street. They knew it wasn't catching. Tim caught up with me after school the next day, just the two of us in an alleyway between brick classrooms.

'Renée? What kind of a name is that? Your dad foreign, is he? My mum says he lives in another country.'

Tim seemed to have more information about my family circumstances than I did. I said nothing but didn't run away.

'Mum says they cut it out in the hospital.' He pointed at my stomach. In hindsight, I'm not sure Mrs Steele had my best interests at heart. 'D'you have a scar? Can I see?'

For the first, but not the last time, I unwisely bared myself. The girls' uniform was a grey jumper with a white blouse and I also had on a vest. I pulled the whole caboodle up and over my face.

'Those are called nipples,' Tim said, the tip of his cold finger touching on my chest. 'I don't see a scar.'

'There.' I put a hand down and pointed to the one-inch line to the right of my belly-button.

'There? Does it still hurt? Can I touch it?'

'It was a bit sore for a while but not now.'

He ran the pad of his thumb over the smooth scar. I lowered my clothes and he gave me a smile. Then he punched me in the stomach and ran off.

'That's what boys do when they like a girl,' Mum explained after I had run home crying. 'The more they like you the more they try to hurt you.'

'Does Daddy try to hurt you?'

'Your father has hurt me, sweetheart, and I'm not sure it'll ever get better.'

She was being melodramatic, I realise now. At the time I thought the noises I had heard, the quiet whimpers and the mysterious rhythmic thumping that used to come from my parents room when Dad had lived there, must have been Dad punching Mum repeatedly in the stomach.

Tim Steele and I became school-friends. He sat next to me on my table in class. His mother may have had the loosest tongue in Cheshire, but Tim never shared what we talked about. It was through talking to Tim that I came to realise Dad had left because of me. I donned the whole weight of everything without question. Mum didn't do much to alleviate the misconception.

It suited her to blame the failed marriage on my cancer rather than on her relationship with Dad.

When I reached my teens Dad began to talk to me in earnest. He had moved to Ireland and I was visiting him in Waterford when he first broached the subject, in a café on the quay.

'You do know why your mother and I split up, don't you?'

I had been trying to elicit some disclosure from him but, now he was about to tell me to my face that I was the cause, I baulked.

'I don't really want to talk about it, Dad. At least, not now. Maybe when I'm older.'

'You are older. Listen, your mother and I were having problems before you got sick. You mustn't think we split up because of your cancer.'

'I don't. Don't be silly, Dad.' But I was crying into my milkshake.

'I know it looks like I did a terrible thing, leaving you at that time.'

'Yep.' I could hardly speak without totally losing it.

'You'll find out for yourself, not all relationships are forever. Your mother and I, well, we reached the end of our respective tethers long before then.'

I looked out of the café window at the old-fashioned high masts and furled sails at their moorings. It was Waterford's turn to host the Tall Ships Race. We were there for Dad, he had an interest in sailing.

'You mean your relationship had run its course? What, before I was born? So why did you have me at all, then?'

It was worse than I thought. My painful existence had been unwanted from the start. Why hadn't Mum had the unborn me removed like a tumour?

'No, no. We began to drift apart a couple of years after you were born, when I started to travel with the job. Some things went on. I'm not proud of my behaviour, but your mother was no angel.'

It sounded like I was about to get a full and sordid confession but I managed to halt it with a raised teenage hand.

'It's unfortunate we came to a crisis point just when you were diagnosed.'

'Unfortunate? UNFORTUNATE?'

The few other customers in the shop looked around at us. They saw a father enduring a tantrum from his teenage daughter. I saw a bastard that had abandoned me in my hour of mortal need.

'Please. I'm trying to explain.'

I could only nod.

'I think I made a mistake in going when I did.'

'You think you should have stayed with us?'

'I should have taken you with me. No, that wouldn't have worked. Your mother would never have…'

He was confused about how he would have rewritten history.

'Listen, Dad. I haven't had a bad childhood. I hardly remember the cancer. I missed you when you weren't there but that made our times together even more special. I have friends at school that have lived through terrible divorces. For what it's worth, I think you did the right thing.'

'You're probably right. You've a wise head on young shoulders.'

It's what comes of carrying the whole weight of everything.

'Did you never think of getting back with Mum at all?'

'No. We still had some feelings for each other but, well, no.'

I had blurry recollections of Mum and Dad having stomach-punching sessions, post-separation, on one or two occasions, such as at Christmas time. It made me shudder. At thirteen, sex was lurking menacingly in the shadows.

'Sorry. The point I want to make is this. I didn't leave because of you. I didn't leave because of your cancer. I left because your mother and I didn't want to live together any more, under any circumstances.'

I put my hand over his and forced a smile. Even through the lens of puberty, I knew my mother could be difficult. And I knew there had been an Uncle Jim and, later, an Uncle Pat, neither of which were blood relatives.

But Dad seemed under the illusion he had taken the burden from my shoulders and thereby healed any damage. His motivation for our little chat may have had an element of selfishness.

Years later a psychiatrist explained to me the lasting damage that had made my character 'needy', as she called it. An ancient peasant becomes bent and stiff from years of pulling his primitive plough through the unyielding soil, but if you retire that plough then the peasant remains bent and stiff. Then, in order to make sense of his stature, knowledge of the plough is required. Even then the peasant might never fully regain his posture. 'Needy' is also the word Ger uses from time to time when I say we don't see enough of each other. I haven't told Ger about my personal plough.

~

Mr McGrath, my consultant oncologist in Dublin, called me negligent. It had been a couple of years since I had sat down with a clinician. He went so far as to phone me himself, last year, but I didn't return his call. When I eventually did get a check-up, and the subsequent MRI scan, McGrath let me off the hook. I had been wrong to let things go, but his opinion was I had saved myself a lot of unpleasant treatment that would have had no positive effect. Riddled with cancer is an expression they use when they open up some old fella for a routine operation and find he's already half-way to St Peter's Gates. McGrath didn't use that expression but his eyes, and the first prescription for morphine, gave the game away. This time I would keep my hair and be buried with it.

God! I hope I can go to my inevitable end without Jo discovering I'm carrying on with her Ger. It's poor repayment for the friendship she's shown me over the past years.

Jo and I first met at a women's society in Kilkenny called the K Club. The name is a swipe at the famous Kildare golf club of the same name that has made golf widows of some of the more well-heeled wives. Jo was there to build her social circle. I was there, on instructions from my psychiatrist, to address my aversion to social gatherings.

In Jo I saw the kind of person I would like to be – gregarious, humorous and popular. We did share some characteristics. Young looking, pretty rather than beautiful, and an air of vulnerability. We were so alike. It had to be we would either become fierce enemies or embrace each other as long-lost sisters. Jo became my surrogate sibling, the one Mum and Dad had denied me.

I can see what attracted Ger, and many other men, to Jo. There's a type of man that goes for the vulnerable woman, wanting to protect her and dominate her at the same time. Not always a particularly nice type. Jo did a good job in selecting Ger from her many suitors, although I know he thinks it was the other way around. Last year I began to get the impression from Jo she thought their relationship had run its course. So, when I caught Ger in a posture of adoration at that dinner party, I didn't have much of a crisis of conscience in deciding to seduce him.

My life needs spice. It needs humour and passion. Without it's just a bland, grey slide into the grave. Ger makes me laugh. He's so funny my cheeks ache after an evening with him, alone or in company. As for romance, he's as mean with that as he is with money. But my instincts were rewarded when I got him in the sack. Ger doesn't talk passion but, by God, he shows it. It's as though my body was made for his adulation. There's not an inch of my skin that hasn't been touched or kissed. The second time we made love, his return confirmed to me it was going to be an affair and not just a one-off and it excited me in a new way. I came twice in the shower and we were going for a third when I had to stop and lie on the floor, my legs too weak to hold me. I thought I was going to have a heart attack and die happy.

We've passed through a predictable, if rapid, cycle in the affair. Ger's infatuation with my skinny body became repetitive. The sensitivity of places rarely touched is due to exactly that. I started to become desensitised. Then I stopped dreaming about him. I shower now without imagining his hands exploring my body, his fingers washing my hair.

Then there was his tireless sexual energy. I should have guessed early on but I was naive of such things. The flushed cheeks and his constant hard-on. One night I saw him take a little pill when he thought my back was turned. So his sexual ardour turned out to be pharmaceutically driven. Does that make me his plaything or he mine?

Recently, we've drifted into some kind of normality. My back has caught me out a few times and I'm having trouble finding a rhythm with the morphine, probably because the cancer is tightening its grip on my spine. Ger's libido is like an on-off switch. Even if he's had one of his pills, any hint of my sore back is an effective deterrent. We've spent evenings together like a normal couple, well, how I imagine a normal couple would be as I've never been part of one. His humour tends to fizzle out without stimulus and that's the worst thing. I need his humour.

Now it's reached the point where I have to tell him about my illness. I'm scared he'll run away. I'm scared Jo will find out and I'll lose her too. And die alone.

A trouble shared

No time to waste, no time to waste. By the time I reach the office, sweating from my Phoenix Park expedition, it's already the early afternoon.

'Ger! We didn't expect to see you until Monday. Why didn't you take the week?'

I respond to Deirdre with a half smile and a flap of the hand. It's surprising how much she's grown in the days I've been away.

'Let me have your doctor's cert when you're ready-uh,' is Brian's greeting as I enter my cubicle.

Shit! I should have gone to the quack like Jo said. But that's all secondary. Right now I need to get stuck in to the business at hand.

'Mr Purcell's office. Lucy speaking. Can I help?' The woman's voice on the phone is interrogatory. A guard dog.

'Hello, Lucy. This is Gerard Mayes. Please tell Mr Purcell I have some urgent mortgage business to transact.' My tones are hushed. The cubicle doesn't provide great privacy.

'Hello? Could you speak up please? I can hardly hear you.'

I repeat my request a little louder.

'I'm sorry, Mr Mayes, but Mr Purcell is on leave until Tuesday. Can I help?'

Bastard bank managers. Never there when you need them.

'I need an appointment first thing Tuesday morning. An urgent investment opportunity that requires finance.' Self-importance is the only way to handle people like Lucy.

'Let me just check his diary, but I'm sure that will be okay. Yes, here we go. How about eleven-thirty?'

'Anything earlier? Nine?'

'Well, he'll only just be back from two weeks' away and there's a lot of work waiting for him.'

'It's really very urgent.' A matter of life and death.

'What sort of amount are you looking to borrow, Mr Mayes?'

I'm not sure if it's something I should discuss with Lucy, but she's clearly the gateway to Purcell.

'A hundred thousand. Or so.'

'Right. Okay. Let's say nine-thirty.'

'Thanks, Lucy. See you then.'

I replace the handset on the phone, let some of the tension drop from my shoulders and stretch back in my chair. But the respite doesn't last for long. If I see Purcell on the Tuesday then what are the chances of having the cash by Thursday evening? Because that's what I need for the Friday rendezvous with Ilie and co. Virtually zero, I would have thought. So I need a plan B. And a cup of tea.

The hot water from the urn splashes my fingers as it gushes into my favourite mug. She's looking good, Vern. For the first time ever it fails to make me laugh. I take my tea into a corner of the room and sit with head in hands. What to do, what to do?

'Are you okay?'

It's Caroline. She has genuine concern on her face and one hand is extended half-way across the table towards me. Hi ho, silver lining. I untangle a hand from my hair and place it on top of hers. It feels cool and smooth.

'You're on fire. You shouldn't have come in today.'

A sudden twist grips my nether regions.

'Sorry, I have to go…'

The toilet is right next to the tea room. Brian comes out as I head in. I can feel the cold sweat coming on. It's happened before, usually when I get out of bed too quickly, having had a skinful the night before. I head into the first of three cubicles, Trap 1 as I like to call it, and push the door up behind me.

There, Brian has left his spoor. Nothing disgusting but just the usual – a fresh, new toilet roll hangs with the dangly bit inside, on the wall side of the roll, precisely positioned. I know from experience he's reset all three cubicles in the same way. With the attack coming I know I should leave it. But life is too short. It pisses him off something mighty when I undo his compulsion. So I pull the centre piece from the toilet roll holder, reverse the direction of the roll so the loose edge is outwards, and replace the thing. Then the same in Trap 2.

In Trap 3 things start to go wrong. I drop the toilet roll and it rolls under the partition between the stalls. My outstretched arm finds it but, when I rise up on my knees to replace the roll, the wall seems to sway away from me. Then my head crash lands on the toilet bowl. Fortunately the seat lid is down. I rest my dizzy, sweating forehead on the plastic and take deep breaths.

'He's in here.'

Caroline's voice comes through the entrance door of the toilet. I manage to reach out an arm and slide home the lock on the cubicle door.

'There, he's in there, I see his feet-uh.'

Now it's Brian. I pull my legs back under the door as I hear the pitter-patter of Brian's size six feet running into Trap 1 and then 2.

'I bloody knew it, Mayes, you bastard-uh.'

I twist my head and see Brian's Neanderthal brow poking over the toilet partition. The squirt must be standing on the toilet. His sloping forehead is wrinkled in anger as he points at the toilet roll still in my hand. I manage a grin.

'Fuck off, Brian.'

'Are you okay in there, Ger?' It's fat Deirdre, in the gents' toilet. Is nothing sacred?

'Fine thanks. I just need a little privacy.'

The main door closes and I'm alone. Almost.

'You fucking prick, Mayes-uh.' Brian, my team leader, bangs on the cubicle door as he leaves. Not very professional, Brian.

I replace the toilet roll, dangly bit away from the wall, raise the seat lid and go about my business. After the flush, I undo Brian's remedial work in Trap 1 and 2 and splash cold water on my face at the sink.

I feel quite fine now, a little sweaty perhaps, but it's an opportunity to head home. No one questions me as I pack up and leave, except Deirdre.

'Post the certificate into the office. Next time, make sure you're well before you come back.'

She's not quite sympathetic. I can almost see the unspoken fine line.

~

There's nothing to be done about the bank until Tuesday. When I get home, having slept most of the way to Bagenalstown, Jo is still at work. Even in this befuddled state I know I need help with plan B, but I don't want to come clean with Jo. That leaves Tom or Renée.

I call Tom. The guitar music starts and I know it's his answer machine.

Tom McMenemy… is not at home… so leave your message… after the tone… then, at his discretion… when he gets in, he'll phone… he surely will.

'Time to change that message,' is my automatic response to his machine. I played the guitar for him on the recording. 'Give me a call, mate.'

~

Renée's BMW is parked outside her house. She always works at home on Fridays, organising appointments. I ring the bell. I don't have a key. Just a cardboard folder in my hand.

The door opens and she leaves it wide, just standing there. We look at each other, like siblings that have unexpectedly, tragically lost a parent. Simultaneously we move to embrace. I drop the folder to the floor. How could she already know what's happened to me? We grip each other, heads and necks intertwining like swans.

'Oh, Ger.' Her lips brush my neck and mine her ear.

Then our mouths lock, her kiss deep.

Upstairs, the lovemaking is slow, gentle. My fingers slide along the back of her arms, over her hands and between her fingers as she lies face-down on the bed. I'm rubbing against her, inside, outside, inside. This is her favourite position. Her hands grip mine hard and I see she's crying.

'Renée?'

She rolls me off and climbs on top. Her hands press down on my chest as she grinds her pelvis back and forth, excruciating for us both. Her hand is in her hair, pulling her own head back, and she cries out as if in pain. That image of Renée burns into my memory like an eclipse of the sun.

Then, instead of us falling asleep, she's up and walking into the bathroom. When Renée stands, her ribcage is visible in her bare back. I see her waif-like thinness as if for the first time. Then a rattle of a pill bottle and the shower switches on.

~

'You beat a crippled beggar to death with an iron bar and it's going to cost you a hundred thousand euro? Tell me this is some kind of sick joke. Isn't it?'

We sit on her sofa, holding misted glasses of cold Italian white wine.

'You come here, talking nonsense about some fantasy world, whilst the real world crumbles ….'

'What can be more real than smashing in the skull of some penniless, immigrant beggar, albeit in self-defence, and then being blackmailed over it?'

She takes a deep breath.

'I have cancer.'

'You what?'

'My back. Those pains over the last few months. It's a tumour, malignant.'

I fight the impulse to recoil. To jump up, run out of the house.

'No. No, there must be some mistake. Get a second opinion.'

'Ha! I trust my Oncologist and I'm no stranger to cancer.'

I look at Renée's uncommon expression. Do I really know anything about her?

'There are a lot of things I haven't told you. I've been battling with cancer since I was four years old.'

The clock on the mantelpiece, even though it's electric, emits an audible tick with each increment of the second hand.

'I don't know what to say.'

I look at Renée's face but what I see is a woman's body hanging at the end of a rope, the creak of wooden beams under the weight. I swallow hard, push the image from my mind, focus on my hands grasped together like claws.

'I'm sorry to lay this on you. Maybe I shouldn't have told you.'

'Don't apologise. God! What now?'

The grip of the noose loosens from under the chin, from the back of the ears.

'You're my rock. Now, what the hell are you talking about? Sorry, but you're just too normal and boring to be blackmailed for murder. I can't believe what you're saying.'

Until a week ago I might have agreed with her.

'Cancer?' is all I manage to say.

'Yes, fucking cancer. It could be a month, it could be a year.'

'Surely they can treat it? An operation or drugs?'

'Surgery is out of the question, it's wrapped around my spinal cord. Radiotherapy wouldn't be helpful.

And I'm not going to have chemo unless there's a chance of survival, which there isn't. Morphine is your only man.'

'Now you're the one who must be joking.'

'Get used to it, lover boy. You're going to be down to one woman before the year is out. Possibly a lot sooner.'

Her smile is brave. It says she's going to take charge of the situation, as she always does. There will be no nausea, hair loss, wheelchairs or wasting away for her. Renée will take a one-way ticket on the fast train to oblivion when she feels the time is right. It's the attitude of the hanging woman.

A tragic situation, right enough. Inescapable. But I have a situation as well, one that might be managed. So I have to be selfish and make a dying girlfriend focus on my blackmail problem. It'll probably be a welcome distraction for her.

I reach for the folder of news cuttings and internet articles about Alin's murder and spread them on the coffee table.

'Come off it. Have you lost your mind? Why not pick a less macabre fantasy?'

I remember the death blow, my shoulders straining to add every ounce of strength as I cleaved the cold night air and Alin's upper vertebrae with that heavy bar. The merciful silence that followed.

'For God's sake! I was seen throwing his body into the river. They have the metal bar I killed him with. There's no element of fantasy in this.'

Tick, tick, tick.

'Why?' Her voice is gentle. 'You've risked everything. What possessed you?'

'You saw the bruises I had last week. I tell you, the guy was trying to kill me. It was him or me. I got lucky and he didn't. It was just bad luck I was seen by the girl.'

'Have you done this sort of thing before?'

'Oh yes, I make a habit of it. Clearing the streets of vermin. Ger Mayes, the Caped Crusader. What do you think?'

'I take that as a no.'

I bite my tongue, waiting for her to continue.

'So, you need a hundred grand by Friday. God, I thought this sort of thing only happened in films! Well, you can't go to the Guards, out of the question. And can you trust these people not to ask for more money?'

'I wouldn't be an expert on Romanian extortionists, but I think this is the only cash they want from me. They said the other thing won't be money.'

'And you believe them?'

'I do. I can't explain why, it's a sort of honour amongst thieves thing.'

'It sounds like Fagin's den in Oliver Twist.'

'There's something of that to it, right enough.'

'And what do you think the other thing is?'

'I dread to think. For now I'm just focused on the money.'

'Tom. He's your best bet.'

'Tom? But I thought you might…'

'Me? If I had a credit card with a hundred grand limit then I'd go get it right now. The fact is all my credit cards are up to the hilt, my current account is redder than a robin's breast and I've no savings. The only thing I have is a life policy that's worth nothing while I'm alive. Tom, on the other hand…'

'I guess you're right. I've seen him lose a few grand at the casino without a bother.'

'Definitely. He's minted. Into all sorts of deals isn't he?'

No time to waste. I pull the mobile phone from my pocket and hit redial.

Tom McMenemy…is not at home…

I hang up.

'Not there?'

'No, just his answering machine. I'll try again later. Listen, I'd better be getting back.'

'Right. And I have to be packing, it's my college weekend. Are you going to tell Jo about your …about this situation?'

'You mean…'

'I mean the hundred grand. The other thing…well, that's for me to work out.'

I look at Renée and understand her fearful expression. If I'm truthful with Jo, if I start being truthful with Jo, will I be able to limit it to details of the blackmail? Or will I end up confessing our affair as well? Not to mention God knows what other smaller deceits.

'No. Not at the moment. With a bit of luck I'll be able to wrap this up without her ever knowing.'

She nods and we both hope, without saying, our sordid secret will go with Renée to her grave.

~

The next morning.

'Just what is your problem?'

My mobile has flown across the room, landed on the sofa and bounced onto the floor, battery and SIM card flying off in different directions.

'Shit, shit!' I scramble the pieces of phone back together and switch it on again. Still working, thank God.

'What's the matter with you?' Jo's standing over me.

'I need to speak to Tom.'

'Tom, is it?' She grabs the phone from my hand and punches the buttons, scrutinising the display.

She knows about Renée. Has probably known for some time.

'Have you forgotten we're going up to Dublin this weekend? To see my parents? Plus it's Alex's birthday.'

Alex, my favourite brother-in-law.

'And we'll be back tomorrow night, right? Sunday?'

'No, Monday. It's a Bank Holiday. Don't you remember anything?'

Monday is a Bank Holiday. Tom, the money. Does he keep cash in his house or at the bank? Why isn't he answering the phone?

'I can't go.'

'What do you mean, you can't?'

'I have to see Tom about something. This weekend.'

'You have to see Tom. About what exactly?'

'I can't say. A surprise, yes, a surprise. I can't tell you, it'll spoil the surprise.'

'You're a bad liar and an idiot!'

It's a rare event, Jo losing her rag. But when she does, oh boy.

'Come on. I just have to see Tom.'

'Stupid fucking prick!' is her parting shot as she races upstairs.

Doors are slammed and feet stomp above in our bedroom. I head out to the kitchen and take a cold beer out of the fridge. If I confront her now then it'll all come out and that won't help.

Why should we waste our weekend on her bloody family, especially Alex the golden boy. As if he doesn't get enough attention. I'm entitled to be angry as well.

The front door slams and she roars away in the Passat before I can say another word. There'll be a conciliatory text over the weekend. Sent by me. And a return message by Jo, apologising for her outburst. Then we'll pretend it didn't happen. Until the next time.

I've now a weekend of freedom. That puts a different complexion on things. The top is barely off the second bottle of beer when my maltreated phone gives a strangled warble.

'Hello, matey! How are things?'

'Tom! Where are you? I've been trying to reach you since last night.'

'I'm down in Kerry, for the long weekend. Visiting a few old haunts. What's the story, captain?'

'I have a problem. A really big problem. I was hoping you might be able to help me out.'

'What sort of problem? The usual? Women.' Tom has frequently advised me on that topic. 'Work. Money? It's money.'

'Well, both really. But yes, money is the main problem. When are you back?'

'Jesus! It sounds serious. Is it a matter of life and death? Only it's like this, mate, I'm down here for the weekend and, well, I've met someone.'

'Hey, that's great news. No, not life and death. Just a small matter of a hundred grand.'

'A hundred k? You're joking me.'

'Wish I was. By next Friday. Cash. I don't know who else to turn to.'

'What have you gotten yourself into? No, don't tell me. I'll be there in four hours.'

I think of Tom and Richie. Poor old Richie. And now Tom is finally getting a life.

'No, don't. I just need to know if you can help. Can you?'

Please, please, please lend me a hundred grand.

'By when? Friday?'

I take a few seconds to think.

'Ger? Are you still there?'

'Thursday evening.'

'I can do it. But I'll need to know the details. Seriously. Everything.'

'Sure. That's great. God! Yes, everything. Thanks. You've saved my life.'

'It might cost you more than your life, captain.'

'Listen, stay down in Kerry and get your hole there. I'll see you when you get back.'

'Monday. I'll be back Monday.'

'Ah! I could have gone to Dublin after all.'

'What's that?'

'It's just…I had a big fall out with Jo and she's gone to Dublin for the weekend.'

'Go and spend the weekend with Renée.'

'I…what?'

'Spend the weekend with her.'

I think Tom must know about Renee's cancer. He would never normally encourage me to cheat on Jo.

'Yes, will do. Thanks. Thanks for everything.'

'Thank me next week. Tell me all on Monday.'

'Will do. Have a good weekend. Don't do anything I wouldn't do.'

'I intend to. See you, mate.'

'Thanks. Lifesaver. See you.'

I hit Renée's mobile number and wait in excitement for her to answer.

'Ger?'

'Hi. I got hold of Tom and he says he can help.'

'Hey, that's great, isn't it?'

'Yeah! Let's go celebrate.'

'How do you mean?'

'Well, Jo's gone to Dublin for the weekend. What'll we do? Pub? And then a restaurant. There's that new one in Kilkenny.'

'I'm in Belfast. Remember?'

I'd forgotten, even though she mentioned it last night. Renée spends one weekend a month up there on a Masters course.

'Oh yeah. Ah, that's a shame. Never mind, let's get a weekend together soon.'

'How will you manage that?'

'I'll think of something.'

There's a clatter of noise in the background.

'We're on break. Class is starting up again. Gotta go. Okay?'

'Okay. See you. I…'

'See you.'

I nearly said it.

Now, I could eat humble pie and drive up to Dublin. Jo's family will know by now we've had a row.

No, I'll stay here on my own. But I know I'm never really alone. Dad and Mum are with me always.

Major Tom

What a weekend! I had no expectations of Kerry, apart from getting very drunk and wandering up and around Carrantuohill in the mist. It's been an annual pilgrimage for me since Richie passed, because that was how we met. Murphy's bar in Killarney. So long ago but the memory is vivid, like a battle scar.

My specialty is, was helping lads out of the closet. Such chemistry can be violent and I've had my share of black eyes and bloody noses from macho men in denial.

All those years ago in Murphy's I had walked up to the bar and engaged a tall stranger in conversation. Mine was just one of a number of heads that turned when he and his friends had walked in.

'Here for the beer? Or for the walking?'

'Both, for the weekend. You a local yokel?'

It was a north of England accent. His tourist status, the boisterous companions and a wedding band all pointed to a secretive weekend fling for me at best, a punch in the face at worst.

'Not exactly. A visitor, like yourself. From up the country. Where's that accent from? Manchester?'

'Yep, spot on, pal. What about you?'

Hint to a stranger that you find their accent interesting and you have their attention. He had mine from the moment he stepped in the door. Lithe when he moved, poised when he stood.

'Carlow, south west of Dublin, down the country.'

My Bacardi coke arrived at the same time as a handful of pints. The window of opportunity was closing.

'Sláinte,' I raised my glass. 'Tom's the name.'

'Sláinte,' he returned. 'Nice to meet you, Tom. I'm Richie.'

A fella appeared behind Richie's shoulder. In contrast he was short, about my height, sandy haired and a bit rounded. Nondescript except for unusual eyes that seemed to be every colour and no colour.

'Let me help you with those pints, Rich.'

Another interesting accent.

'Sure. Good news, mate – the natives are friendly. This here's Tom. Tom, Ger.'

We did a little round of handshakes at Ger's instigation, very British.

'Nice to meet you, Tom. Don't confuse me with these English lads, though. I'm Scottish.'

A sharp little character, that Ger. He knew the Irish don't like the English. But I was prepared to make an exception for Richie.

'Enjoy your evening. See you later.' I watched Richie's face and saw his pupils bounce in a way that confirmed I'd made a hit. Then I returned to my old college crowd in the corner.

I didn't go near him again that night, except once in the toilets.

'You lads off up Carrantuohill in the morning then, at a guess?' I asked as we stood pissing up against the wall of the ancient urinal.

'Yep, but we'll be back on the beer as soon as we get down again.'

'Well, no shortage of pubs in Killarney, but Murphy's here is one of the best. My favourite. Good for the Craíc.'

I turned and held his eyes for a couple of seconds. Dark brown, they were, warm and loving. He couldn't help dropping his to my cock and then back up again. A worried smile creased his crows' feet and I knew we'd see us again the next night.

On the Saturday evening it was mayhem in the pub. Butterflies in my stomach, the Bacardi coke wasn't going down well. The Brits didn't show, not until nearly ten. Then they walked in, Richie looking around, his hair still wet from the shower. He saw me in a far corner and I raised my glass, receiving a smile in return.

I caught up with him at the bar and expressed interest in how his day had gone. The group had lost their way and spent twice as long as they had planned on the mountain. All the time he was talking I watched his wide, sensual mouth.

Our first kiss was in a dark cobbled alleyway, near the back of Killarney's only gay bar. A safe place for two men to make out without fear of discovery or a beating. Richie didn't know where we were. He was off his face drunk, to be honest. I woke up the next morning with a sore neck, from craning up to his six feet height, and a mobile phone number on a piece of paper in my jeans pocket. The excitement of our unrequited sexual urges was still with me the next day, and I think I had a permanent hard-on for a month until we met up again in England's Lake District.

Richie's situation was clichéd – childhood sweethearts, an affectionate marriage with sex for procreation, two young children that kept him from leaving. I opened his eyes to a suppressed sexuality and we became lovers. Then partners. I'm not proud that I took him away from his kids but I believe that he enjoyed his new life. At least, until that drunk driver put him in the ground.

~

So, lightning has struck twice in County Kerry. I'm ten years older, twenty the wiser. Philip, the guy I met this weekend, he's just a young thing. I had to pull out the stops with the older, sophisticated man image. There's a lot about him that reminds me of Richie. His hair hangs straight and dark like a curtain, and he has cheekbones that could grace any fashion magazine. I'm under no romantic illusion, but there's a spark there that I thought Richie took with him to the grave. Perhaps I'll see Philip again. He doesn't live so far away, Kildare is less than an hour from my place back here in Carlow.

Ger, he seems to have put himself in something of a situation. It was a weird phone conversation with him on Saturday morning. Like an over-excited child trying to explain something to a grandparent. How on earth could old Ger have got himself into a hundred grand of trouble? I'm about to find out, because that's his car pulling up in the driveway.

'What's the story, matey?' I shake his hand. He still likes the ritual.

'Great you're back. Thanks. I hope you didn't cut anything short.'

'No, no. I had an action packed weekend. And I mean action. Nearly glad to get home for a rest.'

'I can't imagine.'

'Go on. Try and imagine.' I like to tease Ger. Like most straight men, he's a bit squeamish about gay sex. 'How is Renée, by the way?'

'She's still up in Belfast, has been all weekend. Coming home tonight, as I understand it.'

'Shit! You've been alone all weekend, with this money thing festering? Perhaps I should have come home on Saturday after all.'

'No, no. But if you can help me...I really need help. This is a real mess.'

'Tell me all about it.' I pour a glass of scotch and pass it to him.

'Thanks. Well, I'm being blackmailed.'

'For a hundred grand? What have you ever done that's worth that much money to cover up?'

'I killed someone.'

'You're kidding. Not...'

'No. Not hit and run.'

Thank God. I know Ger wouldn't do that. Not after what happened to Richie. I wait for him to tell more.

'I had a fight with a guy and he died.'

'Jesus fucking Christ! You're kidding me?'

'Straight up.'

'This was your mugging, right?'

'Right.'

'Who started it?'

'Well, he did.'

'So self defence then. Why the blackmail?'

'Please don't get all legalistic. Look, I was getting a bit of a pasting. Then I hit the guy with an iron bar, knocked him down. Then I hit him again, a lot of times. Then the coup de grace.'

Ger is up on his feet, re-enacting the scene. I can see the problem.

'He must have been a monster, a big guy right?'

'Well no, not exactly.'

'A maniac then, a drug-crazed thug.'

'No. A one-legged beggar.'

'What!'

'Not one-legged actually, but crippled. With crutches, you know.'

'God! Where did it happen? Did anyone see you? Presumably somebody saw you if it's blackmail?'

'A girl saw me. It was late, after pub closing, behind Heuston Station.'

'A girl? Shit! I was going to say we could sort it out with an Irish solution. If it's blackmail they clearly haven't told the Guards anything yet. But a girl? I can't exactly get some heads to bump off a girl.'

The wide-eyed look on Ger's face tells me I should have kept those thoughts to myself. Well, he's stepped into the real world now, big time.

'There's a bit more to it. There's a gang of them. Romanian beggars. And they have the metal bar I did the guy in with.'

I say nothing, chewing on the knuckle of my forefinger as I pace in front of the sofa where he's now sitting. This is serious shit Ger has landed himself in. Heavy, serious shit.

'Tom? What am I going to do? You've got to help me.'

'You said they want money, right? A hundred grand? Tell me about it.'

'Right. Well, when I went back to work he was waiting for me on the bridge.'

'Who was waiting for you?'

'Ilie. The twin of the guy I bashed with the bar.'

'Ilie. Like Ilie Nastase the tennis player?'

'Yep. He had the iron bar in a bag and I had to follow them into the Park.'

'There were others there?'

'You're getting the picture. A whole clan of Romanians. I thought I was dead. No, actually I didn't have any feeling they were going to kill me. Ilie said I have to bring a hundred grand in cash, this Friday.'

'And then the subject is closed? Do you believe them? This gang of beggars?'

'Ilie said they wouldn't ask for more money. But there's something else I have to do for them. Something illegal. I won't find out what it is until Friday.'

'Holy shit! This could go on for the rest of your life. Why not go to the Guards, confess?'

'Don't think I haven't thought about it. Not at first, when I thought I'd got away with it...'

He pauses and looks up at me from the sofa. I shake my head, letting him off the hook. This isn't the same as that drunk driver who drove on into the night and left Richie dying in the middle of the road.

'...But when I saw they had the bar, and one of them had seen everything. I know I'll be sunk if I go to the Guards with this. Everything will turn to shit. It'll destroy my life. Then Jo's, and Renée's, what's left of it. And it wasn't my fault. The bastard attacked me. No, I can't risk ten or twenty years in jail. I'm going to pay them and do whatever else it is they want.'

'Is there a way you can get an idea of what else they want, before you hand over the hundred grand?'

'No, I don't think so. I have to make the rendezvous, with the cash, to find out the next step.'

I give my eyebrows a good rub. They need trimming again.

'Listen. I think the Guards are your best bet. You might get off with manslaughter and just a few years in Portlaoise. Would you not think about it?'

'I can't do it. No, I'd rather jump in the river. You've got to help me.'

'Okay, I'll help. But you have to keep me totally in the picture. I can call the bank tomorrow and they'll have the cash ready on Wednesday.'

'Oh God! Thanks. I'll pay you back soon - I'm arranging a re-mortgage on the house.'

He knocks back the remains of his scotch. There's a flush in his cheeks and I realise I love this man. I'll do anything for him.

Finger on the pulse

Tom is a top bloke. Tomorrow, Wednesday, he'll be at his bank or wherever, collecting my money.

This morning I have to meet with Philip Purcell, my bank manager.

'Mr Mayes, nice to see you. It's been quite a while. Yes, yes. Please, take a seat.'

Like undertakers, I try to avoid bank managers. They give me the same feeling of doom. Unlike a funeral director, though, Purcell has a healthy glow to his face. I assume it's a result of his holiday, but I'm not going to ask in case he decides to share his holiday snaps. Keep it business.

'Thanks. Please, call me Ger.'

'Yes, yes. Good, good. What can I do for you, Ger?'

I remember Purcell now. Jo used to call him the Yes man. Now here comes the crunch. I spent the previous day working all this out with Tom.

'I'm looking to raise some money with a re-mortgage on the house.'

'Right, yes, and what is your plan for the money?

'Three things – home improvements, a new car and a lump sum into my pension fund.'

'Yes, yes, and what sort of amount are you looking for?'

'Well, the home improvements add up to fifty thousand. All new windows and doors and a small extension on the kitchen. Fifty thousand into the pension and probably about forty for the car.'

I place a set of drawings on the desk that Jo and I had made up a couple of years ago, when we were actually considering work on the house. Tom has carefully doctored the date to make them look recent.

'Yes, so, a hundred and forty thousand in total. Right, let's see what we have there.'

He opens up the large sheet of paper and briefly studies the plans.

'Yes, uh-huh. Pretty straightforward, yes.'

Then he folds it back together, opens up a file on his desk and moves some papers around.

'Hmm. Yes, well, there are a couple of problems here. Your house in Bagenalstown, a good size and in a sought-after location, but the value is probably only about three-fifty in the current market. You already have a mortgage of one hundred and eighty. Add another one-fifty and you would be mortgaged to over ninety percent of the property value. You see the problem, yes?'

I listen to Purcell and nod slowly. His valuation of the house seems low.

'Yes, well. It would be in contravention of our lending rules. Another problem is we wouldn't normally make a re-mortgage to finance vehicle purchase. You see, a car has a short life compared to the duration of the mortgage. Presumably you would want the term of the re-mortgage to match the existing loan, yes?'

'Right, yes.'

'So,' shuffle of papers again, 'yes, fifteen years from now. You'll have changed your car another one or two times during the interim. So no, no, we definitely can't do the car part of the re-mortgage. You would have to apply separately for a car loan.'

'Okay, I can do that.'

Although the car loan is just a sacrificial lamb for negotiation, I quite like the idea of a new car.

'Yes, good. Removes the problem of the ninety percent threshold. And Mrs Mayes is still working as a ...local government official, yes?'

'She is, yes.'

'Okay, yes. So multiple of income is okay. How about the pension, is that with us? No, I see you're with Irish Life and Permanent. Yes, yes, a good company. No, I can't honestly say there'd be any benefit to you in switching to our pension scheme.'

I nod again at his sound advice. It sounds like Tom's strategy is working.

'When might I be able to get the funds?'

'Yes, it could take up to four weeks. Of course, if you're in a rush?'

'Well, I want to get the home improvements completed before autumn and they'll want staged payments, you know how it is. Any way things could be moved along?'

'Yes, yes, I could prioritise the application and that would release the funds in about ten to fourteen days. Of course you'll need to extend your life insurance to cover the re-mortgage. Yes. It'll require Mrs Mayes' signature.'

'No problem.' A slight problem. I'll have to practice forging Jo's scrawl.

'Okay. Good, yes. I'll complete the mortgage forms while you talk to our insurance specialist. Then we'll need Mrs Mayes to come in and countersign.'

'Oh, that might be difficult. She's up in Dublin on a course for the next fortnight.' A quickly thought up bluff.

'Is she at home in the evenings? I guess her signature is all we need. Yes, yes, you're both known customers. No problem there, yes.'

Purcell picks up his phone and tells someone called Jean to expect me in a couple of minutes.

'Just one more thing?'

I meekly raise my eyebrows.

'Yes, you see, these home improvement companies can be real cowboys. Shoddy work, hidden extras and so on. Yes, I hear a lot of nightmare stories from our bank's customers.' He reached into a desk draw and pulled out a business card. 'Well, I know this company, it's very reputable. Yes, mention my name and you'll probably get some classy extra features thrown in for free.'

I hold the card carefully and read the writing on it. Country Home Improvements – prop. Tony Purcell. Good to know nepotism isn't totally dead in Ireland.

'Thanks, Philip.' Brother Tony won't be getting any of my virtual home improvement business.

Purcell rises from his leather swivel chair and leads me from his office into another, with a brief knock on the door before we enter.

'Jean, this is Mr Mayes. He needs a hundred thousand life cover for a re-mortgage. Yes, yes, it's a priority case. Ger, I'll leave you in Jean's capable hands. I'll have the other forms brought in to you. Yes, thanks for your business, Ger.'

Purcell pumps my hand and leaves as the tallish woman stands up and walks around her desk, hand extended.

'Pleased to meet you, Mr Mayes. Jean Morrison.'

First impressions – she's freckled and slightly tanned, pretty. Curvy but slim, as though she has recently lost weight. The handshake is cool, firm and bony.

'Would you like tea or coffee, Mr Mayes?'

'Please, call me Ger. I'll take a tea thanks.'

'How do you like it?'

There's a slight smile on her lips.

'Milk, no sugar.'

She leaves the room and returns a couple of minutes later with two paper cups. The woman doesn't have enough status to be served beverages. And I only warrant a paper cup. The tea is sweet with sugar.

During the course of our conversation I manage to find out Jean Morrison is recently divorced and definitely on the market. I watch her hands and chest during most of her questions but, when it comes to giving the last few details, I take up direct eye contact and sense definite interest.

'You show unusual foresight if I may say so, putting a lump sum into a pension fund. There are just a couple of questions about health.'

She reads the questions and as she speaks her elegant, long nose moves, the tip twitching up and down with the words. That's a real turn off - I can't stand a wiggly nose. I profess myself to be in perfect health, take all the forms from her for Jo's signature at home, including the ones from Purcell which have been brought in by a young male clerk, and make my exit.

The rest of the day is mine. After the toilet scene at work last Friday, Deirdre still considers me to be ill. A doctor's note will be needed but no problem there. Old Dr Fothergill will sign anything for fifty euro.

My first thoughts of recreation turn to Renée. She came home from Belfast yesterday but she knew I was tied up in scheming with Tom. Tuesdays are a field day for Renée, though, so she won't be home until later. On the short drive home I ponder the female landscape of my life. Sure, I'm no oil painting but I seem to have something certain women like. Physically I'm out of shape, so why not use this opportunity to do something about it?

Twenty minutes later, after digging old faithful sports gear out of various drawers, I find myself at the leisure club.

The fella at the reception desk looks unfamiliar and has a foreign accent. How long is it since I was last here? And the door to the changing rooms now has a security code. I don my sports gear, careful to get the socks looking right in my runners. One or two other people are about. Bodybuilders or security guys in-between shifts. Shaven heads and serious muscles. Solid looking bellies. Not a skinny six-pack in sight.

On the stairs to the exercise room I take myself in at the full-length wall mirror and what I see is not particularly encouraging. Pasty white legs, slight paunch, drooping shoulders, just a hint of man boobs, receding hair. In need of a makeover. The guy behind me, one of the muscle men, pauses to pose and flex his muscles. He doesn't even see me, I'm invisible. I look again in the mirror. At least I'm comfortable in my favourite sports gear.

Before the fling with Renée I was a sporadic gym visitor. There was one purple patch when I trained twice every week and managed to build up to five miles on the treadmill at quite a respectable speed. So no reason why I shouldn't be able to do it again now. Like riding a bike.

The first minute is tough but that's always the way. I know I'll get my second wind. From time to time I grasp the metal handles that measure the pulse rate. A constant 130 is my fat-burning target. There are three other people running, each lost in their own little world. The skinhead weightlifters pay us no mind, as if we are a physically inferior type of monkey.

Three minutes, the breathing is easier and I start to glow, a trickle of sweat running down each temple. I've settled into the groove, pulse rate 130. There's some anonymous soap opera on the multiple TV screens of the gym. Gaudy colours, canned laughter. I start my favourite game of fantasy fuck. Wouldn't, wouldn't, would, wouldn't, wouldn't.

Then I look down at the display of the machine and find my last pulse measurement was 140. It's getting very hot in the room and I feel rivulets of sweat running down my back. The measurement handles are slippery in my hands. It takes a few seconds to take the reading and then it's 155. I slow the machine.

The dyed blondes on the TV screen are blurring. It's sweat running in my eyes. I can feel the pulse in my neck without touching it. The display shows 185.

Now I can hear the heartbeat in my ears. Okay, emergency stop.

'Are you okay? Do you need medical assistance?'

One of the bodybuilders has his hand on my shoulder. The fact that my top is wringing with sweat doesn't seem to bother him. I'm on my knees on the rubber belt of the running machine, body trembling. I look up and see a concerned expression. Perhaps he wants to give me mouth-to-mouth.

'No, I'll be okay, just… just overdid it a bit. Thanks.'

A woman in dark blue gym clothes hands me a paper cup of water and I sip from it.

'You sure you're okay?' The big guy helps me off the machine and I stand leaning against the water fountain.

'Yep, I'll be fine. Thanks.'

I head downstairs to the changing rooms, concentrating on the metal steps and holding the stainless steel handrail. My favourite sports clothes are wringing wet when I take them off. The old gym routine was run, lift weights and then take alternating sessions in the sauna and steam room to sweat out the inevitable alcohol of the night before, but I think I've sweated enough for one day.

Instead I stand in the cold shower for five minutes until the icy grip reaches into my chest and other parts. Then a couple of minutes in a regular shower to shake off the chill. The drive home feels like the last leg of a marathon and I fall into bed like a true invalid.

Three hours later I'm woken from a deep, sweaty sleep by the shrill tone of my mobile phone.

'Hello.' My voice sounds croaky.

'Ger? It's me, I'm home early. Are you okay? You sound like you're in bed. How did it go at the bank?'

It's Renée.

'Oh, hi. Yeah, I'm in bed, just having a snooze. Everything went to plan. Tom's a genius.'

'Come over and tell me all about it, can you?'

'Would you come to me? Just for a change.'

'Oh. I guess I could, couldn't I?'

'Sure, we'll be fine for a couple of hours.'

'See you in a few minutes then, okay?'

About twenty minutes later the door bell rings. I peek from behind the bedroom curtains to check it's Renée and then go downstairs in my underwear.

'Ooh! I see you're all ready.'

She steps in and pushes the door closed. Her tongue licks that Cupid upper lip as her slim fingers run across my shoulders and down my chest. The sensual touch turns investigatory as she reaches round and smoothes her palms down my back.

'Didn't you get a shower at the gym? You're still sweating. Let's get you upstairs.'

I'm led by the hand. The plain oak feels cool under my feet.

Renée has occasionally stayed over at our house, in the spare room, but not since we started the affair. It used to tease the hell out of me, that my fantasy fuck was just a few feet away.

'I want to use this shower. Okay?'

She leads me into the main bathroom, which is virtually unused. Jo and I always shower in our en-suite. Renée knows how to work the shower and sets it to a low pressure stream, then stands in front of me expectantly. I look down at her shoes and she slips them off, losing an inch in height. Our eyes are now level. She raises her arms above her head and I slide her work blouse upwards and off. A hand fiddles at the side of her pencil skirt and I tug it down over her bottom and bare legs, letting it drop to her ankles.

The water falling from the big, stainless steel shower head sounds like rain. On cue, there's a rumble of thunder from outside and the daylight darkens.

Renée takes a step back and strikes a pose of false modesty, with a coquettish smile, in just her bra and knickers. The lingerie looks expensive, like a part of her. She reaches hands around to unfasten her bra and lets it slip over one wrist and to the floor, the other hand sliding her knickers down and off with easy grace. A private show, just for me.

I feel clumsy and awkward in my Marks and Spencers' briefs, but only for a second. Renée takes two steps forward and runs her tongue down my throat and chest.

'Mmm. Mr Mayes, you taste salty. Let's get you out of those.'

She tugs on my reluctant underwear and gets it down and off. Then my lad gets the full attention of her busy tongue. I'm just wondering whether we'll make it into the shower before I come, when she withdraws.

The shower cubicle is a big glass figure of eight with no door, just a step in. Renée presses a button on the control and pushes me under the now gushing water. I close my eyes. It's like standing in a monsoon. Then the water subsides to a trickle and

Renée rubs shampoo into my hair, her fingers firm but soothing on my scalp. There's an odour that reminds me of beeswax.

'You're like a big baby,' she laughs, lifting my chin and kissing me when the shampoo is washed out of my hair. 'Now, turn around please, sir.'

I oblige, placing my hands on the wall in front of me. Compared to the intimate head massage, her hands feel small and weak on my shoulders and back. The cleansing is methodical but intimate, no crevice left un-probed as she works downwards. Before she turns me, I feel her breasts press against my back and she washes my front by reaching her hands around. Then I'm spun around and she has me at her mercy again. The water falls gently onto her hair and face as she goes down and gives me every man's dream, making me come in her mouth. She's never looked more beautiful. The sound of the storm outside and the rain of the shower are joined by my racing pulse as it makes itself audible. I took a Cialis when Renée said she would come over.

'Oh! You are an excitable boy, aren't you?'

There's a tremor in my hands as I guide her under the shower and pick up the shampoo bottle. I think the label reads contains Royal Jelly but my vision is blurred by water. Her hair is so fine and the shampoo smooth as cream. She dips her head into my chest and sighs in ecstasy as I firmly massage her head. I feel so protective towards this woman, she's vulnerable in my hands.

When the shampoo is washed out I smooth conditioner onto her hair, slicking it back. She raises her chin and we kiss deeply.

'You're shaking. Are you okay?'

'I'm fine. You'll be shaking yourself in a minute.'

I push her head back into the water to rinse the conditioner and then reach around for a bright orange container of shower gel. It's a men's brand but I know the smell of it drives Renée crazy. She puts her arms above her head and leans back against the wall as I wash her, neck to toes. When the suds are mostly gone, I stand and touch her ear with my tongue, chasing down her chin, throat and shoulder, lingering at each breast. Then I repay the compliment, finding my way along the narrow strip of shaven hair to the Renée control centre. The shower gel makes my mouth and lips tingle. She comes almost immediately as I tug, suck and probe.

'Oh, Ger! My God! Oh!'

I stand and we embrace under the water, kissing long and hard before I turn her and rub gel on her shoulders and back. When I reach her bottom she pushes hard into me and bends forward, bracing her hands against the wall but first turning up the pressure on the shower. I can see the bones of her back outlined through the milk and honey skin. Her leg muscles are like fine wood and her waist is tiny as I grasp it with both hands.

I don't know how long we make love like that, both desensitised by the numbing shower gel but aroused beyond words. We climb the mountain together and when we reach the peak, Renée is kneeling on the base of the shower with me collapsed behind, my chest lying upon her back.

'My legs are trembling,' she laughs as we drape bath towels around each other.

Then we fall into the bed, a few gentle kisses before drifting, hand-in-hand, into unconsciousness.

~

'Ger? I have to go, okay?'

I feel dizzy in the bed. A cool hand feels my brow and then musses my hair. Lips pepper kisses on my face, soft on my still closed eyes, too heavy to open. Then I groan as my lad is grasped tight in a fist.

'You took one of those tablets again, didn't you?'

Renée admonishes me like a little boy caught masturbating.

'I did. I didn't want to disappoint you.'

'Well, you'll just have to enjoy the rest of it on your own in Dublin, won't you?'

I mentioned earlier to her I'll be stopping out with Tom at his casino tomorrow night.

She releases her grip and swings her slim legs over the edge of the bed. I watch the search for clothes. As she stoops to pick up her bra, there's a jerkiness to the movement that suggests pain. Renée's cancer has entered the room, an insidious assailant. In bra and knickers she takes her handbag into the bathroom and I see her fill a glass of water and swallow some tablets from a brown bottle.

'Are you okay?' I call lamely from the bed.

'Yep, I'm okay. Thanks.'

I throw back the duvet and roll out of bed. My dick is aching with hardness but there's no feeling of passion associated with it. I get clean underwear from the closet and then pull on my jeans and a T-shirt. Renée has emerged from the bathroom and is struggling to fasten the pencil skirt around her waist, it seems to be a bit tight. She slips on her blouse and steps into one high heel, lifting the other foot behind her calf to fix the other. Now I'm at a height disadvantage.

'You look like a naughty secretary.'

'You look like a bit of rough.'

I step forward and take her in my arms. She folds into me and lays her head on my neck. I can feel her tears on my skin.

'I'm sorry. You don't need this.'

As she pulls back, there's a single tear running down her cheek. I wipe it with my thumb.

'Renée, I…'

'Shh.' She places her forefinger on my lips. 'I really have to go. Jo will be coming home soon, won't she?'

I nod. She leans in, kisses me once and turns away. Her heels clatter down the stairs and I hear the front door pull closed. Then nothing. Just the tick, tick of the heart-shaped clock on Jo's bedside table.

Winner takes all

I had planned to take the early train on my first day back at work, to show the bottom dwellers my renewed vigour, but last night was heavy. It's not just the gym experience and Renée's conjugal visit that has sapped my energy, but also something atmospheric seems to have left me wading through thick air. Rain threatens as I board the late train in Bagenalstown.

Sure enough, the heavens open half way to Dublin. There are groans throughout the carriage. Not much sign of coats or umbrellas amongst my fellow passengers. I, on the other hand, always have a brolly in my backpack.

After a couple of stops a woman that I've seen before boards the train. She's petite and demure, with the perfect face of an old-style film star. Dark and beautiful, Natalie Wood. The train is crowded so she has to take the only seat available in the carriage, exactly opposite from me. It's funny how the last empty seat is nearly always near me. A huge man in flowery shorts extrudes himself from the aisle seat to let her in. His accent sounds German. So far I've managed to keep him there by extending my legs under the table, which means I'm slouching right down. Nat looks ridiculously small next to the fat tourist and she forces down the armrest as a safety barrier to avoid being crushed. I appreciate her position and try to convey it with my facial expression.

Her mouth is content. I look at her bony hands fiddling with the MP3 player and deduce she's older than I thought. Her neatness is almost dapper rather than stylish. There's no band on her finger. I make a last attempt at humour and blow out my cheeks into a fat face.

'All is okay, my friend?' the tourist barks at me, very loud. Rather frightening. It feels like my hair is standing on end.

'Yes thanks.' I deflate my cheeks. Nat has a smile on her perfect lips, eyes shut, listening to the music. I think I've made a breakthrough there. I can pick up a conversation with her next time. Remember the loud fat guy?

At Heuston it's more than just raining, it's worked up into a storm. I stand beneath the canopy of the station and watch people scurry around, trying to avoid the sheets of rain blowing down the river and across the city. There are women with their compact umbrellas blown inside out. Men running with the collars of suit jackets held up around their necks. Everyone is getting soaked. I'm better prepared than most but there's no escaping a day of sitting in the office with soaking wet trousers and shoes.

Cursing, I spring open my umbrella, hoist it into position and step out into the weather. With the right angle and a firm grip I'm able to successfully brace against the rain. It slaps against the black fabric like handfuls of thrown gravel. Before I'm even across the bridge my suit trousers are drenched from the shins down. At least there are no beggars to trip over. Jesus, I hate the weather in this country!

The first thing to do when I reach the safe haven of the office is to get a mug of hot tea and let the worst of the rain drip onto the floor of the tea room. There I discover Caroline sitting alone.

'Hi. Mind if I join you?'

'Work away, Ger. Work away.' Which is Irish for sure, no problem.

She seems distracted and doesn't look me in the eye. I think over my research of the previous week and decide on horses as a topic.

'Do you ride?'

'I beg your pardon?'

I have her attention now but it's hostile.

'Horses. Do you ride horses by any chance?'

'Yes. Actually yes. How did you know? Are you saying I look horsey?'

As far as I know horsey is a derogatory term one woman might use against another. I think it means equine, like a horse's head. Big teeth and all. Maybe legs.

'No, quite the opposite. But there's something about the way you walk.'

'Now you're saying I'm bandy?'

Quite the contrary, as she knows herself. Caroline's legs are exquisite, athletic. I can imagine them gripping the flanks of a charging beast, urging it on.

'No, no. Just I can picture you...'

'In riding boots with a whip?'

'Well, I...yes, but really horse riding, you know.'

She finally gives a grin and lets me off the hook.

'Yes. We have horses at home. Show jumping and dressage. I ride competitively.'

I'm sure she does.

'What about you, Ger?'

'A long time ago I gave it a try. Even started jumping a little.'

'And did you enjoy it?'

'I did. Exhilarating. I've tried quite a few things, skiing, light aircraft, but I have to say riding was something special. It felt so natural. The horse seemed to sense which way I wanted to go.' I surprise myself with my genuine enthusiasm. The whole experience comes to life from memory.

'It sounds like you're a natural. Why didn't you continue with it?'

'Jo didn't like it, so we switched to badminton instead.'

'Jo. Your wife?'

'Yes. Eight years married. Time flies.'

'My husband isn't too supportive of my riding either. He doesn't see the attraction it holds for me.'

Wow, I seem to have struck a common note of spousal discord.

'Perhaps we could ride together sometime? A hack across the countryside or something?'

'I don't know. Not boasting but I doubt you're up to my standard. And I don't think Feargal would approve.'

'Your husband? Do you need his approval every time you ride?'

She lets out a laugh. It's embarrassingly loud and distinctive, drawing the attention of the other three people in the room. Everyone has a fault, I guess. I wonder what mine is. She stands, leans in, lowers her voice.

'Listen, Ger. We're not riding together anytime soon, okay?'

And she's gone.

I look into my tea mug with a silly smile on my face. One of three women sitting at a table across the way looks up from their huddle and there's a snigger. Office affairs are never private.

Back at the desk I think over my options. The best plan would be to get away with Caroline on a conference or a training course. Somewhere remote and romantic, like Ballybofey. It will have to appear as a coincidence.

I spend most of my lunchtime surfing the shared drive until I find the lists of people enrolled for training courses, but her name doesn't appear anywhere. There's a customer relationship skills course scheduled this month in Killarney, so I'll hatch a scheme for that. I block the days in my calendar. Fat Deirdre wanders by the desk.

'Hi, Ger. Don't forget to take your lunch,' she smiles approvingly at my apparent new-found work dedication. So I head over the road for a break.

They've begun to pack up the sandwich bar in the pub and I get a strange mixture of leftovers in the only bread available, a poppy seed white roll. Munching away in a corner, I decide on a course of action with Caroline that'll take the week to realise. For today I'll leave her alone to reflect upon our flirtatious tea break conversation.

After lunch, Brian comes sliming by and tries to annoy me.

'Good to see you working hard for a change, Ger-uh.'

But today I'm immune to his snide sarcasm.

Because of the late lunch it seems like just a few minutes pass by before people start to leave the office for the day. Five o'clock comes and the last few file past my desk, like visitors in a hospital.

'See you, Ger,' Caroline smiles and did she wink?

'Missed your train-uh? Stuck in a time warp-uh?' Brian slopes off to his slug infested abode.

'Good work, Ger. See you tomorrow,' Deirdre says. She has no idea if my work is good. Off she pants to the lift, pulling a chocolate bar from her handbag.

The office is silent now, except for my tapping of the computer keyboard. I pull up Caroline's facebook page and check my friend request – no response. Then I pick up the phone and call Renée. We don't often speak for long on the phone, usually just to arrange a rendezvous. She's tired.

'Are you okay?'

'It's just a headache.'

'Good job I can't come around tonight then.'

'Very funny, not.'

At last the clock creeps round to six-thirty. I take up my backpack and pull out clothes for the evening. A pair of beige chinos and a candy striped shirt. My latest wardrobe additions. It's a thrill to change in the open office. I imagine Caroline coming back to work and finding me in a state of undress. Then there's a bang of a door. I zip and button up in a panic, but it's just the cleaner, heading for the tea room.

Downstairs I have trouble getting out of the front door. There's a security button to press and it takes me a while to find it, half hidden on the doorframe. This is the first time I've been so late out of the building. I feel like I own the place.

Out on the street and it's already becoming a different quarter to the daytime. There are few suits to be seen. I didn't realise how many pubs there are on Parkgate Street. Men loiter outside them, smoking, their skin the colour of ash. The people walking the streets are a poorer crowd than during daytime working hours, the older with worn, grubby clothes and the younger in flashy sports gear. A group of three lads come towards me and there's laughter that appears to be at my expense. They don't jostle me but there's an undertone of threat. This is their territory in the evenings.

I look across the bridge and a Luas is on its way down from James's, so I step out to meet it at the Heuston stop. Folk are sitting on the metal benches but they have no intention of catching the tram. I take them in as my head turns from the ticket machine. Two men together, faces telling a story of neglect. They're probably in their mid-thirties, same as me, but the lines and the bones look different to mine. The human body can withstand decades of misuse and abuse. A woman with a face like a bag of chisels walks up to them with another, stouter man who has the rosy face of a drinker. She herself is holding a can of the cheapest no-brand beer. The three males look at her as if she is royalty.

There's a clashing of bells and the Luas pulls up. It's busy and I have to push my way in, past a group of young girls. The Luas moves on across Heuston Bridge and towards the next stop at the Michael Collins Barracks Museum.

All the way into town, wherever there is a seat on the street, delinquents are gathered in small numbers. The Luas moves into the city proper and movements in dark alleys reveal where the drunks have spent their day. A rotund female form emerges at the Four Courts stop and squeezes on close to where I'm standing. She doesn't smell of alcohol but she's not very fragrant.

'I'll see ya tomorrow. I'm heading over to the hostel, bye, bye, bye, bye, bye' the dishevelled woman barks into her battered mobile phone.

I get off at Abbey Street and head south across O'Connell Bridge. The crowd is totally different now, a few business people striding home, some others heading out on the town like me. Gaggles of Japanese moving in packs, armed with cameras, as ever. I work my way up Grafton Street, slow with shoppers and tourists, and take a side road where I find the pub Tom has described to me, The Old Stand on Exchequer Street.

It's not a large establishment and there's no sign of Tom. I feel conspicuous and wonder about my choice of clothes. There are one or two older gentlemen in expensive overcoats sitting at the bar, reading newspapers. The other customers are twenties to thirties, couples and singles. It's relatively quiet, just a murmur of conversation with no music.

I take a stool at the bar and order a Guinness. The stool's feet drag on the floor of black and white diamond tiles. Of course, it takes ages for my pint of stout to be delivered. The barman goes for the triple pour technique and five minutes later I'm still looking at my hands, wondering if Tom has stood me up, wishing I was somewhere else or that I'd ordered an instant pint of something easier. Finally the barman delivers and I take a deep draught.

'Good stuff,' the reader nearest me comments.

'Aye,' I respond, bravado.

'You're not from round here. Northern?'

'Scotland. Port Glasgow.' I allow my old accent to break through for effect.

'Ah yes, Glasgow. Tough weather. Tough men. Real men.'

There's something acquisitive in his tone. I give him the once over and see the man is exceptionally well dressed. In fact, he's altogether too well groomed.

'You beat me here, matey.' Tom's hand claps me on the shoulder and his voice turns to my companion. 'Bill, how are things?'

'Ah, you're with Tom. Yes. I'm well thanks, Tom, well. Three's a crowd so I'll leave you to it. Enjoy your evening, gents.' Bill folds up his paper and moves off.

The penny drops.

'Is this a gay pub you had me wait in?'

'Not particularly, don't be so straight. Gay bars aren't to everybody's taste. Some, like Bill, just prefer an ordinary pub. I'll have a Guinness thanks.'

Another five minutes wait and we finally raise glasses in a toast to the evening.

'So, what's the plan?'

'Well, we can go straight to the casino after this or we can get half a skinful of Dutch courage.'

'Half a skinful of Dutch courage,' I answer without hesitation. Now we're close to the gambling I'm losing my nerve.

'Right you are. Dave?' Tom gestures to the barman who slowly sets about another round. I look at Tom's glass and see it's half empty already.

'Jesus, you have a thirst on you. Have you checked into the hotel?'

'I have.'

'And have you…'

'I have. But I don't think you should. Not the first time. I don't want to get you into too much trouble. Wait and see how it goes.'

I feel a bit left out but Tom is right. Mixing cocaine, alcohol and casino on my first visit? Not a good idea. The second pint slides down as well as the first and we head out and around the corner to the next pub. It has a markedly younger clientele and thumping music issues from somewhere above head level. Tom grabs my arm when I'm at the bar.

'Let's move on from this one. Too loud.'

But I've already ordered two pints in my enthusiasm to keep the beer flowing. So we take the Guinness, which is poured quickly without due process, out to the front of the pub where there are a few tables and chairs for smokers.

'Makes you feel old, doesn't it?' Tom indicates some young ones tottering down the street on high heels, sturdy Irish thighs tinted by bottles of whatever the latest tanning potion is called.

A lad in a group next to us throws out a shrill wolf whistle whilst his mates laugh and lust after the girls, which is the whole idea, to draw attention to each other. The fellas are all aged around twenty, each taller than myself and Tom. Not a grey hair or paunch in sight.

'I feel like an uncle at a wedding,' I confess. Tom laughs.

'So how are things, captain?' He means my love life.

'Steady. Grand. You know.'

Tom never lectures me.

He draws my attention to a group approaching the pub.

'Now there's something.'

Three men and two women. One of the men is very good looking and there's something indefinable about his engagement in banter with the girls.

'Don't tell me. The guy with the perfect sideburns.'

'Yep. I doubt he even knows it himself but it's obvious. He's more at home with the women than the fellas.'

We agree to take another pint but, during the few minutes Tom is at the bar, I feel a complete spare standing outside on my own. Instead of feeling like a casual observer, I'm a voyeur as I sup on the remains of my Guinness and surreptitiously eye the girls on the street. They don't see me. Tom returns with the beer and my cloak of invisibility slips away.

'So what happens now at the casino?'

My worst fear is I'll be rejected. After all, I don't really have the money or the attitude for this gambling carry-on.

'You brought your photo ID? Passport or driving licence, right?'

'Right.' I pull my passport from my trouser pocket and show the photo page.

'Nice. Real nice.'

There are no good passport photographs but mine is a humdinger from around seven years ago, when David Beckham had that stupid gelled Mohican hairstyle and everybody thought it was okay to copy it. These days I don't exactly have enough on top to replicate the photo.

'They'll take a copy and then you have to give your thumbprint on a scanner. You pay twenty-five Euro membership and get the same back in chips on the first visit. You buy a few more chips from the cashier. Then the fun starts.'

I give him a blank look. What fun? Maybe this is a mistake. Maybe I could lose a lot of money I don't have.

'Getting cold feet? Listen, we don't have to go if you don't want to. But you'll have a great time once you get warmed up. Trust me.'

'I do trust you.'

'And remember, drinks are free for anyone playing the tables. This is the last drink we'll pay for tonight.'

He raises his glass and I clink mine against it.

~

The Dublin Gentlemen's Club is just a stone's throw from the pub and two large men in top hats greet us at the door, looking like Odd-Job twins. Their local accents remind me they're hired muscle and the over-familiarity tells me we're not considered serious players.

'First time? Stick your thumb on there, boss. Got your passport? Jim, take a copy will ya? Twenty-five Euro. You'll be getting a confirmation letter and your membership card in the post, so don't forget to put ya address on the form.'

As I struggle to fill out the yellow form with a stubby blue biro that looks like it was filched from Argos, I notice my writing skills are seriously impaired by those four pints of Dutch courage.

Tom is already at the foot of the red carpeted stairs. He's virtually twitching to get started. I complete my task and the talkative doorman points me up the stairs with a heavy hand on my shoulder.

'Give this slip to the cashier and you'll get your free chips, boss. Good luck.'

We round the top of the flight of stairs and the acoustics change completely. The double doors ahead are padded with buttoned red leather. Like a high class brothel. I'm expecting dancing girls. As Tom reaches for the handle it moves towards him and a tall uniformed girl with a very serious expression walks through. She pauses to acknowledge us with a forced smile and then swiftly passes on and through another door marked Staff only.

'One of the croupiers,' Tom explains. 'Just been taken off a table for making a mistake by the look of it.'

I follow him through the doors. We're greeted by the gentle hum of numerous voices at low volume and unfamiliar sounds that turn out to be the dealing of cards, stacking of chips and roll of roulette balls on the wheel. There's a horseshoe bar and I'm drawn to it but Tom pulls my arm.

'First we get the chips. They'll take our drink orders when we're seated at a table.'

We walk the length of the room and I pass my slip of paper to a man seated behind a grilled window. He slides five plastic discs back to me.

'Do you want to buy more?'

I look at Tom and he shrugs. So I pass a fifty Euro note under the grill and receive a further five discs of a different colour. I'm trying to be cool but it's like playing Monopoly. Tom pulls a wad of notes from his right pocket and exchanges them for a handful of chips of various colours. Then he turns.

'What do you want to try?'

'What is there?'

'Blackjack. Do you know how to play Blackjack?'

I shake my head.

'Brag? How about Brag? Surely you know how that's played?'

'Sure, we played as a family when I was a kid. Brag. Right then.'

I feel pretty confident. I was a dab hand at Brag, always beat Mum and Dad. Tom leads me over to a table but there's only one free seat.

'Go ahead. I'll just watch for the start.'

I hover on Tom's shoulder and try to follow what goes on. A waitress appears and takes our order. When the drinks arrive the guy next to Tom picks up his chips and graciously offers me his seat. I watch Tom play a couple of hands and then try myself, quickly losing the twenty-five Euro of free chips and starting into the extra fifty I purchased. It confuses me. Somehow playing against family is different to playing against the casino. In fact I'm not sure what's going on. That must be pretty clear to the others at the table.

'Fluctuate your bets,' suggests a tall coffee-coloured woman next to me. Boyish haircut, androgynous. Her accent sounds South American, her tone professional. 'If you lose then increase the bet, if you win go lower.'

I take her advice and the small pile of chips in front of me dwindles, grows, dwindles, grows some more. I'm back up to my fifty plus the free twenty-five Euros. Next hand and I win another fifty, the following hand I lose twenty-five and again on the next one. This isn't working for me, I don't understand how I'm winning and losing. I place fifty worth of chips in my shirt pocket and resolve not to walk out with a loss. A waitress delivers my next Bacardi and coke.

'Listen, I'm going to try something else.'

I stand and raise a hand to the croupier, who nods lightly, and I wander across to another table.

'Blackjack,' says a man seated at the table, looking up as I step closer. A huge pile of chips towers in front of him. English accent. 'Take a seat.'

I accept his invitation.

'Things going well?' I ask, as the guy seems open to conversation.

'Not any more. I came in with three grand and took it downstairs to the poker tables. Won another eight but I'm managing to get rid of it here.' He watches the croupier turn over a card and take away what looks like two hundred Euro of chips from a spot on the table.

I sit and observe for a few minutes. The she-male who was advising me at the Brag table appears. She stands by another tall, dark figure in a body-hugging frock, all bony shoulders and no hips. This one has longer hair but a very unusual face. S/he looks like a victim of plastic surgery.

'Looking for business, those two. They've seen my pile of cash,' the Englishman says.

'Well, good luck.' I stand to leave and, as I do so, he gets dealt the card he needs and rakes in a pile of chips with reserved exultation.

I take in the remainder of the room. Roulette looks like something I should be able to handle. There are four different tables in play, crowds around each. I watch again and see many players are betting just tens of cents on individual numbers. A tall guy reaches across the crowd and puts two hundred on red, his Basil Fawlty legs stepping across the room to wager on one of the other tables. The croupier calls a halt to bets and rolls the ball. It lands on red and a long arm comes over my shoulder to collect the original two hundred plus his two hundred win. It's that easy. I find I've slid up close to the table.

Twenty-five Euro of chips is in my hand and I place it on red. Last spin it was black, so this time red, right?

I'm right and up twenty-five.

I put ten on black and win again. Then twenty on red and it's lost. Thirty on black and win again. I follow the up-down betting pattern suggested by the South American she-male and claw my way up to two hundred. Then I risk one-fifty on black and win.

The tall guy's arm comes in to place two hundred again and he gives me a look of slightly fevered camaraderie. I match him and we take two hundred winnings each. I drop to fifty and lose.

'Sorry, table limit two hundred,' the dapper male croupier says to me, pointing to a sign on the wall.

I've just tried to bet three hundred and so I have to withdraw one chip. Embarrassing.

'Perhaps you would like to try downstairs? They have much higher limits there.'

I wonder if I should. It seems I have this game licked. Then the ball spins and I lose the two hundred. There are groans from the small-time gamblers that have been placing fifty cent bets. I didn't realise I had an audience. They look at me to see what a professional gambler should do next. I follow my rule and place a hundred on black only to lose it again. Two-fifty left in chips. The arm of the wandering comrade comes over again and puts two hundred on red. Last time I followed him and lost. So I return my original fifty to my shirt pocket for safekeeping and place the remaining two hundred on black.

There's palpable tension at the table as the wheel spins. The house cannot lose. Either they take the red bet, the black bet or maybe the ball could land on green and the house takes both stakes. So it's head to head between me and the tall guy. Pling, pling, pling. The ball bounces in and out of the slots of the wheel and into green, then my psychometric powers will it into black. Which number I don't know, it's only the colour that matters to me. The silence of the crowd breaks and they share my celebration. I pick up the chips and turn to commiserate with my adversary but he has already moved back to the other table where he's won again.

Across the room I see Tom has moved to the Blackjack table and he briefly catches my eye with a look asking if everything is okay. I return a thumbs up and it flicks a switch in my mind. Quit while I'm ahead. I take the chips to the window grill and cash in. Four hundred and fifty. A clear profit of four hundred.

'Hey, gonna join me in Blackjack?'

I take a stool next to Tom but I've no chips to play with.

'No, I'll just watch and learn.'

'In that case, learn from my mistakes,' he says, indicating his dwindling pile of chips.

We get through another two Bacardi and cokes before Tom's penultimate chip is lost. He gives his last to the croupier as a tip and he's done.

'Well, that's me. Down a grand, I'm calling it quits. Have you anything left to cash in?'

'Already did.'

'What's the story?'

'Four hundred up.'

'Hey, not bad for a first timer! You see? Easy money, captain. Well, you deserve to enjoy some of it.'

Tom leads the way out. Near the door I stagger into the tall South American who gave me the advice that underpinned my successful technique. I try to thank her but she swiftly gives Tom the once over, glances at me and moves on without a word.

Outside the cool night air lets me know I'm three sheets to the wind on beer and Bacardi.

'Just around here, if I recall.'

Tom leads me to a black Victorian doorway. He presses the bell and a bald man in dinner jacket opens to admit us.

'Hi, Tom. New friend?' The doorman shakes my hand. 'You're free in as a friend of Tom's. First drink is on the house. My name is Fred'

Another place that knows Tom by name. We walk up to the bar, the lighting subdued, music in the background but with a heavy rhythm. Tom orders two Bacardi cokes and, as they are poured, a girl appears at my shoulder. A real girl, not a she-male.

I find myself lured into a dark corner of the room where I drunkenly interrogate the girl about herself. I feign interest in her but, to be honest, what I'm really looking for is her lithe body naked and close to my face. Her name is Krystal. She pretends to want to know about me but what interests her is my money. She asks about my evening and I let her know I had some luck at the casino. Two hundred euro of luck. Even drunk I have a talent for being economical with the truth.

Two hours later and my pocket is three hundred lighter, my heart is beating at what feels like two hundred per minute and I'm heading for the door. There's been no real intimacy, just semi-naked titillation, but it feels like money's worth.

Tom sees me and bids farewell to a couple of girls he has been chatting with. They seem to be genuine friends of his. He slips a twenty euro tip to the barman who takes it with a smile, his fingertips brushing Tom's palm.

Fred lets us out through the heavy front door into the early morning glow.

'Well?' Tom asks me, a laugh in his voice.

'Well. Well indeed. Very well.'

We grab a cab over to the Four Seasons where Tom has booked us a twin-bedded room. I drift off to sleep, my mind rambling over the events of the night. Life for Ger Mayes is definitely on the up.

I'm in the money

Breakfast at the Four Seasons, thanks to Tom having shaken me awake just before ten. My mouth still tastes of Bacardi and the nausea has yet to set in.

'Get some food inside you, you'll be grand.'

I tuck away everything on the plate. They certainly know how to scramble eggs.

Tom slips a couple of tablets across the table to me.

'That'll help you get through. There's a car coming at ten-thirty.'

'Thanks.'

Tom is like the gay big brother I never had. Back in our room I've just time to brush my teeth before the reception calls to say my car is waiting.

'Catch you later,' I call to Tom who is now sitting on the balcony, looking out over the rumbling city whilst puffing on a spliff.

'See you this evening. I'll have the money for you.'

The car is a long, dark Mercedes. Not a stretch limo but definitely class all the same. I enjoy the glances of pedestrians and motorists alike as they try to look through the blackened windows, to see which VIP might be lurking inside. Twenty minutes later and I step out at my place of work. The driver declines a tip.

'No, sir. It's our policy. Everything is on account. Have a good day now.'

I take the stairs instead of the lift and encounter Deirdre puffing downwards.

'Nice of you to join us,' she snarls. 'There's plenty of work waiting for you up there in Complaints.'

I look at the sweat beading on her brow at the effort of descent and feel pity and warmth. The warmth is coming from her overheated body.

'Better late than never, Dee.' I've heard Caroline call her Dee. 'Unavoidable transport delay,' I add. Then she's gone.

In the tea room I encounter Caroline, on her way out.

'Nice outfit. Did you sleep in it?'

'Thanks. Yes, actually.'

There's a warm, musty smell rising from inside my candy striped shirt but I'm comfortable with it. Today is a happy day.

The hours roll by. There are some particularly challenging complaints on my desk but I handle them with aplomb, calling the individuals to listen patiently to their woes. I inform them that I'll confirm our conversation in a response letter, leaving them with a feeling someone cares about their individual railway-related problems.

Lunchtime soon approaches. I buy a chicken caesar wrap, a packet of cheese and onion crisps and a kitkat from the sandwich bar across the road and carry it up past the Criminal Courts and into the Phoenix Park. This is a walk I ought to do more often, helps the waistline.

The sun is sparkling off the granite crystals of the Wellington Memorial, like tiny daytime stars. Those huge steps up to the base of the giant stone obelisk are a good place to take lunch.

At the top a couple are in a clinch. He's wearing suit trousers and a business shirt. She's wearing office clothes. They both sport wedding bands but instinct tells me they're having a tryst. I walk on and around the corner to find a spot in the sun where I can sit and eat.

Then it's suddenly an hour later. I see, through blurry eyes, that the wrapping paper of my lunch has blown down onto the grass below. The granite radiates warmth and I let it carry me off again for a few more minutes. Then I rise and chase the paper across the field as the wind blows it beyond the reach of hand and foot.

Traffic is busy down on Coyningham Road and I have to wait a long time for a chance to cross back over from the park. The same breeze that had me chasing my sandwich wrapper now carries a complex melody. Ilie must be playing his guitar down by the bridge. I don't worry about him and his compatriots. Tom told me he'll have the cash for me this evening. Ilie's music sounds like the background to one of those TV programs about holiday homes in the sun. The notes tickle my ears all the way back to the office.

By three o'clock I've cleared all the work from my desk and decide to head for an early train. Deirdre bars my way.

'Ger, we've received some complaints.'

'Well, no surprise there, Dee. This is the Complaints Section after all. First thing in the morning, I'll be right onto it.'

I swerve artfully around her and float down the stairs. I want to get a good seat on the train. As I pull the stairwell door sharply inwards, Caroline falls against me, obviously not expecting someone to be on the other side. Her momentum brings her into my personal space, pressing me briefly to the wall, and our eyes lock. She inhales, steps back, pulls the skirt straight and drops her eyes in embarrassment.

'See you tomorrow.' I edge around her and out the door. Playing hard to get. It's guaranteed success.

~

On the Friday I nervously board the early train with a sniffling nose and my rucksack full of money. It was a hell of a job to put it back in neat bundles after Renée and I frolicked naked amongst the fifty euro notes. Undeniably worth the experience, though.

Each and every person on the train looks like a robber, confidence trickster or Garda officer. I might as well write swag or loot or unmarked bank notes on the rucksack. It's justifiable to be paranoid when you have a third of your house's value with you on public transport. In the normal run of things I would place my bag nonchalantly on the luggage rack overhead, but on this trip I keep it close, under my seat, with one leg entangled in the straps. By the time we reach Heuston I've unbearable cramp in my calf and foot.

How does the river look this morning? I have no idea, no time even to scan the river bed for bodies, only eyes for the streets crowded with villains, thieves, lawmen. Carrying three years' net salary on my back, I cross the bridge and there he is.

Ilie eyes the heavy pack approvingly. His cup is, as usual, completely empty.

'Five o'clock,' he says

I give a slight nod, reciprocated, before proceeding on up the road to my place of work.

In the office I open the outer compartment of my back pack and lay out supplies on the desk of my cubicle in an orderly fashion.

'Having a picnic-uh?' Brian snarks.

After four hours a visit to the bathroom is unavoidable. I take my bag of loot with me. Two chaps from the Communications Department are standing at the urinals in the toilet. I sneak past them and into a cubicle.

One of them stops at my desk later to admire the triple-decker sandwich I'm holding. 'What's in the backpack? The Crown Jewels?' The backpack is on the floor and my leg is, once again, entwined in the straps.

'Something like that, yeah,' I mumble through a mouthful of ham, tomato, cheese and pickle.

At precisely five p.m. I leave the building, the money bag having been within my sight the entire day and never more than one meter away. At the street entrance to our building I hesitate and look down towards the bridge where Ilie is just rising from his pitch. He makes good speed up the road towards me and murmurs as he passes by.

'Follow, but stay fifty meters behind.'

We take the same route as a fortnight previously. I keep telling myself the ordeal will soon be over, but then remember my promise to fulfil a further, illegal request. As people walk by I feel like shouting at them. But what will I shout? This man is blackmailing me for a murder I committed? Excuse me but do you think I can trust a Romanian beggar not to continue this extortion for the rest of my life? Does he appear to you like a man of his word?

The long walk of last week is repeated. When Ilie leaves the park thoroughfare near the Castleknock exit and disappears behind the bushes I hasten my pace to catch up with him. He crosses the small clearing in the bushes, walks towards the wall of the park and knocks on an old green painted wooden door. The door opens inwards and Ilie beckons me in. I hurry across the green swathe of grass and slip in through the door. It closes behind me with a clatter of old wood against stone. A shadowy figure slides home archaic bolts that would keep out a giant.

There must be many such houses backing onto the ancient parkland, their Victorian grandeur shielded from the public park eye by twelve foot walls and foliage. Mature trees with broad circles of bare earth beneath them. The thin grass of the lawn is losing a battle with dark green moss. A witch's garden.

Should I be afraid? I could be slaughtered, diced and dug into the vegetable patch. But all I can focus on is the mysterious bargain that awaits me. With one hundred thousand euro in a rucksack, I follow Ilie in through the kitchen door at the side of the house. He takes a seat at the head of a large, rustic wooden table. It looks like all the characters that had encircled me a fortnight previously are here. There's an empty chair next to Ilie, and he motions for me to take it. A young girl appears at my elbow and places a cup of what looks like hot brown tea on the bare table.

'Drink,' Ilie insists. 'It will relax you.' My life in their hands. What do I have to lose? I drink. It tastes slightly herby, refreshing.

'You brought the money, of course.'

It isn't a question but I nod at the backpack. He gestures for me to place the money on the table. I take the bundles of cash out and lay them neatly, one by one. A woman in a traditional headscarf reaches over and performs a rapid count of one bunch of notes by flicking through them with her thumb. Then she tests them with some kind of invisible marker pen I've seen used in stores for checking counterfeits. A quick count of the bundles and she says something to Ilie that I don't understand. This all seems to take only a matter of seconds, but it may have been longer. The tea likely contains some kind of narcotic. I feel spaced out and compliant.

'Good.' Ilie affirms. 'We have achieved the first task together. There is trust.'

He gathers up the money and I feel a slight pang of loss, despite the soothing tea. Then he unceremoniously sweeps the bundles back into the bag, which I hadn't expected. Somehow it is easier to give away the money than my bag. Apart from the fact it contains various personal odds and ends, my bag and I have a considerable shared history. But my dismay is short lived, confusion taking its place as Ilie hands me back the rucksack complete with the money.

'You need this for the second task. This money,' he lays his hand on the strap of the bag, 'is our money now. We will invest it. Your task is to make that investment for us.'

What am I now, an investment advisor for Romanian criminal gangs?

'If you manage to complete what we ask then we will return your money to you,' Ilie continues, his hands opening either side of the backpack as if revealing a present. Merry Christmas.

I'm not sure what they have in mind by way of speculation. Can it be a bet on a horse race or something else that's been fixed? Doubtlessly it's illegal and I'm expected to take the risk as part of my penance. So it has to be something heavy. How bad can it be? Insider dealing? I have no expertise in stock markets, no access to any confidential information that might be used to advantage. If it's some kind of fixed race then I've no prior knowledge so that's not illegal. Perhaps a visit to the casino? Somehow that seems the likeliest.

'Write down your email address here.' Ilie hands me a pen and paper. 'We will send you instructions and you must follow exactly. I tell you the truth when I say your money will come back to you when you complete what we ask.'

I'm writing down my stuff when an internal door to the kitchen opens and three men walk in. The middle of the three steps forward and, from the respectful postures of the others in the room, I gather he is their patriarch. His black suit is expensive but gently worn. The two bruisers accompanying him are clearly minders. Ilie meets the patriarch's gaze and gives a confirmatory nod, returned. The man looks in my face with a smile, both warm and threatening. Then he turns on his heel and leaves, followed by the two henchmen. The room itself seems to breathe a sigh of relief.

'Gerard Mayes,' Ilie resumes, 'If you fail then we will be very disappointed. Your wife and relatives will also be beyond our protection.'

I was not aware until this point that I and my family were under Ilie's protection, but the message is clear. It's a pound of flesh deal with the patriarch. The thought crosses my mind of offering the mother-in-law for that particular sacrifice.

'You will be successful,' Ilie says confidently as he leads me out of the kitchen by my elbow. I reach for my cup on my way out and down the remnants.

'I will fulfil my promise,' I say, having no idea what I've promised.

The gatekeeper leads me back down the garden path and under the trees. Before passing through the door in the wall, I turn back and take in the huge house. It's exactly the kind of place Jo and I have always dreamed of owning. There's no way of telling what the building looks like from the street but I can probably identify it from aerial photographs if I need to. Numerous windows look down onto the garden from several floors. It could contain any number of rooms and quite possibly most of the Romanian beggars in Dublin. I'm dipping my toes into a complete underworld.

Back inside the park, I float downstream towards the Parkgate entrance. Whatever these Romanian folk are up to, it seems to me I'm just one task away from closing a sticky chapter in the Ger Mayes history. Swiping the ID card to gain entry to the offices, I climb the stairs to the third floor, enjoying the exertion and feeling the money on my back is as good as mine. Up in my cubicle all is quiet and the floor deserted. I start up the computer and log on to the anonymously named internet-based email address I gave to Ilie. It's an email address Jo doesn't know about and I use it for stuff like communications with Renée.

There are three new mails. One is an allegedly funny attachment from an old girlfriend that I save for later. A second is an offer to sell me tablets that will enhance my sexual performance. One look at the price tells me my current supplier is cheaper. The third email has arrived in the last five minutes and is from a Romanian address with the name of Alin, my victim. It explains, in quite badly written but understandable English, exactly what I am to do to complete the second task. I must travel to Amsterdam in seven days, purchase two kilograms of pure cocaine and bring it back into Ireland.

Out of my depth

'Two kilos of pure cocaine?' Tom says. 'One hundred thousand euro seems a fair price. They'll probably make six times that when it's sold.'

I'm not surprised Tom knows this stuff, he's been indulging for some time. Handy because I'm totally out of my depth and scared stiff by Ilie's demands.

'From the small quantity it looks to me like they're testing a new line of supply,' he continues. 'Matey, you've got yourself involved in some serious shit here!'

Too right. Acting as courier for what looks like a major Class A drugs ring. The kind of people that habitually feud with each other and carry out roadside executions in Ireland's major cities.

'I've never heard of Romanians being involved in this kind of thing before. Either they're working for an existing gang or they're trying to break into the market.'

My face feels like marble.

'Don't panic. There's a great opportunity here. You'll get your money back and clear the slate. I'll go with you and help you along the way. All I ask for is a little chance for personal speculation. When we meet the contact we'll negotiate a second transaction for another two kilos.'

Tom has a look of glee on his face. I know he likes to use cocaine sporadically but two kilos of pure cocaine will probably be more than he can consume in his remaining lifetime which, with his AIDS at the stage it is, will be short. So he obviously intends to deal the drug.

'I can cut two kilos into twelve and get rid of most of it through my social circle. That would make a cool half a million profit.'

Not that he needs it. A sudden thought crosses my mind. I'm soon to come into some money myself. About a hundred grand.

'Hey, sounds like a plan,' I say with enthusiasm, and Tom's face brightens even further with my lightening mood.

'Don't tell me. You want to borrow a hundred grand from me against your own money and buy two kilos for yourself?'

'Yes. Hell, yes!'

'Well, if I can get rid of two kilos I guess I could get rid of four. If you're sure?'

'I'm sure. I went to such trouble to get the money it seems like a waste to just pay it back to the bank. It's not everyday I have a hundred grand lying around.' The logic is irresistible.

'But if it all goes pear shaped then you'll owe another hundred to an unscrupulous lender.' Tom gives me a wicked grin. I know he'll never ask for the money back if that happens. Earlier in the evening he was talking about his will and I'll be a beneficiary. This grim disclosure has put us into a devil may care mood. The future is unimportant and what matters is the here and now.

'If it goes pear shaped then I'm toast. I have to complete the collection and delivery. Do you think the contact will have a problem with us asking for three times the quantity?'

'Not at all. These guys have access to tons of the stuff. We just have to make it clear that it's a separate transaction. They'll agree confidentiality, especially as the second deal is twice the size of the first. In a few months you'll have your half a million too. No problem.'

We celebrate with a little of the aforementioned substance and a few Bacardi and cokes. Tom reads through the email instructions again.

'They're going to provide a car but we won't use it except on the handover. What we'll do is take the ferry to Wales with my car, drive to London and then on through the Chunnel to Amsterdam. There are no real customs checks on any of that route, especially for respectable business people like us.'

Tom is clearly an old hand at this and a question arises in my mind as to how much of his property development earnings have actually come from narcotics deals. But that's unimportant. What is important is his advice and experience.

~

The next Monday I walk past a begging Ilie on Parkgate Street, making no contribution as usual. He makes a gesture with his finger that suggests I should wait by the river wall a few meters away. I lean against the stone for the next ten minutes as the lines of worker ants pass by on their way to their hives. How different I feel, singled out for greatness. This is just the first of many speculative activities I've contemplated over the previous nights, lying half awake in bed with Jo snoring gently beside me. Ger Mayes is on the road to riches.

During those minutes I see three other people stop by Ilie and place paper money in the cup. Two men, one woman. Each time he deftly palms the money. That goes some way to explaining why the cup is always empty.

Then, as a fourth approaches, I see the truth of the exchange. Twenty euro is placed into the cup and, as Ilie's hand moves down to collect the note, a small package is pushed into the palm of the contributor. Ilie is selling something, most likely drugs, right there on the street and under the nose of the passing public and authorities.

My eyes lift from the transaction to meet those of Ilie who gives me a knowing grin. He beckons me and holds out the cup. I stretch out my hand as if dropping change and my fingers feel something larger and heavier than a coin. I pull out a car key on a fob and slip it into my pocket.

'You find it in the park,' he says and I move on.

Twenty-five minutes later I find the car, parked legally on the Phoenix Park thoroughfare. It's a 1997 Nissan Almera, the old green paint of the bodywork faded by more than a decade of exposure to the Irish elements. On the rear panel I notice a letter D next to the model name that indicates it's a diesel engine, something that was pretty rare in 1997. A glance at the windscreen shows the tax, insurance and NCT road test discs are all up to date. Important as I certainly don't want to attract the attention of the Guards.

The remote central locking button on the key opens the doors, unlike the previous nineteen Nissan cars I've already tried. Ilie has provided a particularly common, nondescript vehicle. The old car has threadbare upholstery of an indeterminate colour and an interior that reeks of cigarettes. I insert the key in the ignition and turn it. The Japanese engine hesitates and then burbles into life. Apart from a delicate sprinkling of cigarette ash, and an ice scraper, the car contains nothing. I switch off, step out and relock the doors.

The email instructions demand I drive this same car all the way to Amsterdam and back but, as already suggested by Tom, this is no longer our plan. The cover story, for all other parties including Jo and Renée, is that Tom and I are going for a lads' weekend away in the Peak District of Northern England. It's quite plausible for us to take Tom's car across on the ferry and head for a few days of beer swilling in Cumbrian villages and hiking in the fells.

Leaving the car in situ, I return to Parkgate Street, half an hour later than usual for work. All day I indulge in a sweet fantasy that this might be my last appearance in the job, thanks to fabulous riches awaiting me in my new life as a drugs baron.

~

The week passes in a blur. Renée calls upon my services a couple of times when she feels up for it. Jo is increasingly occupied by her own sporting activities.

At work I effortlessly develop my enigmatic character, hinting mysteriously that future attendance and availability for meetings might be limited or curtailed. Complainants to the Railway Procurement Agency benefit from my mood as I make promises of improved future services and experiences. It feels like I'm working voluntarily for a charity. I even put my pursuit of Caroline on simmer. I'm treading water, waiting for the big wave that I'm going to surf to the shore of destiny.

Friday mid afternoon in Deirdre's office.

'Ger, are you happy in your work at the moment?'

'Happy enough, for the present,' is my enigmatic reply. 'Why do you ask?'

'Well, a few people have noticed that you've been acting a little strange recently.'

'Oh, you mean that thing with the rucksack last week? I had a lot of cash in there. On reflection I was perhaps a little paranoid, but you can't be too careful.'

'Why would you be carrying a lot of cash in a rucksack to work?'

'For a business investment.'

The look on Deirdre's face suggests my paranoia is accompanied by delusion.

'Are you planning to leave us any time soon?'

Ah, so someone does pay attention to my behaviour after all. Very astute of Deirdre.

'It would be useful for workforce planning if I knew in advance that you had your own plans,' she continues in a kind tone to let me know I'm a valued and essential member of the team.

'Who knows what the future holds?'

'Well, I think you should consider taking some time off to relax. In fact I insist. We have a stress management counsellor I would like you to see.

Here's your schedule of counselling appointments over the next two weeks.' She hands me a printed sheet of paper. 'You'll still be paid and you don't have to take any leave, just attend the appointments. I have someone lined up to cover your work while you're out. Then, after that, we'll review how best to proceed.'

I'm highly surprised. Of course, I've heard of such things in the workplace, work-life balance and so on. Maybe this is an initiative driven by Deirdre as a newly promoted supervisor.

'Why, thank you. I'll make the most of this opportunity. Much appreciated.'

I shake her damp hand as I exit the supervisor's office and return to my cubicle. Looking at the paper Deirdre has given me, I can see the counselling appointments are on a daily schedule over the next fortnight but, other than those two hour sessions, my time will be free. Fortune is indeed smiling upon me. I draft a quick email to Deirdre to remind her I have leave the following Monday and will be unable to meet the counsellor until the Tuesday. The exact wording occupies me for some time. I want to hit just the right tone.

At five-thirty I'm still in my cubicle, the rest of the team having long since abandoned their posts for the weekend. I have the faithful rucksack under my desk, this time packed for the weekend away. Tom is bringing the original cash plus a further two hundred grand in his car.

I change my clothes in the gents' toilets. It's a bit unsavoury but there might be people still in the building. When I come back to my cubicle someone has been there and changed the name tag to Lucy O'Malley. Deirdre moves swiftly when she wants to.

Out on the street, I feel a bit more comfortable in my jeans, runners and hoodie than I did on the casino night. The sky is fading and pavements are lighting up from takeaway joints on Parkgate Street and the headlights of passing cars. I trot across a break in traffic and over to the criminal courts. Above me the smoked glass of the tiered building is dark except for a few offices near the top. It looks like a giant, modernist wedding cake.

I see the Nissan from about a quarter mile away on the main drag through Phoenix Park. It's the only car parked on the road at this time of the day, all the commuters have gone. That means the car has sat alone in the park for a week. I should have come by and started the engine or taken it for a drive. Hopefully it'll start okay.

Something yellow is stuck to the windscreen. I look around for signs of parking restrictions but there aren't any. When I reach the car I see what it is. A large piece of paper with GARDAI AWARE written large. Brilliant. Some Guard has noticed the car and suspects it's abandoned. I'm lucky they haven't towed it away. The sticker leaves two lines of gooey mess when I pull it from the glass.

On impulse I decide to check the luggage compartment. There just might be a Romanian hiding in there, to make sure I keep to the instructions. With some trepidation I lift the lid of the boot but it's completely empty except for a ratty looking spare tire.

The engine starts without hesitation, my fears unfounded. Indefatigable. Rumbling through the park, I head for the Castleknock exit. The steering is incredibly light, as if I'm driving in an arcade game. It's not real, this is an adventure.

Tom is waiting for me in the open air Quickpark at Dublin airport. We'll leave the Nissan there and travel in his three year old Mercedes E320. To add authenticity, Tom's placed a Homburg on the parcel shelf and strapped a child seat into the rear. Two gentlemen on a trip to the races or some such, escaping from their families for the weekend. We'll hardly merit a second glance from the customs officials.

'Nice car,' Tom says with sarcasm, briefly looking over the Nissan as I retrieve my backpack from the boot.

'A rarity,' I say. '1997 diesel Almera. These days everybody buys diesel engines but, back in the nineties, they weren't so popular. This one drives pretty well, almost the same as a petrol engine.'

Did I mention I'm something of a car aficionado?

Tom whisks us away from the airport and down through the tunnel to Dublin port for the late ferry. It's my first time in the tunnel, even though the thing has been open for a couple of years. The vague hum of the Merc's engine takes on a different tone as the earth swallows us. Nick Cave's Murder Ballads shares its deadly contents on the CD player.

'Why are we taking the ferry?' I ask.

'It's more reliable than the catamaran. If a storm blew up we'd be stuck.'

I'm glad Tom is driving. Dublin docklands is a mess of desolate warehouses and kerbsides obscured by parked commercial vehicles. He clearly knows his way around and soon we're dwarfed by an army of trucks lined up to crawl onto the bloated ship. It feels like we are entering the stomach of a great whale.

I fight a touch of panic on the car deck, the stench of exhaust from revving engines and reverberation of clanking ramps. Narrow white metal stairs lead up to fading daylight. We fight an urge to hit the bar. Instead, Tom leads me to the Premium Lounge where he's reserved recliners.

'Nice one, Tom.'

The man does everything with a touch of class. I guess this comes with money and I look forward to acquiring both.

~

The vessel docks soon after midnight at Holyhead on the Welsh island of Anglesey. It's been a calm crossing and we are both in reasonably good shape after our catnaps on the boat. Tom sets the Merc rolling along a dual carriageway towards the mainland and drives for an hour and a half, bringing us near to Chester. An overnight stop is tempting but the schedule doesn't allow it. I take the next stint of driving, caffeine fuelled, and thunder on down the motorway. After Birmingham I pull us into a service station, just before the M6 joins the M1. Tom takes the wheel again and the next thing I remember is waking up in a multi-storey car park near St Pancras Station in central London.

The EuroStar train runs from London, through the channel tunnel and on to the continent. We have a relaxed and seamless journey, first class of course, during which we enjoy a full English breakfast, a lengthy sleep and a distinct lack of attention from any customs officials. Our rucksacks and travel bags don't even merit a glance during the whole outward journey. So far so good.

At Brussels a change of train to another intercity express takes us straight to Amsterdam. Tom has booked us into the improbably named Amsterdam Cok Hotel, close to the railway station. Like almost everywhere in Amsterdam, the Cok is well connected to the city centre by tram. An early check-in lets us catch up on a bit of sleep during the afternoon. The rooms are Spartan but modern in that strange fashion of the Dutch.

I wake before Tom and decide to take a walk. Passing the railway station, I come across beggars and degenerates in similar quantity to Heuston but feel no urge to contribute; it's the road to hell. Tom is up and about on my return and we formulate our battle plan over a couple of large cold beers in the hotel bar. It's Saturday mid-afternoon and the instructions are to rendezvous with the contact at eleven p.m. in a coffee shop named De Rokerij. The main challenge is to stay sober. Getting stoned is also a serious risk.

Seven hours is a considerable time to kill and one good way to do that is a large, slow meal accompanied by draughts of good beer. We find both in an Argentinean restaurant not too distant from the rendezvous. The earlier beer in the hotel has hit upon our empty stomachs and we order a lot of food to compensate, eating leisurely. This stretches out the experience to a good four hours, four left to kill.

It's too early to contemplate window shopping. Most of the ladies don't pull back their curtains until the early hours. The bars are quite empty and we sample a couple of them before finally relenting and seeking out the coffee shop known as De Rokerij. Now, I don't smoke cigarettes and the whole inhalation concept seems unnatural to me, like standing around a bonfire and breathing in the fumes. But in a coffee shop there's little else to do. Tom, as ever, shows himself to be a seasoned professional and heads straight to the punk haired guy in the corner booth where he buys a slice of Moroccan black and a bag of cannabis leaf. The different bars of dope are lined up on the shelves and the vendor cuts and weighs Tom's order like a man in an old fashioned sweet shop.

I decline to partake for the first half hour and get just a little high from the ambient fumes. Then I succumb to Tom's repeated urging and start to share the latest joint he has rolled. It goes down surprisingly well, probably because there's no tobacco in the smoke, a side effect of the stringent anti-tobacco policy that has spread across Europe. It goes so well, in fact, that Tom has me roll my own joint next, an embarrassing result that attracts looks of amusement from other patrons and a giggling fit from Tom. My second effort is much more acceptable and I soon feel like a seasoned coffee shop goer.

The whole experience with the Sock Twins takes on an increasingly hilarious aspect as we enjoy our hash. I mime the death blow with the iron bar for

Tom and he nearly wets his pants with laughter. This sounds ridiculous and shameful and I would like to explain what aspects of beating a crippled beggar to death are so amusing to us but I can't.

Eleven o'clock approaches like the umbra of a cloud crawling indeterminately across a mountain range and we glance with increasing frequency at the old clock on the wall, a sure sign to any knowing observer that we are there for a meeting. On the stroke of eleven I rise with a wobble, like an oversized soap bubble, and float over to the punk in the corner store, placing a cryptic order for a slice of Romanov. He says to return to our table and wait. As I do so he sends a text message from his mobile. For the next twenty minutes we wait, smoking our spliffs and becoming increasingly paranoid. Without an alternative plan, but fearing things have gone awry, we prepare to leave and I rise again, only to find a large hand force me gently but firmly back into my seat.

The deal

Three hulking white Dutchmen squash into our booth. Tom is nearly obliterated beneath two of the raw boned giants with angular faces.

'So, what is it you want?' asks the guy sitting next to me, just a bit too close for comfort. The Dutch have this way of talking which is strangely smooth. They suck the English words until all the corners come off.

'A slice of Romanov,' I answer, keeping to the codeword. 'Please,' I add. A little courtesy costs nothing.

'Why are there two of you? I expected only one. Well, we go upstairs anyway.' He's clearly my man.

We rise to our feet and Romanov, the smallest of the three, towers over me. It's official, Netherlanders are the tallest race on the planet, male and female. Sandwiched between our new friends and separated by Romanov, Tom and I find ourselves hustled through a fire exit and up a flight of stairs. In a few seconds we are trying to relax on dark red leather couches.

'So, Paddy, let's cut to the chase. You're here for some of our excellent wholesale cocaine.'

'Let's see it,' Tom says. I'm happy for him to take the lead and do the talking. I've never bought drugs of any sort, except my little performance pills.

Romanov disappears from the room for a minute, during which the other two less charismatic

Dutchmen try to intimidate us with their six inch height advantage, even when seated, permanent tans and admirable musculature. It works on me but Tom appears not to be phased. When Romanov returns he holds a bright white package the size of a house brick. It's hard to the touch.

'Of course you want to sample it?' The tone of his question strongly suggests against the offer but Tom nods. 'Don't taste too much, it will be a little strange,' the Dutchman advises him.

Tom, following Romanov's direction, puts his forefinger in through the plastic valve at one end of the package. There is a gasping sound as the vacuum pack pulls in air and the package loses its brick shape. He withdraws his finger, thinly covered in the white powder, sucks it and winces.

'Very strong. Quite bitter.'

'Yes, that you can expect. Don't take any more,' Romanov reemphasises. 'So, you are happy? Where's the hundred thousand?'

Tom and I look at each other. Of course, we hadn't taken the money with us when we left the Cok Hotel. The plan was to return to the Cok before eleven and bring the money direct to De Rokerij but a few smokes have caused us to forget this small matter and the cash is still in the safe in Tom's room. Tom gives me a look that says don't worry, I've got this.

'We're happy, no problem. Very happy, so we want to increase the order with an additional four kilos for another customer. Tomorrow we bring the money for all six kilos.'

'Another four kilos? Exactly the same as this? Same package everything? Are you really sure?'

Tom and I nod in unison.

'Hey, you can take ten kilos if you want,' Romanov offers. 'If you take ten kilos I will give you a discount of five percent. It will anyway take me a day to prepare it to be the same as this, so no problem if you bring the money tomorrow.'

'Just another four kilos,' Tom says.

'Okay, come back the same time tomorrow, Sunday. We will have everything ready.'

Romanov shakes our hands sternly. It's clear we're not to leave town until we've completed the deal. The plan doesn't take us home until Monday so no problem. Romanov leaves the room, taking the packet of cocaine with him. The two goons remain until Romanov returns again with a small mirrored platter and several lines of cocaine. All three then leave and, as we indulge in the free offer, two ladies enter the room.

Neither of them are Dutch, that's immediately clear. One is oriental and Tom pats the seat next to him on the sofa. The other looks Russian and takes her place next to me. We share the coke with them and things relax considerably. Tom engages in some fashion talk and his girl gets the message straight away. The Russian and I do indulge in an amount of tonsil tickling but, to my frustration, she gently informs me it's neither the time nor place for anything further.

We subsequently bid the ladies farewell and head downstairs, out of De Rokerij and into the night. Time has stretched out into the small hours and, to my delight, the windows are in business. When it comes to Amsterdam I'm definitely in the category of voyeur rather than punter. I can walk around looking at semi-naked women for hours but there's no way you'll find me taking a three minute turn in the production line sex of Amsterdam's Rossebuurt windows.

'Everything is not as it seems, matey,' Tom says as I slyly eye an Amazonian specimen. 'You'd get a surprise with that one.'

Really, they should have some sort of description of contents for the naive punter like me.

Around four in the morning our stamina gives up, the drugs wear off and, with Tom complaining of stomach cramps, we thread our way along the cobbled alleyways to the Cok and a long sleep.

~

Breakfast at the Cok finishes at ten and, needless to say, we don't manage to make it. Continental breakfast leaves a lot to be desired, in my opinion, especially the Dutch version. There's only so much bland cheese and variations on spam a man can take, and the unsalted butter on tasteless bread rolls with tepid tea. No thank you.

It's well past noon when Tom and I show our faces on the streets, looking for sustenance. Thus the quandary of single, mature men at leisure. Too late for breakfast, in time for lunch but the bars already open. How do you survive the day without steadily drinking yourself into a stupor? Well, you might say, surely there's a multitude of things to see and do in a major European city such as Amsterdam? Yes, true but we're not on a tourist trip.

This is business. Also Tom's exhibiting all the symptoms of having eaten something nasty. He has spasmodic stomach cramps that make him very bad tempered and is looking rather pale, sweating slightly. I have a healthy hunger upon me and Tom should have as well but, when we settle in a pizza place to take lunch, his appetite deserts him. We discuss our diet of the previous day and the main difference is a prawn sandwich he ate on the train from Brussels. Our combined medical knowledge associates food poisoning most commonly with seafood, so the prawns seem the likely culprit. But it's strange he hasn't thrown up at all. Tom concludes it was the late hour at which he took his AIDS medication after our night out. Poor discipline with his prescribed drugs has led to all kinds of symptoms in the past.

I really get stuck in to my pizza. Tom groans as I plough through a chef's special accompanied by garlic bread with cheese and a large bowl of salad. The chef has loaded the pizza with salami and olives, even a few anchovies. My mouth waters in between slices. All accompanied by breakfast beer, the main qualifying criterion for a lads' weekend away. Tom chews vaguely on a dry bread roll and sips a Seven Up with ice.

It's three p.m. when we pay and leave the restaurant. Eight hours to kill. I persuade Tom to take a canal tour, although I can see he really just wants to go back to the hotel room and crash out for a few more hours. We wander the streets until the canal comes into sight and then follow the bank, looking for the start of a tour. During this time I have a distinct feeling we're being observed. There are a lot of people on the streets but once or twice, when crossing at junctions, I think I catch sight of the massive square shoulders that belong to one or other of Romanov's companions from the previous evening.

We decide on the Canal Hopper, which is really the canal bus rather than a tour boat. A day pass at €18 will let us stay on the boat all day if we want to. Tickets purchased, we sit in the boat and discuss tactics for the evening in low tones. This time we plan to stay off the dope and moderate our alcohol intake. A little before eleven we'll return to the Cok for our cash and take a taxi direct to De Rokerij, have the taxi wait outside for us and then return to the hotel with our purchases. After that, we'll stay in the hotel until the early morning, then walk the short distance to the railway station. Once that plan is established, Tom, still feeling a bit off colour, manages to sleep all the way around Amsterdam's waterways. I lose count of how many times we make the circuit but three hours are frittered away before my friend wakes up.

When we disembark, I notice a disgruntled looking giant heave his bulk stiffly out of a seat at the rear of the boat. Romanov's minder has definitely been tailing us all day but he was seated too far away on the Canal Hopper to hear the details of our plan, not that I suppose it matters if he had.

Do you ever have the desire to fast forward your life to overcome a stressful or unsavoury event? I just want to be back in Ireland with my wife and girlfriend, rich and unfettered.

The sleep seems to have rejuvenated Tom and we hit a bar after leaving the canal. He manages to drink a large beer, sipping it slowly over a couple of hours, during which time I consume three. Then, heading back to the hotel, Tom feels desperate for something really savoury, as if recovering from a hangover. So we grab a couple of doner kebabs from a Turkish takeaway. All the time Romanov's friend lurks discreetly in the background.

We choose Tom's room to eat the kebabs in. Wiping the chilli sauce from his hands, he brings the money out of the room safe and lays it on the bed to take a last look.

'Are you sure you want to go ahead with this?' Tom holds up a wad of notes, thumbing through it.

'Well, for my part, I don't have any choice. And I don't think you do either. I saw the gorilla downstairs in the lobby.'

'Okay then.' We shake hands on it. 'I'm just going to check our return travel arrangements, to avoid any unpleasant surprises.'

Tom picks up the remote keyboard and tries to surf the internet on the TV screen for travel news and sea conditions. The internet connection isn't working. I offer to repack the money in a rucksack. The way I look at it the cash is two thirds mine. Never mind that I've borrowed it all from the bank and Tom. We haven't made too much of a mess with the notes, there's been no rolling naked in it, so I'm able to re-bundle the few loose fifty euro notes back into bunches of two hundred. Thirty neat wedges of happiness.

Tom heads into the bathroom to freshen up. I begin stacking the money in my backpack, nice and neatly, but there's something inside his bag that spoils the geometry, a cold and heavy something. My hand finds it and pulls out a grey pistol. When Tom comes out of the bathroom he finds me sat there cradling the firearm. I look up at him like a schoolboy who has found something unspeakable whilst sneaking about in his parents' bedroom. Like a condom. I want to try it.

'Tom, what the hell?'

'We're travelling with three hundred thousand euro in cash. Tonight we'll have one and a half million worth of cocaine on our hands. That's the only insurance available for this kind of risk. Don't worry, I have a license for it. You won't need to use it.'

I put the gun back in the rucksack. My friend Tom, the gun-slinger. I had no idea. Bashing someone on the head with an iron bar in a drunken fight is a long way from being an armed drug smuggler.

I'm entrusted with organising the taxi, which I do downstairs at the hotel reception. I also ask them to enable the internet connection in Tom's room. Before going back upstairs I make a visit to the hotel bar and take a whisky for Dutch courage. Romanov's man is sitting there, sipping on a coffee. He looks up at me and gives a curt nod before standing and leaving. The whisky puts fire into my veins but soon after I begin to feel the uprising heartburn, which is the main reason I don't normally drink whisky. This prompts my return to Tom's room, seeking a remedy from his traveller's pharmacy. In a mirror next to the elevator I can see the gorilla is at the reception desk, talking to the girl.

It makes sense not to hang around in public with a large amount of cash in a bag. So we don't leave Tom's room with the money until the reception calls to say our taxi is waiting.

In the lift, on the way down to the lobby, we examine ourselves in the mirrored walls and exchange confident looks. Two seasoned professionals, out to make a deal. I consider that this could be just the first of many such deals. We're big-time players with sound financial backing and firearms for personal protection.

The girl on the reception signals us out to a car waiting at the kerb. From her face I can tell she doesn't see two confident international drug dealers. She sees two pale northern Europeans, casually dressed in slightly bad taste, one carrying a backpack that looks a little heavy. So maybe it's a little surprising to her that Mr Romanov has offered his private Range Rover in place of the taxi that was requested by me.

On the street, Romanov's gorilla holds open the rear door of the black windowed SUV. Tom gives me a look that says keep calm, don't worry. Romanov is ensuring our attendance at De Rokerij. Once we are onboard, the car is manhandled down the street and through narrow cobbled alleyways to De Rokerij. It's driven in the same way Romanov's minders walk, wide and intimidating, rapid but almost silent.

Pulling up onto the kerb outside De Rokerij, the vehicle bounces to a halt. We're let out then ushered through a door next to the shop front. Both gorillas accompany us, leaving a sharp looking younger man to stand guard over the car.

It must be only a few minutes since we left Tom's hotel room with our bag of money and here we are already in Romanov's den. The man himself waits for us in the same room as before, relaxing on one of the red leather sofas with the Russian girl who speaks in tongues. I feel a stirring but she stands and leaves without a glance. Romanov gestures for us to sit down. He leaves us with the minders and they remain standing, one at each of the two doors to the room.

In seconds Romanov comes back with a tray upon which sit three large brick shaped packages.

'Gentlemen, six kilos as requested. The original package that you examined yesterday and two others, specially prepared to order. All identical. Feel free to sample, if you wish.'

Tom nods and Romanov inserts a tiny spoon through the vacuum valve at the end of each package, one after another. There is a hiss from each as he does so and the bags lose their cuboid shape. He places a minute quantity from each bag onto a small mirror and holds it out to Tom, who licks a finger to pick up the tiny white grains. He winces at the taste but nods his head again in acceptance.

'This is nearly pure. Dangerous stuff,' Romanov advises.

He signals to the gorilla at the far door and the man disappears, returning shortly with some equipment that he deposits on the table. Romanov places one of the three bags into a square box and closes the lid. He then attaches a small pump to the valve of the bag that is accessible through the end of the box and works the handle of the pump for a few seconds. The bag is removed, again rigid and brick shaped. This he repeats with the other two bags. Each brick is then placed on a digital scale that shows the weight to be precisely two kilos and sixty five grams.

'The packing weighs sixty five grams,' he informs us. 'You can see you are getting exactly what you are paying for. I have an excellent reputation in this regard. If there are any discrepancies then you know where to find me.' He waves his hand around to indicate that De Rokerij is his business abode. 'You guys, on the other hand, I don't know if I will see you again. So please forgive me that my friends kept an eye on you since our meeting yesterday. You placed a special order and I had to ensure you would collect. Now, the money.'

As he speaks his henchman removes the equipment from the room.

Tom lifts the rucksack and begins to place the thirty bundles on the table.

'It's all there, fifty euro notes,' Tom says.

'I know, we checked it already.'

Tom and I look at each other. The bastards must have been in his hotel room, in his safe. Why then hadn't they simply taken the money?

'Don't be surprised, gentlemen. We have no intention of robbing you, but try to be more careful in future. That's a nice gun you have there,' he indicates the undisclosed contents of the backpack. 'I guess you know how to use it?'

'Sure,' Tom replies. He seems to be contemplating pulling out the weapon and testing it on Romanov. I'm praying he won't.

'You need insurance in this business.'

Tom silently loads the three bricks of cocaine into the backpack.

'I hope we see each other again, for future business,' Romanov concludes, standing and offering his hand.

We both shake. Tom shakes Romanov's hand and I just shake.

'Our pleasure,' Tom adds.

There's no cocaine fuelled fondling with women on this occasion. We are shepherded out to the waiting Range Rover by the henchmen and returned to the hotel with the same haste as our outward trip. One gorilla remains at the hotel, lurking in the bar. We repair back upstairs to Tom's room again.

'That's the life threatening part over with,' he quips. 'Now we just have to get back into Ireland.'

He tries the internet again. I see him search the EuroStar website for security arrangements. In the meantime I order us some food and champagne. It's just eleven thirty and the hotel offers room service up until midnight.

'Shit!' the exclamation comes from Tom. 'Shit, shit, shit! They've resumed security checks of all baggage going through the Chunnel. We'll have to take the ferry.'

A spanner in the works for our schedule. He checks the websites for European rail travel and the fast ferry crossings. We'll have to change train at Lille in France and travel from there to Calais. We book onto the Sally Viking Line fast catamaran from Calais to Dover. Altogether it adds five hours to our journey and delays our return to Ireland until Tuesday morning, so that ferry has to be rebooked as well. I vaguely remember I've a stress counselling session booked for Tuesday morning that I'll now miss. The stress is certainly mounting. In addition, the weather forecast is crap, putting the ferry crossings in doubt.

Once the travel arrangements are reorganised, Tom visibly relaxes. He even removes the ammunition from his pistol, and answers my unspoken question.

'Yes, I would have used it, but only as a last resort, if our lives were threatened. Now we don't need protection any more. Romanov's guy downstairs will escort us safely out of town.'

'What's the plan with the coke then?' I ask. 'Do we repackage it somehow?'

'We just release the vacuum. That'll make it easier to conceal the bags in our luggage.'

He inserts his forefinger into the valve of each two kilo package in turn and the three bricks change into shapeless plastic bags full of powder.

'We could always try a little now.' He sucks his finger.

'No, I think I'll stick to the champagne.' I'm still not totally relaxed about being in a hotel bedroom with cocaine having a street value four times that of my house.

Tom shrugs and places the bags on the bed. Then he removes a long thin package from his other travel bag. It turns out to be a roll of cling film, and he wraps the bags of cocaine with multiple layers of the film.

'There'll be police dogs in some of these places and they can pick up the slightest scent,' he explains.

How can Tom be so relaxed? Because he's done it before, obviously. I'm not even sure what the penalty is for trafficking class A drugs in the Netherlands, or France or the UK or Ireland for that matter. But it has to be a long, long prison term. I start to worry about this and then remember something about a murdered beggar and a debt to pay. A knock on the door makes me jump. Tom has just finished wrapping the cocaine and he slides the mummified packages onto the floor behind the bed.

'Room service,' a sonorous Dutch voice announces from outside the door.

I open up to find Romanov's man next to a trolley. He hands me the champagne, complete with ice bucket, and the food which consists of two club sandwiches and a pizza. Then he steps into the room and takes a look around, his eyes lingering on the box of cling-film.

'Enjoy yourselves. Don't get too drunk. You are a long way from home.'

There is something threatening in his tone that causes Tom a change of heart. Once the Dutchman has left, Tom retrieves his pistol from the bag and reloads it.

'We'll sleep in shifts,' he advises. I tend to trust Romanov but not too sure about the minder.

I'm the first to sleep, having gorged myself on pizza, sandwiches and champagne. My appetite for food or sleep is rarely affected by my state of mind. Tom eats little, complaining again of stomach cramps. I'm deep in a dream when a shrill ringing from the wake-up call returns me to dizzying consciousness.

Handover

Our return from Amsterdam is tortuous. Tom is intermittently ill, at one point threatening to go home on a direct flight and leave me to my own devices with the cocaine. Fortunately for me, he rallies and leads us through the maze of deception that enables a foot passenger to arrive in the UK from continental Europe with several kilos of hard drugs.

Tom packs the drugs in privacy, figuring I'll be less nervous if I don't know their exact location. Six kilos is obviously too much for anyone's back passage so I guess it's cleverly concealed in our luggage. At one point a police officer with a dog takes great interest in one bag and, to my shame, I try to shuffle away and disassociate myself from the smuggler. But Tom produces his pistol, in a locked case, and then the necessary permit. He threw the forbidden ammunition from an earlier train. It's the weapon that has raised the hound's interest. The policeman perfunctorily searches the bag containing the gun case and, satisfied Tom is simply a travelling gun club member, lets us through.

Another point worthy of note is the diabolical sea voyage. We have to take the late slow ferry from Calais as a threatened gale confines the catamaran to its berth. Four hours of heaving seas challenge many a stomach and we are just another two amongst the throng of green faced passengers when the ship docks in Dover. It's the early hours of Tuesday when we eventually arrive back in London and retrieve Tom's car from the multi-storey car park at St Pancras.

I have to take the initial turn at the wheel as Tom lurches back into the stupor that has followed each bout of stomach cramps. His health has begun to worry me, as both a friend and a partner in crime. We still have some drug-laden island hopping to complete. Also my private stash of two kilos is going to be of little use if my main channel to market expires.

True to form, Tom recovers in a couple of hours and we find a quiet location off the M6 motorway for him to go about the job of concealing the cocaine in his car. There are numerous places to hide three large flat bags of powder in a large Mercedes saloon. When the contraband is fully concealed I'm allowed to return to the car and take a nap, Tom soon joining me. Two grown men sleeping in a car in a field in the breaking light of dawn.

The ferry from the Welsh island of Anglesey is almost as terrible as the channel crossing and two very tired and raggedy men pick up the old green Nissan Almera from Dublin airport Quickpark late Tuesday afternoon. By this stage I'm beginning to feel pretty achy. Tom seems to be over the worst of his illness.

I had the presence of mind to call Jo the previous evening and explain we were delayed by bad sea conditions. Now I call her again to say there are some business matters to attend to and I'm not sure when I'll make it home. Tom and I drive the two cars away from the prying CCTV of Quickpark and a little further out into the sticks in order to redistribute the drugs. He keeps two of the packages and passes the third to me which I place in the tyre well of the Almera's boot.

The next step is to arrange the rendezvous. I phone a number that was in the original email instructions and a man with a Cork accent answers.

'What's the story?' his voice lilts.

'A delivery from Romanov,' I reply.

He informs me that I'm required to drive the Almera down to a location in West Cork County, near the coast.

'Don't have the fuel tank too full when you arrive,' he says.

That stresses me. I always like to travel with a safe margin of fuel. I'll have to estimate the fuel consumption of an unknown car for an unspecified distance to the south coast of Ireland.

'It sounds like they're planning to take it somewhere by boat,' Tom suggests. 'I'm coming with you.'

'They're not expecting anyone else.'

'No, I'm coming with you. We didn't go this far together just for you to be ripped off or worse. Let's stop off at my place on the way.'

I'm comforted by Tom's support. It takes us a good two and a half hours to get to Carlow, it being evening rush hour in Dublin. I drive the Almera sedately, not wanting to over-rev its diesel engine. The dashboard has no rev counter but the old car runs very smoothly. Nevertheless, accumulated fatigue is wearing me down and an old habit of driving with just my left hand on the steering wheel makes my arm ache. At Tom's we have some coffee and he removes our four kilos, placing them in a safe in his sitting room. Then he opens the gun cabinet and reloads the pistol.

The journey to West Cork is going to be another long stretch so we stop in on Jo as we pass Bagenalstown. I hide the Almera around the corner and we pull up in Tom's Merc.

'Jesus! You look like shit,' my wife compliments. 'And you smell too. You're not much better,' she adds turning to Tom.

I spin a yarn about an early meeting planned for the morning in Cork. Tom's taking me down in his car and we'll be back the following night. Jo isn't too impressed.

~

Driving down to West Cork is a bit of an adventure at any time. Travelling down in the dark through driving rain in an old car with no radio and two kilos of cocaine in the boot is a little more so. Tom trails the Almera in his Merc as we work our way slowly down country. At Fermoy we have to take the old road through the town as I've no change in the Almera for the motorway toll.

The fuel holds up well, the tank having been full when I originally collected the car from the Phoenix Park. At some time close to midnight we approach Bandon and then, an hour deeper into West Cork and following my own scribbled directions from the earlier phone call, I take a series of side roads that lead through increasingly remote wooded valleys. The road takes a steady rise and crests a ridge, stopping at a T junction. Before us an oily sea spreads out in the moonlight, not enough breeze to raise a wave. I pull over at a bus shelter close to the junction and a man steps out from the shadows.

'Romanov?' he asks when I lower the passenger window.

The man looks Irish, short and thick set. He has on rough gloves, deck shoes, dark trousers, a thick jumper and a woolly hat. A fisherman, perhaps.

'Delivery from Romanov,' I confirm.

The Fisherman gives me an enquiring look and I signal towards the boot of the car, pulling the internal release lever. He fiddles around in there for a minute or two, examining the package of cocaine. I step out to check on him as whatever he is up to seems to be taking a long time. When I reach the rear of the car he is struggling with his rough gloves to replace the multiple layers of cling-film but seems satisfied. We both get into the Almera and the Fisherman makes himself comfortable in the passenger seat. He brings with him an odour of old shellfish and marine engine oil.

'We have a little drive ahead of us,' the Fisherman says in a high pitched Cork sing-song. I had expected the old salt to be gruff. He leans over to look at the fuel gauge. 'Not enough in there. We'll need some more. There's a late garage down the road a bit.'

I'm annoyed. He specifically told me to arrive with a nearly empty tank and now it isn't enough. I start up the engine again and move off, just catching sight of Tom as he trails us at a distance, driving on sidelights.

In ten minutes we reach an old-style petrol station with two ancient pumps outside and a feebly lit sign above. To my alarm a Garda car is parked outside the small kiosk.

'Don't panic. They always come by here about this time. I know them. We won't arouse any suspicion. I'll get the fuel, you stay in the car.' Despite the situation I have to suppress my mirth at the intonation of his accent.

I stay put behind the steering wheel and nearly jumped out of my skin when the driver's door is suddenly wrenched open.

'What's it, petrol or diesel?' It's the Fisherman.

'Diesel,' I confirm, happy not to handle the greasy, smelly diesel pump myself.

'A tenner should do it then.' He closes the door.

It seems to take an inordinately long time to put the fuel in the car, but probably just the pace time moves at when you're a few meters away from law officers with two kilos of hard drugs in your possession. Finally the ten euro of fuel is dispensed into the tank and the Fisherman goes to pay. I see him make conversation with the Guards in the shop and they appear to share a joke. He's still chuckling when he gets back into the car.

We move off slowly and quietly from the station, the dim sidelights of Tom's car just visible in the rear view mirror. Our headlights aren't much brighter. The old Almera only manages to produce a vague glow in front of us and I realise we are heading into a patch of fog. Sea mist. There comes a steady incline in the road and the car seems to struggle slightly. Tiredness threatens to overwhelm me. We have just crested the hill when the engine gives a splutter and dies.

'Holy Mary! That's all we need,' the Fisherman exclaims.

I pull up the handbrake. We both step out of the car and survey the vehicle in the moonlight. I reopen the driver's door, locate and pull the bonnet release lever under the dashboard. The Fisherman fumbles in the near darkness for the external release mechanism, lifts and props up the bonnet. The two of us then give the vehicle the full benefit of our joint mechanical expertise, which is minimal. There's nothing visibly obvious. And then it dawns on us, simultaneously, that we are looking at an old and rather small engine. Certainly not a diesel engine. There is a strong, choking smell of diesel fuel emanating from the engine compartment and a slight darkness to the mist that swirls under the bonnet. I feel suddenly culpable.

'Back at the station there, you did say to put in diesel, right?'

'Yes, well, yes I did,' I admit.

Moving to the rear of the car I look at the Almera decal and the D next to it.

'I don't recall ever seeing an Almera D before,' the Fisherman comments. 'Diesel cars would have been pretty rare when this old motor was new. How did you manage to get all the way to Amsterdam and back if you were putting diesel in it?'

The Fisherman has a very suspicious look on his face now. Reaching out to the car I poke at the D which falls off onto the ground. The exhaust pipe, which protrudes from below the rear bumper, is dripping oil. We've filled up a petrol engine with diesel fuel. Bad news.

My first thought is all is not lost. Tom won't be far behind and, with a little explanation to the Fisherman, we can continue to our destination in his car.

'I have an idea,' I say. 'Just wait here a minute.'

I begin to walk towards the brow of the hill and can hear Tom's car approaching from the other side. It sounds like he's driving his engine hard.

There being no footpath, I'm walking on the road when dazzling headlights crest the hill and bear down on me. They swerve and so do I, fortunately in opposite directions. As the sharp pain of bedazzlement fades, I catch the image of a Garda car flying past me and a startled man in uniform looking out of the passenger window.

The Garda car screeches to a halt and the passenger door opens but no one gets out. I freeze. The engine idles and its fog lights, much more effective than the Almera's headlights, beam two fans of brightness along the ground at the scene ahead. The Fisherman is clearly outlined against the open boot of the Almera, a floppy white package in his hands. The cocaine. When the Guard's passenger door swings shut, I make a decision to walk on. The Fisherman has the cocaine and it's up to him now. I'm sure the Guards haven't seen my face clearly and I have a good chance of escape.

Once over the hill I can just make out Tom's Merc creeping along with fog lights skimming the surface of the road in front of it. I wave but, at that moment, he flashes his headlamps twice, turns off to my left and follows a lane along the edge of an adjacent field. In confusion I stop and turn back towards where the Almera stands stranded, wondering what to do next.

The Garda car is pulled up close to the Almera with various lights flashing, spreading blue luminescence through the mist. In the murkiness I can make out the uniformed and capped figures of two Guards looking into the open luggage compartment of the abandoned Nissan. One of them raises his head and gives a shout, pointing in my direction. I feel a wave of panic, but the Guard's gesture is not directed at me. A sound of rapid breathing approaches and the Fisherman appears in a field on my left, on the other side of a hedge. He's cradling the bag of cocaine like a baby.

'Better do a runner,' he advises, unnecessarily. 'You go that way,' he breathlessly adds, pointing to the field on the other side of the road. 'I'm off down here. Good luck.'

'Right. Good luck yourself,' I reply and, needing no further persuasion, head across the road.

Well, I don't know if you've ever tried to run through a boggy ploughed field cradling a floppy two kilo bag in your arms. Probably not. Suffice to say, the Fisherman's progress is not rapid and, although he has the initial element of surprise, the Guards are soon upon him. They catch up with him before I've entered the field on the other side of the road. My trousers get snagged on the hedge that bars my way.

'Give it up, Jim,' one of the uniformed officers shouts.

The three men stand several meters apart, panting heavily. Those Guards clearly know the Fisherman.

'Sure, can't run with it anyway,' concedes the Fisherman. 'Here, Ger. Catch!'

I'm hoping one of the two Guards is named Ger but realise with horror the bag has been thrown towards me. The Fisherman has committed the amateur villain's basic error, naming his accomplice. However, his skill at throwing a floppy two kilo bag is equal to his underworld etiquette and the package falls well short of the hedge on his side of the road. I half expect it to burst and shower them all in pure cocaine but the multiple layers of cling-film prevent that and the bag falls with a squelch into the soggy mess of the field.

The Guards' attention is now pulled in three directions: the Fisherman, the contraband and the accomplice, namely me. At first the Guard who called out Jim's name heads towards the Fisherman and the other heads in my direction.

Then the one coming towards me calls over his shoulder.

'Eugene, you get the bag of stuff. We know where to find you, Jim.'

'That'll be Acapulco, Eamonn,' retorts the Fisherman, turning to flee.

Garda Eugene hesitates between chasing Fisherman Jim and collecting the contraband evidence, and then stoops to retrieve the cocaine. Meanwhile Fisherman Jim, now unencumbered by the bag of cocaine, lopes off down the slope of the field at surprising speed. Garda Eamonn has made a clear decision to pursue me, and attempts to hurdle the rough hedge that separates his field from the road.

This all happens so quickly I'm still struggling to free my trousers from the hedge on my side. As a result I'm able to witness Garda Eamonn's athletic prowess. With great energy he throws one foot forward over the hedge, large lumps of mud flying off his size eleven Garda footwear. His second foot doesn't clear the obstacle, the shoe appearing to have a couple of kilos of mud still attached to the sole. He lands astride the hedge, which is mostly gorse, but the momentum pulls his body down and through the prickles and barbs until the top of his head touches the bumpy tarmac edge of the road with a reassuring thump.

'Alright, Eamonn?' the other Guard calls.

'Alright, Eugene,' Garda Eamonn responds.

Irish men are made of sturdy stuff, brought up on Gaelic football, hurling and the like. Garda Eamonn soon recovers and, scrambling onto the road, heads in my direction. Well, that's what I assume happens because, before I hear any further sounds of pursuit, I'm half way across the field. Two factors are in my favour. Firstly, I'm quite a fast runner, especially when my liberty, family and everything else I take for granted is under threat. Secondly, the field on my side of the road is fallow, firm and relatively dry.

Like a champion hurdler, and far superior to Garda Eamonn's effort, I bound towards the five bar gate at the far side of the field and clear it in one leap. Turning briefly to check the safety margin, I see the silhouette of the Guard limping painfully across the field at some distance. This brief respite gives my body a chance to react to the general excitement and exertion. Leaning on the gate I throw up and a great tremor runs through my body, starting at the ankles, moving up through the legs and ending at my scalp. I shake it off but my left arm is still aching mercilessly.

'Jump in then.' Tom has crept up behind me in his Merc.

With a final cough I collapse into the back seat of his car.

'There's a blanket back there, make yourself comfortable.'

As we quietly pull away, I chance a last look at my pursuer and see Garda Eamonn slowly picking himself up from a fall in the field. Hopefully he hasn't seen Tom's car.

The Merc gains speed and we find ourselves climbing up onto high ground that affords an early view of dawn breaking across the sea. A ragged shoreline is visible down below the steeply sloping fields.

'There goes your friend,' Tom says, pointing out beyond the shore.

A small fishing boat is heading at speed out to sea, a bear-like figure at the helm. Soon the Fisherman will be concealed amongst the myriad small fishing boats out for their early morning catch.

~

We encounter only one Garda check point on the way back from West Cork, but it's perfunctory. The Guard checks Tom's tax and insurance discs but, as Tom tells me later, doesn't look inside the car where I'm lying concealed on the back seat under a blanket the same colour as the brown leather upholstery. Apart from that we speak little during the journey. I've failed in my mission for the Romanians.

It's mid morning Wednesday when we finally pull up outside Tom's house. I'm groggy with sleep but Tom has passed the pain barrier and he's animated. He clearly needs to talk before I can expect to collapse into one of his guest beds.

'So tell me again, exactly what happened? You went to the petrol station and then…?'

'He asked me if the car took petrol or diesel. I told him diesel. Then it seemed to take a long time to put in the diesel. He paid, joked with the Guards and came back. We drove a couple of miles up the road and the car conked out.'

'Then the Guards came upon you?'

'Yep. I had gone to look for you for a lift. The Guards went to the car then chased him and he threw the cocaine towards me, calling out my name. The bag fell in the field and the Guards grabbed it. But we both got away. Happy days.'

'Not exactly. You screwed up. They'll come looking for you.'

'Who? The Guards? They don't even know me or anything.'

In my defence I'm very tired at this point.

'No. The Romanians. You failed to deliver. The Guards have the drugs. Romanov has the money. The hundred grand has gone with nothing in return. You even lost the car.'

Yes. Not happy days at all.

Tom continues. 'What I don't understand is how he could have put diesel into a petrol car.'

'Well, I have to take the blame. I told him it was diesel.'

'No, what I mean is the nozzle of a diesel pump won't fit into the filler of a petrol tank because it's too big. It's intentionally made that way to prevent people from accidentally pumping diesel into petrol tanks.'

'What about the other way round?'

'Well, petrol used to be predominant so petrol users were protected first.'

'Maybe that Nissan was too old to have a small bore filler?'

'No way. All petrol cars in Europe have had a fixed gauge fuel filler dimension for a couple of decades.'

And I thought I was the car bore.

'Well, maybe he had a funnel or something. He is the Fisherman, after all. Fishermen have funnels and things.'

Tom laughs.

'Or maybe he just knows about boats and doesn't know about cars,' I offer. 'Either way, it was my stupid fault.'

'This Fisherman, he knew those Guards, was friendly with them in the petrol station. And he called you by your name and tried to throw the drugs to you when they cornered him. It sounds like a setup to me. They tried to set you up for cocaine smuggling, in revenge for the murder.'

I've honestly forgotten about the murder of Alin. It's a sobering thought that I may have narrowly avoided such an elaborate plan of revenge. Then I find a flaw in Tom's hypothesis.

'But what about the hundred thousand? They would lose all that if the plan had worked. They've lost it anyway, even though I escaped.'

'Whose money? That was your hundred grand, mortgaged against your home. They've lost nothing.'

This stumps me. Yes, it was the money from my bank. Well, from Tom.

'So, if it was revenge to set me up for twenty years in prison for cocaine smuggling then they've failed and they're still likely to come after me. Alternatively, if it was a genuine plan to smuggle drugs, I've botched it and they're likely to come after me.'

I recall Ilie's words in the house in Phoenix Park. If you fail then we will be disappointed. Your wife and relatives will also be beyond my protection. This is bad. Very bad.

'There is a way out, though.'

I look at Tom blankly. An honourable way out? Discharging his loaded pistol into my head, for example?

'You still have your two kilos of cocaine in my safe. If it isn't a setup then you could give them that and they'll probably walk away.'

'And if it is a setup?'

'Then they're unlikely to come for you. It's already cost you your hundred grand and they won't want to be implicated in the drugs haul. But the Guards might like to talk to you.'

My brain starts to clear slightly.

'Let's assume the Guards can't trace me. After all I don't have a criminal record and I don't think they caught proper sight of me. So if it's a setup I'm out a hundred grand and hopefully the Romanians are satisfied. If it's not a setup then they'll want their drugs. I give them my two kilos and, with a bit of smooth talking about why I have a spare two kilos of cocaine, they're satisfied. Then I'm out of pocket for the original hundred grand and I owe you another hundred.'

'We can work something out,' Tom smiles. I've a feeling his working something out might involve another trip to Amsterdam. 'Plus you have the opportunity cost of the four hundred grand you would have made if we'd sold on your two kilos.'

'Yeah, thanks for reminding me. So, I'm down either a hundred, or two hundred or six hundred grand depending how you look at it. The Romanians are probably looking for me and, either way, the Guards are definitely looking for me.'

'Sounds like a fair summary,' Tom concedes, standing and moving over to the large flat-screen TV on the wall. 'At the moment, however, you're safe here and we have a million euro of cocaine at our disposal.'

Sliding the TV away from the wall, he reveals the built-in safe and opens the combination. He takes out one package from the safe and places it on the designer coffee table in front of the sofas. The cling-film has already been removed. Then he slides open a shallow drawer in the coffee table and produces from within it a mirror, a long spoon and some other accoutrements.

'So I think we should celebrate the present and take an inspired approach to the future.' He inserts the long spoon into the bag, through the vacuum valve that he holds open with a pencil, and withdraws a heaped quantity which is then deposited in a pile on the mirror. 'Care to join me?'

I'm exhausted, paranoid and agitated all at the same time. The little common sense I have left tells me sleep, and not cocaine, is needed.

'No thanks, mate.'

I walk over to the bag and lift it from the coffee table, hefting it in one hand. It could be flour or sugar for all I know. So much trouble over a bag of powder.

As I switch it to my other hand I feel something small and lumpy in the middle of the bag.

'Hey. What's this?' I ask, showing him the lump.

He takes the bag back from me and carefully reinserts the long spoon until he locates the lump and is able to withdraw it through the valve. Clingfilm surrounding something the size of a button. Tom hands it to me and continues to prepare his treat, cutting in some other white power with the cocaine. I unwrap the cling-film with some difficulty. A large square of the stuff, wrapped many times around a small hard disc that has a few numbers and letters printed on it.

'I've really no idea. Looks like some kind of battery,' I suggest.

Tom briefly inspects the foreign object. 'Probably some kind of production marker, identifying the batch. Manufacturing cocaine is a regular industrial process these days, you know. There's probably one in the other bag too.' And he turns back to his coke, disinterested.

I go over to the safe and fondle the other two kilo bag, locating the small lumpy package within it and confirming Tom's hunch. Then I slip the first button, battery or whatever it is into my pocket, after rewrapping it in the sheet of cling film.

'Be careful what you do with that,' he advises, looking up from his preparations. 'It'll be covered with traces of cocaine.'

I'll dump the thing after making some further investigations. Can't explain exactly why but it seems important that I know what the disc is.

'Are you sure you won't join me?'

'No thanks. And I forgot to say this, but thanks, mate. Thanks for helping me through this mess.'

'More than welcome. Anything for my best friend.' He lines up the powder and prepares to sniff it. Hesitating, he first returns the bag to the safe, spins the combination and slides the TV back into place. 'Best if I don't overindulge. Sure you won't share?'

I shake my head and smile my last smile at Tom McMenemy.

When I wake up several hours later he's dead.

Get out of that

Mid-afternoon, emerging from the guestroom, I wander into the living area looking for Tom. A strange smell greets me. From the look on Tom's face it's obvious that the last few hours of his life were considerably uncomfortable. He lies on the ground in a foetal position with small amounts of blood around his mouth and nose. The odour reminds me of something from childhood, when my father had to eradicate an infestation in our large garage. The smell of dead, poisoned rodents.

Later, at the inquest and in the press, it will be reported that rat poison is sometimes mixed with cocaine. I've done my own internet research on the subject. Some say this as an urban myth. Others confirm the deliberate lacing of cocaine with Warfarin in order to either heighten efficacy or further refine it into an especially potent form of crack cocaine. Whatever the truth, it's a fact that Tom McMenemy died from the cocaine he took whilst I was asleep in his house.

After a few minutes of shocked reflection, and an extended but unsuccessful attempt to open Tom's safe, I call the ambulance service. In turn they're obliged to inform the Guards because of the drugs. I do the emergency services the courtesy of sharing the fact that Tom had AIDS.

Fucking disaster all round. I've lost my best mate, my route to market and two of the six kilos of cocaine. There's the remaining four kilos locked in a safe for which I don't have the combination. One million euro of cocaine. If I can just get the stuff out of the house and sell it.

A female Guard questions me in a corner of the large sitting room, after Tom's body has been removed.

'So, Mr Mayes, you found Mr McMenemy in this room at approximately two o'clock this afternoon?'

'Yes, that's right.'

'And what condition was he in when you found him.'

'In the same state as you saw him. The blood, eyes wide open, no sign of life.'

'How long after that did you call the ambulance, Mr Mayes?'

'About ten minutes.'

'Why the delay? Didn't you want to try and save your friend?'

'He was already dead. I checked his pulse and breathing. His eyes were fixed and he was already quite cold. I think he must have died a few hours earlier.'

'The Coroner will decide, Mr Mayes. Was Mr McMenemy already taking the drugs when you went to bed?'

'Yes. He had a quantity of drugs on the table and was just getting started.'

'And did you join him?'

'No. I prefer alcohol but I'd already had enough over the weekend so I went back to bed.'

'You say back to bed?'

'Yes, we got back late from a long weekend away and I was worn out, so I hit the sack around two in the morning. Tom came home around nine. He'd stayed out all night.'

Okay, I'm being a little wily in my grief. Here's my chance to substitute Tom in my place down in Cork, but if I do so explicitly then the Guards will link him to the cocaine seizure and definitely search every inch of the house with a fine toothed comb. So I restrain the urge and just place him out of the house overnight.

'Were you and Mr McMenemy partners, Mr Mayes?'

Partners in crime? No, the Guard is intimating something else.

'No, we were friends. Best friends. Tom was Godfather to my children.' Having confirmed my masculinity this would normally be the time to try hitting upon the attractive female Guard, but the thought isn't appealing. I must be overtired or genuinely distressed. Rare event.

'Did Mr McMenemy have any more drugs in the house, to your knowledge?'

'I didn't see any.' And please don't go looking for my four kilos of cocaine behind the TV screen on the wall over there. 'Oh, except for his prescription medicine. Tom had AIDS.'

'Okay, Mr Mayes. That's all the questions I have for you right now. We have to wait for the post mortem result but, at the moment, Mr McMenemy's death is not being treated as suspicious.'

I thank the Guard, make my excuses and leave, picking up my denim jacket from the row of coat hooks in the hallway. During the ten minute walk to the train station I toy with the cling film wrapped button in one jacket pocket and Tom's spare keys in the other.

Mid-afternoon there is a train every hour or so from Carlow to Waterford and I'm able to get down the line to Bagenalstown and home by five. Jo is still at work so I have a little peace and quiet to think things over. Sitting in the garden, I watch the wasps burrowing into the plums on the tree. Somehow the summer has passed me by and our small fruit orchard is neglected. Fifteen minutes of pondering the situation and I conclude that the most neglected thing in this entire situation is Ger Mayes. So I resolve to call on Renée. I make a decoy call from my mobile to our house phone and leave a message for Jo to say I'll be a couple more hours and something terrible has happened to Tom.

Renée puts me straight into the shower but she doesn't join me, somehow sensing the doom I carry on my shoulders, as palpable as the disease destroying her body.

'Something has happened to you. I can tell,' she says after I dress in a change of clothes I always keep at her house.

'It's not me, it's Tom. He died this morning of a drugs overdose. I was sleeping off a heavy weekend at his house and when I got up he was, well, he was dead.'

'God! Was it an accident? I mean, he was dying wasn't he? People who are dying sometimes want to have a controlled exit.' Renée's face has a queer look.

'No, I'm sure Tom didn't do it deliberately. He wasn't ready to go.'

Too bloody right he wasn't ready. We had a million euro of cocaine to sell. That's the only thing I can think about. Perhaps Renée has some contacts I could use.

'Have you ever taken cocaine?' I ask hopefully.

'No, and I'm not about to start either. I'll be long gone before I need anything like that.'

Yes, I'm looking at another legacy in the not too distant future. Tom's death in itself means money to me. He promised I was taken care of in his will. But the general subjects of death and terminal illness are doing nothing for my libido. I plead exhaustion and get away with it. What's happening to me? I can't even get it up with my mistress any more! It's time for one of those little yellow Cialis pills but I don't have any to hand.

We make a date for Saturday night. I'll get a pass out from Jo and go on the beer with a couple of mates. The usual ruse. Then I'll accidentally bump into Renée in the pub, staggering back to my deep-sleeping wife just before sunrise.

I make my way home from Renée's, via a circuitous route that avoids Jo's work journey and any possible shopping runs, and pull up outside our house just before eight.

Jo is already home, having first made a visit to the off-license. Once again the weekends-only alcohol vow is cast aside as we share a bottle of cool white Italian wine on a Wednesday night. She wants the full gruesome details of Tom's death and I oblige.

'I can't believe he's gone,' Jo says. She hasn't shed a tear. That'll come later.

I feel like I'm going to implode.

'He wasn't ready to go. I know that for a fact. It was an accident with the bloody cocaine.'

'Talking of accidents, apparently you're going to have one if you don't get up to Dublin for that stress counselling. I had another call for you today, that's the fifth. The girl said your attendance is mandatory.'

Shit! I've forgotten all about my work situation.

'Don't worry, I'll go up tomorrow. I've a cast iron excuse, what with the delayed ferry back from…' I have to remember to keep my story straight, '…back from Anglesey and Tom, well what happened today.'

'Well, if you're going up there you should look in on Aunt Mary.'

I groan. One of the disadvantages of working in Dublin is Jo occasionally uses me to fulfil her family visitation obligations by proxy. A little trip out to Raheny is required. It'll involve waiting at bus stops with the hoi polloi, interspersed with an hour and a half of Aunt Mary. In company I quite enjoy her acerbic wit, but on a one-to-one basis it's difficult to hold a conversation. We'll sit for an hour and a half in front of her electric fire with the imitation coal, trying to find common ground for discussion. Punctuated by two cups of tea and two visits to the toilet, from which she'll return with an ever increasing odour of urine.

So that's the plan. Up to Dublin with the late morning train for my first stress counselling session, then over to Raheny and Aunt Mary, finally back to Carlow. Enter Tom's house, open the safe and drive home to Bagenalstown with the cocaine in his Mercedes. Then? No idea. To regain possession of the million euro of cocaine is my immediate goal.

Jo gives me a squinty-eyed look.

'I know it's mundane. It's terrible, what's happened with Tom. But…'

'Life goes on?'

'Yes. I'm worried about you. Worried about your job. You've gotta get a grip.'

Getting a grip involves drinking every drop of wine in the house and a drunken night of sex as if it were our last.

Make yourself comfortable

The postman arrives quite early the following morning before Jo or I have left the house. There's an official looking registered letter with my name on it that requires a signature. I do love receiving post, especially unexpected missals or packages. Bad news usually comes in the form of regular post i.e. bills. But my delight is short lived. This is bad and confusing news. My employer informs me that written explanation of my non-attendance at the first two stress counselling sessions is required by return. Failure to do so will lead to disciplinary proceedings and dismissal. This is my second written warning. The suspension from work has been extended by another week and a new schedule of counselling appointments is enclosed, starting immediately.

It has to be a mistake. I'm not aware there has been a first written warning. Jo reads the letter and then hands me the first warning from the letter rack. It arrived yesterday, after I missed the first session without apology. Makes no sense, unless I forgot to send that email to fat Deirdre. Anyway, not to worry. Now I'm back in the saddle I'll clear up all this misunderstanding.

The late train is full of twittering old ladies. They all whistle through their teeth as they talk. By the time we arrive into Dublin at around one thirty, I've been driven near demented by an hour and a half chorus of octogenarian budgerigars.

I have half an hour to get the Luas into town, walk up O'Connell Street to Parnell Square and find the counselling offices. Catching the Luas is not without risk. I've no idea what the Romanians' next move might be and can't afford to bump into them. So, when my train arrives, I walk steadily down the platform and take a side exit from the station that leads out to Dr. Steevens' Hospital, the opposite side from Heuston Bridge and the river. Then I sneak around the grounds of Dr. Steevens', up the Luas tracks past St Patrick's Mental Hospital and onto James's Street where I pick up the Luas outside St James's Hospital. A lot of hospitals in the area. As the Luas takes me back down the route I've just walked, I wonder if it might be a better course of action to check myself into St Patrick's.

It's standing room only on the tram and I'm well concealed by the crush of bodies. In any case, I'm not sure Ilie, Deirdre or my mother would recognise me. Heavy denim jacket with a mock sheepskin lining, lumberjack shirt, baggy jeans, old black working boots, five days of stubble, baseball cap and dark sunglasses. I catch sight of my own reflection in the glass of the tram's window and have a sudden shock. Just for a second I think he's standing on the other side of the window. But he isn't. Except for the boots, and two normal legs, I'm a reasonable facsimile of Ilie.

The fifteen minute tram journey passes without incident, although the jacket's unbearably warm. Disembarking at Abbey Street, I turn onto the main thoroughfare and struggle through the throng of business people and tourists on O'Connell Street.

There are thousands of them, all moving in the opposite direction to me, so it seems. They move with a lack of body rhythm, facial features distorting slightly each time a foot hits the ground.

By the time I reach Parnell Square I'm already late as it's ten past two. The square is a misnomer, more like a block in the middle of which stands the old Rotunda Hospital. The omens aren't good. This adventure is going to end in a hospital of some kind or other.

In a heavy sweat, I push open the door of the counselling offices and climb the three flights of stairs. There's no lift. A young girl seated behind the reception desk takes my name and points to a hard plastic chair. From behind the dark glasses I can freely ogle the receptionist. She's very slim with a face of some beauty. It could be radiant if she smiles, but my toothy grin fails to elicit the response. Instead she gives a closed mouth twist bordering on mockery. After a couple of minutes a door opens and a short, red-haired woman steps through it.

'Mr Mayes?'

From the cultured but flattened accent I can tell she's Scottish, perhaps from Edinburgh.

I attempt the poshest Port Glasgow accent I can manage.

'Yes. Dr Livingstone, I presume?' For that is indeed her name.

I offer my hand, which Dr Livingstone shakes with a detectable reluctance. She gestures into the room behind the doorway and I enter. I have to laugh at the leather chaise longue to which she directs me.

'Yes, something of a cliché, isn't it? But very comfortable. Please sit, however you find suits you best.'

I sit on the couch with my back against the upright end, legs and boots extended out along the upholstery.

'Now, Mr Mayes. You work as a senior office administrator. Is that correct?'

'Indeed it is. Please call me Ger.' This is going to be a cinch. Comfort, courtesy and a cute receptionist upon whom I have two weeks to work my irresistible charm. With a daily dose of Ger Mayes they'll all become putty in my hands.

'Thank you, Ger. You may call me Dr Livingstone. And your clothes, how charming. So, are you in disguise today?'

'Well, yes, I suppose I am. No, actually, this is my normal casual attire.'

Dr Livingstone nearly gained the upper hand there but I have things back under control.

'From whom are you disguising yourself? By the way, I can see your eyes moving behind those sunglasses, so why don't you remove them?'

I thought my eyes were free to roam in secrecy behind the shades. That explains why the receptionist snarled at me. I take off the sunglasses and the baseball cap.

'That's better. Now, once again, who are you trying to avoid with this disguise?'

I'm on the verge of divulging everything to the good doctor. She's very good. Although she's being brusque with me, I find it appropriate and feel a sudden wave of attraction to this diminutive but dominant Scotswoman. A small smile plays on her lips.

'There are some people in Dublin from whom I wish to conceal my whereabouts,' I say.

'Why would that be?'

'They might, well they most probably do wish me harm.'

Already too much honesty. I can see from Dr Livingstone's expression that, rather than making an enigmatic impression, I'm appearing deluded and paranoid.

'In any case, Dr Livingstone, this isn't a psychoanalysis session. This is a stress counselling session. Isn't it?'

'Thank you for reminding me of that. But I do find it useful to set the context for the individual. Now, you were scheduled to arrive here on the previous three days but didn't appear. I trust you're well?'

'A little tired. A little stressed perhaps. But I do have a cast iron excuse or two. The first two days I was stranded abroad by bad sea conditions.'

'Right. The same thing happened to me a couple of years ago.'

'Then yesterday I woke up in my friend's house in Carlow to find he had died during the night.'

'How awful for you. My sincere condolences. What time did you find your friend?'

'Around two in the afternoon....'

'Which means you had no intention of coming here at two o'clock yesterday or informing us that you couldn't attend.'

'Well, I...'

'What did your friend die of? And what was his name?'

'Tom. If you have to know, he died of a drugs overdose.'

'Ah yes. That could explain a lot. I'm sincerely sorry about Tom but your employer has stipulated your attendance here is mandatory. They've told me to inform you that if you don't complete this course of...counselling...then they will terminate your employment.'

Silence ensues, except for the squeak of my rocking on the chaise longue.

'How do you feel now?'

'Stressed,' I manage to say through gritted teeth.

'Good. Well, at least we understand each other and the circumstances. Now, I would like you to talk me through some of your recent behaviour in the office.'

We traipse over the same stuff that Deirdre brought up. My apparent mood swings, obsession with order in the workplace and how disorder brings me to apoplexy, and about the day I brought one hundred thousand euro cash to work in a backpack. After an hour of dissection I have to concede my behaviour at work has been a little odd. This disappoints me because I thought I'd covered well for life's recent events. The gambling, the murdering, the drug smuggling.

Dr Livingstone bids me farewell and I fairly look forward to our next meeting. We should achieve mutual first name terms within a day or two and, if I smarten myself up, I can extract a telephone number from that svelte receptionist within a week. To make a start I ask the young lady for a short cut to the Luas line and she points out a route on foot that circumnavigates the Jervis shopping centre.

When the Luas approaches Heuston I feel nervous again. Shall I continue on to James's and sneak back on foot along the Luas line again? Will Ilie be there on his pitch? He isn't, so I step out at Heuston. I figure he might be lying low himself.

There's a train to Carlow departing in ten minutes and I bless my luck, heading for the platform. To my surprise one of the rare Garda checks is in place at the gate. A Guard stands with a Garda dog, letting the animal have a good sniff of every person and every bag that tries to pass through. I have no concerns. The four kilos of cocaine are in Tom's safe, which is where I'm heading next.

Imagine my surprise then when, as I approach, the dog starts to go crazy, sniffing the air like a wolf on the trail of an injured sheep. I think over what will happen if the Guard orders me aside and has me empty out my pockets. Apart from my wallet, phone, Tom's keys and the plastic button thing I have nothing strange. Of course! The plastic button wrapped in cling film has been sitting in the middle of two kilos of pure cocaine. Fortunately the queue for the gate is something of a melee and I can slip away without being noticed.

That little event actually does me another service. I'd forgotten to visit Aunt Mary. So back onto the Luas and then down to Eden Quay to pick up the number 31 bus to Raheny. On the top deck of the bus I study the plastic button. It looks like some kind of electronic component. From my childhood fascination for electronics I know such devices used to be made from ceramic, so why not plastic? I try bending the thing and then prising it apart but it's very resilient. The join around the edge seems to be welded. The numbers and letters printed on it don't make any particular sense to me but I copy them onto a piece of paper anyway for future reference.

The streets of Dublin look very different from the top of a double-decker bus. You can see over the top of the high brick walls that block the view of pedestrians and motorists. There are private little squares buried in the side streets and concealed gardens of surprising size behind some of the plain looking houses fronting onto the street. Aunt Mary's house is one such dwelling.

She greets me with initial enthusiasm and a hug of condolence that challenges the bounds of acceptable intimacy with a ninety year old. We are soon ensconced in front of the fake coal fire and I answer a long stream of questions about Tom's demise then the usual queries relating to home, family and garden. Jo hasn't spoken to her aunt for a couple of weeks and so there are many updates and items of small gossip to share on both sides. The tea tray appears with biscuits.

'Nobody seems to eat biscuits anymore.' Aunt Mary always complains.

While she visits upstairs to use the bathroom for a second time, I take the chance to steal into the front parlour, a museum to late Edwardian splendour. Always kept locked but with the key in the door. I find it, as ever, immaculately clean but blatantly unused. Kept for best. The kind of room no event or visitor is ever good enough for.

I lift the lid of a silver plated tureen up on a high shelf behind a glass cabinet door and drop the cling-film wrapped disc into it. Then I thoroughly wash my hands in the kitchen, scrubbing at them with a rough brush. Finally, I turn the pocket of my denim jacket inside out and give it a good wash with some detergent I hope will prove unattractive to sniffer dogs.

'What on earth are you doing, dear?' Aunt Mary has been watching me from the hallway.

'Just cleaning up a little.'

'Well, you could start by having a bit of a shave. And, while we're on the subject, what's with the clothes? You look like an unemployed lumberjack. Don't tell me you've lost your job?'

'On the contrary. I'm on the verge of great riches.'

'Get rich quick, get poor quick. Just be patient. You and Jo will get a little nest egg when I'm gone.'

I hate it when old people talk about all the money they're going to leave you when they die. It's not that I find it vulgar. Not at all. But you know they're going to hang on for ever and never die, just to punish your greed.

An hour and a half has passed, my duty completed. If I want to catch the last train to Carlow then it really is time to go. I've already missed the last train to Bagenalstown but Tom's Merc will bring me home.

The return bus and tram reaches Heuston just in time to get the train. No Guard or sniffer dog in position, but I'm too late to get a seat. The wet pocket of my jacket has drenched the lumberjack shirt and the only standing room, between carriages, is very draughty. Cold wet cotton across my ribs all the way to Carlow. Real lumberjacks are made of sturdier stuff. To top it all, the weather takes a turn for the worse and I'm drenched by lashing rain on the ten minute walk from Carlow station to Tom's house.

When someone dies on TV the cops tape off the crime scene and draw a chalk outline around the body. I expected to see all that at Tom's house and I'm prepared to sneak in like a criminal. But Tom's large, detached and secluded Carlow house looks just the same as usual, with the Mercedes parked in the drive. So I slosh up to the front door and make to open it with the key but that's neither possible nor necessary. The entire cylinder of the front door lock is missing and the door stands slightly ajar. Someone has got there before me.

Bolt the stable door

Shavings of metal and wood litter Tom's hallway. Someone has opened the front door like a can of beans. From further inside comes a strange smell that tastes damp and dusty at the same time. The smell of building or rather, in this case, demolition. With a sinking feeling I walk into the sitting room and the odour becomes stronger.

Tom's huge flat screen TV sits on one of the leather sofas. So the intruders didn't come for that. Everything is covered in a fine grey dust.

My primary objective in returning to Tom's house is to try and locate the code to his safe or else, rather unrealistically, to crack the combination or whatever I need to open it. Now all that is academic. There's a gaping hole in the wall where the safe used to be.

The back of the hole leads straight through into the kitchen. I walk back into the hall and around to the kitchen to find the concrete blocks at the rear of the safe have been removed from that side.

I collapse onto a kitchen chair. Initial shock is replaced with conjecture. Who did it? The work is tidy, economical and methodical. That rules out the Guards. It seems to me the Guards would have drilled the safe open on site rather than dig it out of the concrete. But unless Tom's death was suspicious would they have posthumously invaded his privacy?

Then something catches my eye in the void where the safe had been. Stepping over the crushed plaster and fragments of concrete, I reach into the space and grasp the item. A Bewley's coffee cup. Inside, a five cent coin. So, the Romanians have my cocaine.

As I drive the few miles from Carlow to Bagenalstown in Tom's Mercedes, a wave of true relaxation flows over me for the first time in weeks and I laugh out loud. No life of drug dealing for me. Deep down I knew conversion of four kilos of pure cocaine into a million euro of cash was beyond my capabilities. This turn of events has saved me from the situation. As for the Romanians, they will surely be content with their haul. Perhaps I should change job and remove myself from any chance encounters with them. To be perfectly honest with myself for a moment, it seems unavoidable. A job change is on the way. Then, in a few weeks, Tom's estate should be settled and I'll be in for a bit of a windfall. That'll hopefully clear off the hundred thousand I've re-mortgaged on the house and perhaps a little extra. Yes, life is starting to look sweet again for Ger Mayes.

'What do you think you're doing with Tom's car?' Jo asks when I arrive home.

I look at the Mercedes, then at the bunch of keys in my hand and then back at Jo. The car, it seemed a reasonable thing to do. After all, he was my best friend and would've wanted me to use the car. Wouldn't he?

'You can't just go and take a dead person's possessions! We'll have to take the car back. Anyway, it doesn't look right outside our house. People will think we've won the lottery or you've become a drug dealer or something. And why are you dressed as a lumberjack? What's that on your clothes? Plaster? Have you been working on a building site? Have you lost your job in Dublin? Ger?'

I smile dumbly and shake my head in the sure knowledge that my drug dealing days are over. And the lumberjack disguise does make me look like a builder.

Jo and I drive back to Carlow in convoy. I switch off the radio in the Merc and put on the CD at high volume. He had great taste in music. I don't know classical very well but the pieces are evocative. After a couple of minutes it's excruciating and, by the time I pull up outside the old bastard's house, the tears are coursing down my cheeks. So this is what it feels like to lose your best friend.

'Come on.' Jo hugs me outside the house and then opens the passenger door of our car.

'I'll just put his keys back,' I head for the front door, intending to post them through the letter box. Of course, it's a bit pointless as the front door is still ajar and can't be locked from outside. If I leave the keys there then I may as well put a steal me sign on the Mercedes. So I enter the house and pull the front door closed behind me, locking it with the deadbolts on the inside. Tom always had his place done up like Fort Knox. Then, walking through to the kitchen, I unlock the back door and leave, relocking the door behind me. Once back at the front of the house I do this time post the keys through the front door and then climb into the passenger seat of our car.

'What was all that about?' asks Jo as we pull out of the driveway.

'Someone broke in through the front door.'

'Is the place a mess?'

'A bit. All they took was the safe. Cut it out of the wall.'

'Then we'd better report it to the Guards. Maybe it was them anyway. What was in the safe, do you know?'

'No idea.' A million euro of cocaine that belongs to me but I'm glad it's gone. 'Hopefully not Tom's will.'

We both laugh. Not in a disrespectful way, but in the way Tom himself would have laughed at the situation.

Once back in Bagenalstown I manage to relax. Then I take Jo out to a restaurant for dinner, for the first time in months. We have a very enjoyable evening and I begin to think perhaps there can be a future for us after Renée.

~

The next morning I have a leisurely start, once again targeting the late morning train in order to meet my stress counsellor for the second time. Jo and I breakfast together and, still wearing my dressing gown, I actually kiss her as she leaves for work, something that hasn't happened in a long time.

Although I've convinced myself the whole Romanian episode is over, it feels wise to keep a low profile for a bit longer and so I put together another disguise. First I rifle through the previous day's lumberjack outfit, extracting my train ticket, money etc. Then I find it. A piece of paper with some letters and numbers scribbled on it. The inscription from the button sized plastic disc. That disc is the only remaining link between me and the cocaine.

'Hello?' Jo answers her mobile phone on the second ring.

'Hi. It's me.'

'Ger? Is everything okay? Are you still at home?'

'Sure. I just wanted to let you know I'm going to call in on Aunt Mary again. She seemed a little frail yesterday and I'm sure she'd appreciate it.'

'That's very considerate of you. Well, make sure you don't miss the last train. And watch out or she'll be expecting to see you every day you're on the course.'

I've no intention of visiting Raheny regularly during the counselling period. I simply want to retrieve and dump the cling-film wrapped plastic disc.

'Will do. I'll tell her I'm just securing our inheritance.'

Jo laughs, knowing Aunt Mary will appreciate such cynicism. I join her in the laughter and feel light hearted once again. My troubles are so nearly over.

The train arrives a little early in Heuston and I take the daring move of walking directly out to the Luas stop. This time I'm even less recognisable. A charcoal trench coat, with padded shoulders, worn over a black polo neck and black jeans. Chelsea boots with a high heel and my stubble shaved down to an elegant goatee beard. All topped off with a pair of reading glasses and a black leather cowboy hat. Taking a seat on the Luas, I stretch out my legs and let fellow travellers be impressed by the enigmatic image.

On O'Connell Street the tide of people parts before me like the waters of the Red Sea before Moses. It's amazing what an extra six inches in height and three in width can do for your self esteem. These circumstances conspire to make me five minutes early for Dr Livingstone and I let the receptionist have the full benefit of today's persona.

'Good afternoon. Do you have an appointment?'

'I do indeed. Two o'clock with Dr Livingstone.'

'Mr Mayes?' She sounds surprised. My attempts at disguise are effective.

'Yes, but please call me Ger.'

At this point I take off my reading glasses and let the girl have the full benefit. I've been told the Mayes eyes are my best feature.

'Ger then. Could I have your mobile phone number please?'

She smiles and it increases her radiance to undeniable beauty. Now I have her hooked, so quick and easy. Clothes maketh the man.

'Sure.' I begin to write my number with the paper and pen she offers to me, like signing an autograph. 'And what's your name?'

'Gobnait.'

Now Gobnait is a good old, honest name for an Irish girl but to me it always detracts from the bearer. It causes something strange to happen. As her smile widens I think I see a tooth is missing at the side and her eye takes on the craftiness of a peasant .

'Thanks, Ger. I might just give you a call on that number…'

Gobnait recovers from her metamorphosis and I resume my role as enigmatic seducer.

'…the next time you're late or don't turn up at all. Your employer has insisted that we inform them on a day to day basis of your attendance so we don't want you forgetting to turn up.'

The svelte Gobnait is turning out to be as dominant as the diminutive Dr Livingstone. I'm spoilt for choice.

'Ger, nice to see you again.' Dr Livingstone has come out of her office and gives me her limp handshake.

'Nice outfit,' she compliments as I make myself comfortable on the chaise longue. 'Please, take off your hat and coat.'

I stand again and place my hat and coat on a stand by the door.

'Is that kohl pencil on your beard? You applied it very well, I would hardly notice. Still in disguise?'

It pains me that Dr Livingstone feels it necessary to peel back my layers of camouflage in such a fashion.

'I already explained why I don't wish to be recognised in Dublin. But the good news is this masquerade is coming to an end. Next week you'll see me in my normal guise.'

'I can hardly wait. Now, I hope the previous twenty four hours have been a little less stressful for you than the start of the week.'

'Well, I suffered a substantial personal financial loss. But I feel I've been released from a burden. So, yes, considerably less stressed.'

'Right. And this financial loss, does it have any ramifications for you? Will you have to take on additional debt or look for extra income?'

'No. It was more a loss of potential wealth. I can write it off without any material impact. However, I'm still likely to receive a legacy in the near future and that will compensate.'

'It appears to be a world of high finance you occupy, Ger. With substantial losses, anticipated legacies and, what was it? A hundred thousand euro in cash for an investment opportunity? I have difficulty in reconciling this with your job which has a salary of only a fraction of that cash amount.'

'Yes. Well, some of us have a net worth, a personal wealth, that isn't in keeping with our salary.' What am I talking about? I can't stop myself being inventive. 'Successful investments, family money, old money, Dr Livingstone.'

'Are you a gambler?'

That question puts me in a tizz. I've recently become a full and frequent member of Tom's casino. How can I deny it?

'I've invested in opportunities that guaranteed the return of my original investment.' That's mostly true. Even Ilie has promised me my money back. And hold on a minute. If Ilie and friends now have the cocaine, albeit actually my personal cocaine, then they owe me my one hundred grand at least, if not two hundred. Will I seek them out and ask for the money? Probably not.

Dr Livingstone doesn't want to let me off the hook about those guaranteed returns.

'Roulette, you mean? Red then black then red. Double the stake until you win?'

Again she has me. That's the simple strategy that won me hundreds of euro at the casino. It's lost me hundreds too.

'Business transactions. I had business transactions in partnership with my late friend Tom McMenemy. But it's over, since his death. And the final transaction fell through, yesterday evening. So, no, I'm not a gambler.'

The good Doctor makes some notes and then changes the course of our conversation. We speak about relationships. She accuses me of hitting on the receptionist. I can only assume it's jealousy on her part. Then I'm probed about my relationship with Jo and tricked into admitting I have a girlfriend.

'But she's dying of cancer,' I protest as though that minimises my philandering. 'It's likely I'll receive a legacy there as well. You see, Dr Livingstone, money just seems to follow me around no matter what I do.'

After the second session I don't have a good feeling. Getting things off your chest is meant to be therapeutic but Dr Livingstone, with her slippery questions, seems to have tricked me into divulging my gambling habits, infidelity and shaky marital situation.

Back at reception, Gobnait hands me my mobile phone. It's a rule of the practice that all phones are shepherded at reception during consultations. If the phone is left on then Gobnait is empowered to field any incoming calls.

'Jo called,' Gobnait informs me with her disarming smile.

'Ah. My wife. What did she say?'

'Your wife, but I…'

The poor girl is crushed. I could ease her pain by claiming it's a marriage of convenience and I'm a free spirit.

'You thought I was single.'

Available for you, Gobnait. I'll take you to the moon and back.

'Well, with all the dressing up and eyeliner on your chin…I thought you were ultimately unavailable.' As my jaw hits the ground she continues. 'Okay. Jo. Your wife. She says Aunt Mary isn't answering the phone so maybe you should leave your visit until another day.'

Not a chance. I need to get hold of that plastic disc and dump it. I bid fair Gobnait good afternoon and exit the building in a swirl of trench coat tails. Now that Gobnait mentions it, perhaps I am a little too slim and good looking for this Don Juan disguise. It might give the wrong impression.

Difficult to keep a low profile on the number 31 bus to Raheny, dressed from head to toe in black with high heels and a cowboy hat. I resolve to have a brief makeover at Aunt Mary's and at least remove the eye liner pencil that I used to flesh out my goatee. Aunt Mary can be expected to have something to say about my erratic attire, but I'll just have to endure it together with an hour and a half of tea and toilet trips.

Jo's right. Aunt Mary doesn't seem to be home. I ring the doorbell several times and call through the letterbox to no avail. But there's something about the feeling of the house that tells me she's home. I can hear the TV chattering away in the back room and catch a glimpse through the letterbox of clutter in the kitchen. Aunt Mary would never go out and leave the house in anything other than silent orderliness. Most likely she's enjoying one of her mid-afternoon naps.

I try the side gate and find it unlocked. This is the first time I've actually set foot in Aunt Mary's back garden. It's sizeable. The old metal framed French windows of the sitting room face a square gravel path around a bed of rose bushes in full bloom. The scent is stunning. I've always liked roses. Their thick, silky blooms and heady aroma make me understand how someone could want to roll naked in their petals. I doubt Aunt Mary has cultivated the flowers for that purpose but who knows? Pushing my face close to the dappled glass of the doors, I can make out her form, fast asleep in her favourite reclining armchair. Gently I tap on the window but it isn't enough to rouse her.

The kitchen door is, surprisingly, unlocked. I walk noisily through the kitchen, not wanting to surprise or scare Aunt Mary. Then I fill the kettle and set it to boil. She's becoming an increasing fan of sleeping pills and has started to take them occasionally during the daytime, so I could probably drop all the pots and pans on the floor without waking her.

'Cup of tea, Aunt Mary? It's Ger,' I call, close to shouting, as I move through to the sitting room with the teapot and two cups and saucers on a tray. I've forgotten the biscuits and will be in trouble for it.

Returning to the kitchen for the biscuits, something in the hallway catches my eye. The door of the front parlour, slightly open. Highly unusual.

Setting the tea tray down on the low table, I move over to Aunt Mary and lay a hand on hers to gently wake her, but then jerk mine away in surprise. She's quite cool. And her face has a slightly blue tinge to it. I'm not a pathologist but I would say she's been dead for a few hours. Well, she looks peaceful and quite composed except her mouth is gaping slightly. I have an urge to lift her chin and close her mouth. My hand moves towards her face and then stops. There's something on Aunt Mary's tongue. It looks like a communion host.

I reach in with thumb and forefinger and withdraw something that is instantly recognisable to me. A small plastic disc, the reason for my visit.

Another one bites the dust

'Jo, it's me.'

'Hi, honey.'

Honey! Things are certainly looking up in the Mayes household.

'I'm at Aunt Mary's. There's no easy way to say this. I'm afraid she's dead. Looks like she passed away in her sleep, lying in that favourite recliner of hers in the sitting room, quite peaceful.'

With a cocaine covered calling card on her tongue.

Silence.

'What should I do?'

Women know what to do when someone dies, is born, marries, has a holy communion. All of those things. The innate knowledge of how best to handle such eventualities is missing from the male brain. Well, it is from mine anyway.

'Oh my God! That's terrible.' A few muffled sobs then, 'Call in on Mrs Jaspersen. She'll fetch an ambulance, tidy the house and initiate the funeral arrangements. I'll have to come up tomorrow for a few days, to be with Ma and Da. The removal will probably be about next Wednesday and the funeral mass on Thursday.'

You see what I mean? I can't remember the last time Jo was at a funeral, so how does she know all this stuff? Trustingly, I follow instructions and call on the next door neighbour, Mrs Jaspersen, who is a lot younger than Aunt Mary at just seventy. Same procedure as with Jo. After a few moments of sorrow, Mrs Jaspersen turns into a veritable whirlwind. By the time the ambulance arrives the house has been cleaned and dusted to perfection. Well, to a certain height anyway, as Mrs Jaspersen is only about four feet and eight inches tall. If this was any kind of a crime scene then all trace evidence left by short perpetrators would have been totally eradicated.

The ambulance crew are courteous but brief. Aunt Mary is checked and pronounced dead, stretchered and carried out well within the hour and a half I've allowed for my visit. They have to lay her body on its side on the stretcher as the rigor mortis has moulded her to the shape of the reclining armchair. She more resembles a waxworks dummy than the acid tongued old lady who recently graced our dining table. During all this I feel a total spare. I can't even assume the mundane duty of making tea. The ambulance crew refuses it and Mrs Jaspersen has already washed up the teapot and made me tea in a mug. As they leave I hear one of them ask Mrs Jaspersen who the cowboy is.

Thanking Mrs Jaspersen for everything, I take another turn around the back garden before I leave. These beautiful roses and all the rest of it will probably come into Jo's possession through Aunt Mary's will. Yet another reason to reinforce my shaky marriage.

Thinking of Jo, she'll have a torturous time up in Dublin with her family during and after the funeral. I'll be expected to put in a few personal cameo appearances at certain times and places. It's Friday afternoon and Jo will likely travel up to Dublin the next morning.

That reminds me of my planned rendezvous with Renée on Saturday night. My head tells me it's time to call it a day with Renée. On the other hand, that would be more than a little cruel considering the late stage of her cancer. The great fatalist that I am, I trust the situation will resolve itself in the not too distant future.

'Single to Eden Quay,' I tell the bus driver at the stop outside Aunt Mary's house.

'Been to a party?' he asks in an African baritone.

'No.'

'Going to a party?'

'Wrong again. My Aunt just died.'

'Oh, very sorry. You are wearing mourning clothes. My respects, sir.'

In all the excitement I've neglected to tone down my appearance. It's a strange trip back to Bagenalstown. Some college students on the train have a few good laughs at my expense, but nothing I can take them to task over. A few seats down an overly well-dressed businessman tries to catch my eye several times and smiles. When I visit the onboard toilet he stands behind the door as I exit and I have to push uncomfortably close to him. I'm afraid to say he does in fact touch me up as I pass, even more embarrassing as I have the rendezvous with Renée on my mind and am experiencing a surge.

The reason for that rare visit to the train toilet was to complete my Raheny mission. Disposal of the plastic disc. Forced through a gap in the unyielding toilet window, the mystery item lies anonymously on or near the railway line somewhere outside Newbridge.

When the train pulls into Bagenalstown I have a feeling, reinforced by the blustery rain blowing at forty five degrees across the tracks, that life is returning to routine. I haven't said much about Bagenalstown but it's a small place. The kind of place where you might have trouble killing an hour or two. Before Jo and I moved there I had the pleasure to try and kill an hour or two in Bagenalstown. There was a bookshop but it was closed for lunch. The only pub I could find didn't suit my tastes. A café looked like it could have been promising had it not been closed down. I found another bookshop but the display on the shelves was more reminiscent of a bring-and-buy sale. On impulse I bought a ream of printer paper from the old lady who ran the shop and the paper wrapper was palpably damp. That's Bagenalstown.

Jo decided we would live in that town, because you could get a lot more house for your money than in Kilkenny, which was the only other option she would consider. Her choice made perfect sense. We had a substantial dwelling by any standards. Unfortunately the children we anticipated were not conceived and we remain the only childless couple in a close of similarly large houses, just busy enough to deny us the privacy we now crave. At least there's a rail connection within walking distance.

I make the short walk, trying to hold my umbrella at the magic angle. I've never had an umbrella turn inside out on me, a point of personal pride. But I've forgotten and left behind countless numbers of the things in taxis, on buses and in pubs. The slanting, drenching weather soaks my black jeans in a four inch band between the hem of the charcoal trench coat and my boots. Other than that, I'm weatherproof, unlike most of the other travellers who get soaked just running to their parked cars in their shirts, blouses and jackets. Slightly smug, I walk in the front door to find Jo in a whirl of packing for the trip to Dublin.

Give a woman a dead body and she knows exactly what to do. Ask her to quickly pack for a few days away and the world comes to an end. I know this is true and so I do the only thing I can which is to dry off with a cup of coffee and then go to the fish and chip shop for comfort food.

'Hey. I'm going to the chipper to get us tea. Salad burger and chips?'

'Yep, thanks. Get me mushy peas and a bottle of something fizzy. I need the sugar.'

We dine in great splendour. Salad burger and chips, chicken snack box with breast, mushy peas, baked beans and Pepsi. And for dessert, two chocolate bars and a bottle of Rioja.

'Hey, you sure know how to show a girl a good time,' Jo grins, wiping the grease from her mouth and hands on a paper kitchen towel.

'My pleasure. What time are you heading off tomorrow?'

'Mid morning, after a lazy breakfast. I probably won't be back until after the funeral, okay?'

'Sure. Do whatever you have to.'

'I have a few days off work. Ma is pretty upset. Aunt Mary was the last on her side of the family. I'll confirm the date and time of the funeral and you can show your face then.'

Five or six days left to my own devices. The prospect is both exciting and a little scary. Come to think of it, I haven't actually been alone for such a length of time since I can remember. Amsterdam was with Tom. Other trips I've made were with Jo or Renée or work colleagues. What will I do with all that time?

'Here's a list of jobs for you to get done while I'm away,' Jo leans across the sofa and thrusts a piece of paper into my hand. She's way ahead of me, as usual. I look at the column of manly tasks. Replace light bulb. Clean windows. Unblock sink. Fix leaking shower door. Sleep with mistress. Sleep with mistress?

'Just joking.'

'Yeah, well thanks for the permission anyway.'

I'm not sure if the joke is on me or her. I pocket the list, resolving to fulfil all her requests. Our conversation turns a little melancholy as the red wine takes effect.

'Oh, poor Aunt Mary. She probably took a few too many sleeping pills. At least it was peaceful and dignified.'

I wonder how Jo would react if she knew a cocaine covered plastic disc had been placed by person or persons unknown onto Aunt Mary's tongue. She takes my silence on the subject as respectful, knowing I normally seize any chance to make a joke at the old bat's expense.

'I think we were almost the only ones who spent any time with her,' Jo continues. 'The rest of Ma's family, well, she rubbed them up the wrong way. And she wasn't great with children. That and Philomena.

Nobody ever talked about it but I think that's why they kept their distance.'

I think of all the years I've endured Aunt Mary's caustic wit and merciless dissection of all things sentimental. She's been a mentor through modern life's excesses of sentimentality. I'll genuinely miss the old dear. Getting close to showing my grief, I remain silent.

'If Aunt Mary was true to her word, and I've no reason to doubt, then we'll benefit from her will. I wouldn't be surprised if she's left us the house.'

We look at each other. Mood change.

'High five!' I shout, Borat style, and we slap hands.

'Here's to good old Aunt Mary. D'you know what? With Tom's will, and now Aunt Mary's, we're going to be well off.'

'Maybe I can get a job closer to home, if we don't need the money?' I suggest.

'Maybe, yes. But watch out. One dead person is an accident. Two is a coincidence....'

'And three would just be careless. But it's got nothing to do with us. The world and his mate can pop their clogs and leave us their riches as far as I'm concerned. I'll tell you what. When it's all sorted out, let's treat ourselves to a trip away. Where would you like to go?'

'I don't know. Prague maybe. Or Vienna? I know! How about Amsterdam?'

She gives me her funny little smile. The one where her lips purse but the corners of her mouth turn up in the smile. Does she know everything? Where would that leave me if she did? The moment passes and we carry on drinking and recalling Aunt Mary's worst excesses of verbal cruelty.

Wine, grief, we cement our bond. We take it upstairs and, with no real hope of overcoming my fertility problems, do our damnedest to give the little mutants their best chance of success.

~

I wake the next morning and Jo is already downstairs, singing away happily to herself as she cooks breakfast. Scrambled eggs, sausages, mushrooms and tomatoes. The delicious aroma roused me.

'Hi,' she greets me, a fresh breeze.

'Hi, honey.' Now I'm into the honey thing.

After breakfast she takes a quick shower and even lets me join her but it's purely a mutual cleansing experience.

'I have a special feeling about last night. Let's take it easy and wait and see.'

I feel like wrapping her in cotton wool. I take Jo's bag out to the car and off she goes, up to Dublin to pay her respects. Then it's off to the bank machine for me and I withdraw all the spare cash for a wild weekend with Renée, some nine hundred euro.

You only live once.

While the cat's away

Apparently the internet is a cornucopia of information on any subject, accessible within seconds, if you know how to search it. I'm not imbued with such knowledge but I know someone who is – Renée Martin. Within an hour of Jo's departure I'm round at Renée's house with my query.

I find her looking pale and complaining of nausea. She tells me she's declined treatment for the cancer and instead has chosen to medicate the pain with medication.

Renée offers tea instead of her normal favourite freshly brewed coffee and we take it up to the spare room where she has a home office. I look at the letters and numbers on the small piece of paper in my hand.

'How would you describe this thing?' she asks.

'A button? A disc? Plastic? Small?'

'No, come on. That's no good. How would the manufacturer describe it? Or a retailer? Try and think of a product description.'

'I really have no idea.'

I really do have no idea. The thing about working in a public administration office is I have very little contact with the world of commerce, industry and consumer goods.

'Describe it again to me, will you?'

She's barely patient with me. This is going to be a real fun weekend.

'Well, it's small, round and thin. A disc. About the size of one of those flat, thin batteries or a large button.'

'And what do you think it might be?'

'Some kind of a batch identifier was Tom's guess. I've a feeling it's something active, miniaturised perhaps.'

'Miniature device,' Renée says aloud as she types into the computer. 'No, still no sense.'

'Oh well, it's gone now anyway.'

'You don't get off the hook so easily, Mr Mayes. When Renée Martin is on the case she always gets her man!'

The spark is back. A miraculous recovery. It's as if she wasn't at death's door just a few minutes earlier.

'Those letters and numbers you have on the paper. Were they all together or in groups?'

'Groups. Three lines of alphanumeric text.'

'Right. That would probably be product type, serial number and batch or something. Let me have just the first group of letters and numbers.'

I read them out from the scrap of paper in my hand.

'AX 3927 miniature device,' says Renée as she retypes the search criteria. 'Nothing in Ireland. I'll try worldwide.'

We wait for a few seconds and then just one result appears on the screen.

'This isn't it, it's just a link to a blog,' she says. Then she opens the blog and lets out a cry. 'Bingo. There's a link to a web page. Here we go.'

A photograph of the mystery disc appears on the screen.

'It's a miniature GPS tracking device, type number AX 3927, manufactured by a company called Covet. What do you make of that?'

As this news sinks in to my brain, Renée tries to find a link to the company's home page.

'They're based in a town called Accident in Maryland. Covert operations equipment. That blog gave us an inside link, so it's somehow confidential information. You're looking at one of the smallest tracking devices on the market. Incredible! We have trackers in our company vehicles and they're about twenty times the size.'

'So what does that mean, exactly?' I ask my technical expert.

'It means somebody was able to track those packages using the devices planted in them, doesn't it?'

A cold realisation indeed. Tom's safe. Aunt Mary's tongue. The Almera and the Fisherman. All located by satellite or something.

They must have traced the device to Aunt Mary's and found the old dear dead in her armchair. Was it the Romanians? Or Romanov? Or someone as yet unknown?

'Ger? Ger, tell me, do you have any more of these things in your possession?'

'No, they're all gone. It's over.'

At this point Renée knows everything I've been up to.

'Well, anyone who was tracking them knows all about you. So I wouldn't say it's over, rather it's wait and see now. If it was the authorities then you'll find out soon enough. If it was the Romanians then they have what they need, don't they?'

'What if it was someone else?

'Like Romanov or the drug manufacturer? I don't know. Maybe it was just to make sure the packages reached their destination. This may sound like a stupid question but when you and Tom bought the extra four kilos did you ask for tracking devices to be put inside them?'

I try to remember back to Amsterdam, through the pot haze of De Rokerij.

Another four kilos? Exactly the same as this? Same package everything?

And then the next day it was:

Gentlemen, six kilos as requested. The original package you examined yesterday and two others, specially prepared to order. All identical.

All identical. Two kilo packets of pure cocaine, each containing a miniature GPS tracking device and a cut of rat poison. Who said we were amateurs? We weren't even that good.

'Yes, I guess we did, but we didn't realise what we were asking for.'

'What a pair of lemons!'

I have to agree and want to laugh at our stupidity, for it's too late to cry over it. Whatever the purpose of those tracking devices, it's out of my hands.

We take a drive out in the car, Renée's BMW, across the Blackstairs Mountains to a secluded beach on the Wexford coast. She has an inexplicable urge to visit the seaside and walk on the beach, although the weather is foul. Then, on the return journey, she has us walk to the top of Mount Leinster. Like some kind of outward bound course.

'I just want to feel alive,' she shouts to me through the high winds that swirl the rain around our heads. 'Do you feel it?'

All I feel is numb. Numb from the cold wind and rain, numb from the thought someone may have tracked my smuggling efforts across Europe, numb because I need to finish this relationship with Renée and devote myself to my wife and future family.

Back in her car the heater helps to dispel the numbness, which turns out to be mostly physical. My left arm retains an ache, a niggling hangover from all the driving Tom and I did earlier in the week. The track up Leinster has taken its toll on my energy and I doze in the passenger seat much of the way back to Bagenalstown. Renée, on the other hand, seems energised by the elements.

'Let's make an early start to the evening,' she suggests as we pull up outside her house. 'We'll take my car over to Kilkenny and then taxi home. You can bring me to pick it up in the morning. Okay?'

'Okay, sounds like a plan.' I head upstairs to change.

'First, how about a bath to warm up?' she suggests with a smile more alluring than Gobnait's. And her name is a whole lot prettier.

Another concession of Renée's to personal luxury is her bathroom. She has a big corner bath with Jacuzzi jets and all that kind of thing. I don't like Jacuzzi bubbles because they make me feel flatulent, but her bath has some device that mixes essential oils into the water and swirls it around at just the right temperature. We spend a very relaxing hour in there with a bottle of champagne and quite a bit of fooling around.

At six we're ready to head into Kilkenny, although Renée has drunk a little too much and is risking her driving license.

'Today I don't care about the rules of society, only the rules of nature.' But she drives cautiously to allay my worries.

We park up outside Larkin's chipper and enjoy some chips straight out of the paper with plenty of salt and vinegar, a necessary precaution for the pub crawl Renée has on the cards. Then we stroll down the hill and turn onto the main shopping street. At the far end lies our objective, Irishtown, and a late table booked at Chez Pierre for dinner. The challenge is to take a drink in every pub along the street during the next three and a half hours, starting with the less decorative men's pubs up at the top of the street.

I lead us into the Harp Bar and order two halves of beer. Now, for a woman to drink a half pint in Ireland is widely frowned upon. It's a pint or nothing. And for a man to order himself a half in a real men's pub like The Harp is to invite ridicule. My instincts lean towards pints of Guinness but the laborious pouring process would restrict our progress. So we go for two halves of Heineken. My emasculation is made complete by Renée insisting on paying for everything. I show her the nine hundred euro in my pocket but she's resolute. That night everything will be on her. We down our halves in one and move on to the next bar across the road, The Tholsel.

By the third pub I no longer feel any shame in ordering or drinking the small beers or in Renée being my financial sponsor. We make good progress at four glasses an hour and move past Chez Pierre well ahead of schedule. So it's on to the Irishtown pubs. At the Ana Conda my beer gauge is close to full. Renée concurs.

'I need wine. Let's go to Pierre's. Okay?' She's slurring her speech.

Back on the street, we find ourselves in the midst of a group of colourfully dressed women. Strange scents waft around us and I'm not sure what's happening until Renée presents me with a single red rose she has bought from the women. Abashed, I hug her and we move on.

Pierre greets us with his usual chalk board menu of four dishes, three fish and one meat. He recognises both of us but is surprised for just a second as we haven't been there together before. Then, with that knowing look only Frenchmen have, he gives a little shrug and a smile and continues with his recommendations.

'The halibut is very good tonight. We also have back of rabbit if you would like something rustic. Oh, and by the way, if you like shellfish I have some very meaty scallops as an appetiser.'

We both take his recommendation.

'Do you have champagne?' Renée asks.

'Of course. I will bring it straight away, very cold.'

The good, homely French cooking brings us back from the brink of drunkenness, despite the champagne. There are several minutes without conversation although we exchange looks that suggest important things to be said.

'There's something I have to tell you,' Renée starts, just as I'm trying to find the guts to initiate my own disclosure. 'There's a reason why I was ill earlier today.'

'I know it's a terrible time for you. And I don't want to add to your pain.' I've promised myself to broach the issue and want to get in first. 'I've reached the stage where I need children in my life.'

'Hah! Ironic!'

'Why so?'

'Well, you'd told me it was impossible because of your…problem. Right?'

I roll my eyes around the room, not wanting my problem to be common knowledge.

'Yes, but…'

'Yes, but I'm pregnant. Ten weeks pregnant.'

It would be interesting to have a mirror at this point, because I'm sure my face is showing a medley of disbelief, wonderment, confusion and frustration.

'That should be wonderful news for us but I won't survive this pregnancy. The cancer consultant told me this week the tumour has spread too far. I'll be dead before the end of the second trimester.'

'Your sickness, morning sickness.' My head spins, not from alcohol. I am to be a father. No, I'm not to be a father. There is a baby. There will be no baby.

'I'm sorry, Ger. Nothing can be done.'

What can she mean? That she'll have an abortion? I try to focus on Renée's expression and see a slight shake of the head. Not for further discussion, at least not at Chez Pierre's. My first instinct is to get drunk, not remembering I'm already there. As I down the champagne, which now leaves a bitter aftertaste, the sobering thought hits me that if I'm drunk then so is Renée.

When Pierre lifts the bottle from the ice bucket to top up her glass I place my hand in the way. Transformed into a righteous and indignant expectant father, I hiss at her.

'I don't think you should have any more in your condition. Do you?'

Pierre gives a small, embarrassed laugh and, placing the champagne bottle in the ice bucket, moves away.

'It's a little late now. We've just spent the last four hours on a pub crawl.'

'But that was before I knew you were pregnant with our child!'

'I shouldn't have told you.'

'And then what would you have done? Just hidden yourself away from me? Gone off to an aunt's for nine months like they did in the old days?'

'It's academic. There isn't going to be any nine months. This mother is not going to be alive to give birth. Like I said, I shouldn't have told you. My mistake.'

Her predicament is clear. There's very little good news in this story. The least I can do is be supportive.

'No, I'm glad you did. Here.'

I pour the champagne for her and we toast glasses.

'To what might have been.'

'To what might have been.'

We kiss across the dinner table and I don't care if anyone sees us. I'm going to give Renée the attention she deserves for the time we have left together. Pierre, seeing it's safe, approaches with our deserts.

'I trust everything is okay for you?'

'Yes, thank you,' Renée says.

I simply smile and nod.

After we pay and leave, we wander the streets, calling in one or two further pubs for another drink. One place feels particularly cosy and we stop there, nestling in the deep blue sofa in the back room. It must be close to three in the morning when they finally push us out of a side door. It opens into an ancient alley, the cobbles leading down to the Nore.

'Let's take the river walk,' she says.

'Are you sure? Sometimes there are drunks down there.'

'Well, there'll be two more in a minute.' Renée's laugh sounds like a burbling brook.

The Nore, by comparison, is swollen with run off from the heavy rain of the last few days. A strong, muddy flow surges along, tugging at the precipitous stone banks but finding no purchase.

Contrary to my expectations, there isn't a soul to be seen. Even the druggies and hobos are safely tucked up in their hideaways. We walk as far as we can upstream and then return. There are only a couple of crossings and the length of the river walk is quite limited. At the city limits the stone lined riverbank reverts to grass and there's no safe passage so we have to retrace our steps.

The walk downstream takes us past the weir before it peters out into a boggy track.

'Fancy a swim?' Renée asks.

'You're joking, right?'

There's an annual swim race in the Nore between the two bridges in Kilkenny but not under flood alert conditions. I can see from her face Renée is only half joking and I think it'd be best if we make our way back up to town and the taxi rank. The time now is after four but, with luck, there might be an odd taxi hanging around. The cool night air has sobered us a little.

'You know what? If you can get me pregnant then maybe there's still a chance for you and Jo to start a family.'

'What are you talking about?'

'Children. I know you want them. I do love you, Ger. It's a real shame it can't work out for us, but I'm sure there's still a chance for you and Jo.'

We reach the John Street Bridge and move on towards the taxi rank behind Dunnes Stores. I talk down at the pavement as I walk.

'I don't know. Things with Jo and me are getting better, it's true. But for now we have to take care of you.'

She doesn't answer. I turn and find myself alone. Spinning, I see a figure on the bridge. Renée has climbed onto the parapet. I run towards her.

'Renée, come down. It's dangerous. You'll fall.'

She stands on the stone rail and wobbles with a slight giggle. Then she looks at me, her face serious, blows a kiss and steps backwards off the bridge and into the river.

I run to look down. The brown waters surge a few meters below. There's no sign of her. I raise a knee to climb onto the wall and then stop, pulled back by a hand on my shoulder. A woman in colourful traditional clothes says something to me in a strange accent.

'She's gone. Don't waste your life as well.'

She's right. As many drown trying to save another. One of the Romanian flower sellers holds me by the elbow as I stand back down. I turn my head to the river and see a dark shape below the surface.

When I manage to move from my frozen position, trying to catch another glimpse of the mother of my child sliding over the weir and away out of my life, the gypsy woman has gone. In her place a brown paper carrier bag.

It contains bundles of notes.

Under the microscope

'Good God. Three people within a week of each other.'

'Hmm.' I slurp my wine.

We're close together on the sofa, half watching a film on TV but getting totally sloshed.

It's five days since Renée, on drunken impulse, jumped into the river. She was still wearing her high heels.

The silver lining is that I've managed a week off work and a stay of execution with my stress counselling, thanks to old Dr Fothergill's certificate, the quack.

Jo doesn't understand why Renée and I were getting inebriated while she was up in Raheny for Aunt Mary's funeral. Doubtless this will come back to bite me in the sporran but, at the moment, we're both too drunk with grief and Barolo to countenance accusations of infidelity.

There comes a sharp knock on the door and I lift my head from Jo's lap. I'm almost lucid by the time she returns with a tall man in a crumpled suit, smelling of cigarettes. He has a cardboard file in his left hand.

'This is Detective Inspector McAuliffe.'

'Hello.'

'Mr Mayes? Mr Gerard Mayes?'

'Please, have a seat, and call me Ger.'

DI McAuliffe doesn't take either of those offers.

'Mr Mayes, I need to have a brief chat with you. Perhaps we might, erm, well, talk in private?' He looks apologetically at Jo.

'No problem, but my wife can hear anything that you might have to say.' Not strictly speaking true.

'I'll get some tea,' Jo offers.

Once she has left the room DI McAuliffe does take a seat but remains formal. 'Mr Mayes, I believe you were a close friend of the late Thomas McMenemy of Carlow.'

'Yes, that's right.'

'And also an acquaintance of the recently deceased Renée Martin of Kilkenny.'

Not a question so far.

'Yes, Renée was a good friend of ours.'

'You don't seem very grief struck, Mr Mayes.'

I'm taken aback. I wasn't aware that this was a test of griefstrickenness.

'Well, Detective Inspector,' I sense he has a purpose and am careful to get his rank correct. 'There would be a couple of reasons for that. Firstly I'm Scottish, as you can tell from my accent, and not inclined to public displays of emotion. Secondly, I'm rather drunk and not sure that this isn't a strange dream.'

'Oh, it's strange alright but real enough, Mr Mayes. I understand that you've also experienced another loss. Your wife's aunt, Miss Mary Twomey of Raheny.'

I'm puzzled. He continues.

'It seems that there is a link between these three deaths.'

In true TV detective style he's surely going to say that I'm the connection. Bang to rights, it's a fair cop. I may as well pack my bag for a lifetime in the clink.

'Yes, we both knew all three of them.' Jo returns with the tea.

'I'm aware of that innocuous connection, Mrs Mayes.' McAuliffe opens the cardboard folder and looks at several sheets of paper before continuing. 'What I'm referring to is the fact that each of the three deceased had recently nominated Mr Mayes here as a beneficiary of their sizeable life assurance policies.'

'Happy days!' Jo swaps her coffee cup for wine glass and makes a toast, not quite perceiving the DI's insinuation. 'We could do with the money. Ger has a little problem.'

I would concur. Well, it's part of a yarn that I've spun Jo because she opened the mortgage letter from the bank the other day. I've confessed to imaginary debts at the casino. I haven't quite worked out yet what I'm going to do with the hundred grand in notes that the Romanians gave me in Kilkenny. It's safely hidden in the attic for now.

Jo hands Detective Inspector McAuliffe a cup of strong tea.

'My husband has a gambling problem,' she explains. 'We re-mortgaged the house to pay off the casino debts and our plan is to use the cash from Aunt Mary's inheritance to repay that mortgage. Then there's her house, of course. We'll sell that, clear the rest of our mortgage and buy a holiday home with the remainder. Perhaps even a small yacht.'

'It sounds like you have it all worked out,' McAuliffe says. I don't like his tone. But he has nothing to persecute me with except that Jo and I have been named as beneficiaries in the wills of Aunt Mary, Tom and Renée. Lucky us.

'Tell me, Mrs Mayes, why do you think Thomas McMenemy would have recently changed the nominated beneficiary of his main life policy to be your husband?'

Jo answers without hesitation. 'Tom was a very close friend of ours, Detective Inspector. He knew about our money troubles and wanted to help out but Ger refused to accept anything from him. This would be Tom's way of getting the last laugh.'

That's a stretch. If McAuliffe knew me then he'd realise that Ger Mayes doesn't flatly refuse offers of cash.

'May I ask how much the policy is worth,' I ask, all innocent.

'Half a million euro.' McAuliffe scans our faces for reaction.

Jo's is extreme. She lets out a squeal and involuntarily throws her red wine into the air, most of it landing over me and a little on McAuliffe.

'Oh my God! I'm sorry.'

'No problem,' McAuliffe takes it in his stride. 'Mr. Mayes seems to have borne the brunt of your surprise.'

I make my excuses and return two minutes later in clean clothes, handing McAuliffe a small towel for the few splashes on his crumpled, tobacco laced suit. Perhaps that might persuade him to get the thing dry cleaned.

'And the same question regarding Renée Martin?' McAuliffe addresses Jo again, as if there has been no pause to clean up the wine.

The room has been transported to the Arctic Circle. You can see your breath in the air. I'm a seal floundering under the ice at an air hole. McAuliffe is the Eskimo dangling his rod and Jo is the polar bear about to rake me and McAuliffe with her claws.

'Renée Martin and my husband were having an affair, Detective Inspector.'

There, she's said it. I don't know how long she's known. I shrink my head and neck into my shoulders and shield my eyes with a hand. Fortunately Jo's wine glass is still empty otherwise I'd be looking at a second change of clothes.

Jo is perfectly still. McAuliffe watches us both. He seems to be enjoying my humiliation. I need to move the topic away from me, back to those who have gone before us.

'She was ill, you know. A malignant tumour around her spine. Renée didn't want to suffer a lingering death in a hospice. I believe she deliberately jumped into the river that night, but I didn't know about the life policy at the time.'

Little white lie there.

'Well, I would have pushed her in,' Jo growls.

'There were witnesses on the bridge that night, I understand,' McAuliffe says.

'Yes.'

This has me sweating.

'Not exactly the normal type of witnesses,' McAuliffe adds. 'A group of three women. Street performers and rose sellers, they claim. Gypsy beggars, to my mind.'

I say nothing. So he's a typical provincial policeman, hurling around racial slurs.

'Now, Mr Mayes, I understand you were also present at the passing of Thomas McMenemy in Carlow.'

Jo pinches her lips and looks from me to McAuliffe.

'Thomas McMenemy died in his home from an overdose of cocaine that was laced with rat poison. You were present at his death and you called the ambulance.'

'Yes, that's right.'

'Did you administer that fatal dose of cocaine?'

'No, I did not.'

'Were you aware that it was a fatal dose?'

'No. I wasn't even sure what he was taking. I've very little idea when it comes to drugs.' I throw a glance at Jo as if to say see, it could be worse, at least I'm not into drugs. She shakes her head in exasperation.

'Were you aware that the cocaine used by Thomas McMenemy was of unusual purity and that it matched a consignment of the drug seized earlier that evening in Cork?' McAuliffe watches me carefully. The tips of my fingers curl into my palms and find cold sweat.

'No, I didn't even know it was cocaine until the inquest.'

Jo turns to me, takes my hand and feels the sweat.

'Tell me you're not mixed up in something criminal?'

'No, of course not.' Big fat lie.

'Go on, tell us, Mr Mayes.'

No, I'm not going to tell him.

'So, Mr Mayes, I understand that two weeks ago you spent several days in Amsterdam with the late Thomas McMenemy.' McAuliffe fixes me with a sobering look.

'You told me you were going mountain walking in Cumbria!' Jo rages, with a thump to my already aching left shoulder.

'Would you have let me go if I'd said Amsterdam?'

My shoulder is really quite sore now. McAuliffe has a big grin on his face. I've finally answered to his satisfaction.

'Let me ask you, what exactly did you do in Amsterdam, Mr Mayes?'

'Well, you know. What any red blooded male gets up to in Amsterdam. Beer. A little window shopping. The usual.'

'Did you engage in any illegal activity over there, Mr Mayes?'

That's as dumb as the one on the old US entry form where they ask if you're a member of a terrorist organisation.

'Nothing that broke Dutch laws.' That might be stretching the truth a little thin as I'm not actually sure if buying six kilos of pure cocaine in Amsterdam is illegal. It seems like anything goes over there.

McAuliffe coughs to signify that whatever I've done in the coffee shops and behind the curtained windows of the Rossebuurt is definitely outside Irish law.

I turn to Jo.

'Look, we didn't do anything dodgy in Amsterdam okay? You know me, I just like to look and not touch.'

'And I suppose you spent all day in the coffee shops getting stoned with Tom?'

'You know I don't smoke.'

The DI goes for the killer punch.

'Mr Mayes, it would be very helpful if you would come down the station with me so we can eliminate you from our enquiries.'

'What enquiries are those exactly?' Jo unexpectedly comes to my aid.

'I'm not at liberty to say at the moment.'

No, but I myself have a pretty good idea what they are.

'Detective Inspector, I'm in a rather inebriated state this evening and it wouldn't be a good time to visit the station. I'm happy to answer any further questions you may have here and now. But surely it's accepted protocol for you to share the nature of your investigation before you invite people for voluntary interrogation?'

I've no idea what I'm talking about but there's no way I'm going to the station unless he arrests me. Yes, it sounds like I'm trying to be clever with him, probably not a good idea.

McAuliffe's hand reaches inside his smoke stained jacket and I expect a warrant card. My arms are feeling the urge to push wrists together, ready for the handcuffs. The only uncertainty is exactly which charges will be preferred.

'That's quite alright, Mr Mayes.' McAuliffe draws a handkerchief from his jacket and wipes a watery eye. 'When you're feeling sober please give me a call and we'll have that chat down the station. You're welcome to bring a solicitor if you feel it's necessary.'

He hands me a card with his number and stands to leave. I've escaped the trap.

At the door we receive an apology for the untimely interruption to our evening and I actually shake the man's hand. Disconcertingly short fingers. He has one foot out of the front door and then remembers his folder of Garda papers, quickly retrieving them from the sitting room. Jo gives McAuliffe a steely look on exit and they don't shake hands.

After McAuliffe has gone I push the front door lock into place with a sharp upward turn of the handle and breathe a sigh of relief. There remains the thorny prospect of an interview down the station but I'm becoming accustomed to living with a worrying future.

Jo wants to resume the wine drinking and conduct her own interrogation but, pleading exhaustion, I escape to bed, leaving her to clean up the sitting room.

The next morning we seem to be short of one dirty wine glass.

Grief

So that's how I lost my best friend, my girlfriend and my favourite aunt. Careless of me.

Ilie, to give him credit, has been true to his word in returning my money. The question is what to do with a spare hundred grand in cash, under such circumstances of recent, tragic bereavement. Lay low for a couple of days, wallowing in misery, then crawl to the bank and pay back the recent re-mortgage?

No way. Ger Mayes, happy go lucky, international big time, soon to be independently wealthy, requires some serious retail therapy. I take it to the casino in Dublin on the Sunday evening, Tom's old club. Jo knows that I have to go and repay my debts.

And there I have a big surprise. The top-hatted doormen greet me cordially but, when I place the pad of my forefinger onto the fingerprint reader, they whisk me off into a side room next to the reception and seat me in an armchair. They're extremely apologetic and deferential. Within a minute I'm joined by a debonair young man whom I take to be the casino manager.

'I'm sorry about the delay, sir,' he begins. 'Allow me to introduce myself. Francois Legrand.'

Legrand has a very slight French accent. I go to stand up but he entreats me to remain seated and takes his place in an adjacent chair.

'Is there a problem?' I ask, wondering if I've been mistaken for a debtor or perhaps some kind of VIP.

'Not exactly, Mr Mayes.' He intertwines his fingers. 'We have a privacy and security policy at our casino that is in the members' interest. You will have read the details on your membership form during application.'

I nod but, on the evening of joining, I was already so drunk that focusing on any small print would have been impossible.

Legrand continues. 'The policy states that, should the authorities make enquiries into any individual member of the club, then that member must abjure from our society for a period of not less than four weeks. In return, we guarantee not to release any member's personal information to those authorities unless forced to do so by a court of law.'

Again I nod, not understanding how this can be relevant to me but having a nasty feeling about it.

'Mr Mayes, I'm sorry to inform you we have to apply the policy to yourself and Mr Thomas McMenemy. Two days ago we received a request from the Garda Síochána for our security records regarding yourself and Mr McMenemy, specifically a copy of your fingerprints and the amount you have both gambled during this year. Naturally we refused and, to date, they have not returned with a court order.'

The Guards must have made the link between Tom's death and the cocaine in Cork. I see myself in a striped prisoner's garb and chains, running across the moors with police hounds snapping at my heels.

'Does this sort of thing happen often?'

'Given the nature of some of our more enterprising clientele, it is not an uncommon event. The authorities maintain an unhealthy interest in the source and amount of funds our members gamble with. They have made accusations that our gentlemen's activities here could be abused as a method of laundering ill gotten gains, so to speak.'

The casino manager eyes my backpack pointedly as if his X-ray vision can see the bundles of notes inside. Yes, the trusty backpack is back in business.

'Therefore, we must ask you not to pass through the security system or play the tables today, Mr Mayes. Please make yourself comfortable here. A stewardess will arrive shortly to take your drink order. According to the membership rules, we would ask you to wait until the middle of next month before you return to play again. Bearing in mind the nature of the Gardai enquiries, you might like to leave it a little bit longer.'

They don't want me around in the near future. I decide to dig a little.

'Thank you. May I ask as to the nature of these enquiries?'

Legrand doesn't hesitate. It's clearly a case of us, the casino and members, versus the authorities.

'It appears Mr McMenemy was already known to the Garda Síochána. They were investigating his possible connection with a recent drugs seizure in West Cork. Regarding yourself, they had no particular enquiries but your association with Mr McMenemy was of interest to them.'

Well, the hounds are on the scent.

Legrand repeats his apologies for not letting me enter the club.

'I hope we'll see you again in the near future, Mr Mayes. If you are looking to spend some money this evening,' again he eyes the backpack, this time a little more covetously, 'you might wish to consider another establishment.' He hands me a card. 'The stewardess will be with you shortly. She can also answer any further questions about this other establishment as she works there from 11 pm.'

I stand and shake Legrand's hand as he leaves, then study the card. It describes a gentleman's club of a different nature to the casino. A minute passes and, with a light knock on the door before it opens, a woman floats in on a tide of seductive perfume. Although she carries a tray with drinks and is clearly there to serve, I stand on impulse. In her mid twenties, she's around five nine tall, eastern European origin with a Slavic bone structure and eyes to match mine.

'Mr Mayes, here is your drink. My name is Krystal.'

I invite her to sit where Legrand has previously been and accept the Bacardi and coke with ice. They must keep a record of the members' favourite drinks.

'Krystal, tell me about this Club Arondissement.'

'Well, it's a club for gentlemen who like to relax in comfortable surroundings.'

'And you work there in the late evening?'

'Yes, I'm a stewardess there as well. If you like, I can take you there later.'

I do like, but fear for my backpack.

'What kind of relaxation is on offer?'

'Well, you can talk with friends, with the stewardesses. You can take a drink or have a dance.'

'And is this in an open area or private rooms?'

'There are private rooms upstairs, you can drink champagne.'

From my very limited experience, drink champagne is a euphemism for a private party of the most personal kind.

'How much is a bottle of champagne?'

'If you have to ask then maybe you can't afford it?'

Champagne sounds expensive.

'Come on, how much does champagne start at?'

'Okay. For straightforward champagne the price is one thousand euro. If you want to have some special vintage then we have a complete wine list.'

'That sounds very interesting, but it's still early so I'm going to leave now and go to the club later.'

'You can stay here and have a drink if you like. I have to go back to work but I will come every half an hour to serve you.'

'Thanks but I don't like to drink alone. I'll see you later, Krystal.'

Downing my Bacardi and coke, I head for the door.

'Don't forget,' Krystal places a hand on my arm 'I will be there soon after eleven. Ask for me and I will make sure you get a special welcome as a new member.'

I thank the lovely lady and make my way out of the establishment.

So, do I turn up at the Club Arondissement that evening with my one hundred grand in cash? Do I hell. After all, I'm a Scot who knows how to look after his money. I take a taxi to the Four Seasons Hotel, check into a room and stash ninety five grand in the hotel safe before returning to Krystal and her friends. Then I blow five thousand euro on personal gratification. Because I'm worth it.

~

You'll be pleased to be spared the gory details, suffice to say I crash in my hotel room not long before breakfast after negotiating a late check-out with reception. That gives me a good seven hours sleep, nevertheless I wake with a feeling like jet lag. Even in a place like Club Arondissement five thousand euro buys a considerable amount of misbehaviour.

With ninety-five grand in the backpack I head into the early afternoon city centre by taxi. The remaining cash equates to nineteen more nights at Club Arondissement or a larger quantity of baser debauchery. So share in my personal pride when I tell you I come to my senses and deposit ninety thousand euro in the bank with instructions for it to be paid off against my re-mortgage. And the other five? I pay that in as well but then lodge it electronically with a stockbroker. My long intended love affair with the stock market has commenced.

The bank where I deposit the cash is within walking distance of Parnell Square and I arrive only a few minutes late for the first stress counselling session of the second week. Gobnait gives me a strange look on entering reception. She has a radiance that deserves further study and, when she stands to move some papers, I notice there is a slight tell-tale bulge to her stomach. It's the first time I've seen Gobnait out of her chair and her early pregnancy hits me like a sledgehammer. I'm on the bridge again, watching Renée's body slide over the weir.

Dr Livingstone emerges from the consultation room to find me gaping at Gobnait's abdomen. Unwittingly I've edged closer, contemplating reaching out to the girl.

'Mr Mayes, Ger. Nice to see you out of disguise, if a little dishevelled.'

The good doctor wrinkles her little Edinburgh nose at my mustiness. I opted for extra sleep rather than a shave and shower at the hotel. Club Arondissement is written all over me.

'You look a little bit wasted,' she says as I settle onto the therapist's couch. 'Did you have a stressful weekend?'

Pregnant mistress drowns herself. Guards seek my fingerprints in connection with cocaine haul. High class brothel leaves me exhausted and soiled.

'Well, it wasn't the best.'

'And how about the world of high finance? How is your self worth today?'

'I've received a level return on my investment.'

'And how do you feel about that?'

'Acceptable, under the circumstances.'

'And what circumstances are those?'

I'm tired of these games. Tired of dressing up like an idiot. Tired of role play.

'Look, Doctor Livingstone. I lost another good friend last week. She drowned in the river. I don't want to talk about how I feel anymore. How would you feel if three people you cared for died within a week of each other?'

'Under those circumstances, I really don't think I would be in a condition to return to work. Are you?'

'Well, you begin to understand me at last. And my GP did sign me off for last week.'

'Are you taking care of yourself?'

Late nights, alcohol and drugs, the emotional trauma, Club Arondissement.

'Not particularly well.'

'So it would appear. So it would appear.'

The good doctor makes some notes and then, closing her book, looks up at me.

'Ger, I really need you to attend every session here this week. I need you here on time, dressed appropriately and in good mental and physical condition. No more disguises, no more dead friends or relatives. Can you manage that?'

How heartless! As if the deaths of Tom, Aunt Mary or Renée have anything remotely to do with me. Nevertheless, I do a quick mental stock-take of my few relatives, who are healthy to my knowledge. Then of my friends, which is easy enough as I have none left.

'Yes, I think with a fair wind and God willing I can manage it.'

'No more fantastic stories, no more paranoid behaviour. And no more pestering my receptionist. She's pregnant, for God's sake! Leave the poor girl alone.'

There, something I'm definitely not responsible for.

'If you can't manage then we'll have to change the nature of these counselling sessions. Believe me, we are very close to that point.'

I smile meekly. I don't do meek very well, but I'm trying. The prospect of a series of psychotherapy sessions isn't totally undesirable, especially if my employer will foot the bill.

The rest of the hour passes amiably enough. When Dr Livingstone asks me some questions about stress in the workplace I think of fat Deirdre and her unreasonable demands. Of the other team members, mostly male, who occasionally laugh amongst themselves at my expense. Of Caroline, who hasn't accepted my facebook friend request.

On the way out of the offices I treat Gobnait in a more fatherly fashion. In truth, I feel rather protective towards her. Pregnant women always arouse that instinct in me. Shame, then, I hadn't been better able to protect Renée from herself.

Interrogated

On the return journey from the dominating Dr
Livingstone and her deliciously fertile Gobnait, I give
the entire situation some deep consideration. There's
no need to travel to Raheny for an hour and a half of
banter, biscuits and toilet visits with Aunt Mary, God
rest her soul.

Undoubtedly the Guards will call on me again in
Bagenalstown. If they're really suspicious of my
involvement then my arrest might follow. From the
little I understand of the Irish criminal justice system,
any resulting prosecution would take a year or more
to come to court, during which time I would be
released, probably on bail. Even the most heinous of
murderers and all but the most dangerous of criminals
experience this drawn out process. Some cases have
even been dropped because the prosecution service
has taken an unreasonable length of time to prepare
the file.

In the meantime, as the result of calamitous recent
events, Jo and I will be big time in the legacy stakes.
Aunt Mary, God bless her, has left us a hundred
thousand in cash plus her house in Raheny and the
small proceeds of an ancient life insurance policy.
Renée, God bless her and my unborn child, will have
a fair amount on her life policy that names me as
beneficiary. Suicide doesn't disqualify payment
unless the policy is new. As for good old Tom, his
five hundred grand will bring us close to the magic

million, assuming we sell Aunt Mary's house. A million euro of cash opens up a lot of options.

I arrive home in Bagenalstown to find Jo cooking dinner. She gives me a kiss and wrinkles her nose at my mustiness.

'I'll be dishing up in about fifteen minutes. Why don't you go up and have a shower?'

I do so and when I come down the dinner table is set with candles, wine, the works.

I think back to the dinner party where it all started. Tom kicking me under the table, my flirtation with Renée, trying to keep old Mary's money out of the hands of the charities.

'Ger?'

Jo has been talking to me.

'Sorry. I was thinking.'

'Yes, well. I'll start again and do try to keep up this time.'

'Okay.'

'You know we're both entitled to a career break of up to five years?'

I nod. It's always been a theoretical point.

'You and I. We're going to apply for it and then head off into the sun. Spain. I fancy Spain.'

'Viva Espana. Or how about Canada? California.'

'Brazil. Or just tour until we settle. We've no kids to tie us down.'

We clink glasses and then I realise the last thing she said.

'That's right, no kids. My premonition was wrong. I'm not pregnant.'

We shed tears together for those who have gone before us and those that haven't been born. Of course

Jo has no idea that Renée was pregnant. But we both know Aunt Mary, Tom and Renée would have been delighted to see our boring civil service lives finally being shaken up.

McAuliffe doesn't materialise at our door that evening. I'm expecting a call during the next few days to formalise his outstanding invitation of a chat and a cup of tea at Bagenalstown Garda station. In the meantime, life has to go on, for those of us still breathing.

~

I head for the late train into Dublin and my Tuesday session with the intrepid Dr Livingstone.

Jo leaves for work in a foul mood born of combined hangover and indignation. Last night when we still couldn't find that missing wine glass I accused her of having broken it and hiding the wreckage. It won't have been the first time. Those goblets were my birthday present from Renée the previous year. Waterford Crystal is expensive but Jo treated the goblets like cheap wine glasses. In hindsight it's clear why.

At the train station I hang back from the hoi polloi and step forward only as the train pulls in. Almost nobody gets off in Bagenalstown in the morning unless by mistake. My foot is actually upon the step of the carriage when a smell of tobacco wafts into my nostrils and a firm hand guides me back down onto the platform. It's McAuliffe.

'Mr Mayes. I thought we might bring forward our meeting and get it over with, so to speak.'

The few other regular passengers are wide eyed. It's not often a Columbo look-a-like and two uniformed plods seize a rail commuter in mid step.

'Well, it's hardly convenient,' I manage to say. 'I have an appointment in Parnell Square at two.'

'Oh, I think we can phone ahead and let them know, get you off the hook, at least on that account.'

I think of Gobnait and Dr Livingstone, the looks that will materialise on their face when DI McAuliffe calls to say Ger Mayes is unavailable to attend, Ger Mayes is helping with Garda enquiries. They will think it's me calling, masquerading as a Garda detective inspector, Ger persona of the day.

Of course, if McAuliffe isn't going to arrest me then I can decline the offer and get on the train. But arrest, from the look of the two red-faced culchee boys in blue, is an option here. Forceful arrest, kicking and screaming in front of fellow commuters, neighbours and the parish priest, Father Sean, who has just now poked his head out of the train to take a look at the fugitive. So I go quietly.

We don't go to Bagenalstown Garda station. No, I'm obviously too big a fish. One of McAuliffe's constables drives us in their dark blue Ford to the old square brick station in Kilkenny.

We halt at reception where McAuliffe informs the desk Sergeant of his catch.

'Mr Gerard Mayes has kindly condescended to have a little chat with us over a cup of tea regarding recent events.'

'Certainly, sir. Room three is available.'

We move along a corridor and stop a few doors down. McAuliffe leads me in and, sure enough, I'm furnished with a white mug of steaming tea whilst still taking in the surroundings.

There have been multiple coats of paint over the years and the most recent is holding up well but the general décor, the furniture in particular, predates the Celtic Tiger economy. I lower myself onto the moulded plywood chair and rest my tea on the Formica table.

'Sugar, Mr Mayes?' McAuliffe asks.

'Yes thanks.' Normally I don't but there's nothing normal about this situation.

A woman comes into the room and is introduced to me as Detective Sergeant Faloone. She offers a hand, her left as her right is bandaged. I shake the hand spontaneously, if a little awkwardly, and only afterwards realise this is good cop, bad cop and she's presumably the good one. But then, from her demonstratively firm grip, perhaps she's the bad one. The crushing gesture leaves a pain in my left hand and sends spasms up the arm. DS Faloone looks like a TV police detective. Attractive in a hard way. Feminine of figure but not in her deportment. Nevertheless, she's my type. Two arms, two legs and a head.

We sit all three of us for a few minutes, drinking tea and exchanging looks. I have the feeling they want me to start. Yes, okay, I did it. I murdered Professor Plum in the library with the candlestick. Eventually, realising I'm willing to sit all day and say nothing, McAuliffe decides to break the ice.

'So, Ger. Why do you think we've asked you down here? What's the subject for our little chat over tea?'

So, we're on first name terms. He's my new best friend. But I don't know his Christian name or DS Faloone's and, as far as I'm concerned, it's going to stay that way.

'I imagine you wish to continue our conversation of the other night.'

'In a manner of speaking, yes.'

'Mr Mayes,' the good lady DS commences. 'We were alerted to a connection between three deaths. Thomas McMenemy, Mary Twomey and Renée Martin all had life assurance policies naming you as a beneficiary. All three policies were coincidentally held with the same insurance company. It's their standard practice to inform the authorities when a certain pattern of claims emerges. The information came to us in Kilkenny and here we are.'

'Here we are,' I echo.

'The first to die, Thomas McMenemy, had a possible connection with a recent illegal shipment of cocaine seized in West Cork the night before his death.'

I merely nod innocently, waiting for a question. It comes from Faloone.

'Were you in West Cork with Thomas McMenemy the night before he died?'

It's not an unexpected question. I choose to answer it with another.

'What makes you think I was in West Cork, or Tom McMenemy was there for that matter?'

If they have any firm evidence then surely they would have already arrested me. I consider asking for a solicitor. If they're just fishing then that might look like an admission of guilt. I decide to bluff it out.

'We have descriptions from West Cork of suspects that match yourself and Mr McMenemy,' ventures McAuliffe.

It's a weak gambit from McAuliffe. Tom and I weren't seen together in West Cork.

'There was a vehicle abandoned in West Cork,' continues Faloone. 'An old green Nissan Almera. Have you ever driven such a car?'

'I mostly take the train these days. We do have a family car but it's a Volkswagen Golf. That's green though, if it helps.'

Faloone and McAuliffe look at each other, trying to decide whether I'm dicking them around or just being dense.

'Look. We know you were in West Cork. We know you drove the car. An amount of cocaine was retrieved after a chase across fields. We know you had just come back from Amsterdam with McMenemy. Three people have mysteriously died around you. So you may as well tell us the entire story.'

Four people died. He's forgetting Alin, as have I up until now. Sure, he doesn't even know about Alin. I could tell all, more than he knows. However, the urge to unburden myself just isn't materialising.

'I'd like to help you with this,' I lie. 'It's true. I was in Amsterdam with Tom. You already managed to disclose that to my wife the other night, thank you very much. But I didn't have anything to do with cocaine in West Cork. There's nothing mysterious about the three people that died, it's just tragic. And I've never owned a Nissan.' Most of that is true.

DS Faloone loses her rag.

'You were in West Cork! We can place you there. You drove the car. McMenemy had more cocaine so you broke into his house in Carlow and dug the safe out of the wall!'

McAuliffe glares at Faloone as if she's revealed too much. For a second I'm flummoxed. If they can place me in Cork and in the Nissan then why am I not under arrest? I decide to fight fire with fire.

'I was the one who reported Tom's house as broken into! You can search my house, my garden, my shed, anywhere on this island. I didn't break into Tom's house and I didn't steal his safe. Wherever it is, whatever was in it, I don't know!'

There! Rightly indignant. How dare they accuse me of something I really didn't do! Then it dawns upon me. Jo hasn't broken the Waterford Crystal goblet. It's in the possession of McAuliffe, swiped by him at the end of his visit to us in Bagenalstown. He must have slipped it into his coat pocket on returning to the sitting room to retrieve his folder of papers. I'm sunk!

'This is all very unbelievable,' McAuliffe says, trying to calm the situation.

'You're telling me.' Truth is stranger than fiction.

The two cops exchange a look, stand and leave me alone in the room with my half full mug of tea.

This isn't one of those rooms like you see on TV. There's no one-way mirror from behind which my accusers can observe me. But there is a small camera up in one corner. I raise my hand to drink the remaining brew and then realise I'm about to leave them with a perfect full set of legitimate fingerprints on the smooth white surface of the mug. So I get up and wander nonchalantly into the corner with the camera. Standing underneath the camera, hidden from observation, I drain the mug. The tea is actually quite tasty. I let the sleeves of my shirt slip down over my hands, rub the exterior of the mug clean with the material of my shirt and replace the mug on the table just before McAuliffe and Faloone re-enter the room. Close call.

Faloone sees me standing there with my shirt cuffs down over my hands, like a school kid's jumper on a cold day. The look she gives me is surprisingly similar to Dr Livingstone's regular expression.

'Mr Mayes, we're going to have to talk to you again on these matters. You might wish to consider bringing a solicitor with you next time.'

Indeed I will.

'Am I free to go?'

'You came here of your own volition. Yes, of course you're free to go. But don't leave the country.'

I won't. That bit doesn't come till later.

Legal advice

'It seems Tom was involved with drugs handling down in West Cork. He drove a car down there and I followed in his Mercedes to bring him back. The Guards have the car he drove and apparently they seized some cocaine.'

Jo looks at me as if I'm kidding her.

'McAuliffe and this other one, a woman named Faloone, are trying to implicate me in Tom's dealings.'

Now her eyes squint as she tries to work out if I'm being economical with the truth.

'When you and Tom went to Amsterdam it was for drugs, wasn't it?'

'I think he must have bought the drugs there, yes.'

'Did you know there were drugs in the car he drove to West Cork?'

'I was just driving his car down there for him. He said there was a chap he had to hand the other car over to.'

'Did you handle the drugs? Are your fingerprints on the package or whatever it is?'

'Probably. He showed me a big bag of the stuff in Bagenalstown and snorted some of it. I guess it's the same cocaine the Guards are talking about. And I drove the Nissan down from Dublin to Bagenalstown, so they'll find my prints all over the car.'

'The Waterford crystal. McAuliffe must have taken it. They have your fingerprints on it!'

She's highly disappointed in me, I can tell. But the story is developing nicely. I can blame Tom for everything and just act the dumb courier.

'We need a solicitor, a good one.'

'Agreed, but how do we go about finding one?'

'What was the name of that fella in Waterford who got off the charge of murdering his wife? His solicitor's name, I mean. Coogan, was it? No, Duggan. That's it, Jim Duggan. He did a sterling job and got an innocent man off the hook. Let's look him up.'

She finds him on the internet. James Duggan, Solicitor for Oaths, 7 The Parade, Waterford City. It's nine in the evening but she hands me the phone nevertheless.

'Leave a message on his machine. You have to go and see him in the morning. I've a really bad feeling about all this. How could Tom have led you into this and then left us to face his music?'

How indeed? I do as instructed and advise Jim Duggan's answering machine that I'll be coming to Waterford in the morning in the hope of meeting with him.

We say little else to each other that evening. In bed we both lie awake for what seems the entire night. I'm expecting McAuliffe to ring the doorbell at any moment.

The offices of James Duggan don't match my expectations. There had been such publicity in the murder case of the previous year that I, doubtlessly along with many others, assumed Duggan had made his fortune and would have a shiny new Porsche parked outside plush penthouse offices. But they don't do Porsches outside plush penthouse offices in Waterford. Duggan's digs occupy the second and third floors of a decaying four story townhouse with rickety stairs and small dusty rooms full of papers.

Duggan himself looks more like an accountant than a solicitor. He's short, balding with a Bobby Charlton comb-over and dressed in charcoal.

I've been fortunate enough to already speak with the man himself by phone, earlier on the train. It was a slightly awkward call made from the toilet to ensure privacy. When Duggan heard about the combination of drugs, dead bodies, protested innocence and ability to pay his fees, he had no hesitation in cancelling another appointment to fit me in.

I followed up with another train toilet call to Dr Livingstone's office, once again conveying my apologies. True to his word, McAuliffe did call the previous day to explain my semi-custodial absence. Gobnait's tone suggested my case of stress might be terminal as far as she and Dr Livingstone are concerned.

Now, in front of Duggan the headline grabbing solicitor, I hope to get the kind of stress counselling I really need.

'So, Mr Mayes, the Guards have already questioned you in Kilkenny Garda station. Why didn't you call me then, may I ask?'

'Yes I probably should have done, but it all happened so fast.'

'Right, well we'll be ready for them next time eh, Mr Mayes?'

'Yes. Please call me Ger.'

'And call me Jim. Now, you say you believe they have your fingerprints on a wine glass that DI McAuliffe stole from your house?'

'That's right.'

'And your fingerprints are all over this Nissan Almera and the bag of cocaine?'

'Yes, I'm afraid so.'

'The only reason they haven't arrested you is that they obtained your fingerprints illegally. Is there anything else to place you in the Nissan together with the drugs?

'No, nothing at all.'

'Good. I think we can get you off that one. And now to the subject of the three unfortunate deaths. In each case you were present at the death or you found the deceased?'

'That's right.'

'None of the deaths has been classed as suspicious?'

'No. Tom died from the drugs. Aunt Mary simply passed away and Renée committed suicide. There were witnesses to the last one.'

'So they had all decided to help you out financially in their wills and then all three died within two weeks?'

Duggan looks at me over the top of his glasses.

'It seems like a hell of a coincidence.'

'That's what it is, nothing more.'

'Why did they decide to name you in their wills?'

'Well, we were all close and they knew my situation. I, uh, had a few problems financially.'

'What was the cause of these problems?'

'Gambling. Tom introduced me to gambling and I got in over my head.'

I've decided to stick to the same subset of the truth with Jo, the Guards and Duggan. If I start to tell him the whole story then I'm not sure where it might lead. The Sock Twins, Alin's murder, blackmailed by Romanians, Romanov, the Fisherman, Aunt Mary's tongue. No, that will go with me to the grave and hopefully not yet awhile.

'Oh, I almost forgot. The Guards demanded fingerprints and gambling transactions from the casino. They were refused but the manager said they would have to be provided if a court order was produced.'

'Which casino?'

I tell Duggan the name of the club.

'Ah yes, I know that one. Right, I'll be in touch with them. Okay, so in summary an unfortunate set of coincidences but the only connection is your financial gain. We may have to push the insurance company to pay out but I think that's manageable as well. Now, it is possible that the Guards will want to pull you in for questioning again. If they do, call me on this number.'

He hands me a business card.

'If they find grounds for arrest then we'll have some work to do. The onus will be on them to prove you were knowingly involved with the drugs. I feel confident there won't be a prosecution but it could get a bit ugly. Hopefully we can avoid it.'

He leads me to the door, one hand reassuringly patting my shoulder. Not too much contact but heartening. I leave the building in complete confidence that Jim Duggan will keep me out of prison. I have my story straight and, barring some unforeseen disaster, McAuliffe will have to accept that Tom McMenemy and the Fisherman were the culprits.

Fairly floating on air, I meander along the quays in the direction of the railway station. There are some very stylish yachts moored on private pontoons and one of them is for sale. Jo and I could be in the market for that. I attempt to gain entrance to one pontoon with the intention of viewing a yacht for sale when my mobile phone rings.

'Mr Mayes?'

'Speaking.'

'This is DI McAuliffe. We'd like your assistance with a certain matter. It may be a little unpleasant for you, I'm afraid, but we have no alternative.'

I freeze on the quay like a rabbit in headlights and consider bolting back to the sanctuary of Jim Duggan.

'What is it, Detective Inspector?'

I can hear the tremor in my voice.

'We've recovered a body from the River Nore in Thomastown. Her parents are currently out of the country and so we have to ask you to make the identification.'

Relief. Simply a dead girlfriend.

'Certainly. When and where.'

'Up at St Luke's hospital in Kilkenny. Shall we say two-thirty this afternoon?'

'Very well. I'll be there.'

I hang up. My train back to Bagenalstown will stop at Kilkenny so McAuliffe's suggestion is quite practical. Although I don't relish another meeting with him this is the least I can do for poor Renée.

Glancing at my watch there are another forty five minutes to kill before I need to get to Waterford Plunkett station, so I cross the quays road and ensconce myself in a café to read a paperback I have in my coat pocket.

Several chapters later, and after soup and a sandwich, it's time to go, so I pay up and head for the bridge. The first thing I notice is the traffic has backed up right along the quay. Then, drawing closer, I see the bridge is up. From a riverside seat I watch an old rusting steel ship slowly make its way upstream towards the bridge. In the same period the train draws into the station on the other side of the river, loads up with passengers and heads back in the direction of Kilkenny and Dublin.

McAuliffe answers after one ring.

'Mr Mayes, hello.'

He has my mobile number stored on his phone, not a good sign.

'Hello. I've missed the train from Waterford. I was caught out by the bridge lift. So I won't be able to get to St Luke's until around four.'

'Four it is then, Mr Mayes. Waterford you say? Give my regards to Jim Duggan.'

I hang up. How does he know? Am I being followed? I spend a paranoid two hours waiting for the three o'clock train, trying to discreetly assess every face as an informant, an undercover Guard or whoever else might be McAuliffe's agent. I'm suspicious of everyone, even grannies.

The train arrives on time in Kilkenny and I'm well on my way to St Luke's Hospital in a taxi when my good friend McAuliffe calls again.

'Mr Mayes? We've had contact from Renée Martin's sister and she's identified the body in the past hour. So thanks for offering to help but your assistance is no longer needed.'

I fume. Should I continue and view the body anyway? Will I be allowed? Do I want to see Renée after so many days in the water? Probably not. I mumble some response to McAuliffe and he hangs up this time. He's tooling around with me, as Tom used to say.

That leaves a delightful three hour wait until the next train to Bagenalstown. Although the MacDonagh Junction shopping centre at the railway station in Kilkenny is indeed a leap into the twenty first century, I've little desire for retail therapy and so redirect the taxi homeward for the remaining seventeen miles of my journey. A final bill of seventy euro is my reward. True enough, I'm still being paid a salary and heading for a fortune, but I resent being jerked around. I have to get McAuliffe off my case.

Jo is pleased to hear that Jim Duggan has taken me on. We feel fairly relaxed, knowing such a celebrity lawyer is on call, albeit at a fairly hefty price. Like a force-field of protection against all comers, Duggan's reputation wraps us in a sense of security that is ultimately false. Why? Because I've concocted an economical version of the truth. And because fate has not yet fully revealed its hand.

~

On Wednesday morning Jo has to rise early and get back up to Dublin for some legal business to do with Aunt Mary's estate. I manage to extract myself from under the duvet about nine and Jo is already long gone, her side of the bed cold, as though I've slept alone.

I take the late train to Dublin, resigned to enduring another session with the good doctor in an attempt to retain my employment. The crowd on the late train are becoming my compatriots by this stage. What category of person regularly catches an eleven-forty morning train from Bagenalstown to Dublin? Perhaps we're all heading for therapy.

The trip is enlivened by a few unusual but similar events. First of all, the quiet little railway station suddenly lights up with flashing white and blue lights, three Garda cars arriving as we pull out. The consensus on the train is that some class of fugitive has leapt aboard after eluding a desperate manhunt across the flooded fields of the surrounding countryside. I catch a glimpse through a Garda Mondeo passenger window of a familiar snarling face. McAuliffe obviously has more important villains than me to worry about.

In Carlow we are treated to a second helping of the Kilkenny Keystone Cops. This time five Garda cars screech into the station car park as we pull out. McAuliffe's Ford is the last of them. His driver must have travelled at dangerous speed to reach Carlow station the same time as the train. But, once again, they've missed their man, or woman.

Athy is the next stop and things are calmer. There's a spattering of new passengers who board the half empty train, easily finding seats in the long line of quiet carriages. Two men in suits, looking rather like Mormons, seem unable to decide on where to sit and wander down the aisle between the seats. I see them coming from a way off and they hasten their step, obviously spotting something to their liking. I can't believe it when they insist on crowding me in my booth of four seats. Just on the verge of asking them to move, I straighten up and the one next to me places a hand on my shoulder.

'Mr Mayes, we're getting off at the next stop. Us three. Together.'

I look at him and then his colleague. I've no desire to join the Mormons, in Kildare or any other venue.

'Look, if you must insist on sitting almost on top of me like this then I'm moving.'

With a sigh the one opposite me drops his wallet onto the table top between us and leans forward to whisper conspiratorially.

'Gerard Mayes, I am arresting you under the Offences Against the State Act 1939 on the charge of conspiracy to rob the State…'

I look at the warrant card on the surface in front of me and then up at the fat, pale face of a Guard who has never eaten a vegetable, just plates and plates of pork chops. It's all been for me. The flashing lights. McAuliffe's snarling car chases. Something has changed.

'I believe I'm entitled to call my solicitor.'

'Go ahead,' the Guard next to me concedes. 'Oh, here's the trolley. I'll have a tea and a muffin. Four sugars and three milks.'

'Can I get a cappuccino?' the meat eater asks.

I take a black coffee and stack it full of sugar. Then I drink it whilst holding the cup with a serviette. The Guards look and laugh.

'We'll be taking your prints down the station. Anyway, you're safe there with a cardboard cup.'

I have to call Duggan with the two Guards breathing down my neck. He doesn't seem surprised to hear from me.

'Have you seen the news this morning?'

No, I haven't.

Into the lion's den

The following is my attempted reconstruction, based upon what I later learned from the Guards, Jim Duggan, Jo and media reports.

At 11:30 on Tuesday evening two men leave a pub called O'Faolains in the Dublin suburb of Drumcondra. They've been enjoying a relaxing and habitual pint or three in the comfortable knowledge that the early shift at work doesn't include them. The level of alcohol consumed is above that advisable for driving home. On approaching their cars, a man in dark blue uniform appears and asks them to accompany him to the squad car, a dark blue Ford, and take a breathalyser test.

Beside the Ford is a ubiquitous large white van. As they pass the back of the vehicle, a rear door opens and they find themselves boosted into the back of the van by persons unseen. A Taser gun, or similar device, is then applied to stun and immobilise them.

They're bound and gagged with duct tape, still in the van. The air is hot and stuffy. Four very large men in balaclavas crowd them and there are two others whom they can't see but can hear as they're the only ones who do any talking.

'Gentlemen, my apologies for this rudeness. We wish to discuss a business proposition with you. Secrecy is deemed necessary due to the delicate nature of our request.'

The voice is Eastern European, smooth, confident and cultured with a strangely antiquated turn of phrase. To my mind this is almost certainly the patriarchal figure I met at the Romanians' house in the Phoenix Park.

'I must assure you that we mean no harm, but it's nevertheless necessary for me to impress upon you how earnest we are in our endeavours.'

One of the large men places a laptop computer on the floor in front of the two captives and then stands back. The bound men can see a forest scene on the screen.

'We are almost ready for your persuasive demonstration,' the Patriarch speaks loudly into the air.

A voice comes back from the small built-in speakers of the computer.

'Yes, sir. Tell me when, sir.'

'Gentlemen, you are about to witness what happens to people who betray me.' The captives in the van are now being addressed directly. 'A man has made solemn promises and subsequently broken them. This has cost me the lives of two of my comrades, not to mention a lot of money.' The voice directs itself again into the ether. 'Very well, let us proceed.'

In the forest scene on the computer a masked man appears, roughly dragging another behind him. The second man is not masked but bound, hands behind his back and ankles together. Hauled to his feet and forced to face the camera alone, the fear of the man is palpable.

'You have betrayed your friends, comrades and family,' the Patriarch says loudly in the van. He adds a further couple of sentences in a foreign language that sounds vaguely French, then continues in English. 'This is our response. Carry out the punishment.'

The masked man comes back onto screen with an iron bar and strikes the condemned man in one arm with surprising force. A crack of bone, slightly lagged by a howl of pain. Three further blows follow that likely break all of the unfortunate man's other limbs. But it isn't over. The masked man produces a pistol and, standing over the whimpering figure, fires a bullet through each elbow and knee joint.

The two captives watching in the van jump with each shot.

'Sometimes we take the next step while the traitor is still alive, but it can be rather messy, so…' the Patriarch instructs the masked man again in a foreign tongue. A bullet is fired through the forehead of the broken body that lies on the forest floor.

A minute of silence passes during which the two captive men in the transit van exchange wide-eyed looks. Another man then enters the picture on the computer screen and proceeds to swiftly dismember the body with a large axe. In a few seconds the arms, legs and head are separated from the torso.

'With the family we are more merciful,' the Patriarch explains. The image pans to show the body of a woman and a teenage boy swinging by the neck from ropes in a nearby tree. 'I am sure that you are shocked. It was necessary to show you this so that you do not doubt our resolve. These people were sub-humans who didn't deserve to live. The man betrayed himself and his family. I know you are both totally different to this man. All we require from you is one day of your time and then you are free to continue with your lives. I would even offer you a financial reward but I fear it would identify you as accomplices. Now I leave the details of our request to my esteemed comrade.'

The two drinking buddies are sharing a worst nightmare come true, the one they've been dreading for years.

A new voice addresses them from the van's interior. The Irishmen later describe it as Northern European, either Scandinavian or Dutch. I'm quite sure it's our friend from De Rokerij, Romanov.

'Gentlemen, your families are being treated to a brief stay in luxury accommodation. Mr Murphy, your wife and two children have been taken to the seaside and have a private beach at their disposal. Unfortunately I can't guarantee good weather because this is Ireland.' Romanov pauses to chuckle at his own joke. 'They are accompanied by men whom they believe to be police officers, or Guards as you call them. We have informed them that there is a security alert which necessitates these precautionary measures. Your wife will be concerned but not alarmed and you can call to reassure her.'

Murphy will later tell the media he had a mental vision at this point of his wife and children hanging from a tree.

'Mr Condon, your elderly parents are similarly relaxing in a mountain cottage. We have made sure to bring all their regular medication and have a doctor on standby in case of any problems. Your mother is insisting on force-feeding our men with tea and sandwiches.'

Condon can't help smiling under the duct tape. Even a kidnapping can't suppress his mother's compulsive Irish hospitality.

'Now, all we ask is that you follow exactly the instructions you will receive. This time tomorrow you will be at home with your families and they will have enjoyed a luxury break that I hope will compensate you for the horrors you have just been obliged to witness.' Romanov's voice suggests he is also horrified by the Patriarch's show of persuasion. 'Now, I am sorry about this, but you need to take a brief sleep.'

A very tall, broad man in a balaclava steps towards the two bound Irishmen. He administers an injection to first one and then the other.

When they regain consciousness an hour later, Murphy and Condon are each in their own beds in their own homes. On the bedclothes next to each man official paperwork instructs them to report to a particular work location at eight in the morning. The address is down the country, a good two hours drive away, meaning an early start.

Murphy drives to the depot at five o'clock, picks up the van and then collects Condon from his parents' house in Drumcondra. The two men say little to each other as they join the motorway and head down to Tipperary.

~

The Devil's Bit Mountains spread across North Tipperary County like a barrier against invading hordes from the north. Below the eastern slopes of the

Devil's Bit itself, so named because it gives the visual impression of a monstrous bite taken out of the mountain ridge, lies the town of Templemore, home to some two thousand or more souls. There are another five hundred or so transient citizens who also call it home, as Templemore is the location of the national Garda Síochána College. The campus also houses the Third Field Artillery Regiment of the Irish Army.

Murphy and Condon arrive at the college just before eight in the morning, presenting their paperwork to the Guard on gate duty.

'Morning, lads,' is the greeting.

'Morning, Guard.' Condon hands over the paperwork.

'You'll be wanting Building 13, around the back of the main building and next to the Army barracks. You'll be met at the door and directed to the loading bay.'

Condon and Murphy nod their thanks to the Guard. Murphy drives the private high security van as instructed, around the back of the splendid three story main building and on to Building 13.

Meanwhile, in a large bungalow some six miles outside Templemore, three men stare intently at a computer screen.

'This technology is amazing,' the Patriarch gives his compliments.

'The device is very small,' Ilie says. 'No bigger than this.' He takes a vitamin tablet the size of a large button from a plastic tube and lays it on his tongue, then closes his mouth.

'Yes, it is the latest technology and comes at a price,' Romanov says. 'The only disadvantage is the battery does not last much more than two or three weeks. We are lucky with the timing of this escapade. Another couple of days and the signal would have faded.'

'Luck has nothing to do with it, the schedule is entirely to plan,' the Patriarch corrects the Dutchman.

On their computer screen in the bungalow the location of the security van is clearly indicated by a flashing red symbol on a satellite picture. Another symbol flashes on the screen and the two markers slowly merge together as the van approaches Building 13.

~

In Building 13 there's a lot of activity. The college has been anticipating a relocation of the building's contents to the Garda Síochána National Headquarters in the Phoenix Park for some time. Although five hundred and twenty Guards and the Third Field Artillery Regiment of the Irish Army are a strong notional deterrent, the Chief Superintendent of the college has been uncomfortable with the responsibility. He breathed a sigh of relief when official instructions arrived electronically that morning to transfer the national storage of seized class A drugs up to Dublin. It is later discovered that the order for the transfer was generated by a third party who had hacked into the Garda Síochána national security system. In most such cases, the hacker is never identified, but a subsequently defunct internet provider address in Romania was the source of the intrusion.

CCTV footage shows the bemused faces of Condon and Murphy as the army regiment loads a few hundred kilos of cocaine and heroine into the back of their van. This, of course, includes the two kilo bag the Fisherman jettisoned in a West Cork field, within which sits the miniature GPS tracking device that has led the Patriarch and Romanov to the Templemore location of the drugs store.

'What's taking them so long?' Romanov asks of his Romanian accomplices.

'They'll be having a cup of tea, of course,' Ilie explains, moving to the kitchen of the bungalow and preparing a brew of the same pacifying beverage he served me at the house on the Park.

After forty minutes the marker on the computer screen begins to move again, away from Building 13 and out of the college. It pauses at the gate, much to the frustration of the men in the bungalow.

~

The Chief Superintendent of the college is engaged in a heated argument with Lieutenant Colonel Darcy of the Third Field Artillery Regiment.

'We cannot let this cargo leave without a military escort,' the Lieutenant Colonel insists.

'The instructions are quite precise,' the Chief Superintendent counters. 'There is to be no escort. This is a low profile transfer.'

'I absolutely insist that my men accompany this vehicle.'

'Lieutenant Colonel, I appreciate your concern. But I have authority here. There must be absolutely no discernable presence accompanying the vehicle. This is to remain low profile.'

After ten minutes of debate with the Chief Superintendent, Lieutenant Colonel Darcy eventually stands his men down to their great disappointment. Riding shotgun is one of the few public military displays that most of his men will ever partake in.

The Patriarch, Romanov and Ilie breathe a sigh of relief when the GPS marker finally moves on their computer screen, away from the college and off to the rendezvous point.

Twenty miles from Templemore, the security van pulls into a wooded area and four men in balaclavas unload the drugs into a camper van. Condon and Murphy then drive onwards to Dublin and into the Phoenix Park where they present the confused Guards with the remaining contents of the van, namely paperwork for a shipment of some three hundred kilos of drugs that are conspicuously absent from the interior of the vehicle. Condon and Murphy eventually reunite later that evening with their families after extensive questioning at the Garda Síochána Headquarters in the Phoenix Park.

It isn't known whether the huge haul of drugs stays in the country or is re-exported elsewhere. When the media finally finds out the size of the take they have an absolute field day at the Guards' expense.

Guards Giveaway – an entire year's drugs haul…
Largest robbery in the history of the State etc.

Unfortunately for me, the Guards have quickly tumbled that the most suspicious link to the case is, of course, a two kilo bag of cocaine that was virtually handed to them in West Cork.

Out of the frying pan

Tweedledum and Tweedledee escort me from the train at Kildare as threatened. Not a Gideon bible in sight. I have an hour or more in the back of the marked Garda car to contemplate what might happen next. From where I'm sitting it doesn't make any difference to my story. How can I possibly be implicated in the huge drugs heist that Jim Duggan told me about when I called him from the train? But he's warned me that the Guards are likely to lean heavily as I'm their only lead.

On arrival at Kilkenny Garda station I detect a very different atmosphere compared to the previous visit. Jim Duggan is at my elbow as the Desk Sergeant books me in and completes the charge sheet. My fingerprints are taken this time, under the provision of the Offences Against the State Act 1939. Had they not invoked the Act then I might have withheld my consent to give the prints, but it's anyway time to meet this head on and perhaps even reclaim my Waterford Crystal goblet.

A young Guard escorts me by the arm to an interview room, identical to that of two days previously but deeper inside the station. His enthusiastically firm grip is sore on my left arm. Once in the room McAuliffe and Faloone recommence their double act, but it's bad guy and bad guy this time. I'm very relieved to have Duggan with me.

McAuliffe initiates the interview formalities by starting a tape recorder and then announcing those present and the grounds for arrest, just like on TV. Then he launches straight into it.

'We know you were in West Cork. The evidence will show your fingerprints all over the car and on the bag of cocaine that was retrieved from the field. My advice to you is to come clean now. Something big happened over at Templemore today and we need to eliminate you from that line of enquiry.'

Duggan interjects.

'Are we to assume the use of the Offences Against the State Act 1939 as grounds for my client's arrest means you are accusing him of being an accomplice in the robbery at Templemore?'

Faloone joins the fray but effectively ignores Duggan.

'Persuade us that you weren't involved. We have reason to suspect the cocaine seizure in West Cork is directly related to the much larger crime in Templemore this morning. Do yourself a favour. You drove that Nissan Almera to West Cork. You handed the shipment of cocaine over to another party. Both of you fled the scene, leaving all the evidence behind that we could have wished for. Tell us the full story and show you're not connected to what happened earlier today.'

At this point I don't even suspect the Patriarch and Romanov are behind the Templemore heist. It's a little tempting to ring-fence my liabilities and admit to the relatively small offence of conspiracy to traffic two kilos of cocaine. Duggan looks at my face and I know he can tell I'm contemplating a change of story. Without hesitation, he responds to Faloone.

'My client has a complete and reasonable explanation for his fingerprints being found in the vehicle and on the cocaine package in West Cork. This explanation paints him in a naive and regrettable light but I can assure you that Mr Mayes is an unfortunate victim of this situation and not any kind of hardened drug-dealing criminal.'

I give my best Joe average, normal guy who works in an office smile.

'Alright then, let's hear the explanation,' McAuliffe grins, sitting back and crossing his legs. 'I like a good story. How come your fingerprints are all over the Almera?'

With a look at Duggan, who nods his head in acquiescence, I begin to answer.

'I drove the car from Dublin down to Carlow for Tom McMenemy. He had driven me up there in his Mercedes and I did him a favour by bringing the other car down to his house.'

'Then you drove it on down to West Cork,' Faloone says matter of factly.

'No. In Carlow I swapped cars with Tom.'

'Why would you do that?' McAuliffe wants to know.

'He asked me to.'

'And what would have been his purpose in taking that old Nissan into the wilds of West Cork on a dark and stormy night? Sounds a bit unlikely to me.' Faloone and McAuliffe are alternating their questions like a doubles tennis team.

'He said he had to meet someone and hand the car over to them.'

'What's your take on it now?' McAuliffe raises his eyebrows. I have to play the eedjit at this point to get off the hook.

'Looks like Tom was involved in more than just a second hand car sale.' Blame it all on Tom, God rest his soul.

'And the bag of cocaine?' Faloone asks. 'How would you like to explain your fingerprints all over it?'

'I handled the bag at his house in Carlow.' That much is true. 'He took some and then asked me to put it back in the safe. So my fingerprints will be all over it.'

Duggan again nods in assent. I'm sticking to my story well.

'Tell me. Why would Tom have put the bag of cocaine in the safe? When was this? Just before you headed down to West Cork? Was there another bag of cocaine in Tom's safe? Is that why someone stole his safe?'

I look at Duggan.

'Too many questions, Detective Inspector McAuliffe.'

'I'm sorry, I'll ask again. Did Tom have more than one bag of cocaine in his house?'

Again I look at Duggan. We're on uncharted territory here. My comment about the bag going back in the safe has alerted McAuliffe. Duggan squints his eyes slightly which I take as a sign to proceed carefully with my answer.

'Yes, he did.'

'How many bags of stuff.'

'Three in total.'

'And you touched which one? How can you be sure the one you touched was the one he took to West Cork?' Faloone seems to be enjoying herself.

'Listen. I touched them all okay? It was six kilos of pure cocaine. I'd never even seen so much as a bag of marijuana before. We had a laugh over it. He snorted some, I didn't.'

'My client's presence in the vicinity of the drugs does not make him an accomplice. He did not consume any drugs and did not carry any drugs.' Duggan makes his point.

I decide to add a little. 'As far as I knew he put the whole lot back in the safe. If what you're saying is true then he must have taken a bag down to West Cork in the Almera.'

The detectives look at each other. Faloone speaks.

'We have no way of confirming your story. If it came to a trial by jury then they might find against you on circumstantial evidence.'

'Possible but unlikely,' Duggan murmurs.

'Let's go back to the cars,' McAuliffe suggests. 'Tom McMenemy drove the Almera down to West Cork, you say?'

'That's correct.'

'Then how come his fingerprints were not found anywhere on the vehicle. Not on the steering wheel, the doors, the boot lid. Nowhere. The only fingerprints on the car are yours.'

And the Fisherman's, I think to myself. Then I remember. He was wearing gloves. Good idea.

'Tom wore gloves. In hindsight I think he didn't want to leave his fingerprints on the car.'

Duggan has something to add.

'I think you'll agree that would have been highly understandable behaviour on behalf of Mr McMenemy as his fingerprints were already known to the Garda Síochána.'

It occurs to me that Duggan and Tom may have had a professional relationship of some standing. The casino manager told me the Guards knew Tom but I haven't shared that with Duggan. I try to suppress a smile. My story is gaining in credibility by the second.

Faloone continues. 'You say you drove McMenemy's Mercedes to and from West Cork?'

'Yes, correct.'

'Then how do you explain this?'

She passes a colour printout of a photograph across the table to us. Duggan and I huddle together to view the scene. It is from the toll plaza on the M7 motorway near Fermoy. Tom's face is clearly visible behind the wheel of the Mercedes. I'm torpedoed! My story about Tom having driven down in the Nissan is sinking like Renée's body in the River Nore.

Then Duggan slowly moves a finger across the picture to a set of numbers that show the time. 1:30 a.m. The return journey from West Cork. It comes to me in a flash. We had avoided the toll plaza on the way down as I didn't have any change in the Nissan and instead we had driven through Fermoy.

'That's Tom driving his Mercedes on the way back from West Cork,' I confirm.

'But you just told us you drove his car all the way there and back,' Faloone protests like a child lied to by a parent.

'Not all the way. He took over after a while on the return leg. I was worn out. He should have been too but I guess the cocaine kept him going.'

'So where are you in this picture then?' McAuliffe points to the car with a tobacco stained forefinger.

'There,' I point in turn to the middle of the printout, between the seats. 'See that brown lump on the back seat? It's me having a kip under a blanket in the back.' Sometimes it really helps to tell the truth. The dynamic duo is flummoxed by my explanation. Duggan starts to look a little smug.

By this time it's four in the afternoon. Duggan informed me I could be held for up to twelve hours without charge. I could opt to sleep undisturbed in the station between twelve midnight and eight in the morning but he advises against it, suggesting we should instead try to outlast the Guard's perseverance.

We've already exhausted the evidence available to McAuliffe and Faloone, but they're like two terriers fighting over a bone and proceed to take us over the same material again and again. Just before midnight they finally give up on getting me to repeat my story in an attempt to trip me up. I've been too well rehearsed to fall for it. When Duggan advises them we don't wish to break for the night they confer and decide to release me from custody.

I shake Duggan's hand as we leave the station. I'm a free man and he's a couple of thousand euro richer from my fee. Before he releases my hand he has a piece of parting advice.

'They were just fishing in there today. There's no concrete link between you, West Cork and Templemore. But if something more incriminating comes along then, well, we may have to change our tactics.'

I nod pensively and bid him goodnight. Duggan knows I've only shared a version of the truth.

Hindsight

During the sleepless night following my mammoth interrogation I try to reconstruct what has happened, looking for my true role in this cocaine business and assessing the best course of action for me. And, of course, for Jo in her dual capacity of only remaining friend and love interest.

The death of Alin and my blackmail agreement with Ilie to purchase, in person, a hundred thousand euro of cocaine in Amsterdam was where my involvement became consequential. Events leading up to that point have been of my own making but not earth shattering. My own stupid fault, Renée would have said. Tom was another innocent who I pulled into the picture, albeit he turned out to be less naive than I was. The cocaine purchase had been completed more or less according to instructions, with the two slight twists of alternative transport arrangements and our additional private purchase of four kilos from our friend in De Rokerij.

Romanov had furnished us with a pre-prepared two kilo packet of cocaine containing a miniature GPS tracking device. The cocaine was laced with rat poison but that was coincidental. Nobody expected anyone would consume almost pure cocaine in the way Tom had. Combined with his medication, the lethal consequences were probably predictable. Also Romanov had made a point of asking us if we wanted the additional four kilos to be identical to the first package and we had confirmed, not realising the implications. The upshot was we brought six kilos of cocaine into Ireland in three packages, each one trackable via GPS by persons who knew what they were looking for.

The episode in West Cork with the Fisherman was very peculiar. He had definitely put the wrong fuel in the car and, on reflection, must have knowingly done so. That scene where he and the two Guards went clod hopping across a muddy field must have simply been a way to convincingly jettison the original two kilos of cocaine into Garda custody. Then, a few days later, the GPS tracker device within the bag of cocaine was used to pinpoint the location of the drugs store in Templemore, enabling the villains to snatch a whole year's worth of contraband. It all made good sense.

Then what about the other two tracking devices? Romanov would have informed the Romanians about them. They had traced one to Aunt Mary's house in Raheny, leaving it on her tongue for me to find as a sign that they fully knew what Tom and I had been up to. I had no suspicions that they had murdered her, why would they? The other device led them to Tom's safe which they neatly took away intact, a bounty of four kilos of cocaine inside, leaving the Bewley's cup as another little memento. I received some recompense for this loss in the form of a hundred thousand in cash on John's Bridge in Kilkenny the night Renée jumped to her death. The money completed our bargain and I had not seen or heard from the Romanians since. Case closed.

The Guards, unfortunately, don't share my view of it all being water under the bridge. Yesterday McAuliffe and Faloone worried the bone until there was nothing left, exhausting us all. There are key elements they can't possibly know about but might be suspicious of. For example, how had the thieves known about the stash in Templemore? The security guards Declan Condon and Anton Murphy will definitely be under pressure. Miscellaneous Garda staff in Templemore and Phoenix Park Headquarters, as well as military personnel of the Third Field Artillery Regiment, will come under suspicion in case it was an inside job. The media are crucifying the Garda Síochána over their incompetence. I can't see how the Guards can link me to Templemore. But if they somehow manage to then I can expect no mercy.

So I have to consider the evidence against me. My fingerprints are all over the bag of cocaine and the car in West Cork. This is arguably circumstantial evidence as I have a convincing explanatory story placing the blame squarely on Tom. Poor Tom, who is already known to the Guards and unable to answer questions due to his being dead. But it was a close call in West Cork. Had the chasing Guards been able to positively identify me then I would be toast. And if the chase had not turned out how it did then I would have found myself in custody much earlier. No, the Fisherman didn't do me any favours and the plan hatched by him, Romanov and the others abandoned me to my own devices at the most dangerous point. If I had been caught in West Cork would the Romanians have ever given me my hundred grand back? I doubt it. They jettisoned me together with the cocaine containing the tracking device. That's the extent of their honour!

The more I think it over, the more my anger grows. Tom and I were used as bait for the Templemore heist. We were disposable. I can understand why Ilie might feel this justified, bearing in mind I beat his twin brother to death with an iron bar. The Patriarch exploited the situation but that was to be expected. After all, that's the way those people live.

But Romanov? That's despicable. In De Rokerij people are at liberty to buy drugs without fear of persecution or prosecution. Romanov has betrayed our trust and set us up. If this is Romanov's normal way of working then someone would have used his body to plug a hole in a dyke long before now. No, Romanov betrayed me and Tom. He broke his own code of conduct. My anger focuses on Romanov. I'll dob him in, as we used to say at school. It would make sense, though, to check it through with Duggan. Having made this momentous decision, I finally drift off to sleep.

In the morning I have a brief period of enlightenment during which everything that passed through my mind the previous night still makes sense. I leave a message on Duggan's voice mail asking him to call me. Then, as often happens, the cold light of day evaporates the logic and I begin to wonder if informing on Romanov would be in anyone's interest.

I call Jo in Raheny and persuade her to contact Dr Livingstone's office and tell them I'm too sick to come in for my appointment. Jo isn't too impressed as her mind is on Aunt Mary.

'Tell them I have palpitations.'

When Jo has completed the task she reports back to me.

'Gobnait said they need a doctor's note when next you see them, or else Dr Livingstone will give you more than palpitations.' Yet another threat for me to mishandle.

I take a cup of tea and a biscuit and watch the TV news. Templemore is still the big story.

The phone rings.

'How are you this morning?' It's Duggan returning the message I left on his answering machine twenty minutes earlier.

'Tired. But I've come to a decision.'

'What's that? Not a full confession, I hope.' Duggan laughs.

I decide to try out the new improved story line on my legal advisor.

'There's something I've recalled about the trip to Amsterdam that might be of interest to the Guards.'

The phone line crackles. Duggan makes a noise that sounds like he is drawing in breath through pursed lips.

'We can't discuss this on the phone. Come down to my office in Waterford this morning and we'll talk about it here.'

I take that to mean my telephone might be tapped. Surely there are rules and court orders and things before phones can be interfered with? Maybe my status under the Offences Against the State Act 1939 allows them to do whatever they want. Either way, it's destination Plunkett Station, Waterford. Thank God for the season ticket.

During my walk in the rain to the station a growing ache in my left arm makes itself known. I've slept on it awkwardly, probably. Plus the custodial manhandling I received from that young Guard in the station the previous afternoon won't have helped. I resolve to make some leisure time and finally return to the local gym for a bit of therapeutic exercise. My right buttock feels rather uncomfortable too and I put it down to the previous day's ten hours firmly seated on a hard wooden chair in the Garda interview room. McAuliffe is becoming a regular pain.

In Waterford Duggan welcomes me to his paper-filled office with tea and biscuits. Very nice.

'So, tell me. What is it you know about Amsterdam that you think might be helpful to the Guards?'

'Like I was trying to say on the phone,' I speak through a mouthful of ginger nut biscuit, 'the details of what Tom and I did in Amsterdam might lead them to the cocaine supplier.'

'Did you meet the supplier yourself?'

'I did. In a coffee shop called De Rokerij. He was a big guy, went under the name of Romanov.'

'Romanov? Are you sure?' Duggan definitely reacts strongly to the name.

'Yes, Tom went upstairs with him and two heavies. That's the only opportunity I think Tom had to buy the stuff.' Okay, so it's another partial truth but truth nevertheless.

'I know of De Rokerij. Could you describe this Romanov to me?'

'Sure. He was about six three, raw boned. Collar length dark blond hair and a goatee beard. Maybe about thirty-five years old. Definitely Dutch, although he looked like a veteran California surfer dude.'

'Could you identify him in a line-up?'

I close my eyes for a second and I'm back in the upstairs room of De Rokerij. Romanov stands clearly before me, holding a two kilo brick shaped package of cocaine. Then a Romanian girl sticks her tongue down my throat.

'Yes, I'm pretty sure I could.'

'Okay. Now let's think what you would gain by informing the Garda Síochána about Romanov. They seem to have exhausted their line of enquiry with you. The fingerprint evidence is circumstantial. I don't believe they have other charges to press against you so there's no need for us to negotiate. There's no mileage in telling the Guards about your experiences in Amsterdam.'

'But Romanov is responsible for this, Jim. It's because of him that Tom died. This whole mess is because of him. I know it.'

Duggan looks at me strangely.

'Listen. I've heard of this Romanov character and he's bad news. Big time bad news. The Guards will already suspect Romanov is the supplier so you're not telling them anything new. If you try to give evidence against the Dutchman he will find out and then your wife will be collecting on your life insurance. Believe me.'

I squint at Duggan. His last sentence sounds more like a threat than a warning. Could Duggan have gone over to the Dark Side? Either way, what he said makes sense. Turning State's evidence against Romanov is a seriously dumb idea.

On the way back to Bagenalstown I think over what should happen next. Tom's life insurance is due to pay out any day. Renée's will follow soon after. Then Aunt Mary's will and testament should be executed and we can pick up her money and the house. It will be timely for Jo and I to organise our career breaks and then head for the sun as soon as the funds are in our account.

So this chapter with the Romanians and Romanov is well and truly closed, I decide. However, when the train pulls into Kilkenny, the last stop before Bagenalstown, who should be waiting but my friend McAuliffe.

The geek

Now here's a nice little tale of public spiritedness for you.

Deaglan Donovan is a geek. Sixteen years old, hair down to his shoulders and painfully thin. Unlike some other teenage long hairs, his complexion is quite clear, probably due to an appropriate regime of personal hygiene. If Deaglan lived in the UK then he would fit, physically at least, into a teenage sub-culture group called Emo. This being Ireland, Emo is actually the name of a village in County Offaly and also the brand name of a chain of petrol stations. So Deaglan is simply a geek living in a small housing estate on the edge of a town in County Kildare.

Girls at school and in the street quite like Deaglan for his almost pretty good looks, but he's too shy to engage with them. Local boys are all active in the Gaelic sports of hurling and football, big meaty country lads who see Deaglan as the runt that affirms their genetic physical superiority. But all this is of no consequence to him, for Deaglan is absorbed in his own world of technology.

The top room of the Donovan house is a treasure trove of technological adventure. Everything from metal detectors, parabolic antennae for covert listening, a radio scanner, night vision goggles, laser positioning systems, an old military aircraft radio and a powerful telescope. He understands how each piece works and how to repair it. Then, of course, there's his computer system. At weekends Deaglan works at PC World and has access to all the latest computer gadgets at discount prices. Those items of his technological inventory that can be connected to a computer are linked up to a powerful stack of processing power.

Mr and Mrs Donovan know their son is gifted, although Mrs Donovan often wishes those gifts were more popular with other people of Deaglan's age. They're accustomed to him spending hours in his room and then traipsing out of the house encumbered with all kinds of equipment. Sometimes he wanders across the fields behind the estate or through the nearby woods. Now, at the tail end of the school summer holidays, he often disappears for most of the day or even the night. They feel this is preferable to him having his head stuck into apocalyptic computer games or shuffling around in the street to some irreverent gangster rap music whilst dressed in strange clothes.

It's Tuesday before the Templemore heist and Deaglan is engaged in a new development. It's been in his mind for some time to take his technological interests and abilities above the surface of our planet. The outer atmosphere contains a legion of satellites waiting to do the bidding of those clever enough to access them. And Deaglan is clever enough. He's fascinated by the claims of security forces to be able to visually identify individuals anywhere on the surface of the earth via satellite. To follow the every move of his only human object of fascination, Marie Finnegan, would be a truly worthwhile endeavour. But that's a bit of a stretch as a starter project. Instead he's gathered components to help achieve a more modest initial goal.

By the evening Deaglan has reached the stage where the location of several vehicles on the estate can be identified using equipment he's put together. Wandering around in a hooded coat, receiver box in hand, Deaglan walks up to and identifies the logistics company truck that parks every evening on the estate. Then he locates a security van usually driven daytime by Mr Finnegan down the road, father of Deaglan's fantasy, Marie. Finally, he approaches a dark blue Ford Mondeo parked in a cul-de-sac. The vehicle sticks out like a sore thumb to anyone who knows the estate. As he approaches the car, its passenger window is lowered.

'What have you there, sonny?'

Deaglan looks into the car and, seeing the various equipment inside, recognises it for an unmarked Garda vehicle.

'Just a GPS. Do you have one in your car?' he asks innocently, knowing full well they do. But what he's carrying isn't a simple GPS. It's a homemade GPS detector.

'Sure,' says the plain clothes Guard. 'Have you seen young Kelly?'

They're after Seamus Kelly again. Everyone knows Seamus is your man for substances, not that Deaglan has any interest in chemical stimulation.

'Nope. Probably saw you lot coming,' Deaglan replies, glancing at the flank of the incongruous Ford. 'But I'll tell him you were looking for him.'

'Be a smart lad and piss off,' retorts the other unseen Guard behind the steering wheel.

As usual, Deaglan has failed to make new friends. He wanders back to his house and is heading towards the back door when the device gives another indication where none is expected. Stepping onto a box placed against the prison-like concrete block wall of the back garden, he climbs over and sets off across the fallow fields between the housing estate and the railway line.

It's difficult to find in the gloom. The homemade location equipment only gives him an accuracy of several meters. After ten minutes of searching his back is beginning to cramp and the large, sharp stones around the track are pushing through the soles of his shoes. On the verge of giving up he finds it camouflaged against the light colour of the stones. There, wedged down between the rail track and a small rock is a white plastic disc. He picks it up and walks fifty meters across the field, then checks the locating equipment again. The target has moved across the field with him. His home made GPS tracker has worked well enough. But he'll have to try and improve the resolution down to a meter or so.

The disc feels surprisingly small in his pocket. Those devices installed in the logistics truck, the security van and the unmarked Garda car would be much bigger, at least the size of a paperback book. But now it's late and he needs to get some shut eye. At six he wants to walk out and ogle the young Miss Finnegan on the way to her job at the baker's.

Next morning, after following the girl at a distance and failing yet again to find the courage to approach her, Deaglan returns home and goes searching on the internet. It takes him seconds to find what he is looking for. Miniature GPS tracking device, type number AX 3927, manufactured by a company called Covet in Accident, Maryland. The item isn't commercially available and he wonders how it's found its way onto the railway line.

After a day spent refining his GPS tracking equipment, he flips around various websites, chat rooms and blogs before looking at the news. Templemore has made it onto the front pages worldwide. Deaglan pauses, considering how the villains could have located the drugs store. He knows how he would have done it.

That evening Deaglan wanders out into the street. The Guards are back, this time in an even more conspicuous yellow Mondeo. The same Guard winds down the passenger window.

'Nice colour,' Deaglan indicates the car's flank with a nod.

'Thanks,' the Guard says. 'Kelly?'

'Nope, but I've found something you might be interested in.'

He holds up a small clear plastic bag containing a white disc the size of a large button.

Two minutes later, Mrs Finnegan reports to the Garda station that a young man in the street appears to be buying drugs outside her house from two men in a banana coloured car. She thinks it's that young Donovan from down the road. The creepy one her daughter says has been following her around.

~

And so it comes to pass that Jim Duggan, DI McAuliffe, DS Faloone and I sit together in an interview room in Kilkenny Garda station contemplating a clear plastic bag containing a button sized disc.

A mistake is made

'Something strange here,' McAuliffe kicks off. 'Do you know what this is?'

Duggan holds the bag aloft and eyes me.

'No, Detective Inspector. You tell me.'

'Well. It's a miniature GPS tracking device, type number AX 3927, manufactured by a company called Covet in Accident, Maryland. Your fingerprints are all over it, not to mention traces of cocaine mixed with a small proportion of rat poison.'

'Where did you find it?' Duggan asks.

'A young lad found it next to a railway line just outside Newbridge, which suggests it was thrown from a train.'

'I'm guilty as charged,' I quip, regretting it immediately.

'Of what exactly?' Faloone wants to know.

'My client has no further comment,' Duggan's eyes throw daggers at me. He clearly wants to confer before we get into any deeper discussion with the Guards.

'I'm guilty of littering the railway line outside Newbridge,' I manage to get out just before Duggan kicks me in the shin. It bloody well hurts.

'You admit to handling this?' McAuliffe smells blood.

'Yes. It was in one of Tom's bags of cocaine. I said I would try and find out for him what it was.'

An egg of a lump is developing on my shin from Duggan's repeated kicks.

'Then you threw it out of a train outside Newbridge?' Faloone asks.

'Yes, when I realised what it was I wanted to get rid of it immediately, so out the window it went.'

'You lied to me just now when you said you didn't know what this was.' McAuliffe holds up the bag containing the tracking device again. 'Not a good start to this interview. I need you to be truthful. So you threw this thing out onto the track. Why would you have done that?' McAuliffe has a sly look on his face.

'Because someone might have been using it to track the cocaine.'

Anticipating another kick from Duggan, I move my chair swiftly away from him as I speak. His brown brogue connects sharply with the shin of Detective Sergeant Faloone who lets out a howl.

'Do you think there was a tracking device in the bag of cocaine that was seized in West Cork?' she asks me through gritted teeth, whilst glaring at Duggan.

'It wouldn't be unreasonable to assume so,' is my uninjured answer.

Faloone rubs her shin and glares at Duggan, but addresses me. 'Ger, my man, you are in deep, deep shit. Someone, either you or someone you know, planted one of these,' she holds up the miniature GPS device, 'with the intention of locating the Garda Síochána drug store. Then they orchestrated a raid on Templemore.'

'No! It wasn't me! I didn't even know the device was in there. They set us all up!'

Duggan pushes back his chair and stands.

'I need to speak alone with my client. You've presented new evidence that he and I need to discuss before this interview goes any further.' I'm surprised Duggan has let it go this far. 'I remind you my client has not been rearrested or charged and remains free to leave at any time.'

It's true. McAuliffe hasn't cautioned me, for some reason. He and Faloone go into a huddle and then McAuliffe responds.

'Mr Duggan, you and Mr Mayes may leave the station now but we require Mr Mayes to return tomorrow morning at nine for further questioning. This will be voluntary on your part but don't think of leaving the area or you will be arrested.'

Duggan strong arms me out of the interview room and onto the street, my bad arm aching again. We head for his car and, once we're inside, he locks the doors as if I might try and escape.

'You seemed to be about to change your story in there. What's happening? What's the truth about this GPS device?'

I have to think quickly. No Jo to help me. Tom and Renée both gone. Should I change my story? In part or tell the whole truth?

'I already warned you about Romanov,' Duggan is now puffing on a cigar, the smoke thick and noxious. The windows remain closed. I try to open my passenger window but Duggan has switched off the power. 'If you have information concerning any other party I'd strongly recommend that you keep it to yourself.'

'If the Guards already know about Romanov then I can give them his name and put myself in the clear. How can that be of any detriment to Romanov? I'm going to tell them about Romanov.'

'Don't. I'm telling you now. We go back in tomorrow and you stick to your story of wide eyed innocence. Maybe someone set up your friend McMenemy. That's what you meant by your outburst just now. No other parties named, no trouble, everyone lives happily ever after.'

'Jim, I hear what you say. But I can't carry the burden of this tracking device and its link to Templemore alone. The Guards will crush me. It could look like I was the man who introduced the tracking device to the cocaine in West Cork and that puts me in the picture for Templemore. I'm going to name Romanov.'

Duggan says nothing else to me as he drives me home to Bagenalstown. When we reach my house he unlocks the doors and I open mine.

'Reconsider. You'll open Pandora's box.'

'Sorry, Jim. Romanov deserves it and I need to put myself in the clear.'

'If that's your final decision then be it upon your own head. Don't say I didn't warn you. I'll pick you up at eight thirty tomorrow.'

As I walk up the drive I see a dark Ford parked outside my house with two men inside.

'Mr Mayes,' one of them greets me as I approach. 'DI McAuliffe asked us to keep an eye on you, for your own protection.'

'Thanks very much,' I respond graciously. How kind of McAuliffe.

There's a scrubbing of tires on tarmac. Duggan speeds off down the road, mobile phone held to his head in blatant disregard for the law. He obviously has a call that can't wait.

~

I have some explaining to do when Jo arrives home.

'You knew Tom was buying cocaine in Amsterdam and you're about to betray the supplier to the Guards.' she repeats my words.

Version three of the truth. I still haven't admitted to Jo that Tom and I'd been acting for the Romanians or that we'd each purchased an equivalent amount of the drug. It seems unnecessary to worry her about too many murderous villains.

'You think the Templemore raid is linked to all this and that you're implicated in the biggest robbery in the history of the State.'

I nod.

'Gerard Mayes, either you need some more psychotherapy from Dr Livingstone or I'm married to the biggest idiot in Ireland.'

'The two things are not necessarily mutually exclusive.' Renée would have laughed at that.

'I'll wager that your idea for us both taking a career break is not totally disconnected from this situation you've got yourself into? Well, it might not be a bad idea to take that break.'

My face must show great relief.

'But not if you have charges standing against you,' she continues. 'I'm not going on the run with an international fugitive!'

I'm disappointed with her lack of adventurousness. In fact, fleeing the country before the trial of anyone connected with the whole thing is the mainstay of the career break proposal.

'From what you've told me we have to accept that you might not be around for a while.'

'What d'you mean?'

'Well, if you decide to turn fugitive then I'm not going with you. And if you have done wrong then you'll likely go to prison. You won't be around to provide for us.'

'Us?' The penny drops. I am to be a dad after all. 'But you told me you weren't pregnant.'

'I was wrong. I took the test too soon or something. Yesterday I took another test and it was positive. Unless you get your act together our child will be born with its father in prison or on the run! So get a fucking grip!'

She punches me hard in the shoulder. I'm shocked. Jo has it quite right. I have to get a fucking grip. We discuss for another hour and then I leave for the gym to take a bit of therapeutic exercise and relaxation.

It's been three months since my last visit to the leisure centre. The various torture machines beckon to me but I only managed ten minutes on the cross trainer before I have to stop, quite out of breath. Lack of exercise and too much alcohol has rendered me unfit and misshapen. Middle age calling.

The weights machines are more forgiving. I manage several sets of reps on the pull-down and the pec-deck, moving half my bodyweight in slow, rhythmic movements to stretch and strengthen those muscles that have been sore and tense in the last couple of weeks.

This I follow with half an hour alternating between the sauna and steam room. Relaxation and thinking time. I'll take Duggan's advice, forget Romanov and stick to the version of the story that paints me as a clueless bystander. Hopefully that will keep me out of prison and I can then somehow persuade Jo to bring herself and our unborn child away from it all. Perhaps to Switzerland or another country where we'll be sure of good maternity care in a private clinic. We can surely afford it.

~

Jim Duggan is there outside my house at eight thirty the next morning as promised. I inform him of my change of heart but he's unimpressed.

'You can't keep chopping and changing your story like this. You'll lose all credibility.'

I'm not sure if he means with him or the Guards or someone else.

'You have to learn a lesson today. We agree a course of action and you stick to it. If you deviate, if you ad-lib, then I can't protect you.' And your family. Where have I heard that before?

The unmarked Garda car with its two occupants follows closely when we leave my house. Duggan says nothing else during the rest of our twenty minute drive to Kilkenny Garda station. The silent treatment again. At the station we ask the Desk Sergeant for McAuliffe but it's DS Faloone who appears and escorts us to yet another interview room. She sits down opposite and I have a chance to give the DS a once over. No, she's too hard looking for my liking.

If I have to go on the run without Jo, I won't be taking up with anyone who looks like Faloone. A Gobnait look-alike, on the other hand, would be a different proposition.

The very thought reminds me I haven't made any provision for informing Dr Livingstone, yet again. Most probably Jo will take care of it for me, being a fairly reliable and thorough type of wife. If not, then I can call Gobnait later and say Jo had forgotten to do so. Master of deceit and intrigue I am, the Guards have no hope of nailing me for anything.

McAuliffe turns up after ten minutes with four cardboard cups of coffee.

'Good morning. Thanks for sticking to our appointment. I thought we could start off today in a civilised fashion.'

We accept the coffee and McAuliffe runs me through my entire story again. By this time I could write a book about it. Naive Scotsman Ger Mayes is unwittingly involved in drugs smuggling by Irish ne'er do well Tom McMenemy. He discovers and identifies a miniature GPS tracking device, then jettisons it in fear of being drawn into a situation beyond his control. Ger Mayes is innocent but gormless.

I tell it forwards, backwards and sideways. The dynamic duo is unable to trip me up no matter how they try. After an hour and a half I'm sure the interview will draw to a close. Throughout, Duggan has a strange look on his face like a cat watching a bird.

Then McAuliffe produces his rabbit from the hat.

'So, take me back to the unfortunate Renée Martin. I want to hear exactly what happened according to your recollection.'

I'm a bit confused. Why are we dragging Renée out of the river again? Nevertheless, I can't refuse and so begin.

'We had spent the day together at the beach and in the mountains. Then we went into town and drank heavily. Renée said she was pregnant but that the cancer would get her before the birth.'

'And that you were the father?'

'Yes, I was the father of her unborn child.'

'Did she seem depressed?' Faloone asks.

'On the contrary, she was in high spirits.'

'Then?' McAuliffe prompts.

'Then she climbed onto the parapet of John's Bridge and simply stepped off.

'Did anything happen before Renée stepped off the bridge?' McAuliffe seems to think so.

'Yes, she blew a kiss to me, like this.' I show Faloone the gesture but the look on her face suggests I can go jump off a bridge.

'Did you touch her?' Faloone asks.

'No, I was a few meters away.'

'And this was witnessed by three Romanian women who were starting to cross the bridge?'

'That's right. End of story. Why do you ask?'

McAuliffe fixes me with a challenging look.

'We've been contacted by the witnesses and they've had a crisis of conscience.'

'What do you mean, a crisis of conscience?' I'm flummoxed but Duggan appears calm, simply drinking his coffee.

'They wish to change their statements,' McAuliffe continues. 'The story according to them goes as follows. When they approached the bridge they saw a drunken man and woman arguing. The woman stood on the parapet of the bridge and began shouting at the man. He then approached her and shoved her off the parapet and into the water. When he realised the women had seen everything he approached them. They were in fear of their lives at this point, but the man didn't threaten or attack them. Instead he offered them a sum of money to serve false witness to the woman's suicide jump. Three hundred euro each. It was too much for them to resist and they went along with the lie, until now. That man was you. We know you withdrew nine hundred in cash the day before, probably intended for some other purpose.'

I'm stunned into silence. I try to speak but nothing comes out and I gape like a fish out of water. Faloone picks up the thread.

'You have the motive. A pregnant mistress in a small town. It would ruin your marriage.'

'We'll have you for this, if nothing else.' McAuliffe gives me a sad little smile. I see my liberty fading away, together with the insurance money from Renée's life policy.

Duggan catches my eye. He picks up his cardboard coffee cup and slides it slightly towards me. Then he asks the detectives for a few minutes of privacy with his client to discuss this new matter. McAuliffe and Faloone leave the room. I glanced into Duggan's coffee cup. At the bottom, where there had been coffee, there's a five cent coin. Sign of the Romanians.

'This is an unfortunate development. I hope you now see that a story, whether true or not, should be adhered to. The consequences of casting aspersions on Romanov or any other persons…' At this point he shakes the cardboard cup containing the coin. '…could be most unfortunate.'

I simply nod, totally out of my depth.

'Now I'm sure this change of statement by these Romanian women is a mistake or perhaps even an attempt to extort money from you. I've no doubt that, if we handle everything correctly, they will be able to exonerate you when it comes to identifying the man on the bridge. The description of the man will not match yours.'

I hear what he's saying.

'Unfortunately this confusion over the nature of Ms Martin's death will postpone her insurance company's payout for several months. Like I said, today you have to learn a lesson.'

Mutely I stare at the table. Duggan has clearly gone over to the Dark Side. He's probably been there from the start. I'm totally at their mercy – Romanov, the Patriarch and the other Romanians. Now I'll have to tread with feather light steps over my story.

McAuliffe and Faloone return to the room.

'Are you okay?' Faloone asks, showing apparent genuine concern. 'Your face looks very red.'

'I'm fine, thanks,' I manage to answer, my first words since the Renée murder accusation. But I'm not fine. My arm hurts, my backside hurts, my head hurts.

McAuliffe is, however, merciless. He leads me back through Renée's death again and again. I begin to get flustered. After about half an hour I have a mental image of my hands on Renée's hips, pushing her back and off the bridge. Could it be? No, I had been out of reach.

'No, no, no! I didn't push her! I didn't kill Renée. I loved her for God's sake.'

'Listen,' Faloone says soothingly. 'Give us something else instead and we can get this reduced to manslaughter. A crime of passion.'

'Tell us about your time in West Cork,' McAuliffe coaxes. 'Were you the man who ran across the field away from Garda O'Mahoney? Did Tom McMenemy pick you up in his car at the far side of the field? Garda O'Mahoney caught a glimpse of a car that could have been McMenemy's Mercedes.'

My heart thumps. How can they know? Do they know? The palpitations are for real now.

'No, it wasn't me, it was Tom. He was in the Nissan with the Fisherman!'

Duggan's shoe is hacking at my shin but I can't stop.

'Who's the Fisherman? Who sold the drugs to Tom?'

Do you ever get the feeling your heart is in your throat? You feel your own pulse beating and hear the blood rushing?

'No, I don't know who the Fisherman is. He didn't tell me his name. But it was Romanov who sold us the drugs. In Amsterdam, De Rokerij.'

'Are you okay? Ger?'

It's Faloone, standing over me, laying me down, on the floor. Through my blurred vision she looks almost beautiful as she lowers her lips onto mine. Then I realise I'm not breathing.

Don't pay the ferryman

It was Duggan's fault. He misjudged how I would react under pressure. The little lesson that laid Renée's murder at my door pushed me over the edge. I wake up the next day in the Cardiac Unit of St Luke's Hospital, tubes and wires all over me like some science fiction film.

Jo stands at the foot of the bed, conversing with a man in a suit who turns out to be the Consultant Cardiologist. I can hear them but they haven't noticed that I'm awake.

'Your husband has had a mild heart attack, probably induced by extreme stress, and he needs to rest, Mrs Mayes. The arteries of his heart are diseased but in many such cases it's likely the condition can be alleviated with a fairly routine surgical procedure. I wouldn't say it's too urgent. As long as he avoids excessive exertion and stress, his health should be quite stable.'

'I see. But he's still quite a young man. What might have caused this heart condition?'

'It may be congenital. Is there a history of heart attack at an early age in the Mayes family?'

'Well, a grandparent and a cousin.'

'Other causes could include diabetes, but your husband isn't a diabetic, or bad diet or excessive use of certain drugs, prescription or otherwise.'

Whilst eavesdropping I'm formulating my own combined theory. Faulty genes combined with a couple of performance enhancing Viagra or Cialis every week for the past, well, however long I've known Renée.

I spend five days at the hospital, under observation and enduring numerous tests. It would be an exaggeration to say I was inundated with get well wishes during that period, but there were a few.

Fat Deirdre from work, a place I vaguely remember, is the ringleader in sending a card and flowers from my colleagues. I can imagine her calling individuals into her office and using that threatening bulk and the small fat hands to coerce signatures and donations.

Dr Livingstone and the delicious Gobnait also send their regards and wish me a speedy recovery. I hope they regret the hard time they gave me over my repeated excuses for absence, now justified.

From Jim Duggan I receive a letter and a box of chocolates. The letter explains his regret at having to resign as my legal counsel at such a difficult personal time but, as we have irreconcilable differences in how to proceed, it's his professional obligation to withdraw. Duggan mentions that the invoice for work he has already performed will follow in the next few weeks, once I'm in recuperation. He'd better not hold his breath for my cheque.

I'm not surprised by Duggan's withdrawal. Although he might prefer to stay involved, so he can keep my story under control, I'm sure he knows I would sack him anyway. The way I see it Duggan's behaviour was the catalyst for my medical predicament. The chocolates, well, I throw them in the bin in case they're poisoned.

The good Detectives also show their joint sympathy with a card. No doubt McAuliffe and Faloone are worried that I'll file some kind of damages claim against them but I have no such intention. I recall Faloone's breath coursing into my mouth and filling my lungs, tasting of coffee and cigarettes. Her lips were firm on mine and, as I lay there not breathing, her blouse had hung down and revealed athletic shoulders and a fine bosom encased in a sports bra. I imagine that her torso is lean and muscled, the stomach concavely curving down to a neat waist below. At this point two nurses run to my bedside and check the monitor which shows an unexpectedly elevated heart rate, but it soon subsides back to normal as my mind drifts onto other subjects.

There's little more to say about the hospital stay. This is the first time our expensive medical insurance has been put to use and, although I've experienced the satisfaction of finally getting something from those years of extortionate payments, the private room it affords leaves me isolated and bored. Daytime TV has little to offer in my opinion and, anyway, the channels in the hospital are very limited. Jo comes to see me every day and has brought a couple of her favourite novels along, but they aren't to my taste.

There's one phone call, during the third day of my stay. Duggan. When I recognise his voice I pick up the remote control and mute the sound of the TV.

'Ger, it's Jim Duggan.'

'Jim. How's it going down in Waterford?' Old mates, water under the bridge.

'Fine. Listen. During the interview before your, um, illness…well….you said a few things I hadn't heard from you before.'

'Jim, should we be having this conversation? You've resigned my case so I'm not sure it's appropriate.'

'Believe me, it's appropriate to you and your family.'

'Go on.'

'You mentioned Romanov and De Rokerij. We spoke before about that. You also mentioned someone you called the Fisherman.'

It all comes back to me.

'Ger?'

'Yes, Jim. Ask me a question or tell me more.'

'My advice at the time still stands.'

'What's that, Jim? Please remind me.' I want to hear his explicit threats or offers.

'This is free advice from me to you. Retract the statement about Romanov. You were raving whilst experiencing a heart attack, didn't realise yourself what you were saying. The Fisherman is a figment of your imagination. They don't recognise the name and you won't give a description for them to work with. No further embellishments to the story, no mention of any other characters. Stick to this bit of advice and the death of Renée Martin will not threaten your liberty.'

Lying in my hospital bed this sounds like a very good idea. As I make no reply for several seconds Duggan continues.

'I think it only fair to also advise you that any deviation from this course will impact negatively on you and your family.'

'Are you threatening me, Jim?'

'These are very dangerous people we're talking about. They're all-reaching and ruthless. An office clerk with a heart condition has no chance against them. Don't ruin your life and that of your wife.'

There. He couldn't be more explicit. Except to explain exactly what ruin your life means and I don't want to know. Not really.

'I hear what you're saying, Jim. Loud and clear.'

'We understand each other. That's good. I'll say goodbye now and good luck.'

Duggan hangs up.

After the phone call I know the Guards will be back on my case as soon as they're permitted to do so by the medical staff. There's no sign of them while I'm at the hospital but when, on the third day, I venture out down the corridor to the bathroom for a shower, I see a uniformed Guard stationed outside the door of my private room, presumably since my arrival. Is this for my protection or to restrain my liberty?

Jo takes me home late in the morning of the sixth day. She wheels me in a chair to the car and I shuffle into the passenger seat. Jo's invalid husband. In truth, I feel good, better than I have for weeks. The symptomatic pain in my arm has gone and five days without sitting on those moulded plywood chairs in Kilkenny Garda station has permitted the ache in my backside to disperse. Enjoying the luxury of being chauffeured, I relax as Jo pushes our Volkswagen around the torturous streets of Kilkenny city and down the Carlow Road towards Bagenalstown.

It becomes apparent after a few minutes that a dark blue Ford is following at an exactly safe distance and I know instinctively it's the Garda Síochána. Sure enough, the same vehicle follows us all the way home and takes up its post outside the house, just behind the hedge, which at least affords us a little privacy.

Jo ushers me onto the deep brown leather sofa in our sitting room, covers me with a blanket and provides a mug of tea.

'Right! Let's have the full story. Take your time. I need to understand.'

Version four of the truth.

I tell Jo that my, well, our financial woes have been a little worse than she was aware of. The cause of this is still blamed on my gambling, with no mention of blackmail or compensation for beating a disabled beggar to death with an iron bar. I admit to getting involved in cocaine smuggling to pay off the supposed gambling debts. Also to joining forces with Tom to buy a private batch of cocaine in Amsterdam and thereby make a one off killing, pardon the expression. West Cork I explain to her completely truthfully plus my discovery and disposal of the GPS tracking device. Apart from Alin's murder, the only other major missing component of the story is discovering dead Aunt Mary with a GPS tracking device lying on her tongue. It seems unnecessarily gruesome and I know how much Jo loved her Aunt Mary.

'Well. You have been a busy boy.'

Jo smiles and I see something like admiration in her expression.

'What do you think? Will I get out of this?'

'You mean will we get out of this. I'm with you now. You should have told me everything before.'

'Well, to be honest, there's something further you should know.'

I tell her about Duggan's threatening phone call.

'It sounds straightforward enough to me. We take his good advice and everything remains as it was. You'll have a bit of a tough time with the Guards but then we'll collect on the life policies and the inheritances. You can get your heart re-bored, or whatever, and we head off into the sunset.'

From the smile on her pretty face I know Jo is right. And, in any case, it's a blessing in disguise that this heart condition has manifested itself here in familiar surroundings rather than in the middle of a South American rain forest or some other remote place where I surely would have died. Perhaps Duggan has involuntarily done me a favour.

We rehearse for our next interview with McAuliffe and Faloone. I say we, because Jo is determined to be my guardian. Duggan is out of the picture. We decide only to seek legal counsel if things get hairy and charges seem to be threatening.

On the second day at home there's a knock on the door and Jo answers. A uniformed Guard follows her into the sitting room where I'm once again ensconced on the sofa, quite the old man under his blanket.

'Mr Mayes.'

'Guard.'

'Detective Inspector McAuliffe requests an interview, sir.'

The young Guard looks about twenty and is highly respectful.

'He says it could be carried out here in your home if that's more comfortable for you, sir.'

'Yes, that would be fine,' I answer 'Please advise DI McAuliffe two o'clock this afternoon would be ideal. We'll have the kettle on.'

When the Guard has left I stand and Jo hugs me.

'We'll get this over with. He's willing to come here so I don't think they're looking to arrest you. By this time tomorrow it'll all be over.'

~

McAuliffe and Faloone arrive five minutes early and Jo shows them into the sitting room where they take a seat. Whilst Jo is in the kitchen fixing tea and coffee, I explain that the interview needs to be conducted in my wife's presence.

'Just like the first time,' quips McAuliffe. 'How long ago was that now? About ten days, I believe.'

It feels like ten years.

'Here we go, two coffees and two teas.' Jo brings the beverages in on a wooden tray and lays it on the low oak table in the middle of the sofa and armchairs. 'And this time, Detective Inspector, please don't steal the Waterford Crystal.'

'I don't know what you mean.' McAuliffe throws a glance at the mantelpiece, upon which stands the missing goblet, intact but sparkling clean. Somehow he's managed to return it unobserved. Slight of hand, a useful skill for a lawman.

'Right then. Glad to see you've staged a recovery from your little attack. You had us quite worried there.' McAuliffe is in nice guy mode.

'Yes, never a good outcome for a suspect to expire during questioning,' Faloone adds.

'Only thanks to you.' I smile. Faloone looks particularly sharp today.

'Well,' she retorts, 'If you prove to be in need of resuscitation today I'll allow DI McAuliffe to do the honours.'

'Let's hope that won't be necessary,' McAuliffe says, 'Because my lifesaving skills are limited to the swimming pool.'

Ho, ho. We're a proper bunch of swells having a good old laugh together.

'Now then. Before your collapse you said some new things we wish to know more about.' McAuliffe pulls out his notepad and reads from it. ''No, it wasn't me, it was Tom. He was in the Nissan with the Fisherman' and then 'No, I don't know who the Fisherman is. He didn't tell me his name. But it was Romanov who sold us the drugs. In Amsterdam, De Rokerij.' We have a good idea what happened, Ger. You can help us put the pieces together. Do that and the Renée Martin thing will go away or at least appear to be an accident.'

Jo and I are squeezed together on the sofa. I've abandoned the invalid under a blanket pose. She squints her eyes, warning me not to deviate from the plan. I've a sudden certain feeling Jo is channelling Jim Duggan.

'Listen, Detective Inspector, I was ranting and raving. A few seconds later I was virtually dead, and would have been except for....' I let my eyes drift to Faloone's blouse. Noticing, she tries to take advantage by subtly adjusting her pose so I can catch a glimpse of bra strap.

'Romanov. We know who he is. You just need to confirm this is the man from whom Tom McMenemy bought the cocaine that was seized in West Cork.'

Faloone pulls a photograph out of her bag and lays it on the table. It's a large blow-up of the Dutch surfer dude himself, striding from De Rokerij towards a bulky black car. I don't say anything. Unfortunately I don't have to. The rehearsals with Jo have been purely about the content of what we would say during the interview. We hadn't thought about body language. What I'm doing with my face, arms, legs and body, I may as well shout from the rooftops Yes! That's Romanov! The bastard set us up with two kilos of cocaine containing a GPS tracking device!

'Right then, that's quite clear,' McAuliffe makes notes in his book.

Jo looks alarmed. Things aren't going to plan. I try to communicate with her by telepathy. Don't worry. I didn't verbally identify Romanov. And they can't get me on the Fisherman.

'Now, this man you call the Fisherman. Do you recognise any of these?' Faloone lays a large mug-shot on the table. A ruddy faced young man with a short haircut. Then another, similarly rosy cheeked chap.

'Two happy looking culchees, probably farmers,' I quip. 'They look vaguely familiar.' I'm pretty sure they won't have the Fisherman's portrait.

Then, to my horror, the very man in question appears on the table, photographed in full sea fishing gear. Of course! The two Guards knew him at the petrol station and in the field one of them called him by his name. Jim. And those other two photos, the red faced culchees. Gardas Eamonn and Eugene, the lads that chased us!

Once again, I may as well say all this out loud. McAuliffe's face is one wide grin.

'Thanks,' Faloone says. 'You've done the State a great service. With these characters in the picture the suspicion over you for Templemore will most probably disappear.'

That's it. The dynamic duo, satisfied with my involuntary identification of Romanov and the Fisherman, stand and leave, their abandoned coffee cups half full behind them. When Jo returns to the sitting room after seeing them out she finds me at the fireplace, studying the returned Waterford Crystal wine goblet.

'Don't be too hard on yourself. I can see how it must have been for you during this past week. They seemed pretty sure about Romanov and the Fisherman and they only had to look at your face.'

'Well, I hope the bad guys see it that way.'

We don't know what to do next. Are we allowed to leave Bagenalstown? To leave the country? Two uniformed Guards still sit outside in the dark blue Ford. Probably we should have asked McAuliffe what to do next. Asking Duggan isn't an option.

Three hours later, on the six o'clock news, two familiar faces peer out at us from the screen. The Garda Síochána have gone public with an appeal for information regarding the whereabouts of a Dutch national named Wik Veenstra and a Cork man known as Jim-Jim Murphy. Romanov and the Fisherman. Templemore isn't mentioned but for us the connection is obvious.

'I think maybe we should be taking that career break sooner rather than later.'

Coup de gràce

Jo is right. The Guards are on to Romanov and the Fisherman, with or without my help. I've no personal interest in either of them being apprehended, as their stories will clash badly with my narrative of peripheral involvement in the whole saga. So it's with some trepidation that I receive a phone call the next day from McAuliffe, once again requesting my presence at the Garda station in Kilkenny. We were hoping to have seen the last of the tobacco stained DI and his athletic counterpart. Can it be a line-up? Surely the fugitives haven't been so quickly apprehended?

Jo drives us to Kilkenny, both of us pensive. McAuliffe was vague on the phone. If asked to identify Romanov or the Fisherman I'm on a hiding to nothing. McAuliffe and Faloone saw my spontaneous reaction in Bagenalstown to the photographs. If I do identify them then Duggan's prediction might come to pass.

The afternoon sun shines low and fierce through the windscreen of our Volkswagen. It slices under the sun visor and hurts my eyes, even behind the sunglasses that Renée bought me as a present, God rest her soul. Jo squints until we reached a point where the tree line gives some protection from the glare.

I think back to that last day with Renée, the trip to the beach and then through the mountains. She had been taking a last deep draught of nature's diversity,

349

relishing the ultimate day of life. I wonder at such courage and determination, comparing it with my ineptitude. But here's Jo beside me, in control. A star and a trooper, supporting her ailing husband when he most needs it.

McAuliffe acquiesces to my request that Jo be present during our meeting in the interview room.

'Listen. I know you and Jim Duggan have parted ways, but you might want to consider engaging someone new as legal counsel.'

I stare at McAuliffe. Surely he's gone mad. What can possibly require me to go further on the defensive at this stage? Perhaps the Fisherman, apprehended, has described me as the driver of the Nissan in West Cork. Perhaps Garda O'Mahoney, Eugene or Eamonn whichever, has remembered the Fisherman calling out my name in the field as he threw the bag of cocaine in my direction, a small detail which so far seems to have eluded McAuliffe.

Jo, my moral support, puts one hand over her eyes and then splits the fingers, looking at me through the gap. The telepathy is working well. What now? What else have you done?

'No, Detective Inspector. I think we're okay for now.' Feigned confidence. 'I don't think there are any surprises in store, it's all out in the open as far as I'm concerned.'

'Oh, there's a little surprise, right enough,' Faloone counters as she places an evidence bag on the table.

I pick it up. It looks empty to me. Jo takes a look and doesn't see anything either.

'What's this? The Emperor's new evidence?'

'We had an anonymous phone call yesterday late evening,' McAuliffe says. 'It opened a new line of enquiry relating to recent events. The evidence in that bag was found in Mary Twomey's house in Raheny.'

Frowning, I take the bag from Jo and look more closely. Inside the bag is something almost clear, slightly cloudy, virtually invisible.

'Help us, Detective Inspector,' Jo says.

'Oh, I already tried to help you when I suggested your husband find himself a new solicitor, Mrs Mayes.'

'Do you recognise what's in the bag?' Faloone asks.

'No, I'm afraid I don't.'

'It's a murder weapon.'

Jo's eyes go wide and my pulse does the wild thing. Faloone continues.

'The tip-off call suggested that we search Mary Twomey's house more thoroughly and re-examine the toxicology tests made on the body. There was cocaine in the bloodstream. This evidence was found located high up on a bookshelf in the sitting room. A piece of cling-film.'

'Sorry, I really don't get the picture.' I really don't.

McAuliffe spells it out.

'You said you found Mary Twomey dead in her armchair. From this evidence we know what really happened. You entered your aunt's house via the kitchen door. She was asleep in her armchair, under the heavy influence of a sedative. That's why there was no evidence of a struggle. You then took this sheet of cling-film and placed it over her face, asphyxiating her. From the traces of cocaine my guess is this cling-film was the wrapper for the miniature GPS tracking device you disposed of near Newbridge.'

My eyes are doing an impression of a chameleon, bulging and rolling, independently flicking between the three other people in the room. My mind's eye can see hands unfolding the cling-film over Aunt Mary's face. Surely not? She was dead already, wasn't she? Are they someone else's hands?

Faloone picks up the baton from McAuliffe.

'It's clear from the evidence that this is what happened. The cocaine in Mary Twomey's bloodstream, your fingerprints on the cling-film, the cocaine traces and Mary Twomey's lip prints on that same piece of cling-film. Ger Mayes, I am arresting you for the murder of Mary Twomey. You are not obliged to say anything unless you wish to do so, but whatever you say will be taken down in writing and may be given in evidence.'

'Oh my God, he's gone blue!'

It's Jo who makes the first comment on my metamorphosis. I'm the only one unsurprised by that shade of indigo as, being a chameleon, the hue of my skin has adapted to the colour of Detective Sergeant Faloone's blouse as she comes once more to my aid. This thought is clear in my mind, despite the familiar pain in arm and chest. Before the lack of oxygen and the tearing of my heart muscles completely immobilise me, my tongue gently slithers into DS Faloone's life-saving mouth. I see her recoil and utter the word Bastard with considerable feeling.

~

Waking from this attack I don't have the same lucidity as the first time. Consciousness comes and goes, Jo's hand in mine on occasion, or an anonymous nurse adjusting my plumbing. There are overheard conversations with the Consultant Cardiologist that put my situation into perspective. McAuliffe, Faloone and I have stressed the diseased heart into an irreparable condition. A transplant is my only hope.

In Ireland there are fatal road accidents almost every day. The Consultant sounds almost jolly when he explains that, with my common blood type, there is a good chance of finding a donor in time. I have images of Romanov or the Fisherman or even Ilie being run down by a Garda car and proving to be a tissue match. That would be deepest irony.

Whilst I'm indulging in this fantasy one day, Jo comes to my bedside. Seeing I'm awake she pulls a chair up alongside the bed but doesn't take my hand. Clearly the time for sympathy is over and marital interrogation will now commence.

'Ger, this thing with Aunt Mary. Tell me you didn't do it.'

My voice is weak, someone else's.

'I didn't. She was already dead when I found her.'

'Then how do you explain the cocaine in her system?'

It seems the onus is on me to explain the post-mortem chemical composition of Aunt Mary's blood. Very Patricia Cornwell. So time for version five of the story.

'When I found Aunt Mary there was something on her tongue. The GPS tracking device. I figured the

Romanians had tracked it to her house and, finding her dead, placed it on her tongue for me to find. As a kind of warning.'

'Do you think they might have murdered her?'

'Considering the cling-film has her lip prints, it's rather likely.'

'Then you have to tell the Guards. You can't take the blame for Aunt Mary's death.'

'How can I blame it on the Romanians? The cling-film isn't circumstantial evidence, it's conclusive. There's no sign anyone else was there. And if I start telling the Guards everything about the Romanians then you and I will soon be six feet under.'

'Did you kill her?'

'I guess I did cause her death,' I croak.

'What?'

I see Aunt Mary's face in front of me, pasty, mouth gaping. My hands are on her cheeks. Is the cling-film in my fingers? I can't be sure any more.

'I inadvertently led them to her. I left the tracking device wrapped in cling-film in her front dining room the previous day.'

'Why would you do something like that?'

'Because there were Guards with drugs dogs at Heuston and I knew the device and the cling film were smothered in cocaine.'

Jo shakes her head in dismay.

'Do you realise what this means?'

I wait to be informed. Will we separate? Get divorced? Am I going to jail for murder, amongst other things?

'Aunt Mary's estate is going to be tied up in legal wrangles. You're named with me as a beneficiary and now you're charged with her murder. What's that going to do to the inheritance?'

'God knows,' I mumble.

The Romanians et al have me well and truly stitched up. No insurance money from Renée's death, which now looks like murder by yours truly. Aunt Mary's insurance and her house held up in probate. Another murder by yours truly. My job down the pan. Not that the job matters, as I'm going to prison for the duration. Double murder, premeditated and motivated by life insurance. Off to the clink, throw away the key, abandoning pregnant wife with a big mortgage. Jo and the baby will have to move to a smaller house. God, what a mess.

A rare thing then happens. I cry. Great big blobby tears run hot down my face, like a little schoolboy, unexpectedly wetting his pants.

'Jo,' I blub, 'I'm so sorry. Everything is ruined. All the money's gone and I'm going to prison.'

Jo has never seen me cry before and it doesn't trigger her mothering instinct. Quite the contrary.

'Hah! I don't think you're going to prison! You won't live long enough for the trial. Let's not fool ourselves.'

She's right. I'll suffer divine justice before the legal process has its way. Surely I'll get a better deal at St Peter's Gate than in Dublin's Central Criminal Court? Then again, maybe not. Alin and his shattered skull have to be accounted for.

'What will you do?'

'Oh, don't worry about me. I'll collect my winnings.'

'What do you mean?'

'I took out a life policy on you last year.'

'Why?' This seems a strange thing for Jo to have done, personal finance being as much of a mystery to her as Lego.

'You've been going down the pan for a good while. You had a lot of headaches, complaining about your arm and chest. And we were trying for a baby. What would happen if you died? So I confided in Tom and he suggested I take out a policy while you were still insurable.'

Tom, the old goat. I can hear him having the last laugh from beyond the grave. Still, I'm flabbergasted at her heartlessness.

'How can we get out of this mess? What can I do?'

Jo looks at me, still not touching my hand.

'Just die, Ger. Fucking die.'

I almost do, on the spot. She's always been black and white, has Jo.

They don't let her back in the room. Alerted by my pulse monitor, the nurses witness our final exchange and it's clear that Mrs Mayes is no longer good for my health.

~

Well, things don't improve. A spell of unseasonably good weather has reduced the number of road accident fatalities to a record low for the month. By the end of the second week it's looking like curtains for old Ger. I agree to let Jo back in for a few final taunts, and then perhaps we can part on better terms.

Footsteps approach down the corridor. Amongst my special powers, which include recognising any model of car in the rear view mirror just from its headlight pattern, I also retain the ability to identify an individual's footfall. If I'm not mistaken, my wife is accompanied by the ghostly Tom.

Jo comes in the door followed by Aunt Mary in a long flowing black dress. I screw up my eyes and forced them open again. No, I'm mistaken. It isn't Aunt Mary, it's Renée, her short golden hair catching the sunlight through the window. But no, now it's Alin, dragging his bad leg as he approaches the bed.

'He's in a bad way,' says Father Sean. 'You've done well to call me, Josephine. The end isn't far off, now.'

Rallying a little, I look up into the earnest face of the priest. Father Sean's fair hair is thick and slightly unkempt. He sits awkwardly in the chair, the old fashioned robes catching on the armrest as he tries to find a comfortable position for his bad leg, a souvenir of childhood polio. I've seen this priest a few times before; in previous years when Jo managed to drag me into the local Catholic Church and once, more recently, when McAuliffe hauled me off a train at Bagenalstown station.

Father Sean's accoutrements have been placed on the bedside table and even I recognise their significance. Richly coloured silk, the chalice, a small phial of Oil of Chrism. I'm to receive the Sacraments. Confession, the Eucharist and Anointing of the Sick. The Last Rites as they used to be known.

My wife is calmer than the last time I saw her and ready to dispense her personal absolution. I raise a hand from the bed and she moves to grasp it.

'My son,' the Priest begins, 'Are you ready to confess your sins before God.'

'I am, Father.' I am actually. Best chance of a Peter pass.

He whispers, close enough to me that I can smell his clove-scented breath. It matches his cloven hoof.

'Let's not be too formal about this. I know it's some time since you were at confession. Just share your sins and you will be forgiven.'

'Where shall I start, Father?'

'At the beginning, my son, at the beginning.'

'At the beginning? Very well. The first sin was……'

I see the sequence of events unfold at high speed, in reverse. What was my first sin?

'…the first sin. Yes, Father, I remember now. I gave ten euro to a crippled beggar at Heuston Bridge.'

'That's no sin, my son.'

THE END

PERIL

RUBY BARNES

Connect with me online:

Email: ruby.barnes@marblecitypublishing.com

My Blog: http://rubybarnes.blogspot.com

Twitter: http://twitter.com/Ruby_Barnes

Facebook page: Ruby Barnes

Facebook person: RubyBarnesBooks

I've pedalled the pushbike of life through the Shires' rolling hills, along the folded rocks of Scotland's lochs and out west to the fractured reaches of North Wales. Love found me in the MacGillycuddy's Reeks of Ireland. The Swiss Alps cured me of obsessive compulsion and yielded progeny.

Misfits, rogues and psychopaths take form in Peril, The Baptist and other works. Their voices, they speak to me. I plead with them, but the demons are real. I've carried them on my back across Scandinavia, through the Mid-West, Eastern Seaboard and Deep South of the USA and to the borders of Argentina, Brazil and Paraguay. We teetered together on the brink of the Iguassu Falls and came back.

My writing is dedicated to the memory of my late grandfather Robert 'Ruby' Barnes.

If you've enjoyed Peril then try **The Baptist** by Ruby Barnes.

A contemporary psychological thriller set in Kilkenny, Ireland.

Tight writing, very atmospheric. A chilling tale of real evil.

Dark and disturbing, but oh so good.

Dark and dingy, hot and steamy, everything you need from a novel in one swift download.

Well written and totally convincing, it provides an absorbing insight into the minds of some very strange characters. It's not without humour albeit of the dark kind.

Compelling and very, very different.

I was hooked right from the start and loved the dark and sinister quality of this tale.

He's clever, calculating and uncatchable. If you hear a knocking on your door don't let him in. John Baptist is cleansing a path for the Second Coming.

To deliberately drown your brother in a bathtub is a terrible, if clean, thing. Might it not be excused, if he is the manifest son of Satan? But that wasn't the view of the Authorities, when they committed John to Fairfield Mental Institution. It wasn't all bad; they let him keep his hair long and he met Dirty Mary. Like an institutionalised Bonnie and Clyde, they roamed the Victorian asylum and grounds, fulfilling their deluded fantasies. There were casualties.

John and Mary loved, lost and left. Thank God for Care in the Community.

When God shines a light, it burns.

The last prophet must wander, cleanse.

I am not the One. I am merely sent to prepare a way for the One.

I am **The Baptist**.

The New Author

by

Ruby Barnes

A beginner's self-help guide to novel writing, publishing as an independent author and promoting your brand using social networks.

There are three reasons why you should read and digest this book:

1. you want to be an author;

2. you have already written a novel and want to publish it as an ebook;

3. you want to promote yourself as an author.

With foreword by Jim Williams, author of the Booker Prize nominated *Scherzo*.

Available in ebook and paperback format from all major online bookstores.